12/11

MISERY
BAY

**Center Point
Large Print**

Also by Steve Hamilton
and available from Center Point Large Print:

The Lock Artist

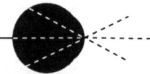

**This Large Print Book carries the
Seal of Approval of N.A.V.H.**

MISERY BAY

STEVE HAMILTON

CENTER POINT PUBLISHING
THORNDIKE, MAINE

This Center Point Large Print edition
is published in the year 2011 by arrangement with
St. Martin's Press.

Copyright © 2011 by Steve Hamilton.

All rights reserved.

This is a work of fiction. All of the characters,
organizations, and events portrayed in
this novel are either products of the author's
imagination or are used fictitiously.

The text of this Large Print edition is unabridged.
In other aspects, this book may vary
from the original edition.
Printed in the United States of America
on permanent paper.
Set in 16-point Times New Roman type.

ISBN: 978-1-61173-192-7

Library of Congress Cataloging-in-Publication Data

Hamilton, Steve, 1961–
Misery bay / Steve Hamilton.
p. cm.
ISBN 978-1-61173-192-7 (library binding : alk. paper)
1. McKnight, Alex (Fictitious character)—Fiction.
  2. Private investigators—Michigan—Upper Peninsula—Fiction.
  3. Upper Peninsula (Mich.)—Fiction. 4. Large type books. I. Title.
PS3558.A44363M57 2011b
813'.54—dc22

                                                      2011021244

To Jane and Jane

ACKNOWLEDGMENTS

Thanks as always to the "usual suspects," new and old: Bill Keller and Frank Hayes, Peter Joseph and everyone at Minotaur Books and St. Martin's Press, Bill Massey and everyone at Orion, Jane Chelius, Maggie Griffin, Mary Alice Kier, and Anna Cottle, Bob Randisi and the Private Eye Writers of America, Bob Kozak and everyone at IBM, David White, Elizabeth Cosin, Joel Clark, Cary Gottlieb, Jeff Allen, Rob Brenner, Jan Long, Larry Queipo, former chief of police, Town of Kingston, New York, Dr. Glenn Hamilton from the Department of Emergency Medicine, Wright State University, and F/Lt. Bruce Smith, Michigan State Police, retired.

A special thanks to Ruth Cavin, my first editor, my friend, and my hero, the one person more responsible than anyone else for this chance to live out my dream. I will miss you and remember you always.

And as always, to Julia, my wife and best friend, to Nicholas the steampunk rock star, and to Antonia, who will one day be a better writer than I could ever hope to be.

PART ONE

CHAPTER ONE

It is the third night of January, two hours past midnight, and everyone is in bed except this man. He is young and there's no earthly reason for him to be here on this shoreline piled with snow with a freezing wind coming in off of Lake Superior, the air so cold here in this lonely place, cold enough to burn a man's skin until he becomes numb and can no longer feel anything at all.

But he is here in this abandoned dead end near the water's edge, twenty-six miles from his home near the college. Twenty-six miles from his warm bed. He is outside his car, with the driver's side door still open and the only light the glow of the dashboard. The headlights are off. The engine is still running.

He is facing the lake, the endless expanse of water. It is not frozen because a small river feeds into the lake here and the motion is enough to keep the ice from forming. A miracle in itself, because otherwise this place feels like the coldest place in the whole world.

The rope is tight around his neck. He swings only slightly in the wind from the lake. The snow will come soon and it will cover the ground along with the car and the crown of his lifeless head.

He will hang here from the branch of this tree for almost thirty-six hours, until his car runs out of gas and the battery dies and his face turns blue from the cold. A man on a snowmobile will finally see him through the trees. He'll make a call on his cell phone and an hour later two deputies will arrive on the scene and the young man will be lowered to the ground.

On that night, I know nothing of this young man or this young man's death. Or what may have led him to tie that noose and to slip it around his neck. I am not there to see it, God knows, and I won't even hear of it until three months later. I live on the shores of the same lake but it would take me five hours to find this place they call Misery Bay. Five hours of driving down empty roads with a good map to find a part of the lake I'd never even heard of.

That's how big this lake is.

"It's not the biggest lake in the world. You guys do know that, right?"

The man was wearing a pink snowmobile suit. He didn't sound like he was from downstate Michigan. Probably Chicago, or one of the rich suburbs just outside of Chicago. The snowmobile suit probably set him back at least five hundred dollars, one of those space-age polymer waterproof-but-breathable suits you find in a catalog, and I'm sure the color was listed as

12

"coral" or "shrimp" or "sea foam" or some such thing. But to me it was as pink as a girl's nursery.

"I mean, I don't want to be a jerk about it and all, but that's all I hear up here. How goddamned big Lake Superior is and how it's the biggest, deepest lake in the world. You guys know it's not, right? That's all I'm saying."

Jackie stopped wiping the glass he was holding. Jackie Connery, the owner of the place, looking and sounding for all time like he just stepped red-faced off a fishing boat from the Outer Hebrides, even if he'd been living here in the Upper Peninsula for over forty years now. Jackie Connery, the man who still drove across the bridge once a week to buy me the real thing, Molson Canadian, brewed in Canada. Not the crap they bottle here in the States and criminally try to pass off as the same thing.

Jackie Connery, the man who wasn't born here, who didn't grow up here. The man who still couldn't cope with the long winters, even after forty years. The one man you did not want to poke with a sharp stick in January or February or March. Or any kind of stick, sharp or dull. Not until the sun came out and he could at least imitate a normal human being again.

"What's that you're saying now?" He was looking at the man in the pink snowmobile suit with a Popeye squint in his right eye. The poor man had no idea what that look meant.

"I'm just saying, you know, to set the record straight. Lake Superior is not the biggest lake in the world. Or the deepest."

Jackie put the glass down and stepped forward. "So which particular lake, pray tell, are you going to suggest is bigger?"

The man leaned back on his stool, maybe two inches.

"Well, technically, that would be the Caspian Sea."

"I thought we were talking about *lakes*."

"Technically speaking. That's what I'm saying. The Caspian Sea is technically a lake and not a sea."

"And it's bigger than Lake Superior."

"Yes," the man said. "Definitely."

"The water in the Caspian Sea," Jackie said, "is it saltwater or fresh?"

The man swallowed. "It's saltwater."

"Okay, then. If it's *technically* a lake, then it's the biggest, deepest *saltwater* lake in the world. Apples and oranges, am I right? Can we agree on that much?"

Jackie turned, and the man should have let it go. But he didn't.

"Well, actually, no."

Jackie stopped.

"Lake Baikal," the man said. "In Russia. That's fresh water. And it's *way* deeper than Lake Superior."

14

"In Russia, you said? Is that where it is?"

"Lake Baikal, yes. I don't know if it has a bigger surface area, but I know it's got a lot more water in it. Like twice as much as Lake Superior. So really, in that respect, it's twice as big."

Jackie nodded his head, like this was actually an interesting fact he had just learned instead of the most ridiculous statement ever uttered by a human being. It would have been like somebody telling him that Mexico is actually more Scottish than Scotland.

I was sitting by the fireplace, of course. On a cold morning on the last day of March, after cutting some wood and touching up the road with my plow, where else would I be? But either way I was close enough to hear the whole exchange, and right about then I was hoping we'd all find a way to end it peacefully.

The man in the pink snowmobile suit started fishing for his wallet. Jackie raised a hand to stop him.

"Don't even bother, sir. Your money's no good here."

The man looked over at me this time, as if I could actually help him.

"A man as smart as you," Jackie said, "it'll be my honor to buy you a drink."

"Well, okay, but come on, don't you—"

"Are you riding today?"

"Uh, yeah," the man said, looking down at his

suit. Like what the hell else would he be doing?

"Silly me. Of course you are. So why don't you head back on out there while we still have some snow left."

"It is pretty light this year. Must be global warming or something."

"Global warming, now. So you mean like our winter might last ten months instead of eleven? Is that the idea? You're like a walking library of knowledge, I swear."

"Listen, is there a problem here? Because I don't—"

"No, no," Jackie said. "No problem. You go on out and enjoy your ride. In fact, you know what? I hear they've got a lot more snow in Russia this year. Up by that real big lake. What was it called again?"

The man didn't answer.

"Lake Baikal," I said.

"I wasn't talking to you, Alex."

"Just trying to help."

"I'm leaving," the man said, already halfway to the door. "And I won't be back."

"When you get to that lake, do me a favor, huh? I'm still not convinced it's deeper, so can you drive your snowmobile and let it sink to the bottom with you still on it? You think you could do that? I'd really appreciate it."

The man slammed the door behind him. Another drinking man turned away for life, not

16

that he'd have any other place to go in Paradise, Michigan. Jackie picked up his towel and threw it at me. I ignored him and turned back to the fire.

They have long, long winters up here. Did I mention that yet? By the time the end of March drags around, everyone's just a few degrees past crazy. Not just Jackie.

The sun was trying to come out as I was driving back up my road. It was an old unpaved logging road, with banks of snow lingering on either side. When the snow started to melt, the road would turn to mud and I'd have a whole new set of problems to deal with. By the time it dried out, it would be time for black fly season.

I passed Vinnie's cabin first. Vinnie "Red Sky" LeBlanc, my only neighbor and maybe my only true friend. Meaning the one person who truly understood me, who never wanted anything from me, and who never tried to change me.

I passed by the first cabin, the one my father and I had built a million years ago—before I went off to play baseball and then become a cop—then the next four cabins, each bigger than the one before it, until I got to the end of the road. There stood the biggest cabin of all, looking almost as good as the original. I'd been rebuilding it for the past year, starting with just the fireplace and chimney my father had built stone by stone. Now it was almost done. Now it was almost as good as it was before somebody burned it down.

I parked the truck and went inside. Vinnie was already there, on his hands and knees in the corner of the kitchen, once again working harder and longer than I ever did myself, making me feel like my debt to him was more than I could ever repay.

"What are you ruining now?" I said to him.

"I'm fixing the trim you put down on this floor." He was in jeans and a white T-shirt, his denim jacket hanging on the back of one of the kitchen chairs. He had a long strip of quarter round molding in his hand, the very same strip I had just tacked down the day before.

"You're ripping it up? How is that fixing it?"

"You used the wrong size trim. You need to start over."

"It's not the wrong size. Damn it, Vinnie, is it any wonder it's taking me forever to finish this place? You wanna rip the ceiling off, too?"

"You got a good half-inch gap here," he said, pointing to the gap between the floor and the lowest log on the wall.

"That's a quarter inch."

"Here it might be, but over on the other side of the room it gets wider. You have to measure the gap at its longest before you go out and buy your trim."

"Vinnie, what the hell's wrong with you?"

"I told you, you bought the wrong size. And as long as you're buying new molding, get something with a little more style, too. Quarter round is boring."

"Nobody's going to notice it. It's on the floor, for God's sake."

He turned away from me, shaking his head. He grabbed another length of molding and ripped it up like he was pulling weeds.

"Something's eating at you," I said. "I can tell."

"I'm fine. I just wish you'd do things right for a change."

First Jackie and now Vinnie. Such a parade of cheerful people in my life. I was truly a lucky man.

"It's actually trying to get nice outside," I said. "We might even have some sunlight soon. Will that make you feel better?"

He didn't look up. "You know one thing that bothers me?"

"What?"

"How long have you been living in this cabin?"

"Ever since I've been working on it. It just makes things easier."

"I think you're done now, Alex. You've got the floor down. You've got the woodstove working. As soon as I redo your trim, this place will be ready to rent out again."

"It's been a bad winter for the snowmobile people. You know that."

"You could have this place rented right now. It's your biggest cabin. You're just wasting money."

"Since when are you my accountant?"

He stopped what he was doing and sat still on the floor. He finally turned to look at me. "You need to move back into your cabin. You can't keep avoiding it."

"I will." It was my turn to look away. "As soon as I'm done here."

Vinnie didn't say anything else. I got down on my knees and helped him tear up the remaining strips of floor molding. An hour later I was on my way to Sault Ste. Marie to buy the new strips, five eighths instead of half inch, cloverleaf instead of quarter round. As I passed that first cabin, I made a point of not even looking at it.

That was how the day went. That last day in March. It started with breakfast at the Glasgow Inn and ended with dinner in the same place. It was like most every other day in Paradise. Vinnie had helped me finish the baseboard trim, then he'd gone over to the rez to sit with his mother for a while. She'd not been feeling like herself lately. Maybe just one more person who was tired of winter. I was hoping that was it, that she'd feel better once the sun came back. That we'd all feel better.

Vinnie gave me a nod as he came through the door. Back from the rez, then a shift at the casino dealing blackjack, stopping in now because that's what you do around here. Every night. Jackie was watching hockey on the television mounted above the bar. Vinnie went over and stood behind him, just like I had told him to do.

"Hey, Jackie," he said, "I heard something interesting today."

"What's that, Vin?"

"Did you know Lake Superior isn't really the biggest lake in the world? Or the deepest?"

Jackie turned and glared at me.

"I'll throw you right out on your ass," he said. "I swear to God I will."

Finally, something to smile about, on a cold, cold night. I looked back into the fire and watched the flames dance. My last hour of peace until everything would change.

We're not supposed to believe in evil anymore, right? It's all about abnormal behavior now. Maladjustment, overcompensation, or my favorite, the antisocial personality disorder. Fancy words I was just starting to hear in that last year on the force, before I looked into the eyes of a madman as he pulled that trigger without even blinking.

In a way, I've never gotten past it. I'm still lying on that floor, watching the light in Franklin's eyes slowly going out. My partner, the man I was supposed to protect at all costs. Later, in the hospital, they pulled two slugs from my body and left the one that was too close to my heart to touch. It's been with me ever since, a constant reminder of the evil I saw that night, all those years ago on a warm summer evening in Detroit. You'd never convince me otherwise. No, I'd seen evil as deep as it could ever get.

But like Jackie and his beloved lake, you'd never know there was something deeper out there until somebody came to you and told you about it. A deeper lake. A lake you've never seen before. Even then, you might not believe it. Not unless he took you there and showed it to you.

It was about to happen. Minutes away, then seconds. Then the door opened and the cold air blew in and the last person I expected to see that night stepped inside, carrying a big problem and looking for my help.

CHAPTER TWO

Chief Roy Maven stood in the doorway of the Glasgow Inn. He was out of uniform, but everything else about him—his clean-shaven face, his buzz cut, his hard eyes, his body language—gave him away as a lifelong cop. He blinked a few times as his eyes adjusted to the light, did a scan around the room, taking it all

22

in. He finally saw me sitting by the fire and came over.

"Chief Maven," I said. "What the hell?"

"McKnight. Can I sit down?"

I nodded to the chair across from me, another overstuffed leather armchair angled toward the fire—just one more reason why a Scottish pub is a thousand percent better than your average American bar.

"This is nice," he said. "I can see why you spend so much time here."

"You knew to find me here?"

"Yeah, it's been an exhausting search. First your cabin. Then your bar."

"Are you gonna tell me why you're here or not?"

He leaned forward in the chair and rested his forearms on his knees. He looked me in the eye and as he did I was already coming up with my own theory. You see, the chief and I had sort of gotten off to a rough start. Genuinely bad chemistry from the first time I laid eyes on him and he laid eyes on me. Then things just went downhill from there, until at one point, he promised me that the day he retired, he'd come out to Paradise to find me so we could settle things between us once and for all. No more badge in the way, just a couple of men who truly didn't like each other, having it out in the parking lot. He was ten years older than me, maybe even fifteen. But I knew it wouldn't be an easy fight. Not by a long shot.

"I came out here to ask for your help," he said.

I stared at him for a moment, waiting for it to make sense. It didn't happen.

"I didn't want to call you," he said. "I figured this is the kind of thing you need to do in person."

Jackie wandered over at that point, a bar towel over his shoulder.

"Who's your friend?"

"This is Roy Maven," I said, "chief of police in the Soo."

"Okay," Jackie said, reaching over to shake the man's hand. "At the risk of being indelicate . . . I was led to believe that you and Alex hate each other."

"Oh, I wouldn't go that far. Just call it a persistent lack of liking each other."

Jackie looked at me for confirmation. I just shrugged.

"Well, as long as we're playing nice here, how 'bout we get you a beer. Alex? A Molson?"

"I'm fine, thanks," Maven said.

"You don't understand," Jackie said. "This is a real Molson, bottled in Canada. From Alex's personal stash. He doesn't drink anything else."

"McKnight, you drive all the way to Canada to get your beer?"

"Hell if he drives," Jackie said. "I do."

"Well, damn," Maven said. "In that case I'll

have to have one. I am out of uniform, after all."

The evening is just about complete, I thought. All we need now is dinner and a movie.

He looked into the fire as we waited for Jackie to come back with the beer. When we both had our bottles, Maven tipped his back and took a long drink.

"That ain't bad," he said. "Not bad at all."

"So seriously," I said, "quit joking around and tell me why you're here."

"You really think I came all the way out here to have a beer with you? I meant what I said. I need your help."

"With what?"

He looked around the place, like somebody else might be listening in on our conversation. Then he pulled out a pack of cigarettes.

"Can I smoke in here?"

"Jackie would prefer that you don't."

He put the cigarettes away. He fidgeted with his bottle for a few seconds, then he stood up.

"Come on," he said. "Let's go outside."

Now we're getting to it, I thought. He really did come here to fight.

"If I don't smoke a cigarette, I'm gonna kill someone," he said. "This is hard enough as it is, believe me."

I made him wait for a three count, then I finally got up and grabbed my coat. Who needs a comfortable chair in front of the fire when you can go freeze your ass off with a man you can't stand?

He opened the door and I followed him into the darkness. He took a few steps along the side of the building, staying out of the wind. He pulled out his cigarettes and his lighter. It was an old-school silver flip lighter. He cupped his hands around the end of his cigarette as he lit it, then he snapped the lighter shut and put it in his pocket. He took a deep draw and let out a stream of smoke.

"So tell me what the hell's going on," I said.

"I told you this wasn't easy. So cut me some slack, eh? I came to ask you to do some work for a friend of mine."

"What kind of work?"

"You still have the private investigator's license?"

"I don't do that anymore."

"Do you still have the license or not?"

"It's a moot point, I told you I don't—"

"Okay, so you have the license. That's good."

"Maven, I swear to God . . ."

"Relax, McKnight. Will you just shut up for once and listen? Here's the situation. I've got this friend, Charles Razniewski. Everybody calls him Raz. I used to ride with him a lot when I was with the state police."

"When was that?"

"Hell, that was what, ten years ago now? I was

26

getting sick of the politics so I left to try something else. Eventually ended up taking the job up here."

"The state police's loss was Sault Ste. Marie's gain, you mean."

"I told you to shut up, okay? So Raz, he ended up leaving, too, just before I did. But in his case he went federal. He's been a U.S. marshal ever since. Based down in Detroit. Your old stomping grounds."

"The marshals had an office on Lafayette. I wonder if he was there when I was."

"Small world, who knows. But here's the point of all this. He's got one kid, Charles Jr."

Maven stopped and looked out into the parking lot. The wind picked up and the pine trees started swaying.

"God damn," he said. "I mean to say, he *had* one kid. Here's the thing. You see, Charlie, he was going to school out at Michigan Tech. Just starting his last semester, right after Christmas break, he goes back up to school for some New Year's Eve party, and then . . ."

He stopped and wiped his eyes with the back of his hand. I waited for him to get to what was obviously a hard thing to say.

"He hanged himself. From a tree. There was some alcohol in his system, I guess, but . . . I mean, he went out on his own and he drove down by the lake and he hanged himself."

"Did he leave a note?"

"No note. There usually isn't."

"I know, but . . ."

But nothing, I thought. The man was right. Despite everything you see in the movies, no matter how somebody kills himself, they almost never leave a note.

"I can't imagine," he said. "I mean, if it was my daughter Olivia . . ."

He took another drag off his cigarette and looked away, shaking his head.

"I don't understand, Chief. I mean, this shouldn't happen to anybody. Your old friend or *anybody's* old friend. But what does this have to do with me?"

"This whole thing has been eating Raz alive, okay? He can't make any sense of it. If the kid was upset about something specific . . . about a girl or something. But no. He's just . . . gone. Like that."

"I still don't see how I can help here."

"He wants to know. That's all. If there's anything to know. He just wants to understand what was going through his kid's head before he died. That's all the man wants."

"How can anybody possibly know that?"

"Maybe you can't. Maybe this whole thing is just a waste of time. But he wants somebody to try. He's already talked to the Houghton County Sheriff's office, but they can't do anything more for him. It's not like they're gonna spend much more time on this. So he's thinking maybe if somebody talks to some of Charlie's friends . . ."

"Wait a minute, are you talking about me going out there and doing that?"

"He can't do it. There's no way he can go out there again. Not yet. Even if he could, there's not much chance they'd really be straight with him. There are some things you just can't talk about with your dead friend's father, you know?"

"But hold on. Time out."

"I can't do it. I've already talked to the sheriff out there. We didn't exactly hit it off, but no matter what, I can't go out there and start grilling people. I mean, I know how I can come across sometimes. I think any of these kids, they'd just feel like they were getting the third degree and there's no way they'd open up to me. What Raz needs is an impartial third party, somebody who's reasonably good at talking to people. And if he hires you on an official basis . . ."

"No. Chief, please. Even if I was going to do this, there's no way I'd take money for it."

"You're not getting it." He was starting to rock back and forth now, shivering from the cold and maybe something else. Some kind of raw energy he was trying to burn off. "Don't you see? He *needs* to hire you. He needs to pay you some money to go talk to these kids. Find out what you can about his son's state of mind. Talk to the

29

sheriff's office, find out if there's anything else they can tell you. About any kind of trouble he might have been in. If he does that, then he's *doing something*. See what I mean? Paying you makes it real to him. So even if you don't find out anything, he can go home feeling like he did everything he could."

"Why me?"

"Well, you've got the license."

"I don't use it. You know that. Why don't you hire Leon Prudell?"

He was the only other game in town. My former sometimes-partner, a man who grew up in the UP and who never wanted to be anything else other than a private investigator. Problem was, he was the fat goofy kid who sat in the back of the classroom and to most people around here, he'd never be anything else.

"Prudell's a clown," Maven said. "At least you *look* competent."

"Gee, thanks. But seriously, Prudell's a lot better than anybody realizes. He'd do a fantastic job with this."

"Look, McKnight, all you have to do is drive out there, talk to a few people, then drive back. Tell Raz what you heard. If that happened to be, 'You know what, your son wasn't depressed at all, there was absolutely no reason he should have killed himself, so it was just a tragic fluke thing, one bad night in his life and I'm awfully sorry . . .' Well, then, I mean if you said that, then everybody would be better off, I think."

"So now you're even telling me what to say? Why bother even going out there? I can just say I did."

"Don't be a wiseass. I'm just saying, if you don't find out anything, that would be a good line to take. Is that too much to ask?"

"Chief . . ."

"And you make your three hundred bucks. Or whatever. I don't see what the problem is."

"You're something else," I said. "You treat me like crap every time I see you, but now you think all you gotta do is wave some money in my face and I'll help you."

He threw his cigarette down onto the gravel and reached out for me. He grabbed me by the coat and drew himself to within a few inches of my face. Here we go, I thought. We're gonna have that fight in the parking lot after all.

"I'm not asking for me," he said, looking me dead in the eye. "I'm asking for my old friend, who's spent the last three months living in hell. Okay? He's going to be in my office tomorrow at ten o'clock. If it's not too much trouble, I'd like you to stop by and at least talk to him. Can you do that?"

"Just once, would it kill you to say please?"

I could feel him tightening his grip on my coat.

"Please, Alex. Okay? Please."

31

Then he pushed me away from him and turned to go.

"Ten o'clock," he said as he got into his car. "Don't be late."

A few hours later, I helped Jackie close up the place for the night. It was starting to snow again when I went out to the truck. The whole town looked even emptier than usual. It actually gets pretty busy up here during prime snowmobile season, but tonight there were no vehicles on the road. The one traffic light blinked yellow above the only main intersection. It was so quiet I could actually hear the yellow bulb clicking on and off.

I got in the truck and started it. I didn't bother turning on the heat. It was only a quarter mile up the main road to my turnoff, then another quarter mile down the old logging road to the first of my cabins. I put the plow down as I rumbled along, past Vinnie's house, then my first cabin. Instead of passing it, I decided to stop this time. I don't know what made me do that, but I pulled up in front of the cabin and looked at it in the glow of my headlights. I could remember setting every single log with my father, back when he was alive and I was a kid who knew everything. I had lived in this cabin ever since coming back up here so many years later, my father long gone, my partner Franklin fresh in the ground with a wife and two little girls left behind, and me off the force by then, just looking to sell off the land and the cabins with it. Finding something up here that seemed to match the way I was feeling inside and deciding to stay. All the things that had happened since, both good and bad—until the day a killer from Toronto came looking for me and found someone else in the cabin instead. How many years later, and yet the feeling had been much the same. More blood, more blame. All on me, no matter what anyone else said. It was all on me.

I hadn't set foot in the place since that day. I had barely looked at it. Vinnie was right, I was avoiding the issue. I was working on every last detail in rebuilding the last cabin at the end of the road, unwilling to face the idea of moving back to where I belonged.

After hearing Maven tell me about his friend living in hell after what had happened to him . . . that night as I looked at my cabin glowing in my headlights, I knew exactly what he was talking about.

I didn't get out of the truck. I couldn't bring myself to do that yet.

I drove to the end of the road and went to sleep. Just another cold night in Paradise.

CHAPTER THREE

In my eight years as a Detroit police officer, I saw maybe half a dozen suicides. I say "maybe" because sometimes you just don't know. Maven was right about them usually not leaving a note. I think the statistic I heard was fifteen percent, so maybe one out of seven will leave a note and the rest will just leave you wondering why. Or even if it was suicide at all. Somebody falls off a building, say—how do you know if it was intentional? Somebody takes too many hard drugs or a few extra sleeping pills. Or the all-time favorite way to kill yourself and leave everybody guessing—the single-car accident. Find yourself a big tree and get up some speed. If the road is dry and you don't leave skid marks, you might be leaving behind that one single clue. But otherwise it'll be a mystery forever.

Hanging yourself from a tree, on the other hand . . . well, there was a hotshot assistant district attorney in Detroit and he had this Latin phrase I'd hear him use at least once a week. *Res ipsa loquitur.* The thing speaks for itself.

I hit the Soo around 9:45 that next morning. Sault Ste. Marie, Michigan, second-largest city in the Upper Peninsula. Sister city to Sault Ste. Marie, Ontario, and site of the Soo locks, where the big freighters line up to go from Lake Huron to Lake Superior, or vice-versa. I usually take Lakeshore Drive instead of the highway, because I like the way it winds around the shoreline, and I usually drive way too fast for my own good, because there isn't a police officer, deputy, or state trooper in the entire Upper Peninsula who'll give me a speeding ticket. It's the one benefit of being an ex-cop who took three bullets on the job. That plus the three-quarter salary for the rest of my life.

The City-County Building sits behind the courthouse on Portage Avenue, as charmless a rectangle as you'll find anywhere in the state. If you were to take a shoebox and cover it with gray paper, then draw a couple doors and some windows, you'd have an exact scale replica. The county sheriff and his deputies all have offices there, and downstairs you'll find the county jail. The Sault Ste. Marie police department has to share space in the same building, even borrow use of the jail, which makes you start to understand why Chief Maven is always so damned unhappy about everything. Add to that the state police barracks on Ashmun Street, the Coast Guard station next to the locks, and the U.S. Customs office at the border, and you see the rest of the picture. The man is as low on the totem pole as you can get, in his very own town.

I parked and went inside. The receptionist told

me to go right back to Chief Maven's office. It was a trip I'd made on five or six occasions, and every single time I'd end up sitting in a hard plastic chair just outside his door for what felt like half a day. Today I was obviously on a different program. Chief Maven was there waiting for me as I came down the hallway.

"McKnight," he said. "You're not late for once."

Maven showed me into the office, a place as welcoming and stylish as always with its four bare cement walls and lack of windows. Another man was already sitting in one of the guest chairs. He stood up when I entered. He was about my age, maybe two or three inches taller. Blond hair cut close, blue eyes. He looked sharp and he looked fit, maybe a little tired now, a little used up. Which wasn't a surprise. Still, I had no trouble believing he was a topnotch U.S. marshal.

"This is Raz," Maven said. "Raz, this is Alex."

"Pleasure to meet you."

"I'm sorry for your loss," I said.

Raz just gave me a tight smile and a nod. Then Maven waved us into our chairs. Nobody said anything for a few seconds, so I figured I should dive in.

"I understand you once rode with the chief," I said. "Way back when."

"We were both at the Lansing post for about two years. Then I left the state police."

"Yeah, that would do it for me." It was out of my mouth before I could even think about what I was saying. I mean, maybe this wasn't the time for making jokes, but Raz gave me half a smile and even half a laugh. For a man who had just lost his son three months before, he seemed to be holding up amazingly well.

"I couldn't stand all the time on the road," Raz said. "Most of it just doing speed patrol."

"Yeah, so he quit to go babysit federal judges," Maven said, falling right back into the pattern. This is what you do to your fellow cop, no matter how many years it's been. "And to drive around handcuffed to gangsters."

"He'll never get it," Raz said to me. "But I understand you were a police officer in Detroit."

"Yes. Third precinct."

"Hell, yeah. Right around the corner."

"I didn't run into many U.S. marshals."

"It's a small office. There aren't that many of us."

"He's a private investigator now," Maven said. "The best in town."

Raz stopped smiling and looked down at his hands. So much for the small talk. It was time to get to it.

"Actually, I'm not," I said. That was Maven's cue to turn the first of many shades of red, but I wanted to level with this man as soon as I could.

"I have a license," I went on, "but I sort of fell

into it by accident. It's a long story, but suffice to say, I haven't actually done much PI work, and I don't want to misrepresent myself. God knows you've been through enough already. You deserve the truth."

"We're not talking about standard PI work," Raz said. "Didn't Maven tell you what I was asking you to do?"

"He did, but I've been thinking about it, and I'm honestly not sure if I can be of much help to you. There does happen to be another private investigator in town, a man named Leon Prudell."

"McKnight, God damn it . . ." Maven was moving through shades two, three, and four.

"Just take it easy," Raz said to him. "You've gotta stop being so upset all the time, Roy. Can you just try that for me, please?"

But Maven was already halfway out of his chair, looking like he was about to come around his desk and strangle me.

"Alex, can we go take a walk so Roy can calm down?"

"It's twenty degrees outside," Maven said. "If you want me to leave, just—"

"Come on," Raz said to me as he stood up. "Come show me the famous locks."

When we were safely outside, I led him down through the locks park to the edge of the St. Marys River. Someone had plowed the walkway, but the whole park was empty. I turned my collar up as a cold wind blew across the snowdrifts, but Raz seemed unfazed by it.

When we got to the observation deck, we climbed up and sat on the bleachers. The metal was cold but at least we were out of the wind now. Through the Plexiglas we could look down on the MacArthur Lock and the Poe Lock just beyond it. It was the first day of April, so everything was still closed down for the season.

"No offense, but this is pretty anticlimactic," he said. It was cold enough for us to see our breath as we spoke.

"Come back in the summer. When a seven-hundred-footer goes through, it's impressive."

"I lived in Michigan most of my life, but this is the first time I've ever been up here. My son was supposed to meet me here last summer, but it never happened. I was thinking maybe next summer . . ."

He stood up with both fists clenched and took a few steps forward. He punched the glass and made the whole thing rattle. He took a few deep breaths and finally turned around to face me.

"I can't cry anymore, Alex. I had a whole lifetime of tears stored up and I spent the last three months crying out every single last one of them. I've got nothing left."

I didn't say anything. I just watched him and listened to what he was saying.

"His mother and I have been apart for a while now. He's been living with me for the past few years. Just the two men, you know? Just me and Charlie. When he decided to switch majors, I was kinda skeptical, but hell, his girlfriend was in the same program, this forestry thing. Managing . . . you know, forests. Trees. Taking care of trees. Tech's got a good program for that, so I thought, okay, why not. Maybe he wasn't cut out for criminal justice. Maybe that was just because of his old man, you know? So I said, sure, go for it. Give it a try, see if it works. But don't complain to me when you get ten feet of snow."

He smiled again for the briefest of moments, then it was gone.

"Okay," he said. "Maybe I wasn't so supportive when he told me about the forestry thing. Maybe I didn't quite get it. The last time I saw him was over Christmas break, and we didn't exactly end things on a good note. But come on."

He looked down at the floor.

"I just want to know what happened to him. That's all I want. I don't think it's too much to ask. Just somebody, please . . . tell me what was going through his head. That's all I want and *nobody will tell me.* You understand, Alex? Nobody will say a word. The only thing they say is that there's no way for anybody to know what he was thinking. I'm sorry, but that's not good enough for me. I will not accept it."

He kept staring at the cold concrete between his feet.

"His girlfriend, and all of his friends . . . they're gonna graduate soon. Then they'll all be gone. They'll forget all about him and they'll move away and start their lives and have families and everything else. So I figure I've got this one chance, while they're all still together in the same place. While it's all still fresh in their minds. I want somebody to sit down with them and go over the last few days of—"

He stopped.

"The last few days of my son's life. So I can, I don't know what, make enough sense of it so I can keep on living myself. Not just give up and join him."

"Raz, come on . . ."

"Try on my boots, Alex. See if you don't feel the same way."

"I can't do that. I never had a son."

He thought about that for a moment.

"You might find this hard to believe," he finally said, "but Roy has a lot of respect for you. He wouldn't have come to you if he didn't."

That one was hard for me to believe, but I wasn't about to argue with him.

"He has a funny way of showing it, I know, but believe me. I wasn't on the force with him for

41

long, but it was enough. It sounds like he treats you exactly the same way he treated me."

"Once again, no surprise you're not a state cop anymore."

"It was actually kind of unusual for us to spend so much time together," he said. "Most troopers lead pretty lonely lives, and if they do end up riding with somebody else, it's usually not the same partner every time. But as soon as I got to Lansing, I think I must have pissed off the wrong lieutenant or something, because I kept ending up in the same car as Sergeant Maven. Don't ever tell him I told you this, but they used to call him 'Sergeant Cooler.' Like we're not sure if we want this guy around anymore, so let's put him with Sergeant Cooler for a while, see how long he lasts."

I had to smile at that. Then he shifted gears.

"Forgive me if I'm hitting too close to home here," he said, "but I understand you've suffered some losses yourself. On the job and—"

"My partner, in Detroit . . ."

"And then someone you loved, not that long ago?"

We sat right here, I thought. The two of us, once upon a time. On another winter's day, right here in this observation booth.

"Yes," I said. "Not that long ago."

"So we have something in common."

"The circumstances were different, but . . ."

"Look me in the eye," he said, "and tell me we don't have something in common."

"We do. I know we do."

"Were you with her when she died?"

I looked at him for a long time. "No," I finally said. "Not at that last moment, no."

"Okay, then. Neither was I."

Through the glass, I could see snowflakes starting to swirl all around us.

"Start at the beginning," I said, "and tell me everything."

I set out early the next day, coming down from Paradise through Newberry to M-28, the main highway that cuts across the middle of the Upper Peninsula. It was twelve degrees, but the sky was clear and there was sunlight gleaming impossibly bright on the unbroken fields of snow.

I hit the infamous "Seney Stretch" that runs right through the middle of the Great Manistique Swamp. It's twenty-five miles of road as straight as a ruler's edge, with absolutely nothing to see on either side but snow-covered trees and such a perfect line ahead of you it's downright hypnotizing.

I stopped for a quick breakfast in Munising, then continued along the shoreline. I didn't see as much ice in the lake as you'd expect in a normal year. It was just a vast expanse of open blue water here in the widest section of Lake Superior, with Canada a good two hundred miles to the north. I hit some actual traffic in Marquette, the biggest city in the UP, then kept going west through Ishpeming, Champion, and Three Lakes. Small towns where you'd buy your gas and your groceries and your fishing tackle and you'd rent your movies for the weekend, all from the same corner store.

In the heart of the day, I was finally getting close to my destination, and I could feel it in the way the road started to rise and fall. The Porcupine Mountains lay far ahead of me. I cut north through L'Anse and Baraga, heading up the eastern coast of the Keweenaw Peninsula. Copper Country. But I wanted to see where it happened first, though, before talking to anyone, so I cut back to the west and headed for Toivola. It's the last real town on the map until you finally hit Misery Bay.

If you ever do find yourself in Toivola, Michigan, I'd recommend stopping at a little place called Toivola Lunch. Of course, it's not like you'd have much choice. There's Toivola Lunch with a little convenience store attached to it on one side of the road, and on the other side there's a small post office attached to a house. That's it. That's Toivola, as far as I could see, anyway. It made Paradise look like a metropolis.

I went inside and had a quick glass of Coke. No

beer for me while I was doing so much driving, and I'm sure they only had American beer, anyway. The old man who served it to me had a slight Finnish accent. I was his only customer, but then the lunch rush was probably already over.

"Misery Bay," I said. "That's right down the road, right?"

"Misery Bay Road, yes."

"You know why they call it that?"

"What, Misery Bay?"

"Yes, is there a story behind the name?"

He scratched his head. "I've heard two stories. Not sure which is true. One is that there was a big Indian battle there, and the other is that a French fur trader got stranded there, and he was so miserable he called it Misery Bay."

"That's it?" With such an evocative name, I was expecting a lot more.

"Yeah, although if it was the French guy, you'd expect it to have a French name, wouldn't you? So maybe the Indian story, except for the fact that it's not an Indian name, either."

"Okay, either way. But it's right down that road."

"Sixteen miles. If you go too far, you'll be in the lake."

I was about to leave. Then I figured there was no harm taking a shot in the dark.

"I heard there was a suicide down there. In January."

The old man's smile evaporated. "Yeah, hell of a thing. A boy from Tech hanged himself."

"Did you know him? Did he ever stop in here?"

The man shook his head. "No, I didn't know him. Hell of a thing, though."

"Thanks for the Coke, sir." Then I was out the door, back in my truck, and heading down that sixteen-mile road.

There was a small sign around the halfway point. It read simply, MISERY BAY, and it had a deer's head beneath the letters. There were thick trees on either side of the road and as I got closer to the end I could see a small river moving through random holes in the ice and snow on the left. The Misery River, feeding into Misery Bay, at the end of Misery Bay Road. It kept bothering me that the man didn't even know where the name came from. I mean, if anybody in the world would have known . . .

Enough, I told myself. You're already letting the place get to you and you haven't even seen it yet.

Then I did. I turned the corner at the end of the road and found the small parking area near the break in the trees. In the summer, this was probably a boat launch, but here in the last month of winter it was just an empty pocket of level ground, mostly cleared of snow, with a view westward across the lake and facing directly into the cold wind. There was a great oak tree at the far end of the lot, and I could see a red ribbon tied around the trunk. This must have been where it happened.

I turned off the truck. I sat there for a moment, listening to the silence, wondering why anyone even bothered plowing this place. I didn't see any snowmobile trails, although I figured there had to be at least one or two out there in the woods somewhere. I didn't see anything but snow piled high in the shadow of the trees and the open water in the lake swirling where the river emptied into it.

As I got out of the truck, I took out the photograph Raz had given me. Young Charlie Jr., not quite as fair as his father, maybe some of his mother's coloring in the mix, but the same strong, confident face. In the picture it's summertime and the young man is standing on the end of a dock, with a fishing pole in his hand. He has turned toward the camera and the sun is going down behind him. I didn't know where the picture was taken. Maybe on another part of this very same lake, on another day not that long ago. Just a matter of months and yet look at where he ended up.

I went over everything Raz had told me. His son came home for Christmas break. He seemed a little down, a little more quiet than usual. He didn't say anything at all about his girlfriend or about his classes. He slept in late every morning.

He went back to school a couple of days early, saying he wanted to hit the New Year's Eve parties. There may have been a few words spoken on the way out the door, about his decision to switch from criminal justice to forestry. The last words his father would ever say to him.

But no, I thought. No way. Sons make their own way and sometimes their fathers don't understand. It's not a big enough reason to end your life before it's even begun. I just don't get it.

I went to the tree where he hanged himself. The red ribbon around the trunk was already weathered from the wind off the lake. I wondered who had put it there as I stood directly below the big branch that extended over the parking lot. This had to be it, I thought. This exact spot, right here.

As I looked up I tried to picture where the rope had gone. It occurred to me then that this wouldn't necessarily have been an easy thing to do. You can't just tie the rope to the branch, after all. You'd probably have to secure one end to something else on the ground, maybe wrapping it around the trunk of the tree, and then dangle just enough of the rope over the branch to give you a noose at just the right height. That's apparently what he did. Sometime between 2:00 and 3:00 A.M., he drove his car the twenty-three miles from Houghton. The rope must have been in the car with him, maybe coiled up right there beside him on the passenger's seat. Was it already tied into a noose? Or did he wait to tie it when he was here?

He backed the car into just the right position to stand on, the noose just close enough for him to slip his neck through. He fell backward off the car and the weight of his body tightened the rope around his neck. With only this short drop, he probably didn't lose consciousness right away. It probably took several seconds for the blood flow to his brain to be reduced, and then for his lungs to start screaming for air. I had to wonder, as I stood under that tree, did he live long enough to regret his choice?

Why the hell do it this way in the first place? Why here? It must have been so cold that night. Why not just take a few dozen sleeping pills and lie down in your warm bed and never wake up?

Or hell, if you had to do it here, why not just stay in your car? Take your pills there, or if you can't find pills, go buy a rifle and put the barrel in your mouth. It's Michigan, after all. You can always buy a rifle somewhere, twenty-four hours a day.

More than anything else, why make such a spectacle of it? Hanging from a tree like this, facing the lake like some sort of horrible sacrifice? I couldn't imagine doing such a thing, even in my darkest hour. Not this way.

I looked at his picture one more time. You see someone's face in a picture like this and you think you can form a basic impression of what kind of person he is. But everything I'd ever know about him would be completely secondhand, and even if I talked to every friend he had, every classmate, every teacher, every person who ever knew him in any way . . . how would I ever know what was really going on inside him?

I stayed there for a long time, taking it all in. There were no houses or other buildings to be seen in any direction. No sign of life at all. Just high drifts of snow and more trees and the lake itself. I started to feel a strange foreboding about the place, and I could only wonder if it was because I came here already knowing what had happened. Would I have felt the same thing if I had just stumbled upon this place by accident?

There was no way to know.

I got back in the truck and started it. I turned up the heat to warm my hands. Then I started driving up to Houghton to see what else I could find out about the late Charlie Razniewski Jr.

CHAPTER FOUR

Houghton, Michigan. If you know your history, you know what this city once meant to the rest of the state. Hell, to the whole country.

The first big mining boom happened here, even before the gold rush out west. Copper Country, they called it. That's how all of the Finns ended up here, along with a few Swedes, Danes, and Norwegians. You can still hear the accents in many of the locals. You can still see some of the heavy equipment standing silent and rusted where the mines were. This is where they took all the copper from the ground and turned it into electrical wire and shipped it all over the world. It all happened right here.

They built the college and it went through several mining-related names until it finally ended up being known as Michigan Technological University. It's not about mining anymore, of course. It's all about science and engineering now. The students come from all over Michigan and besides studying, the one thing they'd better be ready for is snow, because they get a hell of a lot of it. Most years, anyway. I was reminded of that as I drove up into the Keweenaw Peninsula and saw the big sign by the side of the road. It was a measuring stick as tall as a tree, with that winter's current snowfall amount marked at around twelve feet. On the second day of April, usually they'd have at least twice that by now.

As I got closer to the city, I passed a huge set of concrete slabs along the shoreline. Even taller than the snowfall stick, they looked like a giant set of dominoes. More relics from the copper mining, I'm sure, but beyond that I had no idea what they were used for. It made the whole place feel even more foreign to me.

When I got to Houghton itself, that feeling got even stronger. You lose sight of Lake Superior, but as you go inland, you see Portage Lake stretching out across the middle of the Keweenaw. The land rises on either side of the water, and the biggest lift bridge you'll ever see connects Houghton to Hancock, the city to the north. The middle section of the bridge can rise a hundred feet to let ships pass beneath it.

Most strange of all is how the city of Houghton is built on an incline, with streets running parallel to each other and climbing in elevation as you get farther away from the water. It looks like a miniature San Francisco, I swear, and you have to remind yourself that you're still in Michigan.

I passed Michigan Tech on my way into the center of the city, then I found the Houghton County Sheriff's office on the fourth street up from the water. Just like back in the Soo, they seemed to have had the same idea when they put up the building. Start with the county courthouse, the tallest, grandest, most beautiful building in town. Connect another building to that, but make sure this one is a gray concrete box, with all the charm of an air raid shelter.

One of the county plows was touching up the parking lot. I waited for him to finish and gave him a little wave as he left, one plow operator to another. Then I parked the truck and went inside.

The receptionist asked if she could help me, and I picked up yet another Scandinavian accent. I would have guessed Swedish this time, but I wouldn't have put much money on it. I bet if you live out here you can pick them out right away.

"I'd like to talk to the sheriff," I said. "I'm a private investigator visiting from Chippewa County."

I had my license with me, burning a hole in my pocket. It felt strange to refer to myself as a PI.

"He's not in the office right now. I believe the undersheriff's here, if you'd like to speak to him."

"I'd appreciate that."

A minute later, the undersheriff came out looking for me. He was a big man with a perfect cop's mustache. He had a hell of a strong grip.

"Undersheriff Michael Reddy," he said, looking me up and down. "What can I do for you?"

"I don't mean to impose on your time, sir. I just wanted to ask you a couple of questions."

"Can you give me a topic?"

"Charles Razniewski Jr."

I didn't have to say anything else. The undersheriff exchanged a quick look with the receptionist. Then he motioned for me to follow him.

"Come on back," he said. "Let's talk."

A few minutes later, I was sitting on the opposite side of his desk. There were piles of paper everywhere. Organization was obviously not his strong suit, but I was holding a good strong cup of coffee and the man had listened carefully when I had told him why I was there. So I had no complaints.

"How far did you have to come to get here?" he asked.

"I live in Paradise."

"Yeah, I know the place. Over by the Soo, right?"

"Other side of Whitefish Bay, yes."

"Let me ask you, do you happen to know the chief of police there?"

"Roy Maven, you mean?"

"Yeah, that's him. Is he the one who sent you out here?"

"No, sir. You see—"

"Because if it was, I'd like you to explain to me

how one single person can be so charming and persuasive."

"It was the young man's father who sent me," I said. "Charles Razniewski Sr. He and Chief Maven were once state police officers at the same post."

"Okay, now it makes a little more sense. Maven called out here himself a few days ago, is the reason I ask. He didn't say anything about his history. He was too busy grilling me like he'd just caught me trying to steal his car."

"Yeah, that sounds about right."

"Okay, so I won't hold that against you. Just tell him he might want to cool it next time you see him. But you're saying this kid's father sent you all the way out here to find out more about . . . what again? I'm sorry, I still don't quite follow you."

"That's the tough part," I said. "He's not sure what he thinks I can do. He just wants somebody to do something. Find out what I can from people while it's still fresh in their minds."

"He basically wants you to find out why his son killed himself?"

"I guess you could put it that way, yes."

The undersheriff shook his head slowly. "I think he's asking you to do the impossible. Is that something you're usually good at?"

I had to smile. "Generally not. Most days I'm just trying to keep my road clear."

"I had to cut the kid down, you know."

My smile disappeared.

"The EMS guys," he said, "they sorta just put the stretcher underneath him. There was a fire truck there, so we had the ladder, but for some reason I got elected to climb up there and cut the rope. Hell, it wasn't even officially my jurisdiction."

"What do you mean?"

"Misery Bay is actually in Ontonagon County, not Houghton County."

"I didn't realize that. The map made it look like—"

"It's barely over the line. But we always help each other out, you know, and as soon as we found out this kid was one of ours . . ."

"Sounds like a tough day, no matter who's in charge."

"He'd been hanging out there for a day and a half, you realize. Nobody had seen him that whole time. That's how lonely that place is. This time of year, anyway."

"I sort of got that idea," I said. "I drove by there today."

That seemed to surprise him. "You were at Misery Bay?"

"I just wanted to see it."

"Yeah, well, I keep seeing it, too. Every night when I try to go to sleep."

"I understand," I said. "But still. I felt I had to start there."

"What was your impression?"

"Well, I tried to reconstruct the event in my mind. Let me ask you this while I'm thinking of it. How long was the rope?"

The undersheriff picked up a blank pad of paper from the mess on his desk. He picked up a pen and stared down at the pad. It was obvious to me he was coming to some sort of decision.

"Mr. McKnight, I take it you were in law enforcement at some point?"

"Detroit Police Department. Eight years."

He nodded. "And now you're private?"

"On paper, yes, but I'll be honest with you. This feels more like I'm just doing the man a favor. So really, I know I'm just a stranger showing up out of nowhere, asking you all these questions."

"Do you feel that there was something inappropriate about the way we handled this case?"

"No," I said. "God, no. That's not why I'm here."

"Let me tell you what kind of winter it's been for me. A couple nights after New Year's, a kid from Tech drives down to Misery Bay and manages to hang himself from a tree. Like I said, I was the lucky bastard who got to cut him down. Had to look this kid right in the face. He was as frozen as an icicle. Just a couple weeks later, I hear about an old friend of mine, a sergeant down in Iron Mountain. His son shot himself behind the barn. Put a bullet right in his own head."

He paused for a moment, then continued.

"My wife's father killed himself a few years ago, so it's already kind of a hot spot for me."

"I'm sorry to hear that."

"Yeah, he just drove off one day. He found a deserted spot and he tried to run a hose from the exhaust pipe through the window, had it all taped up with duct tape. He didn't realize that new cars don't put out that much carbon monoxide anymore. So it must have taken hours. If he didn't have a full tank, it might not have worked. Although in that case he might have just froze to death. But anyway, he'd been suffering from depression. We had him on some new medicine, but I guess it wasn't doing the job. Takes a while, they said. So meanwhile he has to slip away from us when we're not looking and take all damned day to kill himself. It absolutely destroyed my wife, I'll tell you that much."

He dropped the pad back on the desk. The mess made a little more sense to me now. This man was just trying to keep it all together, and a clean desk was pretty low on his list of priorities.

"It would have been better if her father had died in an accident," he said. "Or hell, even if somebody had broken into the house and killed him. At least that way, you wouldn't have to keep wondering why he did it to himself, you know? I can't imagine a worse thing to have to go through. But anyway, ever since then, every time I hear about a suicide, it just hits me right in the gut, you know? Now two kids killing themselves in the same winter. One of them in my county."

"Look, I'm sorry I'm bringing all this back up. I had no idea this was going to hit so close to home with you."

"You just have to understand. Lately I'm beginning to think that everybody I see is going to find some way to kill themselves."

"Well," I said, "I'm not going to. I promise."

"Okay. That's good to hear. That's a start, I guess. But you know, to tell you the truth . . . maybe it's a good thing I'm the one you got to talk to today. Because maybe most cops wouldn't understand why you'd come all the way out here just to pry into a situation that's obviously not going to change."

I started to protest, but he put up his hand to stop me.

"It's okay, Mr. McKnight. I get it. If it was somebody from my family, I'd be asking the same questions myself. Or else I'd be sending out a wise-looking old cop like yourself to ask the questions for me."

"I'll take that as a compliment, I guess."

"I meant it no other way. And to answer your question, the rope was approximately fifty feet long."

"So more than long enough to tie off around the trunk, and then extend over that big branch."

"That's how he did it, yes. Beyond that, I just wish I could give you more information. We've got so many kids who come up here for college. Then they're gone. I'm afraid that young Mr. Razniewski was just one of those temporary residents."

"His father gave me three names to look up— his girlfriend and two of his other friends."

"You got the phone numbers?"

"I do, yes."

"Then give them a call. On a Wednesday, this time of year, there's not a whole lot to do besides going to class or hanging out in a bar somewhere."

"Sounds familiar," I said. "Except for the going-to-class part."

"This is a terrible thought," he said, his voice lowered, his head leaning toward me. "But sometimes in the dead of winter up here . . . as I get older, I mean, I start to wonder why we don't see even *more* suicides."

There wasn't much I could say to that. So I thanked the man and left him to his pile of papers and his morbid thoughts.

Before I could even get to my truck, it started to snow again.

I checked into a hotel on Shelden Avenue, down in the center of town, close to the water. From my window, I could see the lift bridge and the light stream of traffic crossing in either direction, headlights on as the snow came down harder and dimmed the late afternoon light.

I took out the list of names and numbers Raz had given me. There were only three names— Bradley, Wayne, and Charlie's girlfriend Rebecca. That was it. I started with Rebecca's number and got her voice mail. I left a message, told her who I was and that I just wanted to ask her a couple of quick questions about Charlie. I asked her to call me as soon as she got the chance.

I called Bradley, got his voice mail, and left a similar message. As I called Wayne, I wondered if I was about to get shut out completely. It's quite possible that nobody will talk to you, I said to myself. If they don't want to deal with this, they'll just avoid you.

But Wayne answered the phone. I went down the same path with him, who I was, why I was here in Houghton. When I was done, the line was silent for a few seconds.

"I understand," he finally said. "I don't know what I can do to help you, but . . . I mean, I'll do whatever I can."

"I called his girlfriend, and this other friend of his. Bradley? Do you know him?"

"Yeah, Bradley. We're two of Charlie's apartment-mates. We were, I mean. Anyway, I'll see him in a few minutes. But did you say his girlfriend? You mean Rebecca?"

"Yes, that's the name I have here."

"Your information's a little out of date," he said. "I guess his father didn't know."

"They weren't together anymore?"

"No, not for a while."

"Would it be possible to meet with you for a few minutes? Just to ask you some questions?"

I could hear him letting out a long breath. "Yeah, why not? We're gonna be at the Downtowner tonight. It's right on the end of the main drag, next to the bridge."

"That sounds good. And hey, if you happen to think of anyone else who might have known him well . . ."

"I'll see if I can round up some people," he said. "Say about eight o'clock?"

"That would be fantastic, yes. You'll see if Rebecca can come, too?"

"Yes. Of course. She'll be there."

I hadn't even met the kid yet, but I could tell he was feeling funny about something. It was right there in his voice.

"You and Rebecca . . . ," I said, taking a shot.

"Yeah, we're kinda together now. But she and Charlie were broken up since last fall, I swear."

"You don't have to explain." I thanked him and I told him I'd see the whole gang at the Downtowner at eight.

I hung up the phone and looked out at the snow. Okay, that's one possible reason to kill yourself, I thought. As old as mankind.

I left the hotel around 6:30, figuring I'd get something to eat before talking to Charlie's friends. It was still snowing. The sun was going down and it was getting even colder. I walked down Shelden, feeling my face go numb and the snow collecting in my hair. There were bars and restaurants on either side of the street, each one glowing with warm light and looking more inviting than the last. I saw the Downtowner at the very end of the street, just as Wayne had told me. I stepped inside and saw that it was doing good business that night. Mostly college kids, all hanging around the high tables, drinking beer and talking over the music. There were televisions over the bar, a basketball game on some, a hockey game on the others. The whole place was loud and smoky and basically everything that the Glasgow Inn would never be in a thousand years.

There was a back room with big windows overlooking the bridge. It was a little less noisy and there was room to sit down, so I grabbed a table. When the waitress came over—another college kid, of course—I ordered a hamburger and a beer. She didn't have to card me.

I looked out the window as I ate. There were a

million little lights sparkling on the bridge. Funny how it could be so ugly in the daytime and then a few hours later look like a giant piece of art glowing in the darkness. I thought about what I was going to ask Charlie's friends when they got here. I wasn't so sure about having them all come at once. Normally, when you're interviewing several people, you want to keep them separate as much as possible. There's a group mentality that takes hold when one person gets talking and the others are listening and they each start to chime in and tell the same story. You get each one alone and you usually get a different take on the story from each person telling the tale.

Of course that's the way you play it when you're taking statements. When a crime has been committed and you're trying to sort out the bad guys from the innocent victims. This was nothing like that, so I knew I'd just have to try to ask the right questions, and listen as carefully as I could. Even though at that moment I still had no idea what anyone could say that would make a father feel any better.

At five before eight, a young man and a young woman came into the room. They were obviously looking for someone. And I was obviously the only man in the place more than thirty years old. They spotted me and walked over.

"You must be Mr. McKnight," the young man said. He had long black hair tied in a ponytail. Not exactly what I'd expect at Michigan Tech, but what the hell did I know? "I'm Wayne. We spoke on the phone."

"Please, call me Alex."

"This is Rebecca," he said, indicating the young woman standing next to him. She was pretty in a slightly plain Midwestern way, with blond hair and green eyes. She was already looking a little nervous, and we hadn't even gotten down to business yet.

"It's good to meet you," I said.

She nodded and pursed her lips, but didn't say a word.

"Have a seat," I said. "Can I order you some drinks?"

"Um, I'm afraid I'm not legal yet," Wayne said as they both sat down across from me. "I turn twenty-one next month."

That's when I looked him over and realized how truly young he looked. Rebecca even more so. Hell, I thought, I am sitting in a bar filled with children who have run away from home and are pretending to be college students. They shouldn't be here alone on a cold winter night and I shouldn't be here talking to these two about yet another child who hanged himself from a tree.

"You'll have to excuse me," I said. "I'm not

quite sure how to begin here. So why don't you just tell me about Charlie, okay?"

That seemed to put him at ease a little bit. Rebecca still looked a little anxious, but as soon as Wayne started talking, she relaxed and even found a few words of her own. The picture they painted for me was of a young man who truly didn't have an enemy in the world. One of those kids who light up a room the moment they walk in. It might have been a little bit of exaggeration-as-eulogy, but I got the impression that Charlie Razniewski Jr. would be missed by a lot of people.

He had switched to forestry at the beginning of his junior year, after getting together with Rebecca. Before that, he'd been a criminal justice major, as I already knew, hoping to follow in his father's footsteps. But when Rebecca told him she was a forestry major, well, the whole idea sounded a lot more rewarding to him. More time outside, less time behind a desk. It was just the kind of thing he always secretly knew he wanted to do. At least that's what he told Rebecca.

They were together for their junior year at Tech. But in the summer Rebecca had the chance to do an internship with the U.S. Forest Service, along with Charlie's good friend Wayne. Charlie was still playing catch-up with his new major, so he said good-bye to Rebecca for the summer and they both promised to pick up where they left off come September.

As I was hearing the tale, I already knew what was coming next. By the time they saw each other again, Rebecca had spent the whole summer with Wayne, and Charlie had apparently sort of met somebody else, too. That part was a little fuzzy. Bottom line, there was a big fight and an official breakup and then an okay-let's-be-good-friends a few weeks later. By the time winter break rolled around, everybody was reasonably happy. Or so it seemed.

"I don't think Charlie's father knew anything about the breakup," I said.

"I just feel so bad," she said. "I can't help thinking I had something to do with what happened."

"No, come on," Wayne said. "That's not true at all. You know better."

Wayne sat there rubbing her back for a while as she fought off the tears. That's when a few more of Charlie's friends and classmates showed up. It became a jumble of names and young faces at that point, with lots more stories of how great a guy Charlie was and how nobody ever would have thought he'd be the kind of man to hang himself. There were apparently enough people over twenty-one now, so the beers started getting passed around and everything got a little louder. There was even a little bit of dark humor centered around the fact that Charlie was a forestry major and he decided to hang himself from a tree. That's about when I decided it was time to leave.

Wayne had introduced me to Charlie's two other apartment-mates—Bradley, whose name I already had on my list, and another kid named RJ. They invited me to come back to the apartment to see where Charlie had lived, so a few minutes later we were all outside. The wind had picked up, so we were all trying to shield our faces from the driving snow as we walked up the hill, away from the water. It was Bradley and RJ and me, with Wayne and Rebecca tagging along behind us.

It was a squat little apartment building on the very top of the hill, assaulted by the wind and the snow. I wasn't even sure how it was still standing. They opened up the door and we all went inside and slammed the door behind us, flakes of snow still flying around us in the living room as we took off our coats.

It was everything I expected from a college apartment, with odds and ends and cast-off furniture. Posters for rock bands I'd never heard of on three walls, but on the fourth, in place of the crappy little television and the CD player with the cheap speakers, was a forty-eight-inch hi-def LCD television surrounded by a sleek black sound system. I guess that's the minimum these days, even for four half-starving college kids.

Or rather, make that three. They showed me to the room Charlie shared with Wayne—his half of the room was pretty much empty now.

"The police asked us to box up all his stuff," Bradley said. He was a big kid, maybe fifty or sixty pounds overweight. A late bloomer with bad skin. I didn't imagine he had much of a social life. Not up here where the men outnumber the women by a good seven to one.

"It was just clothes and books and a few CDs," RJ said. He was tall and thin and had dark hair and heavy eyebrows. There was something intense about him, and I'm sure most of the college girls would call him attractive. Unlike Bradley, I was sure he had no trouble finding someone to be with on a lonely Saturday night. "They said they were going to mail it all back to his father."

That makes sense, I thought, and it also means he's already seen it all and gone through it. If there was anything to learn from it, he'd already had that chance.

"It's so weird not having him here," Bradley said. "I mean, it's not like we'd even want somebody else in here. Not that you'd find somebody in the middle of the school year. Heck, I don't even know what I'm talking about."

I sat down on the bare mattress. Then I stood

up and on a whim I lifted up the mattress to see if there was anything hidden underneath. There was nothing. No secret journal into which he poured out his thoughts every night. No answers at all.

When we went back to the living room, the private stash of beer had been tapped into, everybody holding a bottle now and obviously not worrying about the legal drinking age anymore. It had been years since I'd been a cop, of course, and even if I was wearing the uniform that night I wouldn't have said a word to them. They all sat around drinking in total silence and staring at the floor.

"I want to ask you something," Rebecca finally said. "Do you think I can talk to Charlie's father sometime? Just to say how sorry I am?"

"I don't see why not. He's in Sault Ste. Marie tonight, staying with a friend. I can give you his phone number."

"Maybe I should just wait until he goes back home. I don't want to disturb him right now."

I nodded my head and let it go. She didn't really want to talk to the man. At least not for a while. Maybe a year from now, she'll actually call him.

"I really miss him," Wayne said. "This is the kind of night he loved. The worse the weather was, the happier he got."

Everybody smiled at that, and I was sure they

were each bringing up their favorite Charlie memories again. Rebecca started to cry about then, and Wayne told her he'd walk her home. They both shook my hand and thanked me for coming all the way out there to talk to them.

"Tell his father I feel so bad," Wayne said.

"Me, too," Rebecca said, and that was about all she was able to say before they finally wished me a good night and headed out into the wind and the snow.

I put my beer bottle down on the kitchen table and was expecting to head out myself, but then Bradley started talking again.

"It wasn't about her," he said. "I hope you don't think that."

"How do you mean?"

"It wasn't because Charlie and Rebecca broke up. He wasn't really upset about that at all. In fact, he was kind of relieved when she got involved with Wayne."

"Come on, Bradley," RJ said.

"Come on, nothing."

"I swear to God. Don't even go there."

"It's all right," I said. "Go on."

"He knew they weren't gonna work out," Bradley said. "So I'm just saying. It's not like he was all broken up about it or anything."

RJ just looked at the ceiling and shook his head.

"You know why he was so upset," Bradley said

to him. "You were here. He talked to you more than anyone else."

RJ raised his hands in surrender. "I'm not saying anything."

"His father wanted Charlie to be a cop, just like him. When he switched to forestry, his father wasn't happy. Like *at all.* Like he'd say, Charlie was giving up a real career doing something important to be a lumberjack or something. He had absolutely no idea what a forestry degree really means."

I thought back to what Raz had said about the program. Trees, studying trees, he said. Doing things with trees.

"It really got to Charlie, is all I'm saying. He knew his father was totally disappointed with him. They had a really big fight about it."

"I wouldn't go that far," RJ said.

"There's no use sugarcoating it," Bradley said. "That doesn't do anybody any good now. We might as well tell the truth."

"Don't you understand?" RJ said. "Sometimes you don't have to say anything at all. You need to learn that."

"It's the truth and you know it. Charlie was miserable because he thought he was letting his father down."

RJ closed his eyes and put one hand against his forehead.

"I'm not saying he *should* have thought that,"

Bradley said, running out of steam. "I'm not saying it was right. I'm just saying . . ."

Then he stopped. He had wheeled out the great weight and put it there in front of us. It was invisible yet heavy as cast iron and it would crush any man who would try to carry it.

Yet that's what I had to do now. I had to strap that weight to my back and walk out into the cold night.

I shook the hands of each of those two young men and left them there. I knew it would be quiet there in the apartment for a long time to come. When I was outside I turned my collar up against the wind and I went back down the hill toward my hotel. The lights on the bridge were glowing. I didn't feel like sitting in my hotel room yet so I found the loneliest bar on the street, the darkest place to sit and drink with as few people around as possible. No music, no laughter coming from young college kids with their whole lives ahead of them.

I sat at the rail and had my drink. I looked at the dark mirror behind the bottles and I asked that man on the other side of the glass what the hell he was going to do next.

CHAPTER FIVE

When I woke up the next morning, I saw actual sunlight coming through the window. The snow had stopped sometime during the night. Maybe six or seven inches had come down. The bright light bouncing off all that new snow made my head hurt even more, so I took four aspirin and a hot shower.

I grabbed a quick breakfast downstairs, then checked out and hit the road. As I drove down through the Keweenaw Peninsula, I started working it over in my mind. What exactly was I going to tell Raz about his son? The whole idea had been to make him feel better somehow. To give him some kind of closure so he could move on with his life. That it may have been largely his fault, his absolute worst fear come true, was probably not the kind of closure he had in mind.

I was taking the southwestern route out of Copper Country, so whether it was a completely conscious decision or not, I was making a slight detour through Toivola. When I got there, I took a right down that same lonely road to Misery Bay. I just had to see the place one more time. I wasn't even exactly sure why.

Maybe it was because I felt as though I knew the kid so much better now. Like now it would hit me that much harder to see where he breathed his last breath. The new snow hadn't been plowed, so I fishtailed my way down those sixteen miles until I got to the end. I parked in the same spot, got out, and walked over to the same tree with the red ribbon still tied around it. The whole place looked different now with the sun shining. Yet somehow I still had that same raw feeling of uneasiness just being there.

I stood under the same spot and looked up at the branch where he had looped his rope. It was sturdy enough to hold his weight. I could see that much. I had an urge to climb the tree, to work my way out on that branch so I could see the exact spot where the rope came in contact with the bark.

I didn't end up climbing the tree. One fatality here was more than enough. Instead, I went back to the truck, reached in, and opened up the toolbox that was on the passenger's side floor. I found the pair of scissors I used to cut the plastic sheets for the cabin windows. I got out and went back to the tree. There were a few inches of loose red ribbon on either side of the bow. I cut about two inches from one side and looked at it closely. The color was already beginning to fade.

This is all I'll bring back to him, I thought. Just two inches from a red ribbon tied around the tree. I won't bring back the great weight I've been given. I won't bring back the truth about what was really bothering this kid that night. I'll leave it right here forever. Right here on the shores of Misery Bay.

I hit Marquette about two hours later. I stopped to gas up and while I had an actual signal on my cell phone I figured I'd call ahead to Raz. I dialed his cell phone number, listened to it ring a few times. It went through to voice mail.

"This is Alex," I said. "I'm on my way back. I should be in the Soo between two and three o'clock. I'll give you another call when I get closer."

There were a few seconds of dead air while I decided what to say next.

"I hope you're doing okay today," I finally said. "I'll talk to you soon."

I hung up the phone and hit the road again. The sun was still out, but on the open stretches the wind was whipping the snow back and forth across the road. I kept driving, back through all of the little towns I had passed on my way out the day before.

I drove straight through on M-28, all the way into Sault Ste. Marie. If I was going to lie to Raz's face, I wanted to get it done with as soon as possible. I picked up the cell phone and called him again. Once again it went through to voice mail. I hung up and dialed the police department.

I asked for Chief Maven. I had to wait a few minutes, but he finally came onto the line.

"McKnight! Where are you? What's going on?"

"I'm just looking for Raz," I said. "I'm almost back to the Soo."

"Did you call him?"

"Yes, I did." I resisted saying anything else. Like why the hell would I not do that first?

"He's not answering?"

"No," I said. Count to three in your head. "He's not answering."

"Well, he's at my house. Give him a call there. Maybe his cell phone's dead." He gave me the number.

"Okay, I'll try him there."

"How did it go out there, anyway?"

"I found out a few things about his son. He had a lot of great friends."

"Is Raz going to be okay with what you tell him?"

"Yes," I said. "I think he will be."

"McKnight, so help me God, if you add one more ounce of pain to that man's soul . . ."

"Hey, you're the one who asked me to help, remember? So save the attitude."

"All right, relax. I'm just saying . . ."

"It was just like you were thinking, Chief. A total fluke thing. One bad day in his life."

"Are you just saying what you think you're supposed to say?"

You're making this hard, I thought. There's nobody else on this earth who can make things hard like you can.

"It's the truth," I said. "I'll tell that to Raz."

"Okay, then. Give him a call. Tell him I'll be home in a few hours."

"I will, Chief."

I hung up before he could say another word, then dialed his home number. It rang a few times. Then the answering machine came on. It was Roy Maven's wife, telling me they weren't home just then but that they'd like me to leave a number so they could call me back. I'd met the woman exactly one time that I could remember. She seemed quite human and perfectly nice, and at the time I couldn't help wondering how she had ever come to marry outside of her species. Maybe someday I'd get to sit down and ask her, but right now I had other matters to deal with.

For the hell of it, I tried calling Raz's cell phone again. No luck there, so I called Maven again and told him there'd been no answer at his house.

"My wife helps out at the hospital," he said, "so she might be there. But Raz should be at the house. I don't know where else he'd go."

"Where's your house? I'll stop by and see if I can find him."

"McKnight, you're giving me a bad feeling here. How come whenever you're involved in *anything,* I end up getting an ulcer?"

"Just relax, Chief. Give me your address."

He gave me a number on Summit Street.

"I'll call you right back," I said. As I hung up, I tried to shake off the same uneasy feeling. He's out taking a walk, I told myself. Or he's asleep. Or maybe he and Mrs. Maven are out having a late lunch somewhere. There were a hundred different possibilities.

I swung up I-75 and then got off by the college. Down Easterday, past the students outside taking advantage of what passes for a nice day in April around here. I'd seen so many young faces in just the past two days. I made the turn at Summit and went halfway up the block until I found the number I was looking for. I pulled into the driveway.

It was a nicely kept raised ranch. Nothing too extravagant, but then I wouldn't have expected anything approaching extravagance from a man like Roy Maven. The walkway was clear. The shovel was leaned against the house, right next to the front door. I went up the steps and rang the doorbell. There was no answer.

I rang the bell again. Nothing.

I tried the knob. The door was unlocked. I pushed the door open and took one step inside. Under the circumstances, I didn't think Maven would mind.

Okay, maybe he would have, but I did it anyway.

"Hello? Anybody here? Raz?"

The house was silent. I stood there for a while, thinking about what to do next.

That's when the odor came to me. Something I'd smelled before. Organic and metallic at the same time. A basic, instinctive foulness. It was the smell of death.

The whole scene flashed before me in a fraction of a second. I imagined Raz hanging from a rope he had somehow tied to the ceiling. Taking the same way out. Following his own son into the abyss.

Or no. He's a cop. Marshal, ex-trooper, whatever the hell. He's a cop and he'd do it the cop way, by eating his own gun.

I went through the living room to the kitchen. As soon as I turned the corner, I saw Raz's body laid out on the hard tile floor. There was blood all around him. His throat was cut open. He was lying facedown but his body was twisted as if he were still trying to get away. His eyes were still open. He stared right at me as if to accuse me of thinking even for a moment that he'd actually take his own life.

I stood there for a long moment while it all washed over me. Then I pulled out my cell phone and called 911.

I went outside and sat down on the front step. The voice on the other side of 911, a woman's voice, wanted me to stay on the line with her until the police showed up. I told her to send somebody and that I'd wait right here and she started to argue with me so I hung up on her. I sat on the step and I looked out across the street at the other houses. All of them sealed up tight against the winter. We live in such a frozen wasteland for much of the year. That's the strange thought that came to me as I sat and waited. It feels so cold sometimes, you wonder how anyone would choose this place. Yet we do. We live here, some of us for our whole lives, and the one benefit we should receive in return is that the violence from the rest of the world should leave us in our frigid state of peace.

That doesn't seem like too much to ask.

The thought was interrupted by the first squad car. It was a Sault Ste. Marie police officer who got out and came hustling up the walkway. I knew the state police would be here soon, too. For a crime this big in a city this small, they'd all come running.

I didn't recognize this officer, and he turned out to be a youngster right out of the academy, so we had to go through the whole song and dance, with me putting my hands up and him patting me down. I was even thinking he might feel uncertain enough to go ahead and put the cuffs on me and I wasn't about to complain because I knew that's exactly what they taught this kid. He had no idea who I was and he hadn't checked inside the house yet. For all he knew, I could be the killer myself, and I could even have an accomplice waiting inside to jump out and surprise him. So just like they drilled it into his head, whenever you're alone and there's any doubt at all, you put your man in cuffs, even if it's just for a minute while you secure the scene. Even if you have to apologize while you're doing it, you "hook" your man until the backup arrives.

But that's when Maven's car pulled up and I suddenly had bigger things to think about than a pair of handcuffs.

"Chief," I said. "Don't go in the house."

"What's going on here?"

He came up the steps and I tried to block him.

"McKnight, get the hell out of my way."

"Chief, don't. He's dead."

He pushed past me and into the house. I stayed where I was. I didn't follow him inside because I didn't need to see it again, and there was nothing I'd be able to do to help him now. A few seconds passed. When he came back out, his face was white.

"What the hell happened?" He wasn't facing anyone. He was staring out into the middle distance and it looked like he was trying hard to swallow.

"My God," he said. "My God, what the hell—"

Then he stopped dead.

"Where's my wife?" he said. "Has anybody seen my wife?"

There were three more city cops on the scene now. Another car was pulling up, with two state cars close behind. The whole street was fast becoming a riot of red and blue flashing lights.

"Where's my wife, God damn it! Somebody find her right now!"

"Chief," I said, grabbing him by the shoulders, "take it easy. You said she might be at the hospital. Remember?"

He pushed past me again and went into the house. I heard him running up the stairs.

"Call the hospital," I said to the young cop, the same first cop who'd responded, and who was experiencing a hell of a first major crime scene. "I think she volunteers there or something."

"Where is she?" Maven, careening back down the stairs. Halfway down he almost fell and broke his neck. "Somebody find her!"

He ran around the house into the backyard. Finally, the young cop heard back on the radio that they'd located his wife at the hospital. She'd been sitting next to an old woman's bed, reading to her. The other cops had to practically tackle Maven to convince him that his wife was safe. When he finally sat down on the front steps, he was breathing hard and rubbing his hands up and down his thighs. He looked totally undone, something I'd never even imagine seeing from him.

"Tell me," he said to me when he finally got his

wind back. "Give me an explanation for why Raz is lying there in my kitchen like that? Huh? Can you tell me, please?"

I didn't have an answer for him. I just sat there next to him on the cold steps while the madness went on all around us.

I had no idea this was just the beginning.

PART TWO

PART TWO

And we're rolling . . .

. . . Establishing shot. Nice and wide. Here it is. This is where our story begins.

. . . See the normal-looking neighborhood? There are trees and a sidewalk and a blue mailbox on the corner.

. . . Here's a house, here's a house, here's a house.

. . . HERE'S HELL!

. . . Here's a house, here's a house, here's a house.

. . . Here's that blue mailbox again.

. . . End of the street.

And cut.

CHAPTER SIX

It was after nine o'clock at night when they finally interviewed me. I had no idea why I had to wait so long. I sat in that little interview room in the City-County Building, the very same interview room where Chief Maven himself had once tried to give me a good workout. Back when we first found out how much fun it was to have the other as a mortal enemy.

Now the circumstances were a little different. I mean, we weren't going to be picking out china patterns together anytime soon, but at least we seemed to be on the same side for once. We were both trying to help out his old friend Raz, and now we both wanted to know why he ended up slaughtered in Maven's kitchen.

But I didn't see the chief anywhere. That was the first strange thing. Then there was the fact that they had been making me wait around for more than six hours. They were perfectly nice about it. They even brought me some dinner from Frank's Place, one of the better restaurants in town. They apologized a hundred times for keeping me there, but nobody would give me a reason.

Finally, the door opened and a woman came in. She was wearing a dark blue business suit and I could tell in about two seconds she was a serious player. Not from around here, that was for sure. She had a cup of coffee in each hand. She nudged the door shut behind her with her foot, put both cups down on the table, and then reached out her right hand.

"I'm Agent Janet Long," she said. "From the FBI. You must be Alex."

"FBI?"

"Please, have a seat. I'll explain why I'm here."

We sat down and she slid one of the coffees to me. She had brown hair, cut in a short, no-nonsense style. She had nice eyes, but again, everything about her was business first, second, and third. It was hard to imagine her doing anything else but wearing this suit and sitting on the other side of this table.

"I have to apologize, first of all, for making you wait so long. I know this was already a horrible day for you. The wait couldn't have made it any easier."

"It's all right. I understand."

"We had to drive all the way up here from Detroit. Almost six hours."

A hell of a trip, I thought, one I'd made many times myself. But I could never remember looking this alert and ready to go when I got there.

"So let's get right to it so we don't have to take up any more of your time. If you'll start at the beginning and tell me everything that happened—"

"Can I just ask you first why the FBI is involved in this case?"

"Because Charles Razniewski was a U.S. marshal. Any murder of a federal agent, from any law enforcement branch, is automatically under the jurisdiction of the FBI."

"Yeah, that's right. I think I knew that, once upon a time."

"You were a police officer." She didn't have any notes in front of her, but I wasn't surprised she knew that. She had obviously been brought up to full speed on me and I was sure she could tell me a lot more about myself. She probably even knew my career batting average.

"I was," I said. "For eight years."

"Do you mind me asking why you left?"

Okay, I thought, so she doesn't know everything.

"I got shot," I said. "Is this important information for this case?"

"I'm just curious. I apologize."

"No apology necessary."

"Very well, then. So can you tell me what happened? I understand you were out in Houghton, interviewing people about his son's suicide?"

"Not really interviewing. Nothing that official. He just asked me to find out what I could."

90

"And what did you learn out there?"

I hesitated. "According to Charlie's friends, he and his father got into an argument about Charlie switching his major from criminal justice to forestry. Nothing his father had said to me made me believe it was such a big problem between them—nothing more than ordinary father-son stuff—but apparently it was. But I wasn't going to come back and tell him that."

"Why not? Isn't that what he asked you to find out?"

"I don't think it would have done anybody any good. Not that it makes any difference now."

"You didn't get the chance to speak to him before you found him today? You didn't call him?"

"I tried to, but he wasn't answering his cell phone."

"I noticed the cell service isn't very good up here."

"Some days it works better than others, depending on where you are. I did get through to his voice mail."

"Okay," she said, leaning back in her chair. "That's all in line with what I've heard so far. Apparently, you called him just after noon today. You were in Marquette."

"How do you know that?"

"The signal from your cell phone went through the tower there. You called him again around two o'clock, just outside Sault Ste. Marie."

"You guys work fast," I said. "So I'm sure you know the approximate time of death, too."

"Right around noon. So obviously you're eliminated as a suspect."

"That's not why I was asking. I just want to know when it happened."

"Once a cop, always a cop," she said. "So yes, the murder occurred right around the first time you called him. It's possible the killer was still in the room when Mr. Razniewski's cell phone rang."

I thought about that one for a moment. I imagined Raz on the floor, already bleeding, his phone ringing and being unable to answer it. One of the last things he heard before he died.

"So if you'll just go through the entire thing one more time . . ." She pulled out a small black recording device of some kind, no bigger than a matchbook. She spoke into it, said her name and the time. Then as she looked around the room she said she was at the police station in Sault Ste. Marie with Mr. Alex McKnight of Paradise, Michigan. She gave me a quick smile and a nod of her head and then it was my turn to speak. I went over the last forty-eight hours, beginning with Chief Maven's visit to the Glasgow Inn. His request for my help. Meeting Charles Razniewski Sr. and learning more about his son's suicide. Driving out to Houghton, the detour to Misery Bay, my conversation with the undersheriff, then Charlie's friends. Coming back the next day. Finding Raz dead on Chief Maven's floor.

She listened without interrupting. She didn't ask any questions until I was done.

"So just focus for a minute on what actually happened here in Sault Ste. Marie, before and after your trip."

"How do you mean? I only met him briefly before I went out there, and then when I got back, obviously it was only—"

"I understand, but was there anything else that might have happened here that might look out of place now? Something you might not have even noticed at the time?"

I tried to follow her thought, but I wasn't coming up with anything at all.

"Any suspicious strangers hanging around town?" she said. "Or did Mr. Razniewski mention anything, perhaps? Was he uneasy? Did he feel like he was being watched? Anything like that?"

"No. I mean, he was preoccupied with his son when I talked to him. It was just that one conversation."

"One more time, if you can. Please go back over that whole time frame. I know that your trip is the thing that stands out in your mind, but just focus on what might have been going on here in this immediate area. Anything that might have seemed unusual or out of place here. No matter how small. Please think about it carefully."

I shook my head. "I'm sorry. I can't think of anything else."

"Okay," she said, turning her little machine off. "I appreciate you taking so much time here, Mr. McKnight. You realize, I hope, that we had to follow a certain protocol. We had to keep you separated before the interview, even with you being an ex-cop and Chief Maven, of course, still being on the job up here. I hope we didn't inconvenience you too much."

"It's okay. Really."

"I think we've probably kept you and your friend apart for long enough, wouldn't you say? Shall we bring him in here?"

"My friend? Are you referring to—"

"Chief Maven, yes. My partner was talking to him in his office. If they're done, I think we can wrap this up together."

She excused herself and went down the hall. About a minute later, she came back, followed by Chief Maven and a man in a dark blue suit much like hers. It might have even been the exact same fabric, cut from the same bolt. He was young and slick-looking, with a narrow face and sharp eyes. As he entered the room he seemed to be distracted by his cell phone.

"Any day now," he said to the phone. "Is there *any* service up here?"

"This is my partner," Agent Long said to me. "Agent Fleury."

He put down his phone just long enough to shake my hand.

"Mr. McKnight," he said. "Sorry this wasn't a more pleasant occasion."

Chief Maven sat down next to me. He hadn't said a word yet and it didn't look like he was planning on speaking anytime soon. He looked even worse than before—at least twenty years older now, his face drained of color. He kept staring down at the table with half-closed eyes.

"We've been letting you guys do all the talking," Agent Fleury said, "so I figure maybe it's our turn."

He looked over at his partner until she nodded back to him. Then he continued.

"As you know, Mr. Razniewski was a U.S. marshal. I assume you know what that job entails?"

"In general," I said. "I believe so."

Maven didn't look up from the table.

"Mr. Razniewski probably didn't get into specifics, but I can tell you that in the past two years he was involved in some very high-profile cases. He wasn't just transporting detainees. He was closely involved in the actual capture of fugitives. Were you aware that U.S. marshals actually arrest more fugitives than all the other federal branches combined?"

"I didn't know that," I said.

Still nothing from Maven.

"Raz brought down some pretty heavy hitters," the agent said.

Maven finally raised his eyes at that.

"I hope you don't mind me calling him Raz," he said. "I know that was his nickname. We didn't work together, but I'd certainly heard all about him. I mean, even before today."

Maven kept looking at him, but stayed silent.

"In the past six months especially," Agent Long said, "Mr. Razniewski was personally involved in a major case that we feel might be connected to this murder."

"So it had nothing to do with his son's suicide," I said. It was starting to make more sense now— why Agent Long had been so focused on anything that anybody might have noticed here in town, and not so much on my trip to Houghton at all. "Is that what you're saying?"

"I can't imagine any direct connection, no. I mean, how could it?"

"It just seems strange that it would happen three months later."

"Well, that's the thing," Agent Fleury said. "There might not be a direct connection, but it did perhaps create an opportunity for somebody to get to him."

"I don't follow you."

"As a marshal working on these kinds of cases,

it was natural that he'd need to stay in pretty safe company. As long as he was in Detroit, at least."

"Apparently," Agent Long said, "ever since his divorce and his son moving away to college, he'd been sharing his house with two other marshals. Young guys, just out of school. They needed a place and he had the room."

"So between that and the secure workplace," Agent Fleury said, "we figure he must have been a tough target."

"Wait a minute," I said. "Are you saying—"

"Somebody may have been watching him, yes. If they happened to follow him all the way up here . . ."

He put his hands up, like that's all that needed to be said on the matter. I sneaked a quick look at Maven, wondering when he'd finally blow. I was surprised it hadn't happened already.

"We mean no disrespect," Agent Fleury went on. Needlessly. Apparently, he didn't have the skill of knowing when to stop talking. "But you have to admit, if you were looking to take somebody out and you knew they were up here in Sault Ste. Marie . . ."

"We'll be talking to some of your neighbors," Agent Long said. "Just in case somebody saw something. I'm afraid this is going to be a tough one. If they sent a pro to track him down, well, I'm not sure what we're going to be able to find up here."

"If it was a pro," I said, "why the bloodbath? Why not a simple shot to the head?"

Agent Fleury looked over at his partner. I was trying not to read too much into any of this, I swear. I didn't want to believe they were treating us like dumb hick yoopers.

"With a suppressor?" he said. "Make him take his shoes off and get down on his knees?"

"I wasn't going for the whole cliché, no. I'm just saying—"

"There are other players in the game these days, Mr. McKnight. People with very different ideas about how you should kill your enemies. In this case, well, there was obviously a lot of blood involved. It was a lot more dramatic."

Maven kept looking at the agent, but the chief was still doing his best imitation of a granite statue. He hadn't even blinked yet.

"I'm assuming you want it straight, Chief. And I'm sure you realize, it's probably a very good thing that your wife wasn't home today. If this was somebody who tracked him from downstate, I'm sure he wouldn't have hesitated to kill two people instead of one."

"We have other agents working on this from the Detroit end," Agent Long said. She was starting to look a little apprehensive, at least. Unlike her partner. "Maybe they'll find someone who'll be willing to point us in the right direction. That's what we all want, right?"

"In the meantime," Agent Fleury said, "we'll try to stay out of your way as much as possible. You do realize that anything directly relating to this case needs to come through us. We're clear on that?"

On top of everything else, I thought, Chief Maven just got pushed down one more notch on the totem pole. He's so low now it's a wonder he can still see above the dirt.

Without even realizing what I was doing, I started to edge my chair back away from the impending blast zone.

Then he spoke.

"I'll do whatever I can to cooperate with your investigation." Maven's voice was devoid of any anger, any sincerity, anything living at all.

"Very good," Agent Fleury said. He seemed only slightly put off by the robot who'd apparently taken over Chief Maven's body. Agent Long looked at me for some kind of reassurance, but I was even more confused than she was.

"Chief, are you okay?" she said.

"His wife," he said. "Has she been notified?"

"His ex-wife," Agent Fleury said. "Yes, she's been notified."

"Who told her?"

"Another marshal, I believe."

"Okay," Maven said. "Then I think we're done here. Go do your jobs and find out who did this."

99

"You can rest assured we'll do exactly that," Agent Fleury said. "I can't tell you how much we appreciate your cooperation today."

"We'll be staying at the Ojibway if you need us," Agent Long said. "I'm sure we'll be here in town for a couple of days, at the very least. Of course, we'll be in touch as soon as we know anything."

She gave Chief Maven one more look of vague bewilderment, then a quick smile for me. Then they were both out the door.

The chief made no move to get up. I kept sitting there next to him for a long while, waiting for him to say something to me.

"If you send me the bill for your services," he finally said, "I'll make sure you get paid."

"What are you talking about?"

"You made that trip to Houghton on Raz's behalf. He's obviously not here to pay you, so I will."

"I don't want any money."

He didn't answer that. The room was silent again. He kept staring at the door. After another minute passed, he leaned forward, put both hands on the table, and pushed himself to his feet, as slowly as a ninety-year-old man.

"Chief," I said, as I got to my feet. "I'm sorry."

He took two steps and stopped. He didn't look at me.

"It's time for you to go home," he said. "I have work to do."

"What are you planning on doing now?"

He turned and looked me in the eye for the first time since we'd come back to the station. Hell, for the first time since I'd found Raz on his kitchen floor.

"Do you have to ask?"

"You heard what they said, Chief. This isn't your case."

"You're probably right. But let me ask you a question. If it was your old friend, would you let anybody stop you?"

"Chief, come on."

"Answer the question."

I looked at him for a long time. I didn't say yes. I didn't say no. I didn't have to say anything at all, because we both knew the answer.

And we're rolling . . .

. . . Here's my neighbor, Mrs. P. Hello, Mrs. P. How are your roses growing?

. . . Close-up on her face. She's looking at the camera, looking at the camera, that's it.

. . . And then boom, she looks at something behind me.

. . . Her face changes. Yes, that's it. Nice job. You're selling this. It's all in the face.

. . . Meanwhile. Uh-oh. This can't be good, right?

. . . Easy there, don't overdo it, Mrs. P. Your eyes are as big as saucers.

. . . The Monster is standing behind us. Let's not even look. We're too scared to even turn around!

And cut.

CHAPTER SEVEN

I drove home in the dark. The wind kicked up and covered the road with white sheets of snow for yards at a time, rocking my truck back and forth. When I finally got back to Paradise, the yellow light was flashing in the middle of town and the Glasgow Inn was still glowing in the darkness. Beyond that the whole town seemed deserted. Usually there'd be snowmobiles zipping all over the place, but when people downstate get the idea in their heads that we're not getting enough snow, they just don't come. A cruel irony as I put the plow down and pushed six inches of new snow off Jackie's empty parking lot.

When I was done, I sat there with the truck idling and asked myself if I really needed to go inside. I didn't feel like talking about what had happened, but I felt even less like going back to any empty cabin. So I turned off the ignition. Jackie was cleaning up the place and barely looked up when I came in.

"Where have you been?" he said. He poked at the fire with a long iron stick.

"To hell and back," I said. "Although I'm not sure about the 'back' part." I went behind the bar and grabbed a Molson from the bottom row in the cooler. Then I sat down in my usual chair by the fire.

There was a roar inside my head, louder than a jet engine. Louder than the wind howling away outside in the cold night. I closed my eyes and tried to quiet it but it only got louder until I couldn't even imagine hearing anything else.

Three days went by. I could still see the blood on the floor every night when I closed my eyes, but the colors were fading and the scene was shifting and turning into something else entirely. A different floor, with different blood. Then another, until they all blended together. If there was anything like true justice in the universe, I'd be exempt from bloody floors for the rest of my life.

I called Agent Long on the second day and she said they were still chasing leads, which might have meant they were getting absolutely nowhere. There was no way to tell. I called her back the next day and this time she asked me point blank to explain why Chief Maven was such a psychotic jackass. Her exact words for him. I was an unlikely person to defend him, but I asked her to remember what had happened to a man who had once been his partner.

"I hear what you're saying," she said, "but he's driving us absolutely crazy over here."

"How so?" As if I had to ask.

"I thought he understood this was our case, but he's been up and down the street, personally talking to every neighbor. Plus he's got his men rounding up every surveillance camera in town."

"Didn't you guys think of that?"

There was a silence then, as she processed my little dig.

"We've done this a few times before," she finally said. "I think we've got it all covered, thank you very much."

"Do you have anything new since the last time I talked to you?"

"It's still ongoing," she said. Making me wonder, once again, if they had anything at all.

I thanked her all the same, and wished her the best of luck with Chief Maven. Then I called the Soo police station. I asked for the chief and the woman at the desk told me she'd leave a message for him. He didn't call back.

I shrugged it off for the time being and went back to working on the last cabin with Vinnie. It had finally started snowing hard again, like Beboong, the Ojibwa winter spirit, was making up for lost time. I plowed my road. In the evenings I'd buy Vinnie dinner down at the Glasgow. Jackie was still in a bad mood, chasing away customers. Three days since the day I found Raz on Maven's kitchen floor, and now everything was almost back to normal.

So why couldn't I shake the feeling that I was missing something important?

· · ·

It was a Friday morning. As soon as I woke up, I knew there was only one way to get to the bottom of this thing. Only one person who could help me see things in a different way. I took a hot shower and got dressed and headed out. The wind had died down and the sun was trying to come out. It was almost a nice day, but I knew not to fall for it. You think spring is on the way up here and end up with a broken heart. I grabbed some breakfast at the Glasgow, got back in the truck, and then headed east.

When I hit the Soo I drove over to the Custom Motor Shop on Three Mile Road. It was the last place Leon Prudell had worked and I was hoping he'd still be there. But the man at the desk told me Leon was no longer an employee. Judging by the empty parking lot, I could see why. It's hard to keep a full staff in the winter when you're not moving snowmobiles.

I drove down to his house by the airport in Rosedale. I was hoping I wouldn't have to, but I didn't see much choice. The house looked quiet when I got there. The kids were off at school, no doubt, and maybe his wife was out shopping or something. That was my hope. I parked my truck and went to the front door. The old tire swing was still hanging from the tree in the front yard. Now it was covered with as much snow as could balance on its rounded surface. I looked at the rope tied to the thick branch above the tire swing and I couldn't help picturing a young man hanging there. Something that would probably always come to me now, whenever I saw a rope and a tree.

Eleanor answered the door. She was roughly the size of an NFL linebacker, and was probably just as strong. I had seen her lift Leon completely off the ground when he had two broken ankles, and Leon wasn't exactly a ballerina himself.

"Alex," she said, and then I saw the cloud pass over her face. It was the same as ever and this is exactly why I didn't want to be here. The woman loved me, I was sure of that. But she hated to see my face at her door.

The lead story on Leon Prudell is that he grew up wanting to be a private eye. It's the only thing he's ever really wanted to do. We got tangled up, once upon a time, and then we sort of worked together and for a while there he even referred to me as his partner. He even had business cards made up. After that, when I made it clear that I wanted no part in the private investigator business, he opened up his own office in Sault Ste. Marie. That office is closed now, and Leon has held a number of jobs since then. Still, he's never given up on that original dream.

Any time he sees me, that dream is rekindled— which wouldn't be a problem if that dream wasn't completely impractical and occasionally dangerous. In fact, if Eleanor really knew how close I had come to getting Leon killed, well . . . the woman *is* strong enough to kill me with her bare hands.

"I'm just stopping by to see Leon," I said. "I haven't seen him around in a while."

"He's not here. What do you really need him for?" She looked at me the way I used to look at drug buyers when they tried to explain why they just happened to be driving down a certain street.

"I just want to talk to him. I'm not dragging him into anything, I swear."

She opened the door and held out her arms.

"Come here," she said.

I took a breath and waded in for the hug. I saw stars as she squeezed me.

"It's good to see you," she said, "but you know I hate it when you get him into trouble. I end up worrying about both of you."

"I told you, I'm not here for that. How's the rest of the family, anyway? You look good."

"Don't try to butter me up, Alex. It won't work." But she was smiling as she said it.

"Seriously, Eleanor. Where's he working these days?"

"He's up at the movies. He works there a few days a week."

"The movies? You mean, like an usher?"

"They don't have ushers anymore, Alex. What do you think this is, 1948?"

"Well, okay, so he's like a ticket-taker or something?"

"Something like that. Whatever they need him to do. It's just a temporary thing. He's got a few other jobs lined up. Real full-time stuff."

"Good to hear. Okay. Well, maybe I'll wander up there. See how he's doing?"

She gave me the look again.

"Just to say hello," I said. "I promise."

She let me leave without another bear hug. So I was back in my truck with all of my ribs intact, heading back up to the Soo. I was feeling a little guilty. I mean, I hadn't lied to her. I was only going to talk to Leon. Yet the reason I was going to talk to him was because once again I had hit a dead end, and he was the only person I could think of who'd be crazy enough to listen to me. And smart enough to maybe even help me see the answer.

I know most towns in America have a grand old theater that's probably shut down or already turned into something else entirely. If you're lucky, the theater in your town is being reclaimed and cleaned up and turned back into what it was a hundred years ago. In Sault Ste. Marie, that would be the Soo Theater, and yes, it is being restored to its former glory. In the meantime, if you want to see a movie you have to go to the one cineplex out on the main business loop, down the road from the Walmart. It's got the big parking lot and the eight separate screens, and on a lonely weekday in April you can go sit and watch an afternoon matinee on one of the eight screens and be the only person watching.

Leon was standing at the snack bar when I walked in. A big man with untamable orange hair, you'd never miss him, even if he wasn't wearing his trademark flannel. Today, he had an official-looking blue Cineplex shirt on that didn't quite fit him, and he had his name printed on a gold badge. He was staring off into the middle distance when I walked up to the snack bar, so it took a moment for him to notice me.

"Alex! What the hell?"

"Good to see you, Leon."

"What are you doing here? Are you seeing a movie? Can I get you some popcorn or something?"

"No thanks," I said. "I actually just wanted to talk to you for a minute."

"I don't know. As you can see, I'm pretty swamped here."

"Yeah, it's a madhouse," I said, looking around at the movie posters and the ugly carpeting and the velvet ropes. "But maybe you can break free for a minute."

He came out from behind the counter and sat down at one of the little tables they had scattered around the place. He made a sound when he sat down, like an old man on his last legs. He rubbed his eyes and smiled when he caught me looking at him.

"It's been a tough month," he said. "I'm not selling sleds anymore."

"I know. I went by there first. Then I went to your house."

"My wife let you live, I see."

"She did."

"She loves you, you know."

"As long as I'm not asking to borrow one of your guns."

"I was hoping that's why you were here today."

"Nothing that exciting," I said. "I just want to run something by you and get your opinion."

"Okay, shoot."

"You read about the murder at the chief's house?"

"I sure did. Wait a minute, didn't the paper say 'an unidentified local man' found the body? Don't tell me."

"You're looking at the unidentified local man," I said. "The victim was a U.S. marshal named Charles Razniewski Sr. He and Maven used to ride together for the Michigan State Police."

"Okay, and?"

"His son committed suicide in January. And Raz—that's his nickname—Raz hired me to go out to Houghton to find out everything I could about his state of mind that night."

"Are you kidding me? That sounds impossible."

"I told him to hire you, Leon. I really did."

He waved it away. "Come on, like Ellie would let me go do something like that."

"It wasn't dangerous. It was just talking to people."

"It still would have been me trying to be a PI again," he said, looking away. "That would have been enough. But anyway, what's the problem?"

"You mean besides coming back and finding the client dead on Chief Maven's kitchen floor?"

"Besides that, yes. I assume there's more."

"That's just it," I said. "I don't know *what* it is. It's just a feeling I've had that I've somehow missed something."

"Do you think there's a connection between the suicide and the murder?"

"I don't know. The FBI doesn't think so. They think Raz was murdered because of some high-profile cases he's been working on down in Detroit. He's been a marshal down there for the past ten years."

"I read that part in the paper, yes."

I smiled and shook my head. "Do you normally memorize everything you read in the paper?"

"When it's about a local murder, yes. But go on. You say the FBI doesn't see a link?"

"Not that they'd talk about. They haven't really said much to me at all."

"When you went out there to look into the suicide," he said, "did you find anything suspicious?"

"You mean to indicate it wasn't a suicide at all? No, I didn't. Not really."

"Not really?"

"Well, I mean, I just got this feeling that something wasn't quite right about it. I didn't find anything concrete."

"But your instincts told you something was wrong," he said. "You should definitely listen to that."

"That's the thing. I've been wondering if maybe Raz himself had an instinct about it."

Leon narrowed his eyes and leaned in close, like I was finally getting to the good stuff.

"I mean think about it," I said. "Your son kills himself, right? It's the worst thing that could ever happen. Obviously. But why try to find out more about it? It's not going to fix anything."

"Maybe he just wanted to know. So he didn't have to wonder anymore."

"That's what he said. It made sense at the time, but ever since then, I don't know. I'm just thinking maybe there was something else. Like maybe he himself knew that the idea just didn't make any sense."

"How could it *ever* make sense? For anyone?"

"Think about everyone you know," I said. "Out of all those people, there are some that simply would not kill themselves. You know what I mean? Those people, if somebody told you . . . you just wouldn't believe it. Am I right?"

"Whereas some people . . . ," he said, leaning back in his chair. "You might still be shocked, but that doesn't mean you wouldn't ultimately believe it."

"Exactly. Maybe that was part of why Raz couldn't leave it alone."

"Even if it was just a half-conscious thing, you mean. Interesting."

"It's just a gut feeling. I'm probably wrong."

"I bet you're not. So tell me what you found out when you went out there."

"All right," I said. "Here's what happened . . ."

I gave him the same rundown I'd given to Agent Long. Everything I did, from the moment I met Raz to the moment I came back to town and found him dead on the floor. Leon sat absolutely still, watching my face as I talked and absorbing every single word. Even Agent Long, who presumably interviewed people almost every day, didn't seem to be listening with half the attention that Leon was giving me.

When I was done, he thought about it for a while.

"The kid was drunk. Yet somehow he was able to string up a rope just right, stand on the back of his car when it was snowing, and it was probably zero degrees at that point, then he stepped off and hanged himself."

"Correct."

"I understand why you'd have a problem with that," he said, "but it's probably not impossible. Not if you really wanted to do it."

"Not impossible, no. But it still bothers me."

He thought about it some more.

"There might be something else," he finally said. "Something you haven't told me yet."

"I told you everything. Why would I leave anything out?"

"Because you don't think it's important. Even though it might be exactly what you're looking for."

I threw up my hands.

"Tell me everything again," he said. "But this time, don't leave anything out. Tell me about every second. Everything you saw. Every word that was said, as best as you can remember."

I let out a long breath.

"Okay," I said. "Uh, let's see. I started driving out there on Wednesday morning . . ."

"No, go back. Start with the first time you met your client."

"That was the day before. I met him at Chief Maven's office."

I told him everything I could remember. I played it all back in my mind, trying to pick up every word he said. How he asked me to do this thing for him. Then, the next day, driving out to Houghton, making my detour to Misery Bay.

Even the way I asked the old man at the diner why the place had gotten that name, and how he didn't have a good answer. When I got to the place itself, Leon made me slow down and describe every detail. Where the tree was in relation to the parking lot. Where the lake was.

"There were no buildings in sight?" he asked. "No summer houses or anything?"

"Not that I could see. I mean, I knew there were a few up the road."

"No trails leading to the parking lot? Just the road?"

"I think there might have been a snowmobile trail in the woods, but it didn't look like it had been used recently."

"You said there was fresh snowfall that day. Either way, that has nothing to do with what might have happened three months ago."

"Granted. Good point."

"Okay, so go on."

I continued with my conversation with the undersheriff. Everything he told me about being the one who had to climb up the ladder to cut Charlie down, and his answers to all of my questions. The length of the rope. The way the car was discovered with the driver's side door open, the key still in the ignition. The car out of gas and the battery dead.

I was about to move on to the interviews with the friends, but then I remembered what the undersheriff had told me about his own personal experience with suicide. When I was done with that, Leon stopped me.

"Tell me that part again," he said. "Slow down even more and tell me everything."

"He just said it seemed like a lot of suicides going on. There was this other kid who had killed himself, down in—where was it? Iron Mountain, I think he said. The son of somebody he knew, or worked with, or whatever. Then he told me about his own father-in-law, how he ran away one day and killed himself in his car."

"His father-in-law—that wasn't this winter, was it?"

"No, that was a while ago, I think. Some years ago."

"Okay, so put that one aside for a minute. Tell me more about this other suicide. Think hard. What exactly did he say?"

I closed my eyes and put myself back in that office. The undersheriff sitting across from me, with that pained look on his face as he talked about young men killing themselves.

"It was definitely Iron Mountain," I said. "This winter. I think he said like two weeks after Charlie hanged himself. Something about going back behind his barn and shooting himself in the head. Yeah, that was it. But then he went right into talking about his father-in-law."

"Because that was the thing that was important

in his own experience. That was the connection. But not for you, right? Not at all. For you, it's just this one other suicide that happened to take place two weeks later. You said the kid's father was what again?"

"Somebody he knew down in Iron Mountain," I said. "Somebody who . . . no, wait, it was a *sergeant.* I remember that now. He said it was a sergeant's son."

"A sergeant, as in someone in the military? Or in the state police?"

"I got the feeling he was talking about another cop. But if he's a sergeant, yeah. He couldn't be another county guy. He didn't say sheriff or deputy. He said sergeant."

"So now you have two sons of state police officers, killing themselves within two weeks of each other."

"But Raz was only a state guy for like two years. A long time ago."

"Okay, but either way, it's still two men in law enforcement, right? Could it just be a coincidence? Maybe. Maybe not."

"Damn," I said. "Of course. It was right there, but I just wasn't seeing it. You're amazing, Leon. Yet again."

"I think you would have worked it out. Now that you see it, what are you going to do?"

"I guess I could try to find out more about this other suicide. Maybe give the undersheriff a call, although the FBI was pretty adamant about keeping this case to themselves. They wouldn't even let Chief Maven anywhere near it."

"You said they were investigating the murder of the father. Who says that has anything to do with the son? Besides, didn't he pay you to look into it?"

"He never got the chance. Not that I would have taken any money from him."

"But even now," Leon said, "you could theoretically send a bill to his estate."

"I'd never do that."

"But you could."

"What are you getting at?"

He waited patiently for it to come to me. The snow fell outside and the wind blew and the earth turned a few degrees and then I finally got it.

"He hired me to look into his son's suicide," I said. "If I feel like there are still unanswered questions . . ."

"Then you're still on the case."

"No. This is crazy. Come on."

He leaned forward and put both hands flat on the table.

"You know I'm right," he said, drawing out each word. "As long as you don't have your answers yet, you are still on this case."

I felt bad leaving him there. I could see in his eyes how much he missed working on a case.

Any case at all. And it was obvious to me, more than ever, that he was way better at this than I would ever be. He didn't deserve to be standing behind a snack bar, serving popcorn to teenagers. I couldn't help wondering if my visit had made him feel even worse.

With that cheery thought in my head, I drove over to the other side of town and parked next to the City-County Building. I went inside and asked the receptionist if I could see the chief.

"He's not here right now," she said. "Can I take a message?"

"How about the FBI agents?" I said, remembering how well that message business worked the last time I called him. "Are they here?"

"They left for Detroit this morning. I think they were all done with their work up here."

That surprised me a little bit. I mean, it's not like I expected them to come back and fill me in on everything, but damn. Did they hit a big dead end up here? Or did they just get tired of the weather?

"Where's the chief right now?" I asked. "Is there any way I can reach him?"

She looked both ways before lowering her voice. "I think he's actually out on some kind of administrative leave. I haven't seen him at all for two days straight."

"The chief? Out on leave? Are you kidding me?"

"They just told me to take messages for him, and to refer anything important to the county. Which I've never done before."

"That is definitely strange." I thanked her and went back outside. There was only one other place I could think of going, so that's exactly where I went. Down Easterday Avenue, past the college, to Summit Street. To Chief Maven's house.

Three days had passed since the last time I had been there. The police cars were all gone now, of course. Even the crime scene tape had been taken down. You'd have no way of knowing anything unusual had happened inside the house.

I went to the front door and knocked. I was about to knock again when the door opened and I saw Chief Maven standing there holding a paint roller.

"What do you want?" he said.

"I left you a message. You never called me back."

He shook his head and turned away from me. "Come on in." He was wearing old jeans and a T-shirt speckled with paint. "Wipe your feet."

I went inside and did as I was told. There were plastic drop cloths everywhere, and the unventilated smell of paint was almost overwhelming. It took me back to my days right after baseball, when I kept from starving by painting houses.

"I'm kind of busy here," he said, his voice coming to me from the kitchen. "So make it quick."

"Good to see you, too."

"What was that?"

"Nothing," I said, turning the corner. The kitchen had been virtually taken apart. The table and chairs were gone, and everything else that wasn't bolted down had been removed. Beneath the paint smell I caught a strong undercurrent of bleach. There was a plastic tarp on the floor and from the bare wood along the edges I could tell he had ripped up all of the tiles.

The chief poured more cream-colored paint into his tray. It looked like he was about halfway done with his first coat.

"How's your wife?" I said.

"She's in Amsterdam."

"Really?"

"My daughter's been traveling around Europe since right after Christmas," he said, rolling the paint on the wall. "Kind of a lifelong dream. When this happened here . . ."

He paused for just a half second to look down on the floor, at the exact spot where Raz breathed his last breath.

"When this happened, my wife took the chance to go over and spend some time with her."

"That sounds like a good thing." I tried to remember what I knew about Chief Maven's daughter and came up with only one thing. The very first time I sat in his office, I saw the picture of a young girl on his desk and asked him if it had come with the frame.

"Do you know how much it costs to fly to Amsterdam at the last minute? Take a guess."

"I have no idea."

"Soo to Detroit. Detroit to New York. New York to Amsterdam. Twenty-three-hundred dollars."

"That's impressive."

"It was worth every penny to get her out of this place. I don't know how she'll ever be able to live here again."

"What about you?" I said. "It looks like you've been here nonstop. Do you think that's a good idea?"

He looked up at me as he went to put more paint on his roller.

"Where the hell else am I going to go? They took away my badge, you know."

"I hear you were driving those FBI agents a little crazy."

"The FBI can kiss my ass. They can't touch me. But the mayor, that little spineless weasel, he kinda suggested that maybe I'd be better off taking a personal leave of absence for a while."

"That doesn't sound like taking away your badge."

"Don't be an idiot. They forced me out. Like what the hell else am I supposed to do with myself? The job is all I know anymore."

That much was true, I thought. It was hard to imagine him doing anything else.

I watched him paint. He accidentally got some

wall paint on the white ceiling and spent the next five minutes trying to fix it. He was getting more and more aggravated and I knew he'd blow up at me if I stayed there. But for some reason I knew I couldn't leave.

What he was doing . . . it was something I knew so well myself. He had already cleaned the place within an inch of its life and now he was painting, and if I left him there he'd probably start knocking down the walls. Anything to change the one thing that couldn't be changed.

"I can't believe I'm about to say this," I said, "but I wonder if you'd like to help me keep my promise to Raz."

He stopped painting. "What are you talking about?

"I'll tell you the whole story, but first I need to use your phone."

"For what? Who are you calling?"

"The undersheriff of Houghton County."

An hour later, we were making our plans. We'd be leaving early the next morning and driving all the way out to Iron Mountain. A long trip with such an unlikely passenger, but we both knew it was something we needed to do. We had to see it with our own eyes, this place behind a barn in a forgotten corner of the Upper Peninsula. One more cold and lonely place where one more young man somehow decided to end his own life.

And we're rolling . . .

. . . These are the Monster's instruments. Pan slowly here.

. . . One man's leather belt, size 38.

. . . One big metal spoon.

. . . One broom, minus the broom. Just the handle, I mean.

. . . Then this thing. I have no idea what this is.

. . . But it would probably hurt more than all the other things put together.

. . . If it was real.

. . . Good thing these are just movie props, eh?

And cut.

CHAPTER EIGHT

On a cold morning in April in this part of the world, the sun doesn't come up until seven o'clock, so it was still dark as he came walking down his driveway and got in the truck. He was wearing a green blanket-lined parka, dungarees with extra wide cuffs, and heavy-duty work boots. Like we were about to go hunting, or maybe even go work on an oil rig. To complete the outfit, he was sporting an original Stormy Kromer hat, with the elastic band you can pull down over your ears if they get cold. I suppose it was exactly the kind of hat I would have imagined Roy Maven wearing, aside from his chief's hat.

As he got in, I saw that he was carrying an old-school silver thermos. Probably the same one he had brought with him his first day on the job. It went perfectly with the hat and the buzz cut underneath it, not to mention the silver flip-top lighter in his hip pocket along with the Marlboro Reds.

"Good morning, Chief." I waited until he closed the door and then I gunned it.

"You're gonna get us killed before we even leave the Soo?"

"You can't even write me a ticket. It must be killing you."

"I'm only on leave, McKnight. I can still run your ass right up the flagpole."

"Tell you what," I said, settling down to somewhere near the speed limit. "It's gonna be a long trip. How 'bout we try not to drive each other crazy?"

He shook his head at that and settled in for the ride. We left the city and headed due west, the sun finally starting to come up behind us. When we hit the main highway, he opened up his thermos. The cab of the truck was filled with the aroma of strong black coffee. He filled up the cap of the thermos and then put that in the cup holder. Then he reached into his coat pocket and pulled out a travel mug. He filled it with more coffee and handed it to me.

"Thanks," I said.

"I don't know how good it is. My wife usually makes it for me."

"Have you talked to her since she went over to—where was it again?"

"Amsterdam. That's where they'll be this week, anyway. I think they're going to Germany next."

"That sounds great."

"Yeah, I talked to her, to answer your question. She sounded tired. But Olivia is with her, so it's all good."

"Olivia, that's your daughter."

He nodded. We rode for another full minute before he spoke again.

"She's thirty years old now. She had kind of a rough patch for a while. Just got out of a bad marriage. Finally. So she decided to go travel around for a while."

"No grandkids?"

"No, not yet. There's still time."

We were sounding like two human beings actually talking to each other. The first of many surprises we'd run into that day. I headed out to Newberry and it was starting to feel like the trip I had just made a week before to Houghton. This time, instead of that ruler-straight shot across the UP, we cut south and headed down toward Lake Michigan, passing through a string of small towns along the southern coast. Gulliver, Manistique, Thompson, and Cooks, places I hardly ever had any reason to see. As we drove, I gave him all the details from my two phone calls.

"The undersheriff was very helpful," I said. "He didn't understand why I'd want to know more about this other suicide, but I just told him I had a gut feeling that I wanted to follow up on. That was enough for him. He gave me the man's name and number. Donald Steele. He's a sergeant in the state police, stationed at the Iron Mountain post."

"So you talked to him next?"

"Well, I called, but he wasn't at the post. I gave the guy on the phone the undersheriff's name, told him he had sent me, and he was nice enough to give me Sergeant Steele's home number. Steele wasn't at home either, but I talked to his wife. I wasn't so sure about pressing her for details. I mean, it's only been a couple of months since it happened, but she seemed to want to talk to *somebody* about it. So I just listened."

"Another kid kills himself. Two more parents going through God knows what. I can't imagine and I hope I never have to."

"I hope so, too."

"You don't have any kids, McKnight."

"I was talking about you," I said. Thinking, okay, here we go, so much for talking like two human beings. "I'm hoping you never have to live through something like that."

"I apologize." As far I could remember, the first time he ever said those two words together in my presence. "Continue."

"Their son's name is Brandon. He killed himself on January fifteenth."

"Two weeks after Charlie."

"Yes. Although in this case, he didn't hang himself. He shot himself in the head."

"Damn, and she's telling you all this?"

"It just started coming out. I got the whole story. He was target shooting behind their barn. That afternoon he went out to shoot, and about an hour later, they notice that they're not hearing the gunshots anymore. When they went out

129

there, he was lying on the ground. One bullet right to the temple."

"No note?"

"No note. But as you already know . . ."

"They usually don't. Yeah, I know. But still. Did she say anything about any troubles he might have been having?"

"She didn't get that far," I said. "By that time, I was wishing we were there in person. It just doesn't feel right to ask somebody these kinds of questions over the phone."

"So we're driving all the way out here just to drag these poor people through their misery again? Is that what you're telling me?"

"I didn't force you to come, Chief."

He didn't answer that. He looked out the window at the snow on the trees and the rocks and the great nothingness that lies between the towns.

"You have the same feeling I do," I said. "Am I right?"

"Yes, you're right. Something's not adding up."

"She did ask me to make her a promise."

"Who, Mrs. Steele?"

"Yeah. When I asked her if we could come out and talk to her, she said we could, as long as we promised to do one thing for her in return."

"And what's that?"

"She wouldn't tell me. I guess we'll find out when we get there."

• • •

We kept hugging the shoreline as we made our way around the bottom rim of the UP, Lake Huron looking calmer and bluer than Lake Superior. We hit Escanaba, the closest thing to a real city we'd seen since leaving Sault Ste. Marie, stopped for gas and a bathroom break. We'd been on the road for a good three hours, with another hour to go. I had told Mrs. Steele we'd be there around eleven o'clock, but as we were ordering our food to go I remembered the thing about the Michigan time zones. With virtually the entire state on Eastern time, it's easy to forget that there are four counties, all bordering Wisconsin, that are on Central time. So we'd be picking up an hour before we got to Iron Mountain. As tough as this visit would be, there was no reason to make it worse by arriving an hour early.

So we sat down with our food and Maven told me a few more stories about his old friend and fellow state cop, Charlie Razniewski. He made it sound like being a trooper was all about spending a lot of time in the patrol car, driving up and down I-75. If you do it for a while, you can eventually move on to other things, but Raz just wasn't cut out for it. He wanted to *go go go* every minute of the day, and sitting behind a big rock with a speed gun in his lap was not his idea of time well spent.

"We did have some excitement now and then," Maven said. We were sitting by the window in a place called Elmer's, while the snowplows rumbled by on the main road. "There were a few big arrests. A couple of really terrible accidents. That's when you find out if a rookie recruit can carry his weight."

"And he did?"

"Hell yes. That's when he showed his true colors. I could tell he'd make a fantastic trooper if he stuck with it. It was all the other stuff he couldn't deal with. The paperwork. The riding around all day. Being patient. Putting your time in, you know, playing the game. It's not an easy life if you're not wired for it."

"So tell me," I said, thinking maybe now's the time I can finally ask this question. "When he was killed, you seemed to take it especially hard."

"He was a fellow cop, McKnight. I'm supposed to take care of him."

"I know, I know, but you weren't together for long. And it was a long time ago."

"Spending all that time with me was supposed to be his punishment for mouthing off to a lieutenant, if you can believe that."

I remembered what Raz had told me about Maven being nicknamed "Sergeant Cooler," but I figured I should keep my promise to Raz and not mention it. Even if he was dead now.

"But we ended up hitting it off," Maven went on. "You don't really get a partner when you're with the state police, but that's what it felt like to me. He was my partner. Now all these years later, he comes to me for help and he ends up dead on my kitchen floor. How do you expect me to react?"

"You're right," I said, holding up my hands in surrender. "If he's your partner, he's your partner, no matter what. I would have reacted the same way."

"Except you were there when your partner died."

I let that one hang in the air for a long moment. I looked at him and he looked right back at me. The waitress was about to come over and offer us more coffee but thought better of it and kept on walking.

"What do you mean by that?" I finally said.

"You were with him at the end. I didn't get that chance. That's all I'm saying."

"You didn't get the chance to save him, you mean? The chance I had? Which I didn't use?"

"Easy, McKnight. I wasn't going there."

"It sounds like you were."

"Raz died alone, is all I'm saying. Or with his killer there watching him, which is even worse. I can't stop thinking about it. That's all I meant. Honestly."

"Okay," I said, mostly believing him. I waved at the waitress to bring us our check.

"I'm sorry," he said. The second apology from Chief Maven in one day. "So let's go talk to the Steeles."

If you want to get to Iron Mountain, you need to leave the shoreline at Escanaba and drive straight into the heart of the woods. That's all you'll see for miles on end—trees and more trees. An hour of this and you'll finally see Hermansville and Norway flash by, until you finally come to the very edge of the state. There, on the northern bank of the Menominee River, is the small town of Iron Mountain.

By the time we got this far, the roads were starting to rise and fall again. We were close enough to the Porcupine Mountains to see some real elevation, even though Copper Country was way the hell north of us, on the other end of the UP. It wasn't about copper down here at all, and never had been. As we got close to town we saw an iron miner with a pickax standing two hundred feet above us. It was just a huge billboard, of course, and the sign between the giant miner's legs read, BIG JOHN WELCOMES YOU TO IRON MOUNTAIN IRON MINE!

"Hard to miss that one," Maven said. "I guess that means we're here."

"The Steeles live just south of town," I said. "They've got a farm down by the river."

I found the road and turned off. The road

twisted back and forth through the woods until we were finally going up a big hill. I felt my tires start to slip, and I wondered how many other vehicles had gone into the ditch here. When we got to the top of the hill we were looking down at an old farmhouse with a great red barn just behind it.

"This has got to be it." I stopped there and stared down at the scene below me.

"Yeah? So what's the problem?"

"No problem. I'm just noticing something here. See that barn down there?"

He leaned over toward my side and looked out the window. "Yes?"

"We could sit right here and see everything that's happening behind the barn, would you agree?"

"Uh, yes."

"I'm just saying, if you were trying to figure out if there was any kind of routine, you could drive right by here a few times and observe everything that goes on down there."

I hit the gas and we kept on going. As we looped around to the driveway, I saw that it was covered with a good ten inches of snow, so I put down my plow and started pushing.

"Mighty neighborly of you," Maven said.

"She said she wanted to ask us a favor, right? Maybe this was it."

I ran the length of the driveway, then backed up

to do it all over again. If I'm going to plow, I'm going to do it right. Maven started getting a little impatient, but I finished the job and then we finally got out of the truck.

"Tell me the truth," he said as we walked to the door. "Are you trying to get on their good side? Or would you have done that anyway?"

"I'll pretend you didn't ask that."

I pressed the doorbell and heard a three-note chiming deep within the house. As we waited I looked around and saw nothing but the road curving around the farm, the woods, the barn, an old fence and a piece of rusted farm equipment here and there. Plus a hell of a lot of snow. Besides that there were no signs of life at all.

"Did they tell you they'd be here?" Maven said.

"Mrs. Steele did, yes."

Finally, the door cracked open and we saw a woman's face.

"Mrs. Steele?"

"Yes," she said, pulling the door open a few more inches. She was thin and pale and I got the feeling she wasn't quite as old as she looked. But then she'd been through a hell of a winter. "You must be the man who called."

"I am. Can we bother you to come inside for a moment?"

"Of course." She stepped aside and let us in. She was wearing something that looked almost like a bathrobe. A housecoat, I guess you'd call it. She went through the motions of offering us coffee, but we told her we were good and we didn't want to take up any more of her time than we had to.

"Is Sergeant Steele around today?" I asked. "I was hoping to talk to him at some point."

"No, he's not." She looked away from us as she said it. "He's not here."

"Oh, is he at work today?"

"No, he hasn't been back to work yet. Since it happened." Still not looking at us.

"Um . . . do you expect him back soon?"

She shook her head.

"Why don't we sit down," Maven said, his voice softer than any time I'd ever heard him. "I hope we haven't come at a bad time."

"It's all bad times anymore." We were sort of lingering at the entrance to her kitchen. There was a table full of papers in the middle with four chairs around it. She pulled out the closest chair and sat down.

"Mrs. Steele," I said, "are you all right?"

"No. Of course not."

"Can I get you anything? A drink of water?"

She shook her head again.

"We're terribly sorry to hear about your loss," Maven said. He took one of the other chairs. I did the same.

"I shouldn't have asked to come out here," I said. "I'm sorry. This was clearly a mistake."

"No, it's okay. I'm glad you came. I saw you outside, plowing the driveway. Now I can get out and go to the store."

"Mrs. Steele, where's your husband?"

"I don't have snow tires, you know."

"Mrs. Steele. Your husband."

"He hasn't been spending much time at home," she said. "Ever since it happened. I guess I can't blame him for that much. If I had somewhere to go, I wouldn't be here, either."

"Where is he?"

"Brandon never saw his eighteenth birthday. Did you know that? It happened just a few days before he turned eighteen."

"We didn't know that," I said. "I'm sorry."

I didn't know what else to say. We could have kept on saying we were sorry for a thousand years and it wouldn't have helped her one little bit.

"He liked lemon cake. I was going to make him a lemon cake for his birthday."

She stopped talking for a while. We sat there, one on each side of her. All of us staring at the floor. Then finally she sat up straight and smoothed out her hair.

"Brandon was very much into his guns," she said, her eyes suddenly more alert, her voice more animated. "I wasn't so sure what to think about this, but Donald felt that it would be a healthy activity for him. Something to get him outside and away from the television set. There's a big sand pit behind the barn. If you go out there you won't be able to see much now with the snow, but you'll see where Brandon had put some wooden posts along the edge there, in front of the incline. It was very safe that way. Because he could shoot all he wanted to and none of the bullets could ever go anywhere."

She seemed to lose steam there for a moment.

"It was very safe," she said. "Very safe."

I was sure we were about to lose her again, but then she snapped right back.

"On the day it happened, he went outside with two of his guns. Two pistols. I'm sorry, I don't know what kind they were. What exact caliber or anything like that. All I know is that one was a revolver and one was an automatic. Or a semiautomatic, I think he said. I don't know the difference. Anyway, he went behind the barn to shoot at his cans. I was in here doing the dishes and listening to the shots going off. In the wintertime, it doesn't seem to be so loud. The snow absorbs some of the sound, I guess. He was shooting and shooting, just like always, but then I didn't hear the sound anymore. I was waiting for him to come inside, but he never did, so I went out to see if he was still out there and there he was, lying in the snow."

She stopped again and this time she drummed her fingers together. I looked at Maven and he looked back at me and we both knew there was no way we'd be leaving this place without trying to get her some help. All this time alone in this house, right next to that barn we could see from our chairs, right out that kitchen window. It wasn't good for her to be here.

"We had a service for him up at the church right up there on H Street. We don't have more than a dozen streets in town so why they used letters to name them, I can't even imagine. But that's neither here nor there."

"Mrs. Steele . . . ," I said.

"He's buried out in that place on Old U.S. 141. That's just a number, but it used to be the highway so I guess you can understand it."

"Is there somebody we can call for you?" Maven said. "I'm not sure you want to be here all by yourself, do you?"

"No. No, I don't want to be alone. That's what I wanted to ask you to do for me."

"This is the favor you were talking about," I said. "On the phone, you said you had a favor you wanted to ask us."

"My husband. I want you to bring my husband back. Will you do that for me, please?"

"I don't think you mentioned where he is. If you tell us, I'm sure we can—"

"He's across the river. At his girlfriend's house."

"Mrs. Steele," Maven said, shooting me another

look, "this sounds like it might be a bad situation all the way around. God knows you've got enough to deal with already."

"Just go talk to him. Man-to-man. Tell him this is where he belongs. I know it's not easy, but we have to face it. Tell him I'll let him go forever if he just comes back and helps me get through this. That's all I want him to do. Is that so much? Just be a man and come back until we can find some way to—"

She started waving her arms around, and the tears started coming down her face.

"Tell you what," Maven said. "Let's call his post and get one of the troopers to come down here. Then we can go find your husband."

"No. No trooper. I want my husband."

"I'm just saying, for the time being . . ."

"Did you hear what I said? I said I don't want a trooper in this house. Or anybody else from his little circle of boys up there. All I want is my husband here in this house, where he belongs. Okay?"

"Maybe somebody else? Just for now? A neighbor?"

"Bring him home!" she half yelled, half sobbed. *"Do you hear me?"*

"Okay, okay," he said, reaching out to touch her arm. "We'll bring him home. Just tell us where he is."

"Her name's Donna. She works at the Starlight,

across the border in Niagara. That's where you'll find him."

"Okay. We'll go drag him back here if we have to put him in handcuffs."

I was about to say something, but Maven stood up then and I didn't get the chance to speak until we were outside.

"You made a pretty big promise," I said. "What if we can't find him?"

"You heard her. He's at the Starlight."

"If he doesn't want to come back, what do you plan on doing?"

"Between the two of us I'm sure we'll be able to convince him."

"Somebody should stay here," I said. "She shouldn't be alone."

"She's been alone for days. What she needs is her husband to be a man and to come back home, just like she said."

Okay, I thought, so now we're apparently going to go across a state line and kidnap a sergeant. Not the plan I would have expected from a chief of police, but maybe all those years at the bottom of the totem pole had taught him how to get things done his own way.

"Just give me one minute first," I said. Instead of going to the truck, I made a detour toward the barn, fighting my way through the deep snow.

"Where are you going?"

"I want to see it."

Maven followed in my tracks as I made my way around the barn to the shooting gallery behind it. We both stood there for a while, listening to the wind. It was buried in snow, just like Mrs. Steele had said, but I could see the five wooden posts in the ground, and the way the land rose just behind them.

I got a little taste of that same feeling as I was standing there. That same sense of foreboding I had felt at Misery Bay.

Of course, I had come here already knowing what had happened.

"This is the place," Maven said. "God damn."

"He must have been standing right around here," I said, stepping back to the side of the barn. There was a single window there, with a ledge wide enough to hold a gun or two.

"He had two guns," Maven said, putting his hand on the ledge. "So if he leaves one right here, he can fire with the other."

"I wonder if he was wearing earmuffs."

"Be stupid not to. Your ears would be ringing for days if you didn't."

"If he was just turning eighteen, stupid isn't out of the question," I said. "But either way, it would have been easy to sneak up on him."

"What are you saying?"

"I'm just going through all the possibilities. If you came up on one side of the barn . . ."

I walked over a few steps to the corner and looked back at the scene.

"This side," I said. "If he was right-handed, I mean. From this side, he wouldn't see you coming."

"It's possible. He was already shooting, so one extra gunshot wouldn't have been noticed. You take the other gun and put it against his head."

"Exactly." I stood there and watched the whole thing happening in my head. A few steps, grab the gun. Boom.

"This is why you stopped up there on the road. To show me how easy it would be to watch this place, so you'd know when the kid was back here shooting."

"Right again."

"But there's no way to really know this for sure, McKnight. If there was nobody else here to see it happen . . ."

"I know. It's still just an idea."

"So what do we do now?"

"We go find Sergeant Steele."

The road to Wisconsin took us over a big dam on the Menominee River and the water was rushing through the gates. The town of Niagara was right there on the southern banks of the river, but of course it was a long way from Niagara Falls, so I couldn't tell you how it got its name. The one thing I did learn pretty quickly is that Niagara badly needed a Glasgow Inn. We drove past four different bars before we came to the Starlight, and if I had been an actual customer looking for a nice place to have a drink, I would have kept on driving.

We knew it was bad as soon as we walked in. It was too dark, the tables were too close together, and the jukebox was too loud, even on a Thursday afternoon in the middle of April. We went up to the rail, and on any other day I would have just wondered what the hell were they thinking of in this town, and how could anybody spend more than five minutes in this place without killing somebody, and don't even get me started on calling the place the Starlight with a straight face, not to mention the business about Niagara itself. But today we had more important questions to ask.

"We're looking for Donna," I said. "Actually, we're looking for Sergeant Steele. Are either of them here?"

"Who's asking?" the man said. He was all sideburns and bad attitude. Yet one more reason not to drink here.

"We're friends of Sergeant Steele's wife," I said.

"Haven't seen him." As he was about to turn his back to us, Maven stepped out and flashed his badge.

"We'd appreciate it if you could tell us where

they might be," Maven said. "You think you could manage that?"

Maven didn't keep the badge out for long, and it was too damned dark to see it, anyway. But it did the trick.

"Honestly, guys. I haven't seen either of them in a couple days. If you want to go check her house . . ."

"That's a great idea. If you could just write down an address for us."

"No need. Just go down the main road, about seven or eight miles, until you get to Pembine. Her house is number 1490, on the right."

"That's very helpful, sir. We appreciate your time."

We left the place and got back in the truck.

"I didn't know you could use that badge in a different state," I said as we pulled out onto the road. "You're really full of surprises today."

"You're starting to rub off on me, McKnight. I'm not sure that's such a good thing."

We headed south down the main highway until we saw the little sign letting us know we had hit Pembine. We started watching the numbers go by, 1460, 1470, 1480, until we found the mailbox with the 1490 on it. It was another long driveway with a lot of snow on it, but this time I didn't bother putting my plow down.

"They've been camped out here for a while," Maven said as we came to the house. We could see the sergeant's Michigan State Police car parked next to a beat-up old Cadillac. "There are no tracks at all."

The house was small. It was really more like a cottage that you'd only call a house if you happened to live there year-round. There was a screen door on the side porch and we could see where the snow had blown in and covered the wooden floor. I knocked on the door a few times, but nobody answered.

"I think I see a light on," Maven said. "They've got to be here. Both cars are here."

"Hello!" I said. "Sergeant Steele!"

I knocked on the porch door again, and then I opened it and went inside the porch to the next door. The whole place needed about a hundred hours of sanding and then two or three coats of good paint.

"Donna! Sergeant Steele!"

Maven came up beside me and looked through the window next to the door. I don't know which came first, him seeing the two bodies on the floor or me noticing that the door was slightly ajar and pushing it open. The smell came out, riding on the warmer air from inside the house. It washed over me, turning my stomach inside out.

We had found Sergeant Steele, just like we had promised, but we sure as hell wouldn't be bringing him back home.

Maven got on his cell phone and called 911. I

went outside and stood there with my hands on my knees, trying hard not to throw up.

"They're on their way," he said after he hung up. "Are you all right?"

I shook my head. I wasn't ready to stand up.

"Two sons and two fathers now," he said. "Plus one girlfriend. McKnight, I think we've got something terrible going on here."

And we're rolling . . .

. . . Things are getting a little dark here. We need a bright shot to shift the mood.

. . . This is the Mackinac Bridge, gleaming in the sunlight.

. . . Some bouncy travelogue music would be great here. Don't you think?

. . . Here's the bridge. Here's the way out. Here's all the hope, right here on this one thin ribbon of pavement.

. . . Five miles long. Too far to run. Unless you're the fastest man on earth.

. . . Even then, they'll catch you. They always catch you.

. . . Get the sunlight. So bright it hurts. That's right.

And cut.

CHAPTER NINE

We waited for the police to arrive. The county guys came first, from their post in Marinette, followed closely by the Wisconsin State Police officers from Fond du Lac. They came out of their cars with guns drawn and Maven and I were smart enough to keep our hands in plain sight. When Maven flashed his badge, the guns went back in their holsters, even if some of the confusion remained. Here was a chief of police, after all, not just from across the border but from way the hell on the other side of the state. It would have been like the chief of police from Milwaukee coming to Sault Ste. Marie and calling in a double homicide.

The preliminary identifications were indeed Sergeant Donald Steele, age forty-three, from the Iron Mountain post of the Michigan State Police, and Donna Krimer, age thirty-eight, a waitress from the Starlight Bar and Grill up the road in Niagara. Both victims had been shot with Seargent Steele's service revolver, Sergeant Steele in the back and Ms. Krimer in the head. The revolver had not been recovered.

They estimated that the two had been dead for approximately three days, but we didn't stick around to see the medical examiner do his work. The police took full statements from each of us, and then we were free to go.

"Who's notifying the next of kin?" Maven asked the state detective who seemed to be in charge.

"We've got a couple of men from Sergeant Steele's post on their way down to talk to his wife," he said. "Ms. Krimer is separated from her husband, but we haven't located him yet."

Maven thanked the man and promised him we'd both be available at any time if they needed us. Then we climbed in my truck and got the hell out of there.

"Are we going back to see her?" I said. I didn't have to specify who.

"It was bad enough for her before," he said. "Now she *really* needs somebody else to be there."

I didn't argue. We went back over the river, back to Michigan and to all of the misery waiting for us there. When we got to the Steeles' farm, there was a state squad car in the driveway. It was getting late in the day now. We could hear the unhinged, almost inhuman sound of her crying before we got to the front door.

We introduced ourselves to the troopers. We stayed there for about an hour, trying to help them calm her down. In the end, I saw Maven grab one of the troopers by the collar and make him promise that they wouldn't leave her alone. I'd known enough state cops in my time to know that you don't grab them. Ever. And you don't tell them what to do. Ever. But Maven did both and it seemed to work.

We left the place as the sun was going down. Back up that big curve to the top of the hill, where you could look down and see the whole farm laid out like an early American painting. I kept driving, back through the forest, back along the coastline, back to Sault Ste. Marie, with neither of us saying more than a few words the whole time.

There wasn't much left to say.

It was almost midnight when we pulled up to Maven's house. There was a Soo police car waiting in the driveway. A young officer got out, the very same officer who had been first on the scene when I found Raz on the kitchen floor.

"Good evening, Chief." His eyes looked tired. He'd obviously been waiting there a long time.

"What's going on, Ray?"

"I'm supposed to let you and Mr. McKnight know that the FBI agents will be back in town tomorrow. And that you should plan on making yourselves available to them."

Maven let out a heavy sigh. It was so cold out now, we could see our breath as we stood there shivering in the driveway.

"I don't suppose they gave you a specific time," the chief said.

"No, I'm afraid not."

"You actually had to wait here until we got back, just to tell us that in person?"

"Those were my instructions, yes."

"From the agents? They're the ones who told you to do this?"

"Yes, sir."

"You know, Ray, I know you're new at this, but here's one little tip for you. If somebody who *isn't* in your immediate chain of command tries to tell you to do something, even if that person is a federal agent, you should always at least *consider* the option of telling that person to blow it out their ass."

The poor young officer wasn't sure what to make of that one.

"It's okay," I said, trying to help the kid out. I knew the chief was just as tired and just as shell-shocked as I was. The last thing he should have been doing was giving out career advice. "We'll be around. Just have them call us and we'll come right in."

The officer thanked us and got back in his car. He drove off, presumably to sign off from his shift and go home to bed.

"Those agents are going to try to put us through the ringer tomorrow," Maven said.

"They have no reason to. Not really."

"Since when did that ever stop them?"

"Well, get some sleep," I said. "It's been a long day."

"You can say that again."

I left him there to open the door and to go into his empty house. Then I drove home, trying to keep my eyes open, feeling like I'd seen more than any man should have to see in one day.

Agent Long called me at seven o'clock the next morning.

"We're on our way up," she said. "We need you at the station at one. Please don't be late."

"Good morning to you, too. Thanks for calling so early. Six hours should be just enough time for me to get dressed."

"We'll see you there," she said. Then she hung up.

I went back to sleep for a little while. I'd already spent the entire night dreaming of dead bodies and blood and an unholy smell that had somehow become like a living thing, snaking through a cracked door and trying to wrap itself around me. It was after nine when I finally got up, took a hot shower, and got dressed. I went down to the Glasgow and grabbed a late breakfast, fending off Jackie's complaints about my erratic schedule and how I expected him to reopen the kitchen whenever I waltzed in the place—in other words, the usual routine. Vinnie stopped in and told me he wouldn't be able to help me with the finish work on the cabin that day. His mother was feeling even worse, so he was on his way over to the rez to sit with her. I told him I wouldn't be doing much work that day anyway, which got Jackie going again. By the time I got out of there, I was almost glad to be heading to my FBI grilling.

Chief Maven was already there waiting. As strange as it had been to see him out of uniform the day before, it was doubly strange to see him out of uniform and sitting in his own interview room. I sat down beside him and gave him a nod. He returned the nod and we both stayed quiet. I started to wonder how long the agents would make us wait, but at that very moment the door opened and the two of them walked in.

They put their coats and briefcases down and took all of thirty seconds to settle in before getting down to business. Agent Long sat down in a chair across from us. She had her hair pinned back tight today and I didn't think it suited her, although I sure as hell wasn't going to tell her that. Agent Fleury stayed on his feet. He started pacing back and forth like a caged animal, which was our first indication that this particular meeting was not going to go well.

"Okay, so Chief Maven," he finally said, still pacing. "You know, when we came up here the first time, I think we really did try to treat you like we were all on the same team."

"That wasn't my impression," Maven said, folding his arms. "Thanks for returning my last call, by the way."

"We've been very busy down in Detroit. You know that."

"It takes one minute to return a phone call."

"When we left here, I believe we had established that the FBI would be taking the lead on this case, did we not?"

"This was a different case," I said. "This was my case."

He stopped pacing. "What are you talking about, Mr. McKnight?"

"Mr. Razniewski hired me to look into his son's suicide. Even though he's dead, I felt it my duty to complete that assignment. Chief Maven came with me as a private citizen, out of uniform."

It had sounded good when Leon had said it. In the light of day, with a federal agent standing over me, it was maybe not quite as convincing. But now that I'd hit my ground ball, I had to run it out.

"You are joking, right?"

"No, I'm not."

"And you needed the chief to come with you . . . because you're such good buddies?"

"He was good friends with the young man's father. It's natural he'd have an interest. And since he was asked to go on leave and had a lot of time on his hands . . ."

"He was asked to go on leave because he was actively and aggressively interfering with our investigation into the death of a U.S. marshal. You understand that part of it, right?"

"I thought you said you guys were all on the same team."

"All right, stop," Maven said, uncrossing his arms. "Will you just tell us what you want to tell us so we can get the hell out of here?"

Agent Fleury kept trying to stare me down until Agent Long cleared her throat and joined in.

"If you gentlemen had any other material leads pertaining to either Mr. Razniewski *or* his son, which apparently you did, you should have brought them to us. Especially if those leads involved crossing a state line."

"We had no way of knowing we'd end up in Wisconsin," I said. "But come on, does that really matter? Why are you laying into us, anyway? We were just asking some questions."

"Alex," she said, going with the first name thing now, "do you really think there's some kind of connection between Razniewski and his son's death, and Sergeant Steele and *his* son's death?"

"I don't know. That's what we were trying to find out."

"I understand how you could look at the close timing and think it was kind of suspicious, but take a step back. You've got one young man who has a conflict with his father over his future. He ends up taking his own life. A tragic thing that happens all the time. Every single day. His father

157

is a U.S. marshal, who's actively hunting down some of the worst criminals in the country. He ends up getting murdered in cold blood. Again, it's tragic. Of course. That goes without saying."

I looked over at Maven. He was listening carefully. Once again, I could only marvel at his newfound calm demeanor, and wonder where the hell he had found it.

"In an entirely separate branch of law enforcement, you have Sergeant Donald Steele of the Michigan State Police. His son, as we've learned today, was a bit of a loner. Liked to go back behind his barn and fire his guns. Pretty much every afternoon he did this."

"How did you find that out?"

"We've been in contact with the officers out there. They've been very helpful. I hope this shows you how seriously we're taking this."

"And let me just point out one more time," Agent Fleury cut in, "that if you had simply come to us instead of going out there yourself—"

"They get it," Agent Long said, snapping a quick icy look at her partner. It was the first break I had seen between them. "Anyway, the bottom line is we have another young man with some troubles, who takes his own life. But again, as we all know, it happens."

I was about to speak up on that one. The fact that neither kid had left a note, percentages be damned, and the fact that both suicide scenes gave me the same gut feeling that things just weren't adding up. But then what? They'd ask for some piece of hard evidence that something was amiss in either case, and what would I give them?

"Finally," she said, "in the case of Sergeant Steele himself, and the murder of both him and Ms. Donna Krimer, I assume you were aware that the two of them were involved in a long-term extramarital relationship?"

"We got that impression, yes."

"Were you aware that Ms. Krimer was still legally married to a man with a history of domestic violence?"

"No, we didn't know anything about her."

"No, you didn't," Agent Fleury said. He obviously couldn't resist jumping back in with that one. "Were you aware that Mr. Krimer has been missing ever since the two bodies were discovered?"

"The police mentioned that they hadn't been able to contact him yet."

"Yes, well, they still haven't tracked him down as of this morning. Without presuming any guilt on his part, can we at least try to imagine a likely scenario here? If he were to come back to the house unannounced, say, and find his still lawfully wedded wife in bed with another man?"

"Okay," I said. "I see where you're going. It makes sense."

"Good," he said. "I'm glad we're all on the same page now. So in the meantime, if anything new does come up, I can assure you we'll be right on top of it."

"It sounds like you've already decided that there's no connections between any of these events," Maven said. "You can just go back to Detroit and forget all about it, eh?"

"Is that what you just heard me say?"

It was Maven's turn to get the hard stare now. He returned it without blinking.

"If any further information is developed," Agent Fleury said, slowly, "we'll follow up on it. At this point, if there *is* any connection, not only does it involve the original case with a U.S. marshal, but it also crosses state lines now. In which case, it should be even *more* abundantly clear to you, if it wasn't already, that this falls under our jurisdiction. Are we clear on that point?"

Maven took a few beats to answer him. "Yes, we're clear."

"I don't get it," I said. "You didn't come all the way back up here just for this."

"We're still pursuing leads in the Razniewski case," Agent Long said. "Seeing you gentlemen again was just a bonus."

"We'll be at the Ojibway again," Agent Fleury said. "If you think about chasing down any more leads, maybe you should give us a call instead?"

On that note, they said their good-byes and left us sitting in the interview room. Maven was staring off into space, just like the last time we found ourselves here together. He was the kind of man whose actions I was sure I could predict, a man with clearly marked buttons that you pressed at your own risk. Apparently some kind of alien life force had taken over his mind and body now. There was no other way I could explain his behavior.

"You know why they're back up here," he finally said.

"Why?"

"They're not getting anywhere in Detroit. It's a marshal so there's a lot of pressure to solve the case. But they've got nothing, so they're back up here to start from scratch. They probably have orders not to come back empty-handed this time."

"The case is getting cold," I said. "I don't like their chances."

"Neither do I."

A minute of silence passed. Neither of us moved.

"What do you think?" I said. "Are they right?"

"About what?"

"About all these deaths not having anything to do with each other."

"I don't know, McKnight. If we think differently, I'm not even sure what we can do about it now. They made that pretty clear."

"Well, if you think of something else and you want to run it by me . . ."

He nodded. "I'll keep that in mind."

I got up and grabbed my coat.

"It seems like we sort of ended up on the same team the past couple of days," he said as I went to the door. "That's a little different from our usual arrangement."

"You're right. It is."

He didn't say anything else, so I left. A half hour later, I was driving home in my truck, making that last turn around Whitefish Bay, heading toward Paradise. That's when a thought came to me out of God knows where.

I turned around and gunned it all the way back to the Soo.

Half hour out, half hour back, so I'd only been gone an hour. I didn't know where Chief Maven would be, and I didn't have his cell phone number. Hell, I wasn't even one hundred percent sure he'd carry a cell phone out of uniform. But either way, I didn't figure there were too many places he could be.

I tried the City-County Building first. The receptionist told me he had left just after I did. She didn't know where he was going, and no, she didn't have his cell phone number.

Okay, so he's at his house, I thought. Doing more painting or God knows what else. Or maybe just sleeping it off. We'd both had a pretty rough couple of days.

I drove over there and pulled into his driveway. I didn't see his car. I peeked through the window on the garage door and saw an immaculate set of tools hanging from a set of pegs on the wall, a snowblower, and three snow shovels, and one car that I'm sure belonged to Mrs. Maven. Left there when he took her to the airport, no doubt. But Maven's car was gone.

"Where the hell are you?" I said. I tried to picture him buying groceries or renting a movie at the video store or maybe sitting in a dentist's office. Normal things that everyone does, but I just couldn't see Chief Roy Maven doing any of them. Especially not today. Not with all of this still bouncing around in his head, just like in mine.

I got back in the truck and sat there for a while. Half-waiting for him to show up. Half-trying to figure out where else he could be. It finally dawned on me that there was one place that would make sense. If he *was* there, it would mean that he had had the same thought that I had, at right around the same time. Meaning we were long-lost twins or something strange and mystical like that.

Only one way to find out, I thought. I put the truck in drive and headed for the other side of town.

• • •

The Michigan State Police had something like sixty posts back when I was in Detroit, located all over the state and certainly one in every town as big as the Soo. The post in Sault Ste. Marie is over on the business spur, a few blocks away from the main highway. It's another charmless brick shoe box, but still probably a little bit nicer than the City-County Building, and I'm sure every single office in the place puts Chief Maven's to shame. I recognized a few of the troopers and sergeants, but as far as I could remember I'd never set foot in their building. That was about to change.

I pulled into the lot and parked between two squad cars. These were the old-style "Blue Goose" cars with the single red light on top. I couldn't help wondering if they gave you a less comfortable ride than the new-style squad cars, and how that would set off the inevitable battles over who got assigned to them. All the usual political games that come in any station with more than one cop in it.

As I went around to the front I saw Maven's car taking up the last visitor's spot.

"You stupid son of a bitch," I said. "After all we've been through together."

I went inside and asked the trooper sitting at the desk where Chief Maven was. He was young and he had the typical state-issue haircut, cut so close he might as well be a Marine. I was expecting to get a little bit of runaround from him, asking me who I was, what business I had there. That whole show. I mean, every single trooper I'd ever met in my life was top shelf, but sometimes they can come across as *knowing* they're top shelf just a little too well. God bless them for the job they do, but if I had to deal with troopers every day I'd probably snap.

"Chief Maven's back with Sergeant Coleman," he said. "If you give me your name, I'll let him know you're looking for him."

"Alex McKnight," I said, a little surprised. "Thank you."

"No problem, sir. Sit tight, I'll be right back."

He was back in half a minute.

"Right this way, sir."

I followed him to the back of the building, where Chief Maven and a state man were sitting side by side in front of a computer screen.

"What are you doing here?" Maven said, looking up at me.

"I could ask you the same question."

"This is Sergeant Reed Coleman," he said, indicating the other man. "We go way back."

"Pleased to meet you," the sergeant said, shaking my hand. He was an old-timer, probably close to retirement. "I think I've seen you around town."

"Seriously," I said to Maven, "if you're chasing

something down over here, why didn't you tell me?"

"You heard those FBI agents. They don't want us anywhere near this thing."

"Since when would that stop either of us?"

"Look," he said, "it's bad enough if I screw up my own career here."

"I rent cabins for a living. What can they do to me?"

"They can do plenty, believe me. I didn't want to drag you into this any deeper."

"That's a load of crap, Chief, but we'll talk about it later. Tell me what you guys are working on."

He let out a long breath and rubbed his eyes. "It was just a thought. I mean, I was just thinking . . ."

"You were looking for a link between Raz and Steele," I said. "You figured the only thing they ever had in common was being a state cop."

"Right, and this is the place to come to find out."

"Even though it was a long time ago, and even if you were his only regular partner . . ."

"I was thinking, still, if they came in around the same time . . ."

"Because they're about the same age. So you're wondering if maybe they went to the academy together. There's just one for the whole state, right?"

"Yes."

"So even though they never worked together, they might have run into each other there."

Sergeant Coleman looked between us and couldn't help smiling. "Sounds like the two of you are on the same wavelength," he said.

"Most days I'd take offense to that," I said. "But yes."

Another trooper came by, carrying a cup of coffee. He was looking at us with great curiosity, until Coleman told him to keep on walking.

"The chief has had a problematic relationship with most of the men in this building," Coleman said to me. "I'm not sure any of them can believe he's voluntarily sitting here. Or hell, that I'd even let him through the door."

"All right, knock it off," Maven said. "Everybody here hates me. I got it."

"So what did you find?" I said. "Did Raz and Steele train together?"

"No, that's a dead end," Maven said. "Steele went right in after a couple years of community college. Raz was in the military first, didn't join the police until he was twenty-five. They missed each other by a good five years."

"We can't find any connection at all," Coleman said. "All of Steele's posts were in the UP. Raz did his two years down in Lansing with Roy here. There weren't any special assignments or anything else that would ever bring them together, as far as I can see."

"I take it the chief has explained our general situation," I said.

"He has," the sergeant said. I could see him hesitating about what to say next.

"What's your opinion?"

"Well, we all heard about Sergeant Steele this morning. I didn't know the man very well. I think I only met him once. But it's never easy to hear about one of your fellow officers going down."

I waited him out. He was doing a good job of not answering the question.

"As far as this other man goes, I obviously know nothing about him at all. But the two suicides . . . hell, I don't know, guys. It seems like a big coincidence, but I've seen bigger. That's all I'll say. If you have something else that's concrete, that's a different matter."

"You'd make a good FBI agent," Maven said.

"That's a low blow, Roy."

Maven took a long sip of coffee while another trooper wandered by to gawk at us.

"It's true," the trooper said, "Chief Maven is really here. Did somebody arrest you?"

"Sergeant Fusilli," Maven said. "Always a pleasure. Alex, meet the biggest pain in the ass in Sault Ste. Marie."

"We're just kidding around," the man said, shaking my hand. "We all have the utmost respect for the chief. What are you guys working on, anyway?"

"It's nothing," Coleman said. "Just a little legwork."

Fusilli leaned over and peered at the computer screen.

"Nothing to see here," Maven said. "Go do something useful."

"Sergeant Steele," Fusilli said. "What a shame, huh? He was Iron Mountain, right?"

"Right," Coleman said.

"Didn't his son kill himself, too?"

"A couple of months ago, yeah. Actually, if you'll excuse us—"

"Been a tough winter for old state men in the UP, eh?"

Fusilli said it as he walked away. It took a few seconds for the coin to drop, then Maven and I looked at each other.

"What was that?" Maven said. "What did he just say?"

"Hey, Jim!" Coleman said. "Get back here."

"No, no, you heard the chief. I'm gonna do something useful."

"Get your ass back here," Maven said. "Repeat what you just said."

"Hey," Fusilli said, coming back to us with his hands up, "I didn't mean anything by it. I was just saying, with Sergeant Steele in Iron Mountain, and Haggerty in Marquette . . ."

"Haggerty?" Coleman said. "What do you mean?"

"What about him?" Maven said. "Who is he? What happened?"

"Well, he's been retired for a while now . . ."

"But he was a state cop at one time?"

"He was a forensics guy, up at the lab in Marquette."

"What happened to him?"

"Not to him," Coleman said. "To his daughter. She just died recently. But it was in her sleep, right? A heart attack or something?"

"She was twenty-seven years old," Fusilli said. "You really believed that story about the heart attack?"

"I don't know," Coleman said. "It can happen."

He waved that one off and was about to walk away again.

"Stop," Maven said. "Tell us what happened."

"It's none of your business, Chief. He was a state man and some things stay in the family."

"You're the one who brought it up," Maven said. "Now start talking."

"Jim," Coleman said, putting up both hands to calm everybody down. "This might be important. Please tell us what you heard about Haggerty's daughter."

He worked it over for a moment, then he started talking.

"All right, if you really need to know. This was like two weeks ago now. Up at Northern, in the university housing. Haggerty's daughter was like an associate professor or something. She didn't come to class and when they finally opened up her apartment, she was dead. Apparently, there were some . . . unusual circumstances in terms of the way she died."

"Unusual how?" Maven said.

"I didn't get the details. I just heard it wasn't as simple as a young woman dying of a heart attack. Whatever happened, it may have been self-inflicted, that's all I know. I think the guys at the Marquette post have been so tight-lipped about it in deference to Lieutenant Haggerty. Just out of respect, I mean. He was a very popular guy up there."

"You say this happened two weeks ago?"

"Yes," Fusilli said. "And that's all I know. You want anything else, you're gonna have to talk to the guys in Marquette."

He walked away from us. Maven sat there looking like somebody had just slapped him in the face.

"Where is Haggerty now?" I said. "I mean, is he—"

"I don't know," Coleman said. "I would assume he's still up in Marquette, but I guess I don't know that for sure. I haven't heard anything about him since he retired. Until this."

"Do me one favor," Maven said. "Can you look him up in your records there? See where he's been on the police force?"

Coleman went back to his keyboard and his mouse and started going through the database.

"He started out in St. Ignace," he said. "He was a trooper on the road for what—seven years, I guess, until he transferred to forensics. He was probably taking a lot of extra classes at night or something, because I know that's pretty heavy stuff."

"St. Ignace," Maven said. "Where did we just see that?"

Coleman hit a few more keys.

"Right here," he said. "Sergeant Steele was also stationed in St. Ignace. In fact . . ."

He sat back in his chair and looked at us, one by one. The words and the numbers and the dates glowed on the screen and for the first time the whole thing was coming together before our eyes. It wasn't just a gut feeling anymore. We had a hard connection now and I knew everything was about to change. I felt a sick cold wave rising from the bottom of my throat.

"They were there at the same time," Coleman said. "For seven years, it looks like. Steele and Haggerty were riding out of the same post for seven years."

And we're rolling . . .

. . . This is going to be a tricky shot, but let's try it.

. . . Get as close as you can to the blade of this knife.

. . . Yes, even closer. I want to feel like I'm riding the edge.

. . . Stay in focus, as much as you can. That's it.

. . . Feel that metal? Feel it on your skin? That's how I want it to feel.

. . . We'll need the right sound mix here. A musical note, off-key. Grating and painful, until you're begging it to stop.

. . . All the way up the edge. To the very point. That's right.

. . . This will come across on film. This feeling. I know it.

And cut.

CHAPTER TEN

Nobody said anything for a long time. As Sergeant Coleman sat there looking back and forth between us, the other state policemen kept walking by, grabbing their coffee and heading outside to their cars, like it was just another normal day.

"We have to talk to this guy Haggerty," I said. "I mean, don't we? Do we have any choice?"

"He just lost his daughter two weeks ago. How the hell is he going to be able to talk to *anybody?*"

"We have to find him. If we don't, he may be next."

"It's time to fill me in here," Sergeant Coleman said. "What the hell's going on?"

"Do you know anybody up in the Marquette lab?" I said. "We have to get to this man. Even if he's retired, you must be able to find him, right?"

"Probably," the sergeant said. "But come on, guys. Give me the rest of the story."

Maven and I looked at each other.

"This is going to sound crazy," Maven said, "so promise me you'll hear us out before you say anything."

"Uh, okay," he said, not looking too certain about his ability to keep that promise.

"It all starts with a suicide," Maven said. "Another kid. A son of another former state cop. Out in Misery Bay."

An hour later, we were outside the Soo post, shivering in the cold and wondering what the hell to do next. Sergeant Coleman had told us he'd call the Marquette lab and get back to us as soon as he could. But first, he had to figure out a tactful way to tell whoever answered the phone that he needed to contact a former lieutenant who was certainly just beginning to grieve his dead daughter.

"How long do you think we'll have to wait?" I said to Maven.

He shrugged his shoulders. Then he leaned over to shelter his cigarette while he tried to light it.

"You can't do this again," I said.

"Do what?"

"Go running off without me."

He looked up at me, his cigarette still unlit.

"You have to trust me," I said. "We're both into this now."

"That line you gave the FBI about this still being your case. I know you were just trying to cover for us. You really don't have to do this anymore."

"I told you, we're both in this. Okay?"

He got the cigarette going at last, then stood up and blew a thin plume into the cold air.

175

"Those agents aren't going to be happy if we keep sticking our noses in their business."

"I don't consider this to be their business," I said. "I don't think they even believe there's any connection here."

"You know we have to tell them. This new thing with Haggerty . . . it might change their mind."

"So you're saying what, give this to them and then go home?"

"I'm saying give this to them and see what they can do with it. But the hell with going home."

He gave me a nod and told me to follow him in my truck.

"Where are we going?" I said.

"It's our turn to go ruin *their* day."

I followed Maven across town, all the way north to the frozen St. Marys River. There on Portage Street sat the one and only three-star hotel in Sault Ste. Marie. The Ojibway. As I parked in the lot, I couldn't help running through my own personal history with the place. I had come here a million years ago to spend the night with Natalie and to find out if we could make a future together. If I really wanted to break it down, I could probably trace back to this very building and find my last real happiness here, before it all went to hell. But that was something I didn't have the heart to think about. No, better to just go find the FBI agents who were camping out here so we could share our new horrible secret.

Agent Long was coming out of the business center as we stepped into the lobby. She had glasses on now, and she was holding several pages that had obviously just come off the hotel printer.

"What are you guys doing here?" She couldn't help but flinch as the blast of cold air made it to her side of the room.

"We need to talk to you and your partner," Maven said, stomping off the snow from his boots. "Why don't you get him down here?"

She pulled out her cell phone, hit a speed-dial number and then made the customary cell-phone face as she watched the call trying valiantly to go through. When it finally bounced its way to a tower that was probably across the river in Canada and back to her partner's cell phone upstairs, she told him to come down to the lobby as soon as he could. A month later, I knew she'd see the bill and wonder why it cost five bucks to make a call inside the very same building when she could have just picked up the house phone, but today that was the least of our problems. The elevator door opened and Agent Fleury stepped out, looking seriously unhappy to see us.

"What's this about?" he said. "Didn't we set things straight enough at the station?"

"No," Maven said. "Not straight enough at all. Let's go sit down somewhere."

We went into the dining room. The Freighters, they called the place. Yet more memories I could have dwelled on if I wanted to. There were a handful of people having a late lunch, so Maven asked for a quiet table on the far side of the room. As we sat down, we could see the frozen locks from the big windows. It made me remember standing up there on the observation deck with Raz, listening to him talk about his son. It was the last time I saw him alive.

"We have a conference call in ten minutes," Agent Fleury said, waving the waitress away without even glancing at her. "Make this quick."

"You'd better call and postpone it," Maven said. "You need to hear about a new development in this case."

Agent Long looked at the ceiling and shook her head while Agent Fleury's face went through several shades of red.

"I thought we had reached an understanding," he finally said.

"Just get over yourself and listen to me," Maven said. "We talked to one of the sergeants over at the state police post here in town and we believe we've found another suicide that appears to be connected."

"Why were you talking to the state police?"

"The sergeant and I go way back. Besides, I

didn't exactly see you rushing over there to do the legwork, so give it a rest."

"You're out of line," Fleury said.

"Everybody take it easy," Agent Long said. "Chief, tell us what you found."

He laid it all out for them. The apparent suicide of the young woman in Marquette, now the latest of three. Her father a retired lieutenant from the state lab. Most importantly, the one vital link between Sergeant Steele and Lieutenant Haggerty—their seven years together at the St. Ignace post.

"I still don't see how this ties in with our man Razniewski," she said. "He never worked up there, did he?"

"No, he didn't," Maven said. "But at first we were thinking maybe he ran into them in the past few years, after he became a marshal. I'm sure he doesn't work with Michigan state cops all the time, but maybe once in a while, right? Even that far north?"

"It's possible."

"Yeah, but the time frame doesn't work as well that way. If you go back ten to twelve years, *that's* when Steele and Haggerty were still together in St. Ignace. And *that's* when Raz was a state cop, too. You've got all three men in the same job at the same time, even if it was only for a couple of years."

"But you were on the job, too," Agent Fleury

said. "Am I right? How come you're not involved in this yet?"

I thought Maven had already stared this agent down as hard as a man can be stared down, but I was wrong. Maven had one more gear left and he used it now.

"First of all," he said, slowly, "yes, I was on the job at the same time. But as far as I can remember, I never ran into Steele or Haggerty. And I have a good memory. Second, who's to say I'm *not* involved? Whoever's doing this . . . if it really is one person doing this . . ."

"Then he may have you next on his list? Is that what you're suggesting?"

"Haggerty's the one I'm worried about. According to the pattern, he'd be next. And soon."

"But then what? After that? Does he move on to you?"

Maven let that one hang for a moment. "I don't know," he finally said. "It's possible."

"So this person who's doing what, let's go through the MO. He finds these old state cops from back in the day, and the first thing he does is make that person's son or daughter commit suicide? Is that what you're suggesting?"

"That's the worst possible thing you could do to somebody." I hadn't said a word yet and I figured it was about time. "Think about it. It's even worse than killing somebody straight out. Kill their child first."

"But make it look like suicide."

"Yes," I said. "Exactly. Make it look like suicide."

"Do you know how hard it is to *really* do that? To kill somebody and to fool everybody into thinking the person killed himself? Or herself?"

"I understand," I said, "but it might not be so hard to miss if you're not looking for it."

"I don't know, I'm still skeptical."

"I don't have any kids, but if I did . . . that would be the worst thing you could do to me."

"Maybe." He cocked his head back like he was thinking of what could be worse.

"It would be right up there," I said. "Believing your own flesh and blood doesn't want to live anymore."

"Okay," Agent Fleury said, "so if I buy that, and if Chief Maven is somewhere on that same list . . ."

He turned his attention back to the chief. I had a bad feeling about what might come next.

"What do you say, Chief? Do you have any kids?"

"I have one daughter," he said, his voice going robot-flat again, drained of all color and emotion as it had been in the interview room.

"One daughter," Fleury said. "Okay, then. So you better give her a call, huh? Tell her to stay away from open windows."

It was several days in the brewing, but that finally did it. Maven came out of his chair, faster than I'd ever seen him move. Faster probably than anything he'd done in twenty years. He was already around the table by the time I could get to my feet. He grabbed Agent Fleury by the collar and pulled him close. With his face one inch away he said something that I couldn't hear. I caught up to him and pulled him away, and as I did I could see the fear written clear on Fleury's face.

"You're out of control, Maven!" The fear was gone as quickly as it came. He was upset now. Upset and embarrassed and I knew this was something that wouldn't go away quietly. "It was just a stupid joke, you idiot. I could throw you right in jail, you know that?"

"I'd like to see you try," Maven said.

"What the hell is wrong with you people up here?"

"Hey," I said. "Just knock it off, all right?"

"I just make one stupid little crack and you turn into a maniac?"

One stupid little crack, I thought. Pretty standard cop humor, actually. I'd heard a lot worse, but Fleury picked the wrong man on the wrong day.

"Everybody cool down," I said. "Okay? Can we all just relax?"

Maven shook free from me and straightened his shirt. "If you ever say another word about my daughter, I swear to God . . ."

"You swear to God what? What will you do?"

"Knock it off," Agent Long said. She stood in front of him and pushed him backward. She was strong, I had to give her that much.

Fleury was about to say something, but thought better of it and turned away.

"Who did you guys talk to at the state police post?" Agent Long said.

"A sergeant," I said. "An old friend of the chief."

"Yeah, you already told me that. Give me a name."

"Sergeant Coleman."

"Okay. So we'll go over there right now and get up to speed. We're all over this, and you don't have to worry about it. Is that understood?"

I didn't say anything. Maven sure as hell wasn't going to say anything, either.

"I asked you if it was understood."

"Yes," I said. "We got it. Although I think we've already heard this line once before."

"You have my word," she said. "We'll give it our full attention. Right now."

"Okay," I said, putting my hands up. "In that case, it's all yours."

"Take the chief and get out of here before these guys start throwing chairs, all right?"

I put one hand on the chief's back and he pushed it away. He gave Agent Fleury one more hard look, then turned and walked out of the room. Agent Long gave me a grim smile and a roll of her eyes as I followed behind him. By the time I caught up, he was already through the lobby and out the front door.

"Chief, wait!"

He got into his car, put the key in the ignition, and gunned it. His tires spun a few times on the frozen road. When they finally gained some purchase he veered out into traffic, horns honking all around him.

Then he was gone.

I went home. I didn't hear a word from the chief for the rest of that day. I kept thinking about the retired lieutenant up in Marquette, wondering if he had any idea what kind of mortal danger he might be in. Even as I went down to the Glasgow Inn that night, I kept looking at the phone sitting on the bar. Call information, I thought, get his number, give him a call, tell him to keep his head down or to get the hell out of town, or something. Anything.

Just relax, I told myself. There's nothing you can do right now. The agents are on top of this. Better late than never, but still. They went to the state police post, they got all the information they needed. Surely they've been in contact with the lieutenant by now. Agent Long promised you personally that they'd give this their full attention.

I'd tell myself all of that and it would hold me over for approximately one minute. Then I'd go back to staring at the phone.

There was still no word from the chief when I went home to bed that night. In the morning I broke down and called the Soo post. I asked for Sergeant Coleman, but they told me he was unavailable and would probably remain so for the rest of the day. I asked if he was meeting with the FBI, but whoever was on the phone would not go down that road with me. In the end, I hung up, went outside, and got in the truck.

When I hit the Soo, I tried Maven's house first. He wasn't home. His car was gone. I wrote out a note asking him to call me and wedged it in his front door.

I tried the City-County Building. Nobody had seen Chief Maven that day.

"You know, the chief is on administrative leave," the receptionist reminded me. "He's not supposed to be here at all."

"Like that would stop him." I thanked her and left.

I drove aimlessly around town for the next hour or so. Eventually, I stopped at the state police post and looked for his car in the lot. It wasn't there. I stepped inside, knowing it was probably useless. Sergeant Coleman was not in the building and had not left any word on how to contact him.

As I drove back to Paradise, it was all I could do to not keep going west. Two hours and I'd be in Marquette. At least I'd be doing *something* then, no matter how ill-advised. But I made myself take that last turn north toward home.

There were no messages on my machine. I plowed my road and then went down to the Glasgow to see if I could drive Jackie half as crazy as I was, but that didn't seem to help at all. The sun went down. The wind picked up and started howling and I knew the wind chill would be something like thirty below. Another beautiful April night in Paradise. Then the door opened, just like it had that first night. The night Chief Maven walked in and got me into all of this.

This time, on an even colder night, Maven knew exactly where to find me. He came over to my chair by the fire. He stood looking down at me. After searching for him all day, now that he was here I had no idea what I wanted to say to him.

"I had to get out of here for a while," he said. "It was either that or kill somebody."

"Let me guess," I said. "You went chasing down more leads without me."

"I had to see it."

"See what?"

"Misery Bay," he said. "I had to go there."

"What? Are you serious? You went all the way out there?"

"I was there today. I just got back a little while ago."

"But wait a minute—"

"Why didn't you tell me, McKnight?"

"What are you talking about?"

"That place is even worse than I imagined. If that kid was really hanging there, facing the lake like that. I mean everybody else is dead, I know, but *that place.* My God, McKnight. All of this started right there?"

He stared into the fire. He was still standing.

"Sit down," I said. "Take your coat off."

"I can't. We have to go."

"Excuse me?"

"We have to go talk to Lieutenant Haggerty. Right now."

"Chief, come on."

"As soon as I got home, I had a message from Sergeant Coleman. The agents were at Haggerty's house today, asking him questions. It wasn't a good scene for anybody, I guess. Haggerty was in no shape to hear their crazy ideas."

"But they weren't their ideas . . ."

"I know. That's the thing. He called Coleman and told him he wants to talk to us. You and me. As soon as possible. I just called Haggerty himself to confirm."

"Tonight?"

"We can be there in two hours," Maven said. "Let's go. While he's still alive."

And we're rolling . . .

. . . Open up that closet door, just a few inches. Just like that.

. . . We want the shot as if we're looking out from the closet, watching the Monster.

. . . That's right. Drink that beer. Cigarette. More beer. That's it.

. . . Oh, what's this? A sound behind you?

. . . Camera down. No face here. It's so much better when you don't see the Monster's face. You use your imagination, and the Monster is worse than anything you could ever see in real life. Solid filmmaking right there.

. . . Come around toward the camera. Stagger just a little bit. Good, good.

. . . Just the legs. Don't tilt up. No face. Come closer. Close the door. Just like—

Hey, watch the camera!

CHAPTER ELEVEN

I could see that Maven was dead on his feet, so I made him get in the truck. We left his car there in Jackie's lot and headed west. It was just after nine o'clock. In the UP, in April, that means it's already been dark for hours and it feels like the middle of the night.

"Haggerty's got a place in Au Train," Maven said as we left town. That was a good thirty miles this side of Marquette.

"Is he really expecting us?"

"He is, yes. But I don't know much else. What kind of state of mind he's in. He sounded pretty out of it."

"He's probably going crazy right now."

"His daughter just—"

He stopped short. He couldn't even say it. If the little fracas he had gotten into with Agent Fleury hadn't removed any doubt, I wouldn't want to be the man who ever threatened a hair on Olivia Maven's head.

Maven put his head back and closed his eyes. If he really went all the way out to Misery Bay and then back again that same day . . . well, it was a hell of a day under any circumstances. Now it looked like it was going to go even longer, and this last part would probably be the worst of all.

"So what's the plan?" I said. "What are we going to say to him?"

"I don't know," he said, his eyes still closed. "I guess we'll figure that out when we get there."

It was the same long, straight road stretching across the middle of nowhere, except now in the utter darkness with the wind blowing and all of the death on our minds it was anything but boring. I would have paid big money for boring at that point in my life.

By the time we reached the water again, it felt like dawn should be right around the corner, but it wasn't even 10:30 yet. We had been on the road just over an hour. We drove through Munising, where every sane, normal person was locked up tight in a warm house. Then more empty road until we passed through the town of Christmas. The casino appeared on our left, all lit up in the snow, looking out of place and frankly ridiculous. There were enough cars in the lot to justify being open on a night like this. I could only shake my head in amazement as we drove by. The sudden light woke Maven and he sat up straight, shielding his eyes.

"Where are we?"

"Christmas. I assume you don't want to stop and play some blackjack."

"The day you find me gambling you can go ahead and shoot me."

"I wasn't actually suggesting—"

"Just don't get me started on that," he said. "Au Train's what, just a couple miles ahead, right? Coleman said you gotta take a left at the main intersection and go south for a while."

We hit the center of town and took the left at the blinking light. Maven told me to go down past the falls and then to look for one of those double-decker mailboxes. One at normal height, the other about eight feet in the air—when you see them downstate, the sign on the top mailbox usually says AIRMAIL. Up here it's more likely to say WINTER DELIVERY. Either version stops being funny around the second or third time you see it, but in this case it was a welcome sign of life and humor and I don't know, after driving in the dark it reminded me that there was a real human being who put up those mailboxes and probably thought they were hilarious at the time. Before his whole life got turned inside out.

As I turned down the driveway, I put my plow down. There was half a foot of snow on the ground and you could see some recent tire tracks.

"You said he already talked to the FBI. When, yesterday?"

"So I'm told," Maven said. "That must be their tracks, huh? Probably didn't have the sense to drive a real vehicle."

As if on cue, the driveway turned and we saw the tracks going right off the road. There was a great mess where the snow and ground were churned up and I could imagine Agent Fleury trying to push the car from behind while Agent Long steered. So not a good time for anyone involved. It made me wonder what kind of mess they may have left inside, as well. Maybe Agent Fleury knew how to impersonate a human being when talking to a grieving father, but I wouldn't have bet on it.

"Look at where this place is," Maven said. "He's totally isolated back here."

It was true. His driveway was as long as my logging road, lined on both sides by trees heavy with snow. The headlights from the truck cast an eerie glow over everything and it was as though we were heading down some long tunnel lined with white, all the way down to the dark center of the earth.

Finally, as we came around one more bend we saw the house sitting in a small clearing. It was a good old-fashioned log cabin, obviously built by hand. Many long, loving hours spent right here in the woods, with nobody else in sight. A black Jeep Cherokee was parked by the cabin. The man was long retired by now so naturally he'd have the civilian vehicle and not a state car. I parked behind it and turned off the headlights.

As we got out of the truck the night itself seemed to throw a blanket of absolute quiet over our heads. There was what had to be a frozen pond behind the house, with lights mounted on wooden poles, probably for skating on the pond. But the lights were off tonight and the pond had not been cleared of snow.

We went up the three steps to the front porch and knocked on the front door. There weren't many lights on inside the cabin. We stood there in the darkness, waiting for something to happen. It didn't take long for me to start feeling sick to my stomach. I was pretty sure Maven felt exactly the same way.

"I swear to God," he said, "if that poor son of a bitch is inside this cabin, lying dead on the floor . . ."

The possibility seemed more likely with each passing second. We're too late, I thought. The man's been murdered. Maybe just a few hours ago. Or even minutes. His blood might not even be cold yet.

Then the door opened. It happened quickly and it scared the hell out of me. We saw a man standing there in the doorway with just enough backlighting to form a black silhouette and nothing else.

"Lieutenant Haggerty?" Maven said. "We're sorry to bother you, sir. But I spoke to you on the phone earlier this evening?"

The specter took a step forward. I was already expecting to see a man who had just lived through the worst two weeks of his life, but even so it was a jarring sight. He was unshaven, first of all, and his hair was uncombed. His clothes looked like they had been picked out at random. Baggy pants that might have been pajama bottoms or workout sweats or God knows what. An old cable-knit fisherman's sweater with stretched-out sleeves. Brown corduroy slippers. Overall, the complete outfit of a homeless man, yet here he stood in the doorway of a cabin he may very well have built with his own hands.

But more than anything else, the man's eyes—sunken, half-dead, with dark rings beneath them. If you had kidnapped this man and beaten him and starved him for two weeks straight, this is exactly what he would look like.

"Lieutenant," Maven said again. "May we come inside?"

The man took two steps backward so we could pass. We were in the living room, but it was hard to make out exactly where we were going because it was as dark in here as the night itself. He walked past us, his footsteps strangely quiet on the wooden floor. As we followed him, we could finally see the one source of light in the entire house. It was a small lamp with a crooked shade and a lightbulb that couldn't have been more than forty watts, sitting on a table at the far end of the kitchen. The man went to the table and sat down on one of the chairs. He put his hands together on the table and still did not speak a word. Maven and I stood there watching him for a moment. Then we went to the table and we each moved a pile of catalogs and newspapers from the other chairs and sat down across from him. There was a sour smell of old food and unwashed dishes coming from the sink.

There was a large window next to the table. It was so dark outside it might as well have been painted black. The wind blew and the window flexed, while the man let out a long ragged breath and kept staring at his hands.

This is the man who told Coleman he wants to talk to us, I thought. Who confirmed it himself when Maven called him. Yet now that we're here, he doesn't seem to want to say a single word.

"Lieutenant Haggerty," I said.

"I'm not a lieutenant anymore." His voice was somehow even more tired and more faraway than I would have imagined. "Call me Dean."

"Dean," I said. "I can't tell you how sorry we are for your loss."

He looked up at us, meeting our eyes for the first time.

"You sound like cops. That's exactly what a cop would say."

"I'm the Chief of Police in Sault Ste. Marie," Maven said. "My name's Roy."

"I've heard about you. Everybody says you're an asshole." Like a simple statement of fact, deserving no apology for saying it. Or else he was beyond caring.

"I have my days," Maven said, unshaken. "This is Alex. He was a police officer in Detroit."

He looked at me and nodded.

"The FBI agents were here to talk to you," Maven said. "Is that right?"

"Yes. They were here."

"I don't want to drag you through it again," Maven said, "but what did they actually—"

"They said that you guys have some questions about my daughter's . . . about what happened to her. They said they didn't necessarily . . . what did they say? *Subscribe* to anything unusual themselves, but they had to follow up."

"That doesn't sound like a good way to put it," Maven said, unable to hide his anger. I'm sure he was imagining Agent Fleury sitting right here in the same room, behaving exactly like himself. So much for impersonating a human being. "I'm sorry you had to go through that."

"Feds are different," the lieutenant said. "Always have been."

Maven pursed his lips and nodded. He was rubbing his right fist with his left hand.

"If you don't mind," I said, "can we ask you a few questions?"

"As long as you tell me why you think there's something suspicious about my daughter's . . ."

That's twice now, I thought. You come right up to it and you can't say the words.

"Of course," I said. "We'll tell you everything we know."

"Then go ahead. Ask me your questions. But then I want answers from you. That's the only reason I wanted you to come here."

"Your daughter . . . ," I said. "What's her name, anyway?"

"Dina. Her name is Dina."

"I understand she, um . . ."

Here it is, I thought. The man's still talking about her in the present tense, but I can't do it. I have to say this the right way. The way it really is now.

"I understand she was a teacher at the college," I said.

"Yes."

"Was there any indication that she might have been depressed, or . . . I don't know. Was there any sign at all of this happening?"

"Not that I know of. But she was twenty-seven years old. She lived in town, had her career at the college. I talked to her every week, but . . ." His words trailed off as he looked away.

"We've only heard in general terms that she may have . . ." I hesitated, then plowed ahead. "That she may have taken her own life. But we haven't heard any details beyond that."

"It was a suicide bag."

Maven and I looked at each other.

"I'm sorry," I said. "I don't know what that means."

"A suicide bag is supposedly a quick and

painless way to kill yourself," he said. "It's a very simple device. All you need is a helium tank, the kind you can buy to fill up balloons. A rubber hose, a plastic bag, and some sort of strap or belt or something to tie it off with. You cut a small hole in the bag and you slip the hose through the hole. Then you put the bag over your head and secure it."

He was still looking away as he said this, the words coming out in a rush and it made me remember that he had been a specialist at the crime lab in Marquette. It was the only lab in the Upper Peninsula, so that's where any questions about poison or ballistics or anything else along those lines would inevitably be sent. He was on familiar ground now, even if it never hit so close to home before.

"You turn on the helium. Because it's an inert gas, it helps suppress your suffocation reflex. Within seconds, you lose consciousness. Asphyxia will take place within minutes. Then you're gone."

It took me a few extra seconds to really absorb what he was telling us. There really was something called a "suicide bag." And his daughter had apparently used it on herself. We're sitting here in this dark house while this man is telling us in a perfectly matter-of-fact voice one of the most horrible things I've ever heard.

"How would she have even learned about this?" Maven finally said.

"I'm sure it's out there on the Internet. I've heard of it once or twice, but I've never actually run into a case of . . ."

He stopped. He looked down and I thought he was about to lose it. But he didn't cry. He didn't make the slightest sound. Maybe he was all cried out at that point.

"Lieutenant," I said, "why are you here all by yourself? Isn't there somebody who can . . . be here with you?"

He wiped his nose and looked up at me.

"What, you mean like my family?"

"Yes."

"My brother came right out," he said. "The day after it happened. Then my sister came, with her son. Then two cousins who haven't said a word to me in twenty years. They flew out all the way from California and rented a car and tried to drive out to the cabin and made it about one mile before they went into a ditch. They all invaded the house and tried to clean me up and make me eat and eventually they even tried to drag me out of here."

"Don't you think that would be a good idea? You shouldn't be alone through this."

He snorted at that and shook his head.

"You don't understand," he said. "Forgive me for saying so. You don't get it at all."

"Okay," I said. I wasn't about to fight him over it. "So . . . I'm sorry, if we can just go back one more time . . ."

"Lieutenant," Maven said, "just a couple more questions, I promise."

"Go right ahead. I'm not going anywhere."

"Was there . . . a note by any chance?"

"No note. They just, uh . . . they found her in bed the next day, with the bag over her head, and her arms wrapped around the tank."

"Who's 'they'?"

"A couple friends of hers. They had her key, for when she'd go away and they'd come in and water her plants. Stuff like that. She didn't show up for classes, and she wasn't answering her phone, so . . ."

I didn't want to picture it, but I couldn't keep the image out of my head. A woman alone in her bed, hugging a tank of helium like a lover.

But now it's going to get even worse, I thought. Here's the really hard part . . .

"A device like this," I said, "is it possible to use this on someone against their will?"

He didn't answer that for a while. I thought I saw his hands starting to tremble.

"Yes, I believe that would be possible," he said. "But then there'd probably be some sign of a struggle."

"What if you were asleep?" Maven said.

"That's possible, yes. The suffocation reflex would still have to be suppressed, even if you're asleep. But again, if the inert gas could do that . . ."

Once again, I didn't want to picture it. But I saw a man standing in her bedroom, looking down at her as she slept. He has a tank of helium, a hose, a plastic bag, a strap. He's probably wearing surgical gloves. If he's gone this far, he probably knows not to leave fingerprints.

"This is why I called you," Haggerty said, looking back and forth between us. "I had to hear from you in person. You actually believe that my daughter might have been murdered."

"We're asking you to consider that possibility, yes."

"The possibility that somebody broke into Dina's apartment and killed her in her bed. That's the possibility you're asking me to consider. This is why the FBI agents came to talk to me."

"Did they ask you about your old partner?"

"Donald Steele, yes. I hadn't seen him in a while, but I heard about his son shooting himself behind the barn. Then just a few days ago, he ended up being murdered at his girlfriend's house, right?"

"That's correct."

"That part wasn't a huge surprise, if I'm being honest with you. He always had a wandering eye. But I understand the girlfriend was killed, too. And they suspect her husband."

"They suspect him," Maven said, "but they haven't found him yet. So nobody knows for sure."

"Your idea is that somehow these deaths were all connected?"

"I know this was a number of years ago," Maven said, "but back when you were at St. Ignace with Sergeant Steele, did you ever happen to run into another state cop named Charles Razniewski?"

"The agents asked me the same question," he said, "but I don't remember that name at all. How long was he on the force?"

"Just short of two years. Are you sure you never ran into him? Big blond guy? Most people just called him Raz. He was stationed down at the Lansing post."

"That's a long way from St. Ignace. No, I honestly don't remember him at all. Actually, I do remember *your* name from back then, now that I think of it."

"I was down there, too. I was a sergeant."

"Yeah, I must have seen your name somewhere," he said. "I mean, before you came up here to take the Soo job. I don't think we ever ran into each other on the job, did we?"

Maven shook his head. "No, I don't believe so. I hardly ever got this far north, and I don't imagine you came down to Lansing all that often."

"Not if I could help it."

"I was hoping you could give us something that would tie the three of you together."

"I've got nothing," the lieutenant said. "If you really think there's some connection . . ."

"If there is," I said, "you may be in danger. The pattern would suggest that you're next on the list."

He didn't answer.

"I'm sorry to have to put it that way," I said, "but that's the cold hard reality. I'm just glad we got here before anything happened to you."

"You still don't get it." He shook his head and he was almost smiling.

"What do you mean?"

"Look at me. What do you see?"

"A man who has suffered a great loss," I said.

"Nice try. I appreciate the thought, but no. What you're actually looking at, gentlemen, is a dead man."

"Lieutenant . . ."

"I'm still breathing," he said. "My heart is still beating. But those are just illusions. I know all about death, believe me. I faced it every day when I was in the lab. I studied it inside and out. I know a dead man when I see one, and that's me."

"You have to let us help you," Maven said. "It's natural to think that you don't—"

"No, don't even start. When you lose the only person who makes you get out of bed in the morning, you can come back and talk to me, okay? But for now? You say this guy, whoever he is, he's still out there? He's gonna come for me next? Is that what you're saying?"

"If we're right," Maven said, "then yes. It'll be soon."

"Perfect." He stood up, showing more energy than he had at any point in our conversation. Hell, probably more energy than he'd had in the last two weeks. "Let him come, I say. I'll be right here waiting for him."

"Whoever this guy is," I said, "he's a cold-blooded killer."

"You still don't *get it!*" He slapped his hand down on the table, as loud as a gunshot. Then he regained his composure as quickly as he lost it.

"He can't touch me. Don't you understand? He's already killed me once. He can't do it again. In fact . . ."

He sat back down in his chair.

"I hope he gets here soon," he said. "The sooner the better. I don't have a helium tank, and I don't feel like going out and buying one."

"Lieutenant Haggerty," Maven said, "you need to listen to us."

"Where do you even buy a helium tank, anyway? At a party store? When's the last time I filled up balloons with helium? Dina's birthday party. Sweet Sixteen. Eleven years ago."

"Lieutenant Haggerty . . ."

"Sweet Sixteen. Never been kissed."

"Please," I said, putting one hand on his shoulder. "You have to let us help you."

"Get out." He didn't look at us. "Get out right

now, please. I don't imagine he'll come if you're here."

"We're not leaving."

"Yes, you are. You're leaving right now. You're no longer welcome in my house."

"Then you're coming with us."

"No. No, I'm not. And don't try to send anybody else over here, either. Do you hear me? No matter who it is. Cops, troopers, even asshole FBI agents—I will not let anybody else take one single step onto this property. If this person is really out there, then it's just him and me now. Just him and me."

"You were a cop for a long time," I said, playing my last card. "You know you can't face him alone. The only thing you can do is work with everyone else to catch him, so he can pay for what he did to your daughter. Don't you want that to happen?"

He closed his eyes. He didn't say a word.

Maven and I stood there. Minutes passed. The wind blew and rattled the window and we both seemed to come to the same conclusion without exchanging a word. As we left the room, I took one more look over my shoulder. He stayed in the chair, not moving a muscle, his eyes still closed. Waiting.

"Where are we going?" Maven said.

The headlights swept across the snow-covered trees. As we left Haggerty's driveway,

I pointed the truck north, back to the main road.

"I figure the Marquette post," I said. "No matter what the lieutenant says."

"Makes sense. They know him there. We can get somebody out here to watch over him."

We drove back into Au Train and I made the left turn. We were heading west, along the lake. We'd be in Marquette in half an hour.

"This is what he wants," Maven said. "We just saw it with our own eyes."

"What do you mean?"

"The man who's doing this. Whoever he is. This is what he wants to do to these men, before he kills them. He wants them to suffer."

I couldn't argue. I knew he was right.

"If this does go back to something that happened on the police force . . . ," I said. "Even if there is a connection and we don't see it yet, I still don't get it. What could three cops do that would make somebody come after them, and their families, all these years later?"

"I don't know."

"Raz never killed anyone on the job, did he?"

"I'm pretty sure he never took his gun out of the holster, no. I know I never did myself."

"Which reminds me, I've been meaning to ask you something else. About what Agent Fleury said to you."

He fidgeted in his seat, but otherwise kept his cool. "Yes?"

"We don't know for a fact that you're connected to this. But if you are . . ."

"I called Olivia. I told her to make arrangements to stay in Europe for a while. Just to be safe. Until we know for sure she won't be in any danger."

"Okay," I said. "That's probably a good idea."

I kept driving. It was after midnight now. There wouldn't be many state police officers on duty at the Marquette post, but *somebody* would be there. Somebody would be able to watch over Lieutenant Haggerty, if we explained the situation carefully enough.

"They can't watch him forever," Maven said, as if reading my mind. "They'll send a man out tonight. Then tomorrow night. But who knows how long?"

"We don't even know if Haggerty will be his next target. If you think about it, he's been mixing it up so far. The suicides and the outright murders."

"You're right," Maven said. "It could be another cop's kid. Somebody we don't even know about yet. Who knows how far this goes?"

"So I guess there's only one way to do this."

"Yes," he said, looking straight out the window, into the cold heart of the night. "We have to find this guy and stop him."

And we're rolling . . .

. . . Big scene. Everybody, we gotta nail this one.

. . . Cue the fire. Get it going.

. . . Come on, I said fire! Let's go big here! We're not roasting marshmallows.

. . . There you go. Boom, right out the window. Look at that smoke. Now we're talking.

. . . Must be hot in there, eh? Oh, man. Talk about one well-done Monster.

. . . Fire engines, do your thing. That's right, get in there. Everybody's doing great.

. . . Keep on that fire. Keep going. We'll use all of this, I promise you.

. . . That's a wrap for the Monster! His last scene, give him a hand.

And cut.

CHAPTER TWELVE

It was two days later. I was back home, trying to work on the cabin but unable to focus. I kept thinking about Haggerty sitting alone in his cabin, waiting for a killer to come through the back door. We had been to the Marquette post, of course, and now as far as we knew there was a state car positioned at the head of the driveway whenever possible. That's what they had promised us, anyway. Pretty amazing, if you think about it. Two guys stumbling into the station in the middle of the night, with this crazy story about a killer with a list of former state cops and their children. Yet they bought it. Or at least the sergeant we talked to was willing to give us the benefit of the doubt, especially if it meant his old friend the retired lieutenant might be in any kind of danger.

It was morning. I was back from breakfast at the Glasgow and trying to do something useful so I wouldn't drive myself completely crazy. There was a knock on the door. Way the hell back here, at the end of the road. I had no idea who it could be. It wasn't Vinnie, I knew that much. He had already been by and was on his way to the rez again, and he sure as hell wouldn't knock on the door, anyway. He'd just come on in.

I opened the door and saw Agent Long standing out there in the freezing cold. She was wrapped up tight in a long woolen coat that wasn't nearly thick enough. I could tell she was miserable.

"Come on in," I said. "Are you trying to kill yourself?"

"We do have winters in Detroit, you know," she said. "They just don't stick around until April."

"Come by the fire," I said. "Can I get you anything?"

"No, I was just stopping by. Nice place you got here. Although I wasn't sure which cabin is yours. The man at the gas station said it was the second one."

"Well, I own the second cabin and then everything after it," I said. "I'm living in this one while I finish it."

"You built this yourself?"

"I'm kinda *rebuilding* it." I didn't feel like getting into that story, but I wasn't sure where else to go. "Why, um . . . I mean, to what do I owe this pleasure?"

"I wanted to let you know," she said, finally taking her coat off. There was a warm light coming from the woodstove and it made her look good, I had to admit. For a man who had lost so much, it was a strange thing for me now, this unimaginable fact of feeling attracted to another woman. But she had this slow, careful way of smiling, like she didn't want to give too much of herself away. And she had those eyes.

"They finally tracked down Donna Krimer's husband," she said. "He was hiding out at a friend's house in Green Bay. An off-duty cop spotted him in a bar late last night."

"And?"

"And he says he didn't do it. He says he came home and found two dead bodies on the floor, panicked, and took off."

"Does anybody believe him?"

"Well, normally a story like that told by a man who's been arrested six times before wouldn't exactly hold up. But in this case . . ."

I waited for her to get to the punch line. Instead she took a slow lap around the place, looking it over.

"Tell me," she said finally, "do you really believe this is all one person we're talking about? All these deaths?"

"I think I have to. It would be too much of a coincidence otherwise. Besides that . . ."

"Yes?"

"I don't know. I've been getting the same feeling, every time I talk to somebody or every time I go see where somebody died. If you're really a fellow cop at heart, I don't think I have to explain that."

She looked at me for a long time.

"So what's next?" I said.

"I understand you and the chief talked to Lieutenant Haggerty the other night. Right after we did."

Here it comes, I thought.

"He specifically asked to talk to us," I said. "He wasn't getting the answers he wanted from you and your partner."

"We told him everything we knew. We asked him to do the same."

"Well, maybe he just wanted to hear it from us in person. It was hard enough for him to lose his daughter like that. I can't imagine having somebody come around two weeks later and tell me she might have been murdered instead."

"Did he believe you?"

"I don't think it even matters anymore. Although, actually, I think by the time we left he was anxious to meet this guy. Whoever he is."

"I've been on the job for twelve years," she said. "I've never even heard of anything like this."

"I think I've run into some pretty evil people myself. Even more now that I live way the hell up here, if you can believe it. But yeah, this is a whole different kind of animal we're talking about. It's a shame we can't put our heads together and catch him."

"Yeah, well, that's the other reason I came by. I was hoping we could sort of start over here. I think we all got off on the wrong foot."

"You think 'we' did, huh? Let me ask you something. I've seen I don't know how many partners over the years. When I was down in Detroit and even up here. FBI, DEA, cops in other towns, even state guys, and every time it's the same story. One partner's a human being, and the other one's, well . . . let's say the other one's usually a more colorful character. Every single time."

She couldn't help smiling a little bit. "Agent Fleury's not that bad, believe me."

"I've seen him in action a few times by now, remember? Seriously, do they actually pair you up that way? Separate you into two groups, one from column A, one from column B. Or do you both start out human and then one partner has to go to the dark side?"

"Well, why don't you ask him yourself? He'll be at the state post today, going over some old records with Chief Maven. If you'd like to be a part of that . . ."

"What's the catch?"

"There isn't one. You've helped uncover something important. We need to investigate it as thoroughly as we can, as quickly as we can. So we need your help."

"Your partner's really on board with this?"

"We both had a talk with our boss this morning. Believe me, Agent Fleury's officially on board."

"This I gotta see," I said. "Just tell me what time to be there."

"Noon should be fine."

"Okay, Janet. I'll see you there."

She stopped in the middle of putting on her coat. "When we're all done with this, you can use my first name," she said. "For right now, I'm still Agent Long to you."

I put up my hands in surrender. "I'll see you at noon, Agent Long."

She said good-bye and went back out into the cold. An hour later, I was still thinking about her.

It felt strange to be doing this in the state police post. Maven's office was just down the street, after all. If the wind chill was above zero, we all could have gotten up and walked over there. Instead we were in this too-small interview room at the Soo post, with Maven on one side of the table, and Agent Fleury on the other. It was the only interview room in the building, so I couldn't imagine what the state guys must have thought of this imposition. From the looks I saw walking in, we weren't exactly welcome guests.

No, who am I kidding? It wasn't about having strangers taking over their room at all. By now, the word must have gotten around. If they were like any other cops in the world, they looked out for each other, to the very end. I could only imagine how it must have felt that day, with no official bulletin yet but this vague story floating around about ex-troopers and ex-troopers' kids. Making it twice as bad if you had kids of your own. On top of that, having the FBI taking over the case—because sure, it all started with a U.S. marshal, which made it automatic, and one of the murders happened to take place over state lines. But if this story was true, it was *their family.*

That's why the place felt so cold, and I tried not to take it personally. I followed Agent Long past the front desk, back to the room in question. Maven looked up as we walked in. He was never exactly a magazine model on a good day. Today, he badly needed a shave and about ten hours of sleep.

"Come on in," Agent Fleury said to us. "We were just about to get started."

"How are you, Chief?" I said.

He looked up at me and shrugged.

When we were all sitting down, Agent Fleury waited approximately a tenth of a second and then dove right in. He had a tall stack of loose paper in front of him, but for now he pushed it aside. The man looked freshly scrubbed and caffeinated—in other words, the exact polar opposite of Chief Maven.

"Okay, gentlemen, Agent Long, here's our plan of attack. I've been working this over and it seems like we've got two separate target periods to look at here."

He stood up, went to the white board, and grabbed one of the markers. He tried to write, got nothing, swore at the pen, tried another, got nothing again, swore again. He hit gold on the third pen and he was off. He drew two separate boxes, his pen squeaking with every line. I looked over at Maven and tried to catch his attention, but the chief was staring at the board with bloodshot eyes.

"Okay," Fleury said. "If we take it as a given that our suspect has motivation to commit these crimes based on some connection between the victims, then we have to take a look at where those three victims were during each period. I say three men for now, because so far we only know for sure that Razniewski, Steele, and Haggerty were targeted."

Agent Long took out her pad of paper and started taking notes. I could see her drawing the same boxes. Me, I just sat there and listened.

"So by the time we enter target area one, Donald Steele is already a trooper at the St. Ignace post, Dean Haggerty is a recently promoted sergeant at the same post, and Charles Razniewski is a brand-new recruit at the Lansing post. You with me so far? This is the first day we've got all three men on the job. For the next twenty-two months or so, Trooper Razniewski will be frequently partnered with the veteran Sergeant Roy Maven."

Agent Fleury drew four circles in the first box, and marked them *S, H, R,* and *M.*

"This is the almost two-year period in which all four men were on the job. Although I've been asking around here at the post and apparently once you've completed your first year, you end up spending at least part of the time out on the road, on your own. Would that be fair to say, Chief Maven?"

He cleared his throat and leaned forward.

"Generally, yes," he said, sounding as dead tired as he looked. "During daytime, at least. But Raz never did care for that part of the job. It's why he eventually left."

"But he did spend some time out on the road by himself."

"Sure, of course. We all did."

"So then you have to admit, it's at least theoretically possible that on one of Razniewski's infrequent solo days, he somehow ran into Steele and Haggerty. Or some third party who might be a link to all three."

"Yes, but don't forget," Maven said. "It's Lansing and St. Ignace. They're more than two hundred miles apart."

"Granted. We'll get to that. For now, let's move on to the second target period."

"Razniewski leaves the force at that point," Agent Long said. "So what else is there?"

"Good question," he said, waving the pen at

217

her. "Razniewski is off the force, but Steele and Haggerty are still together in St. Ignace. That will last for approximately three more years, at which point Steele is promoted to sergeant and Haggerty moves to Marquette, where he'll soon become a lieutenant. But during those three years, where is ex-trooper Razniewski?"

"In Detroit," Agent Long said, "working for the marshals' office."

Fleury drew a line through the middle of the second box. He drew two circles in one half, marking them *S* and *H*. Then he drew one circle in the other half, marking it *R*.

"And where's Roy Maven during this time?"

He drew the fourth circle outside the box completely, and marked it *M*.

"He's out of the picture, on his way up to Sault Ste. Marie to accept the position of chief of police."

"Are you saying there still could have been a connection between the three men?" Agent Long said. "Even after Razniewski left the force?"

"As a marshal, he has coverage all over the state of Michigan. Ordinarily, that wouldn't bring him into much contact with the state police, right? But it is possible. We can't rule it out."

Fleury sat down again and started to shuffle through the stack of papers. As he did, I finally caught Maven's eye.

"Agent Fleury is completely on board now," Maven said to me. "As you can see."

"I've always had an open mind," Fleury said, "but recent events have made it obvious that you gentlemen were onto something from the beginning. I apologize if it *seemed* to take longer than it should have."

Emphasis on "seemed," as if he was way ahead of us. Whatever. The important thing, I realized, was that he was finally committed to the case.

"And I have to say," he went on, "that the two of you have done an incredible job with this so far, with limited resources. You bring a great deal of credit to your local police force, Chief Maven. I'll make sure the mayor is aware of that when it's all done. And Alex? Once a cop, always a cop, right? It's too bad you don't have a boss I can send a letter to anymore."

Wait a minute, I thought. I may be slow, but this is finally starting to make sense . . .

"Okay, so moving on to the particulars," Fleury said. "Here's where we really get down to it."

"This is a huge case," I said. "Somebody killing cops? After killing their children? This is the kind of case that if you crack it, you make your career."

Fleury just looked at me.

"That's why you've suddenly seen the light," I said. "It's got nothing to do with your boss talking to you or you suddenly deciding to play

219

nice. You put it all together yourself and what you came up with was the case of a lifetime."

"Alex, come on."

"You haven't even reamed us out for going to talk to Lieutenant Haggerty yet. I figured that would be the first thing on the agenda, but you haven't even mentioned it."

"I didn't think that would—"

"No, I get it now. You can't treat us like dog crap anymore because it finally dawned on you that you need this. Which means you need *us*."

"Leave the man alone," Maven said, finally showing some energy. "I don't care why he did the one-eighty, okay? All I care about is him being on the case, and having the whole bureau behind him. If it makes his career, then good for him. They can throw him a goddamned parade for all I care. As long as he helps us catch this guy."

An uneasy silence reigned for a few seconds.

"Normally, you wouldn't have a place at this table," Fleury finally said. "You're not an active police officer and you have no official standing in this matter. The only reason you're here is because Chief Maven wants you to be here, and because maybe you can help us. I'm sure we can all agree that we have to catch this guy before he kills anyone else. Can we start with that, at least?"

"Yes," I said. "We can start with that."

The chief is going along with this, I told myself. No reason why I can't, too.

"No harm done," Fleury said. "Let's get back to work."

He went back to his papers, separating them into three piles.

"The state guys were good enough to print all this out for me. Even though we're talking about events that happened many years ago, there's always a data trail. In the case of state troopers, that means a lot of time out on the road and a lot of tickets."

He put his hand down heavily on the first pile.

"I hope we can agree this is *probably* not the work of somebody who didn't like getting a speeding ticket ten years ago. So that leaves other events like major arrests or even on-the-job shootings."

"Raz never pulled his gun," Maven said. "At least not when he was a state cop. That first period you were talking about."

"Fair enough. Let's not even worry about him yet. I say, let's start with Steele and Haggerty. We know that if there's one link, it involves both of those men as state cops. So that means it's right here somewhere."

He hit the papers again.

"The marshals are putting together similar information for us right now," Agent Long said. "We should have that by the end of the day."

"I still don't think this goes beyond Raz in a state uniform," Maven said. "It feels like too much of a coincidence otherwise."

"All the more reason to start right here," Fleury said. "So what do you say? Are you ready?"

Maven took out a pair of reading glasses I'd never seen on him before.

"Ready as I'll ever be," he said. "Bring it on."

It was a long afternoon. Steele and Haggerty turned out to be two especially active and energetic state police officers. It was easy to see why they both had such successful careers. On top of that, they happened to be stationed in St. Ignace, one of the busier posts in Michigan. It's the last stop before you get on the Mackinac Bridge, after all, meaning that everybody coming to and from the Upper Peninsula has to pass by your doorstep. They have to go through the toll booth there and pay their money and let you get a good look at them if you happen to be sitting right there in your squad car. So it's the perfect place to camp out and watch for suspicious vehicles. Anyone going too fast or even too slow. Anyone trying way too hard to act natural. You get a feel for it eventually. You watch the people go by and you let your gut tell you if the person is holding his or her breath until you're safely out of their rearview mirror. You pull up behind the vehicle and you run the plates. If something comes back, you light them up. Or hell, anything else you might happen to notice. One of the taillights out, for instance. Or one of those tiny white lights that illuminate the license plate. Those things go all the time and people hardly ever replace them.

Once you've got them stopped, you get out of your car and approach the driver's side window, your right hand ready above your firearm, just in case. You do a quick visual on the backseat. If there's anybody back there acting squirrely, trying to hide something or worse yet, trying to dig out something from under the seat. You watch the driver carefully. You look in the glove compartment when he opens it, the whole time waiting to see that familiar sight of cold blue steel. A hundred different things to process at once and a fraction of a second to react.

That's what a good trooper does. That's what Steele and Haggerty did, again and again, to the point that they developed a reputation for apprehending so many high-profile offenders. The agents went through their official daily logs, one day at a time, finally settling into a rhythm— Agent Fleury with Haggerty's logs, Agent Long with Steele's. They looked for the "A" entries and occasional "F" entries, *A* standing for Arrest and *F* for Fugitive. They passed over all of the "S" for Summons entries, the "V/W" for Verbal Warning entries, and all of the other minor incidents that filled out a state police officer's day. It was amazing to me just how detailed these logs were.

Each arrest had a file class number associated with it, and we ended up seeing some of the same file classes again and again, after, 8041 for driving under the influence of alcohol, 2408 for possession of a stolen vehicle, 5202 for a concealed weapon. Maven had to step out to clarify two or three obscure file classes with the guys in the office, but for the most part it all went by in a blur.

It was just raw data, that was the problem—date, time, file class, name of the arrested party, driver's license number, place of residence, date of birth—there was no room for pictures or for stories. By the end of a long, long afternoon, after we'd gone over hundreds of arrests involving both Donald Steele and Dean Haggerty, not one of those arrests could be cross-referenced to Charles Razniewski's daily logs. Or Roy Maven's either.

No, it would not be that easy.

When the post commander finally showed up, he invaded the room and we had to go through a minute or two of rooster strutting until Agent Long finally sat everybody down and tried to make them play nice. I couldn't help wondering how many times she'd done this same routine before, and whether she ever got fed up with men wearing shiny badges. In the end, we all agreed that the Michigan State Police should be made aware of what the FBI was doing, and that the St. Ignace branch in particular could be a big help. There might have been a few old-timers left down there, after all, who might have memories of Steele and Haggerty and hell, why not? Maybe even a particular suspect who vowed revenge someday. We'd never know if somebody didn't ask.

"You see," Maven said to me when we were finally outside, "that's the problem I keep coming back to. Let's say somebody did get arrested all those years ago and what, he went to prison? He did his time and now he's out? If he's still got a beef, why would it be the cops he goes after? If he went to trial, it was the district attorney who stood up and pointed his finger at him, and told the judge he should be put away. Then of course it was the judge who actually banged his gavel and sentenced him. Why do you think Raz spent so much of his time guarding federal judges, anyway? They're the real targets. Not the poor schlubs just doing their jobs who happened to catch you."

"Still, you might have to testify," I said. "You could still be the one person who makes it all happen. At least, it might feel that way if you're looking at prison time. In fact, we should mention that angle to the agents, have them check the court records."

"I don't know, McKnight." He sounded more tired than ever. "I was hoping I could help find the connection today, but it was like a total waste of time."

"They'll move on to that second time period now, after Raz became a marshal. If there's something to be found, they'll find it. I know Agent Fleury tries to talk a big game sometimes, but I think they're both pretty sharp."

He shook his head and turned his collar up against the wind. There was no good reason for both of us to be standing out there. Maven wasn't even smoking a cigarette.

"You look like hell," I said. "You should go home and get some rest."

"I went back out there."

"Where?"

"To Haggerty's house. I just had to check on him."

I counted to three in my head.

"You promised me you wouldn't go off on your own again," I said. "What happened?"

"There was a state car on the road, by his driveway. I rapped on the guy's window and just about gave him a heart attack. Then I asked him why he wasn't in the house with Haggerty. You know what he said?"

"What?"

"He said Haggerty kicked him out and told him to stay off his property. That's why he had to sit on the road."

"He's still waiting," I said. "He doesn't want anybody else there to keep the killer away."

We both stood there shivering for a while, thinking this over. There wasn't much else to say about it.

"So what now?" I finally said.

"When we were talking about letting the guys at St. Ignace know about this, you know what occurred to me?"

"What?"

"All the time I've been a cop here in the Soo, I've never once set foot in the St. Ignace post."

"It's in a different county," I said. "Why would you ever have business down there?"

"I wouldn't. That's just it. The only time I might have gone there was back in the day, when I was a state cop with Raz and I happened to come up here for something."

"Something you can't remember."

"Right," he said. "But what if . . ."

I waited for him to finish.

"Come on," he said. "It's not that far away. Let's go see if I'm crazy."

Sault Ste. Marie to St. Ignace. From the top of the eastern UP to the bottom. Not even an hour away, straight down I-75. It's the busiest road in the state, the main artery running up from Detroit, all the way into Canada, so it's always the first to be cleared. Plus the speed limit is seventy, so I'll routinely buzz it between 85 and 90, even in wintertime.

It was early evening. I could have been having Jackie's famous beef stew, I thought, along with the first of several cold Canadians. Sitting by the fire with my feet up. Yet I was here with Chief Maven again, and I wanted to see how this played out.

It didn't take long to find the state police post in St. Ignace. It's not a big town—just a few streets with some shops and gas stations and restaurants, and the docks for the ferries that run back and forth to Mackinac Island. When the ice finally melts, anyway.

The state police post was right there on the edge of the water, overlooking the Mackinac Bridge. We pulled up to the building. It was getting dark now, and here where the two peninsulas came together there was a narrow strait where Lake Michigan flowed into Lake Huron. Cars have been blown off the bridge before. It's not an urban legend. It really happened. The wind wasn't strong enough to flip cars that day but still, we could feel it rocking the truck and we both knew that we'd be suffering as soon as we stepped outside.

I took a deep breath and opened the door. The

wind tried to slam it shut so I had to wedge my way through and then I was out in the open air, moving as quickly as I could to the front door. Maven was right behind me. A hundred feet of hell. When we were safely inside, we stomped off our boots and rubbed away the numbness from our ears.

"Remind me again why we live up here year-round," he said.

"Because we're idiots?"

There was another set of doors, to help keep out the elements. When we went through those we were in the main lobby. To me it was like any other police lobby, with the semi-comfortable furniture and the brain-numbing fluorescent lights. There was the standard waist-high barrier keeping everyone safely corralled outside the main offices, with the one narrow gate leading right past the main desk, where a trooper was sitting. The trooper didn't look more than twenty years old.

"Can I help you guys?"

Maven didn't answer him. He kept looking around the room.

"Got a question for you, Trooper," Maven finally said, without looking at him. "Have they redone this place in the past few years?"

"Redone it?"

"Yeah, you know. Redecorated? Made it look different?"

"Oh, sure," the trooper said. "There was a big contest. The best interior designers from all over the world submitted their plans."

Maven locked eyes on him.

"What, are you some kind of joker?"

"Just tell me what's going on, okay?"

Then the young trooper did a double take.

"Wait a minute," he said. "You're Chief Maven from Sault Ste. Marie, right?"

"Have we met before?"

"I don't believe so. But I've seen your picture in the paper."

"That's great," Maven said, "but here's the thing, I was a state man, back when you were in diapers. I'm trying to figure out if I've ever been here before. Hence the question. You want to give me the real answer now?"

"I honestly don't know," the trooper said. "I'm kinda new here."

"Any old-timers around?"

"Sergeant Avery is here. He's forty-five."

"For God's sake," Maven said. "Just let me look around the place, all right?"

Maven went past the desk, down the hallway. I followed him.

"What do you think?" I asked him.

He was lost in thought, going back so many years, trying to remember if he had once walked down this same hallway as a younger man. Being this far north, for whatever reason, with his partner Razniewski. Steele and Haggerty in the building, as well. If he could start with that memory, everything else might come back to him. It had seemed like a crazy idea on the way down here, but now that he was here . . . yeah, it made sense. Or at least it was exactly the kind of thing I'd do myself.

"I don't know," he finally said. "It's a police station, you know? How different can it look from every other one?"

"The agents were going to call down here, remember? With everybody working on it, *somebody's* gonna remember something."

"It's too many years, McKnight. Nobody will remember."

"Come on, let's go."

"Gimme a second." He pushed open the door to the men's room and stepped inside. I figured it wouldn't be a bad idea, with another hour to go before we were back home. So I pushed open the same door and stepped up to the urinal next to him.

He was looking up at the ceiling.

"Look how high that is, McKnight."

I looked up. He was right. The ceiling was a good twenty feet above us, with a wide oblong skylight obscured by the snow. What a strange anomaly in a bathroom where everything else was pretty much standard issue, from the gray tile on the walls to the white porcelain sinks to the automated paper towel dispensers.

"I stood right here," he said. "Raz stood next to me. Right where you're standing now."

"You're sure?"

"Positive."

He stepped away, washed his hands, and took a paper towel from the dispenser.

"It really did happen, McKnight. Whatever it was, it must have happened right here in St. Ignace."

He wadded up the towel and held it tight in his fist.

"So what the hell happened here? Why can't I remember?"

And we're rolling . . .

. . . I think we have just enough light for this.

. . . Yes, with the lake in the background there. That ambient glow should work just fine.

. . . Okay, now cue the rope. Pull on that thing!

. . . Get him up there. That's it. A little higher.

. . . Oh yeah. Now that's a shot. Let's do a walk-around here. That's it.

. . . Close on the face. A few snowflakes. Perfect.

. . . Way to start things off, Charlie. That was wonderful. I'm crying, that was so beautiful.

. . . Now where's that snowmobile? It's cold out here!

And cut.

CHAPTER THIRTEEN

It was after ten o'clock at night when we got back to the Soo. I dropped Maven off at the state post so he could pick up his car. He told me he'd be going over to the Ojibway to find the agents before they went to bed. He had to tell them this one small thing he had figured out, this glimpse into the past. No matter how late it was, he would not be able to sleep until he told them.

I wasn't sure if he'd tell them the exact spot he was standing when he had his little epiphany. But what the hell, maybe he would.

I didn't think I could sleep either. It felt like I was missing some essential part of the story, something that I should have seen already, but I couldn't even begin to figure out what that might be.

There was only one person to talk to. So instead of heading back home, I went to the other side of town. To the movies.

The parking lot was jammed. On a frozen Friday night in Sault Ste. Marie, it was either the movies or a bar. I went inside and saw Leon scooping a tub-sized bucket of popcorn and then squirting what looked like yellow motor oil on top of it. He gave the bucket to a couple of teenagers and they gave him money in return. Then he went on to the next customer. I sat down at one of the little tables and waited. Before long, the customers all disappeared and the lobby was quiet.

"Alex!" Leon said, finally noticing me.

"You got a minute?"

"Yeah, why not?"

He came out to the table. He winced as he sat down and leaned forward to stretch out his back.

"Too much standing in this job," he said.

"Leon, I don't want to keep bothering you every time I get stuck on something."

"You're not bothering me. You know I love this stuff."

"Yeah, I know."

I didn't want to go down that road again, so instead I just launched into my full update. All of the things we had learned since the last time I had spoken with him. Going out to Iron Mountain to talk to Mrs. Steele, finding her husband and his girlfriend both dead in her house in Wisconsin. Then finding out about Haggerty's daughter and that cheerful little trip out to talk to him. The troopers watching his driveway around the clock. Then this whole new information dump from the state police records, leading right up to Maven's almost-breakthrough that very evening.

"We just can't find that one link," I said. "That one person who crossed paths with all four of them."

"I think you're drowning in the details, Alex. You're not the one who's gonna find it, remember. Maven's the one with the memories, and the FBI agents have all the raw data."

"So I'm useless. Yeah, thanks, I feel better now."

"You're the neutral party here," he said. "You're the one who can sorta stand above everything and see it all from a thousand feet."

"I don't know how to do that."

"Think about it. Do your own little profile here."

"That sounds like something the FBI would do."

"It's all common sense, Alex. Just think, okay? Think like him, whoever's doing this. Why are you doing all this?"

"Well, let's see . . ."

"Think, but don't *overthink*. Just say the first thing that comes to you. Right from the gut. That's usually pretty close to the truth. Why are you committing these crimes against these people?"

"Revenge."

"Okay. For what?"

"For what they did to me."

"What did they do?"

I hesitated. "They arrested me. They took me away."

"Why are you killing their children first?"

"Because I want them to suffer before they die."

"So you really must hate them."

"Yes."

"So why are you making these deaths look like suicides?"

"I don't know," I said. "I really don't. At first, I thought it was because that would make it worse somehow. But if I just took them away and then killed them—"

I stopped.

"What is it?" he said.

"Because it happened to me. That's why I'm doing this, Leon. Because the exact same thing happened to me."

His eyes lit up. "That's good. Because you suffered the same loss. So put it all together now. What's the whole story?"

"I was arrested and put in prison. My son killed himself. Or my daughter. While I was in prison."

"Is that really enough of a reason?"

"They died alone, from their own hand. They killed themselves while I was rotting away in a concrete box."

"So now you're having your revenge," he said. "All these years later, right? Why have you waited so long?"

"Because I just got out of prison."

"Maybe." I could see Leon thinking that one

over. "Or there might be some other reason why now is the right time."

"Yeah, maybe I had other reasons to wait. Other things in my life that I didn't want to lose. But maybe now there's nothing stopping me."

"Exactly. So how old are you?"

"Well, if I was arrested what, like ten, eleven years ago . . ."

"And you already had a son or daughter at the time."

"I'm guessing this suicide probably happened fairly close to the time of the arrest," I said. "Otherwise, you wouldn't necessarily connect the two in your mind."

"Okay, so your son or daughter must be of age already. Old enough to commit suicide, anyway."

"If you add it all up, you're talking about somebody who's at least in his midforties?"

"Or older, right."

"But hold on." I flashed back to what Maven and I had already talked about. "We're talking about taking my revenge against the cops who arrested me. What about the judge and the DA and hell, for that matter, even the defense attorney who obviously didn't defend me too well?"

"From everything you've seen, would you say this guy is smart?"

"Smart, yes. Ingenious even, if you think about what he did to Haggerty's daughter with that bag full of helium."

"Would you call him methodical? Is that a word you'd use?"

I thought about it. "Yes. Methodical."

"So who's to say those other people, the judge and the DA and the defense attorney, aren't further down on the list?"

"What, are you saying . . ."

"He's starting at the beginning. And the beginning is what?"

"The cops who arrested him."

Leon didn't say anything else. He leaned back in his chair and looked at me.

"This guy is a smart, patient killer," I said. "And he may only be getting started. That's what we've got here."

"It would seem so."

"But Maven can't even remember him."

"Doesn't matter who remembers him. He remembers *them,* that's all that matters."

Some kid in his twenties, wearing the same uniform as Leon's, came up to us right about then and asked him to get back to work.

"Hey, give us a break," I told him. "This is important."

"Not as important as changing the syrup in the Coke machine," the kid said. "Not when he's on the clock, anyway."

I could have put him right through the window, but Leon put up his hand and told me to take it easy.

"We're about done here," he said to the kid. "I'll go change that syrup."

"Leon, you don't belong here."

"It's only temporary. Don't worry about it. Go help catch that guy and then come back and tell me all about it."

"I can't thank you enough, Leon. Yet again."

"Just be careful, all right? My wife is right, this is no job for a middle-aged man with too much to lose."

"Tell her hello," I said. I thanked him again and left. As I went back out the cold air hit me in the face and I couldn't help thinking to myself, Leon's got something to lose, all right. A wife and two kids. Me, I've got nothing left. So maybe I'm the right man to go chase this killer after all.

When I got to the state police post the next day, Maven's old friend Sergeant Coleman was waiting for me with a cup of coffee.

"I heard you guys weren't exactly the most welcome guests yesterday afternoon," he said. "I hope you can understand why it might have seemed that way."

"It's okay. I know this is a tough situation for everybody."

"We've got everyone in the state on notice. We're all trying to figure out who this guy could be."

"You know I was a Detroit cop myself, right?"

"So I heard."

"I had the chance to interact with a few state cops along the way, and as far as I'm concerned, there's no better police force in the world."

I was leaving out a few personality issues I might have run into, but yeah, overall it was the truth. He thanked me for the compliment and I thanked him for the coffee. Then I joined Chief Maven and the two FBI agents in the interview room.

Agent Fleury was talking to somebody on the house phone while Agent Long and Chief Maven sat on the other end of the table, going over a fresh pile of papers. Maven looked a little better today. Maybe he'd actually gotten a few hours of sleep. Agent Long gave me a quick smile.

"Good morning," she said. I thought I heard a little extra something in the way she spoke to me today. Either that or I was just imagining things.

"Looks like you guys have already gotten started," I said. "Did I misunderstand the schedule?"

"We wanted to get an early jump, because we've actually got something to work with today."

"Oh yeah?"

I sat down next to her.

"Our team in Detroit has been looking at this overnight, and they've identified three men who were all arrested by Steele and Haggerty, right around the time when Chief Maven and Razniewski were still on the force. As you know, we've established that Chief Maven has at least a partial memory of being up at the St. Ignace post at some point. Although we still don't see anything reflected in the official records."

"Sometimes cops assist on arrests but don't show up on the official reports," Maven said. "You know how it is with paperwork. Some days you just don't get it all done the right way."

"I do remember that much," I said. "I used to hate that part of the job."

"We're trying to cross-reference arrests that resulted in significant jail time, and beyond that we've got a general profile that would suggest a suicide in the family right around that same time."

Exactly what Leon and I were talking about last night, I thought. I was going to bring that up as soon as I got here today, but it looks like Agent Long is already way ahead of me.

"It's not easy to make those connections, because the information isn't in one place. But we have people in the Detroit office working on it."

"You say you have some hits already?"

"The three men arrested by Steele and Haggerty working together, yes. All in the right time frame, as I said, and in all three cases, there was a suicide in the family, within the following two years. The only sticking point will be tying in Razniewski and possibly Chief Maven."

"It sounds like the right place to start," I said. "So who are these guys?"

"Well, here's what we have . . ."

She shuffled back through her papers.

"Candidate number one," she said. "Andrew Parizi, age forty-five at the time of his arrest. His vehicle was stopped by Steele and Haggerty just short of the bridge. He was driving a station wagon and they could see all this stuff piled up in the back, lots of boxes and a few television sets. He went racing up to the toll booth, it sounds like, but they caught him before he could go through. He became combative when they tried to cuff him, so they could already add on felony resisting to the felony eluding, to whatever they ended up finding in his car."

"What did they find?"

"The stuff they'd already spotted. The televisions and the stereo equipment and a bunch of other stolen items. Power tools, jewelry. There'd been a string of break-ins in Cedarville and out on Drummond Island. Vacation homes, mostly. This guy was loaded up and heading downstate with it, so they were able to connect him to most of the robberies. He was already a repeat offender, so he got sent away for five years. He did three, it looks like, but about a year and a half in, his son Patrick killed himself. He jumped out a window."

"What was his name? Andrew Parizi? Does that mean anything to you, Chief?"

"No. Agent Long and I have already been through this. The name doesn't ring a bell."

"Neither Razniewski nor Maven were involved in the arrest," she said. "That much we know from checking their daily logs. That was pretty early on in Razniewski's career, actually, so he was definitely in the car with Sergeant Maven all day. From the logs, we can determine that they never went farther north than Mount Pleasant. Of course, we're still keeping open the possibility that they may have had some form of contact with our eventual killer. On a different date, or maybe even out of uniform."

"So it'll be hard to eliminate anybody," I said. "But okay, who's next?"

"Clyde C. Wiley. You may have heard of him before."

"Doesn't ring a bell, no."

"He's an actor," Maven said. "You've probably seen him on TV."

"I don't know," I said. "I don't even watch that much TV anymore."

"This guy's been around forever," Agent Long said. "He did a lot of biker movies, right after *Easy Rider* came out. Did you ever see *Road Hogs*? That was probably his biggest."

"I vaguely remember the title," I said.

"He was kind of a maniac back then, even for Hollywood. He got busted a few times for possession, got in a big fight on a movie set, ended up getting thrown out of town for a while. He did some low-budget horror movies, until he finally worked himself back into television. Whenever some crime show needed somebody to play a psycho tough guy, they'd give him a call. He's got real wild eyes, long hair, tattoos, arms like a body builder. I'm sure you've seen him a million times."

"Honestly, no. I don't own a television."

She looked at me for a moment like she was trying to decide what planet I'd come from.

"You really don't watch TV," she said.

"If there's an important game on, I'll catch it at Jackie's place. That's about it."

"Okay, whatever. Point is, Mr. Wiley's had a long and colorful relationship with law enforcement, going all the way back to before he even went to Hollywood. He grew up here in Michigan, down in Bad Axe."

" 'The Bad Boy of Bad Axe,' " Maven said. "I remember when he got arrested."

"He was in his sixties at the time of this arrest," Agent Long said. "Now he's seventy-two."

"But you say Steele and Haggerty popped him?"

"Flying down I-75. Apparently, he had assaulted

somebody and a tip was called in. They were waiting for him at the bridge, ended up chasing him all the way down to Indian River, until they finally ran him off the road. Then he got into it with both troopers."

"So what happened to him?"

She picked up another sheet of paper.

"Besides the assault, there was a gun in the car. Traces of cocaine, a few bottles of pills. Tack on the eluding, obstruction, another assault or two on the officers, and just for good measure, he was on probation back in California and wasn't supposed to leave the state. So with the violation and the prior offenses, he ended up getting fifteen. Did seven and a half. During that first year his daughter killed herself. It was hard to track that down because she had a different last name, but we found her."

"How did she do it?"

"She cut open both wrists," Agent Long said, then she drew an imaginary line down the length of her forearm. "She even knew to do it the long way to bleed out faster. There was no chance of saving her."

"So what do you think, Chief? This Wiley made it a few miles downstate at least. Any chance you were involved?"

"I told you, I recognized the name right away," Maven said. "But if anybody assisted on that arrest, it would have been out of the Mackinaw

City post, or maybe Gaylord. And hell, if it was me helping to bust a celebrity, I'd certainly remember it."

"Not to mention he's kind of old now to be killing people," Agent Long said. "And according to the logs, neither Razniewski nor Maven had any activity that day at all. It just says 'Admin.'"

"What does that mean?"

"It means running around doing nonsense," Maven said. "We were at the Lansing post, remember, so every once in a while we got to go run errands for the governor."

"Didn't he have a regular attachment for that?"

"The governor had four state guys on a permanent assignment, yes, but you know how it is. There's always somebody from the mansion who needs a ride somewhere, or something stupid like that. You can guess who usually got picked for that exciting duty."

"So maybe you guys were close to the arrest that day," I said, "while you were running an errand. Isn't that possible?"

"If we were in on that arrest, it would be in our daily logs, believe me. And I told you, I'd remember it, anyway."

"All right, all right," I said. "So I guess that's strike two. Who's the third candidate?"

"Here's where it takes a little different turn," she said. "Candidate number three, a man named

Kenny Fraser, was actually a city police officer in St. Ignace. He was charged with a number of aggravated assaults, apparently committed while on duty, and as you can imagine, it would have been tough for one of the other officers in town to arrest him. I mean, the whole force couldn't have been more than a half dozen officers, right? So they called in the state police to make the arrest. You can guess who did that."

"Steele and Haggerty."

"Apparently, Fraser made quite a scene about it. I'm told he even swore to both Steele and Haggerty that they'd pay for breaking the cop code. No matter how long it takes, this guy's yelling as they're taking him away, he'll get even. At least that's what the guys at the St. Ignace post are saying. We found one sergeant this morning who's been around long enough to remember it."

"What kind of assaults are we talking about?"

"We don't have that information yet. The sergeant can't quite recall. But if you think about it, a former cop knows how to use a gun, knows how to access information about other cops . . ."

"What about it, Chief?"

"It's ringing a faint bell," Maven said. "But again, I might have just heard about this guy through other channels."

"The suicide?"

"His son, the same day his father got arrested.

Sixteen years old. Hanged himself in the garage."

"A hanging," I said. "Just like our first suicide."

"On the day of this arrest, it looks like Maven and Razniewski were riding separately. Maven's log shows activity south of Lansing, Razniewski's north of Lansing."

"That sounds promising. How far north?"

"There's nothing logged north of St. Johns, but there's a fair amount of time not accounted for. It doesn't look like Trooper Razniewski was a ticket-writing machine, if you catch my drift."

"I told you guys," Maven said, "he hated that part of the job."

"Okay, so maybe he ended up having some contact with this guy Fraser."

"We don't know that yet. We're still tracking all this down."

"We've got a line on Parizi," Agent Fleury said as he hung up the phone. "We've already got a man heading out to talk to Wiley. The ex-cop, Fraser, is still an unknown."

"What about Dr. Sizemore?" Long said. "Is he on his way up?"

"He'll be here in about two hours."

"Who's Dr. Sizemore?" I said. Whoever he was, he must have hit the road pretty damned early in the morning to be two hours away by now.

"He's our psych man in Detroit. He's going to try hypnotizing Chief Maven to see if we can help him remember any possible connections."

"You're actually going to try hypnosis?"

"Why not?"

I looked over at Chief Maven, who was sitting there with his usual unhappy troll face, or rather an even more unhappy version than usual on account of everything that was happening around him. If I knew anything about the chief, I knew that he liked to be in complete control of things, which would probably make him the worst possible subject in the history of hypnosis.

"I know," she said, apparently understanding exactly what I was thinking. "But we have to try."

"All I can say is good luck, then."

"I'm not sure what else we should do right now," Agent Fleury said. "We'll wait to hear what happens with those three candidates. When Dr. Sizemore gets here, we'll need a quiet room with absolutely no interruptions. Alex, we'll have to ask you to leave at that point. The doctor and Chief Maven will need to be alone."

"No problem," I said. "I understand."

He looked like he was about to say something else to me. He gave Agent Long a quick look and then he turned away. Of course, I knew all too well that they were continuing to break the rules every day, having me here in these meetings. I had done my part and by all rights I should have been debriefed and shown the door. I knew Chief Maven still wanted me here, as strange as that would have seemed to me just a few days ago. Would that be enough? Maybe this was mostly Agent Long's doing. Either way, I knew it could end at any second.

"Let me look at those files again," Maven said. "Maybe I'll remember something on my own, before the stupid goddamned headshrinker gets here."

This poor Dr. Sizemore, I thought. He has no idea what he's about to run into.

Many hours later, when the sun was long gone and the temperature had dropped back toward zero, I was sitting in front of the fire at the Glasgow, a Molson in hand, but my only beer of the night. I was thinking about Haggerty again, sitting alone in his cabin, his life in ruins around him. All his tears cried out and nothing left at all.

That's when the door opened up and the cold air came blasting in. Chief Maven came over and joined me in front of the fire. He didn't sit down. He kept standing and he was looking into the fire and warming himself.

"How did the hypnotism go?" I said.

"He should have tried to hypnotize a cinder block instead. That might have worked a little better."

"Some people don't hypnotize well."

"Some people have actual working memories, too."

"This isn't about your memory, Chief. It was at least ten years ago."

"I came face-to-face with a killer, McKnight, and I can't even remember him."

"Sit down."

He did, but he left his coat on.

"What happened with your three candidates? Did the agents find out any more information?"

"Yes, they did."

I waited a beat. But he didn't continue.

"Chief, what did they find?"

"Parizi's living in Flint. He's the guy who got busted with all the stuff in his car. He's on parole now for another bust, and apparently his parole officer can vouch for his whereabouts."

"His parole officer doesn't live with him."

"No, but he sees him often enough. If you do the math on him getting all the way up here and back, it just doesn't work."

"Okay, what about the actor? What was his name?"

"Clyde C. Wiley? Our seventy-two-year-old actor? He's living in Bad Axe again. I guess he's been working on a film, except he's actually the director this time. Which means, apparently, that he's working almost around the clock. He's got people around him at all times, and there's just no way he could have slipped away for more than a few hours at a time."

"The third man?"

"Fraser, the ex-cop."

I waited again.

"The ex-cop," I said. "What happened with him?"

"He did his time. Finally got out of prison about a year ago."

"Okay, that's perfect. Then what?"

"Then nothing. He's dead. He moved to Florida and died in a car accident, about six months ago."

"They're sure it was him?"

"Yes." He still hadn't looked at me. "They're sure. He's in the ground."

I put my head back and closed my eyes.

"All this running around," he said, "and it comes to nothing. We're right back where we started."

"We'll keep looking."

"Yeah. I know."

I could hear the defeat in his voice. Something I never expected to hear. Of all the things you could say about this man, good or bad, I would never, ever expect him to give up on anything.

"You need a drink," I said.

Maven didn't answer me. He kept staring into the fire while outside in the cold dark night the snow began to fall.

A hundred and fifty miles to the west of us, Lieutenant Dean Haggerty sat in his own chair, with no fire to warm him. At the head of his long driveway, through the blanketed trees, a lonely state trooper sat in his idling patrol car with the heat turned up as the falling snow melted on his hood.

None of us knew it at that moment, but there was one other person sitting in another vehicle, either down the road or on another road entirely but within walking distance of the house. Staying awake, staying warm, and waiting for the right time to move.

And we're rolling . . .

. . . Slow approach to the barn. Nice and easy.

. . . Look at that light. Is that perfect or what?

. . . The camera loves the snow, you gotta admit.

. . . Careful now. Don't rush the shot.

. . . Close to the wall. Let the camera feel it. That's right.

. . . Hello, young Brandon! Mind if I borrow this for a second?

. . . Boom, just like that. Oh, that's beautiful. Look at that.

. . . Bravo, young sir. That's how you do it. That's how you own a scene, people.

. . . Stay on his face. Drink it in. That is so goddamned perfect.

And cut.

CHAPTER FOURTEEN

I got the call at 4:30 in the morning. The fire in the woodstove had gone out and it was cold enough to see my own breath as I stumbled out of bed. I knew the call would not bring good news. No call at 4:30 in the morning is ever good news.

It was Maven who called me. Lieutenant Haggerty had been killed by a single gunshot, sometime between 3:00 and 4:00. The trooper did not hear the gunshot, although there was some question as to how well he'd hear a gunshot a good one hundred yards away, through snow-covered trees, with his windows shut and the engine running.

My first thought was obvious. Yes, he's done it. The killer has struck again. My second thought was, if only Haggerty had let the trooper stay closer to his house. My third thought was, I'm glad I'm not that particular trooper right now.

"The agents are meeting at seven o'clock," Maven said.

"I'll be there."

"This is going to get ugly today."

"I know."

I pulled into the Soo post parking lot at 6:45. The sun hadn't come up yet. It was ten degrees and the air smelled like snow. I walked inside and I could feel the unnatural silence in the place right away. The interview room was empty. I went in and sat down. A trooper I didn't know walked by and gave me a quick look. It wasn't friendly.

Maven came in a few minutes later. He nodded to me as he took his coat off. Then he went back out into the office to get a cup of coffee. Actually, he brought back two cups. He put one down in front of me and sat down.

"Thanks," I said.

He nodded again. He still hadn't said a word. I wasn't about to make him talk until he was ready.

Seven o'clock came and went. Then 7:15. It was almost 7:30 when the agents finally showed up. They came in shivering, each of them carrying folders thick with paper. It took them another minute to take their coats off and get settled with their own cups of coffee. They both looked tired as hell.

"First priority," Agent Long said. "Chief Maven, if we truly understand what's going on here, you could be next on the list. Or rather, your daughter could be."

"I know that."

"We need to ensure her safety."

"She's in Amsterdam, staying with a friend. My wife is over there, too. They'll stay there until it's safe to come home."

"Okay, good," Agent Long said, nodding. "But

until we know who this person is . . . I mean, we don't know what kind of resources he may have. For all we know, he could go all the way to Amsterdam to find her."

"He wouldn't know how to find her. She's staying in a private residence there, and there are only four people in the world who know about it. My daughter and her friend, my wife and myself."

"I'm just saying, if we wanted to contact the authorities in the Netherlands, we could arrange to—"

"You brought up the possibility that it might have been an ex-cop doing this."

"You mean Fraser? But we established that he's dead."

"It's still something to be aware of," Maven said. "Think about it. What if it was another cop? An old trooper even, somebody we used to work with?"

"Don't let those guys outside hear you saying that," Agent Fleury said.

"My point is, I don't want anybody to know where she is. Even you guys. As soon as you tell somebody else, you don't have any control over it."

"This is the FBI you're talking about," Fleury said. "If there's one thing we're good at—"

"That's debatable."

"What's that supposed to mean?"

"Guys," Agent Long said. "Can we stay on the same team here?"

"There is another avenue we might want to think about," Fleury said. "If Maven's daughter did come home and was willing to help us set a trap for this guy . . ."

"Agent, let me stop you right there and ask you a question," Maven said. "Do you have a daughter?"

"No, I don't."

"I didn't think so."

"I'm talking hypothetically," Fleury said. "It would be a very carefully controlled situation."

"Next topic."

Fleury held his gaze for a long moment. Then he shook his head and opened the folder in front of him.

"Actually, before we get to this," he said, "there's one more thing we have to talk about. We have some other agents on their way up here right now. If the weather stays clear, they should be here by noon. Special Agent Kozak will be among them. He'll be taking over the lead on this investigation, and we'll probably be moving to another location."

"Why would you do that?" Maven said. "This is where all of the records are."

"As long as we have access to the computer, we can get to them from anywhere. The real problem is just a matter of space. We're going to

259

have a half dozen people working on this until we have a resolution."

"Okay. Whatever."

"What this also means," Fleury said, looking at me now, "is that our arrangements are going to have to change. Special Agent Kozak is fully aware of the assistance you've been giving us, Mr. McKnight, but when he gets here I'm quite sure he won't understand why you're still sitting in on our meetings."

"If he doesn't understand," Maven said, "then I'll just have to explain it to him."

I put a hand up to stop him. I looked at Agent Long for confirmation.

"I'm afraid it's true," she said. "That's the third thing he's going to do when he gets here. The first is kick Agent Fleury's ass, the second is kick *my* ass. Then the third will be asking us what your official capacity is in this case."

"Nobody's happy right now," Agent Fleury said. "Fair or not, the FBI is mad at the state police for not protecting one of their own. The state police are mad at the FBI for not involving them in this sooner. This is going to end up being a rough day for everyone, Mr. McKnight. I just don't see how they're going to let you stick around."

"All right," I said. "I get it."

"I don't," Maven said. "If they think they can just—"

"Chief, come on. The man's right. This day's going to be bad enough."

"We really do appreciate everything you've done," Agent Long said. "I don't think we'd even have a case without you."

"Just do me one favor," I said. "As long as the big boys aren't here yet, tell me exactly what happened."

Fleury hesitated for a moment. Then he started pulling out papers from his folder.

"All right. As you've probably already heard, Lieutenant Haggerty was killed between three o'clock and four o'clock this morning. One single gunshot to the forehead, at fairly close range judging from the powder burns. He was apparently sitting in a chair in the kitchen. There were no marks on his hands to indicate any attempt to defend himself."

I pictured him sitting there, waiting for exactly this event to happen.

"Or it's possible that he was asleep in the chair," Fleury went on. "We're not sure about that yet. We'll have some forensics later today, but right now it appears to be a .45-caliber round similar to the rounds used to kill Sergeant Steele and Ms. Krimer."

"That was Steele's service weapon," Maven said. "Did he keep it to use again?"

"That's quite possible. We'll know for sure later on. Right now, the one interesting thing we do have is a few fiberglass fibers close to the entry wound. This would suggest some kind of homemade suppressor."

"A homemade suppressor? Are you kidding me?"

"It's possible to make a pretty effective suppressor if you want one bad enough. I'm not talking about the old bleach bottle on the end of the gun thing. I'm talking about a carefully made suppressor, with a PVC pipe and fiberglass matting inside. If you do a good enough job, you can contain the gases very well, and you can even use a wipe barrier to slow down the bullet to subsonic speed. Your accuracy would be compromised, of course, but at such close range . . ."

"How would this guy know how to make something like that?"

"I could find it for you on the Internet in two minutes," Fleury said. "You just need the materials, available at any good hardware store."

"If he knows guns well enough to make a suppressor," I said, "then he probably knows that we'll be able to trace that slug back to Steele's weapon, assuming that's what it was."

"Probably, yes."

"So he'll know that *we'll* know there was a connection between the two shootings. There won't be any pretense of unrelated deaths anymore."

"That's true," Fleury said. "Although he probably already figured out that something was up when he saw that trooper's car at the head of the driveway. The one question is, does he realize we've connected the suicides, as well?"

"I don't see why he wouldn't assume that, too."

"Only one way to know for sure," Agent Long said. "When we catch him, we'll have to ask him."

She opened her own folder and grimaced at what she saw.

"Are those the photos?" I said.

"Yes. Not pretty."

"May I see them?"

"I don't think that's a good idea."

"I've seen crime scene photos before. Come on, let me see them before I get kicked out of here."

"Don't say I didn't warn you."

She slid the folder across the table to me. Maven inched his chair closer so he could see, as well. The first photo showed Lieutenant Haggerty lying on his back, both arms stretched out on the floor as if he were caught in the middle of making a snow angel. The shot was taken from directly above him, a clean hole centered perfectly in his forehead. The blood had drained out through the exit wound and was pooled all around him.

There were several other pictures taken from

different angles. Close up, farther away, his legs draped over the upended chair. Shots of the room. The back door slightly ajar. The new snow on the back porch.

"As you can see, the killer came through the back door," Fleury said. "The exterior light was on, and the door was unlocked. There's another road about a mile back, through the woods. Our man probably parked there and walked."

"How would he know how to get there?"

"Again, the Internet. You can bring up a map of just about anywhere and see every little road, every driveway even."

"Why wasn't there another trooper watching from that back road?"

"There was yet another road about two miles to the east," Fleury said. "He might have come from there instead. How many troopers can you put out there every single night, all night long?"

"They should have been in the house," Maven said. "I don't care if he didn't want them."

"Yeah, well, they're probably telling themselves the same thing right now."

"You have other photos there," I said, nodding at the remaining pile of folders. "Are those the other crime scenes?"

"Yes."

"Even the suicides?"

"Alex," Agent Long said, "I'm serious now. You really don't want to see these."

"Yes, I do. It's the last thing I'll ask."

She let out a long sigh, then pushed the folders over to me one by one. There was one set of photographs for each crime scene, starting with the double homicide of Sergeant Steele and his girlfriend, Donna Krimer—the scene Maven and I had stumbled upon. At the time, we hadn't done much more than peek inside the doorway. Here was the whole thing in living color.

Sergeant Steele was laid out spread eagle on the floor, his arms stretched out like Lieutenant Haggerty's, but in this case, Steele was facedown. There was an obvious entrance wound in the center of his back. The bullet probably passed right through his heart and killed him instantly. Instead of the bright red blood that had surrounded Lieutenant Haggerty's body, the blood here was a different color—darker, duller, almost rust colored. This is what happens to blood when it lies on the floor for two days.

Donna Krimer lay five or six feet away from Steele, in her own pool of dark blood. She was on her side with both arms extended in front of her. You couldn't even see her face. It almost looked like she was doing a dramatic death scene on a stage, every limb arranged just so. Except of course she would never stand up for her curtain call.

The next folder I didn't even need to look at, but I did anyway. It was Charles Razniewski Sr., sprawled out on Chief Maven's kitchen floor, his throat cut wide open, the blood painting everything around him. Chief Maven looked away from the photos, gripping his coffee cup so tightly I was surprised it didn't shatter.

I looked at Razniewski's open eyes one more time before I closed that folder. Photograph or no photograph, I knew I'd be seeing those eyes forever.

"It's like we're going back in time here," I said. "Am I right? We sort of lost sight of that because we found out about everything out of order. But the three apparent suicides actually happened before the three obvious homicides."

"That's right," Agent Long said. "If you think about it . . . the three children, then the three fathers. Maybe it was just those three after all. Maybe this guy's done."

"Or maybe that's the way the opportunities came up for him," Maven said. "My daughter's been out of the country for almost five months."

"I agree we have to act like you're still on the list," Agent Long said. "I'm just saying, it's possible he considers his work to be completed."

"What if Raz hadn't come up here?" I said. "Our killer would have to travel a lot farther to find him. Maybe he'd still be alive now and it would be *him* next on the list."

"I still don't understand how this guy even knew he was here in Sault Ste. Marie," Agent Fleury said. "That part still bugs the hell out of me."

"He obviously knows all about these people," Agent Long said. "He's been watching them all very carefully."

"Or he has access to some special source of information," Maven said, "bringing us back to the idea that he's in law enforcement. Or used to be."

"Yes, as you were saying before," Agent Long said. "That's starting to sound a little more likely now."

I opened up the next folder. Now we were into the suicides. Or what had been considered suicides before this whole case started coming together. The first was Haggerty's daughter, again moving backward through time. She was the most recent. After all the blood of the previous photographs, these were somehow even more disturbing. There was no blood. No signs of violence whatsoever. They were almost . . . I couldn't even bring myself to think it, but yes, they were almost peaceful.

A woman in her bed. It was a double bed, with the woman on one side and on the other side, where another person should have been, instead there was a large helium tank. Like you'd use to blow up balloons at a birthday party. It was the most out-of-place thing I'd ever seen and it made me feel absolutely sick to my stomach. The worst thing of all was that the woman seemed to have her arms wrapped around the tank, like it was . . . damn, like it was a teddy bear or something.

I closed the folder for a moment. I took a few breaths. Maven's face was white. He'd seen his share of crime scene photos over the years, too, but I was sure he had never seen anything like this.

I opened the folder again. Looking closer, I saw the clear plastic bag around her head. The kind of bag you'd find a suit or dress inside when you went to the cleaners. It was wrapped neatly around her head and it appeared to be tied off at the neck with a cord of some type. An electrical cord? No, it looked like fabric, like the cord you'd use to tie back your drapes. Hardly even visible at all was the clear tube that ran from the tank to the bag.

"I told you you didn't have to look at those," Agent Long said.

I didn't answer her. I kept going. I opened the next folder.

It was Sergeant Steele's son. He was lying on the ground, on his back, in the snow. You could tell that it was still snowing when the photographs were taken. The snowflakes were already collected on his face. The left side of his head was ruined from the exit wound and the blood was soaking into the snow beside him. The pistol was in his right hand, his finger still on the trigger.

His eyes were closed. Once again, this time despite the blood and the gore . . . the whole scene almost looked peaceful.

I closed the folder. There was one left. I opened it.

Misery Bay. When I had been there, it had been empty. Now as I looked back in time at this moment captured in the photograph, I saw young Charles Razniewski hanging from the tree. His body was limp, so devoid of life you'd think he was some kind of rag doll or hanging effigy or some other crudely fashioned *thing.* Not a person. This wasn't a child, not a man's beloved son hanging here in the cold. From the spot the photographer had chosen, you could see Lake Superior through the opening in the trees. It was late in the day, so the sun was setting in the western sky and from behind the hanging body was completely in shadow. In the next photograph it was nothing but a dark figure seeming to blot out the sun itself.

The photographer had moved around to the front for the next few shots. Charlie's face was blue. His hair was crowned with snow. There, about three feet in front of him, was this car. It was covered with snow, too. The driver's side door was open.

I kept looking at the photographs. Unlike the others . . . these, for some reason I couldn't stop staring at them. This is where it all began, I thought. This was the first.

"I think that's enough, Alex."

I didn't move. Agent Long had to reach over and close the folder.

"Are you okay?"

"No," I said. "I think it'll be a long time before I'm okay."

We went over the three candidates they'd identified the day before, the three men who'd been arrested by Steele and Haggerty and who had lost children to suicide not long after. The thief, Henry Parizi, with the solid alibi from his current parole officer. The actor/filmmaker, Clyde C. Wiley, working on his next project sixteen hours a day, seven days a week. The ex-cop who had vowed revenge, Kenny Fraser, now deceased. All three had been eliminated, so it was time to pick up the search again, to go through the records with an even closer eye to find another candidate.

I didn't actually see them get that far. By noon the big boys from Detroit had arrived and I was kicked out of the building.

So what the hell was I supposed to do?

I ended up driving around for a while, feeling numb and having no idea where I was going. Eventually, I ended up back in Paradise. I drove right by Jackie's place. I put my plow down and went up my road, not even thinking to avoid looking at that first cabin. If nothing else, at least that particular hang-up had been displaced from my mind for a while.

I parked the truck and went inside. I got the fire going, then I looked around for something else that needed my attention. Eventually I went back outside and started chopping some wood. I had plenty, but swinging a big ax seemed like a good idea.

An hour later, I was tired and my shoulders were sore, but otherwise I didn't feel any different. So I drove down to the Glasgow. Vinnie was sitting at the bar reading the newspaper. I sat next to him.

"How's your mother doing?" I said.

"Not too bad today."

"You got a shift at the casino today?"

"Later, yeah."

I nodded my head. Eventually, I found myself tapping my fingers on the bar top.

"Something bothering you?" he said.

"You still got those boxing gloves?"

"Uh, yeah. Why?"

"I need to hit somebody. And to have somebody hit me back."

"What do you suggest, we box in the parking lot?"

"I don't know, maybe. You still playing in that hockey league?"

"No," he said. "Besides, you made me promise you I'd never ask you to play hockey again, remember?"

"Where's Jackie, anyway?"

"He went out. Should be back soon."

"What, did he leave you in charge of the place?"

Vinnie did a quick scan around the room. We were the only two people there.

"I didn't go to bar management school," he said, "but I think today I can handle it."

"He should be here," I said. "He's the only person I can drive crazy enough to make me feel better. Well, him and Chief Maven, but he's kinda busy right now."

"Alex, I know you've been through a lot lately, but—"

"I can't just sit here, okay? I've got to do something. Anything. I'll see you later."

He watched me walk out the door like he was seriously wondering if I had lost my mind. Which was a fair question at that point.

Agent Long was right, I said to myself as I got back in the truck. I never should have looked at those pictures.

By five o'clock I was debating whether to call Chief Maven on his cell phone. I wanted to know what else had happened that day, if the additional agents from Detroit had helped develop any new breakthroughs. In the end, I decided it was still probably too soon for that. They were probably still catching up with everything.

Call him tomorrow, I told myself. He'll tell you what's going on. You know he will.

By six o'clock I was back at the Glasgow. Vinnie was gone, but Jackie was back. He stood behind the bar and watched me pacing back and forth in front of the fireplace. He started yelling at me to knock it off, but even that didn't make me feel any better.

By seven o'clock I had eaten dinner and had actually sat down in a chair for a while. The problem was I'd keep seeing those pictures whenever I was still for even a moment. I couldn't even say why they bothered me so much. I mean, apart from the obvious fact that seven people were dead. There was something else about the photographs, some horrible thread that ran through all of them.

He's still out there, I thought. I could feel him. He was breathing the same air I was breathing, and he was waiting to do this again.

By eight o'clock I was back in my truck, driving hard toward nowhere. Eventually, I pointed it east and headed into the Soo. I passed the state post and was tempted to park in the lot. Go inside, start asking around, see what was happening. I didn't see Chief Maven's car.

It was almost ten o'clock when I finally pulled in front of the Cineplex. I shouldn't be bothering Leon again, I thought. I'll probably get him fired this time, but I don't know who else to talk to.

I sat there in the truck with the heater still going, looking out at the customers hurrying through the cold air into the theater. They'd sit in the dark and they'd forget all about everything else in their lives for at least that long.

Not a bad idea, I thought. I should try it myself. Maybe it'll even work. But which movie?

I ran down the list on the marquee. All the movies had titles I didn't recognize. Not that it mattered. I could pick one at random and give it a shot.

Then something came to me. I didn't get out of the truck. I didn't go bother Leon. I put it back into drive and I drove across town instead. To Chief Maven's house.

His car was in the driveway. I knocked on the door. When he opened it, I could see that he had his service revolver in his right hand.

"McKnight, what are you doing here?"

"Sorry to bother you, but I figured you'd still be up. Can I come in for a minute?"

He held the door open for me. I went inside. He put the gun away, and as I took my coat off I could smell the bleach coming from one direction and the new paint coming from another.

"You've been busy here," I said.

"Just trying to keep myself from going insane."

"Yeah, I know how that one goes."

"Come on in and sit down."

He led me into the kitchen. It was as bright and clean as an operating room. As I sat down in the chair, I tried not to think about what had happened in this very spot. Right there at my feet.

"How did everything go today?" I said.

"After you left? Well, four more agents showed up, including Long and Fleury's boss. So we blew the rest of the day getting them all up to speed."

"That's what I figured would happen."

"Are you okay? You look a little rattled."

"I'm fine. I'll live."

"Come on, McKnight. Why did you really come out here?"

"I've got something I want to run by you."

"Go ahead."

"I've been thinking about those photographs we saw today."

"Yeah, me, too."

"Here's the thing," I said. "I know this is going to sound crazy. It already sounds crazy in my head and it's going to sound twice as crazy when I say it out loud, but I'm gonna say it anyway, all right?"

He inched up his chair a notch and leaned forward.

"Those photographs," I said. "You saw them, too. I mean, I know you've seen crime scenes before, but was there a little something, I don't know, *extra* in those photographs?"

"Extra what?"

"I don't know, it's just like there was something a little bit too . . . what's the word . . . a little too *composed* about them."

"Composed. I'm sorry, I still don't follow you."

"When I run those pictures through my mind, which I can't stop doing, it feels like each one of those scenes was somehow . . . I don't know, like they were thought out in advance. You know what I mean? With everything in the perfect position. Even the bodies . . ."

"Go on."

"Go back in your mind and picture every one of those bodies, especially the suicides. The so-called suicides. Whatever. Haggerty's daughter in her bed, with the tank. Steele's son in the snow. And more than anything, my God, Raz's son hanging from that tree? The way he was looking out at the lake? Perfectly framed by those trees?"

"You're saying, what . . . that he wanted each crime scene to *look* a certain way? Is that what you're saying?"

"Think about it, Chief. If you were going to fake somebody's suicide, why would you take him all the way down there to Misery Bay? You could hang him almost anywhere, couldn't you? Why there?"

He didn't say anything. I could tell he was

thinking hard about it. He was running all the photos back in his mind, trying to see the same thing I was.

"I told you it was crazy," I said, "but you were there. You stood right in that same spot. What did you feel?"

"At Misery Bay?"

"Yes. What did you *feel* when you stood there?"

"I felt like . . ."

"What? Tell me."

"I felt like I was seeing something out of a bad dream."

I waited for him to complete the thought.

"Or . . . ," he said. "A movie."

"Exactly. That's the same feeling I had."

"Now, wait a minute," he said. "Just because one of those three men we were looking at yesterday happens to be an actor . . ."

"And a filmmaker."

"And a filmmaker. But come on, you're not suggesting this guy is . . . what, filming these people?"

"No, that would be the sickest thing ever," I said. "But if you're the kind of person who's always thinking about putting things together in just the right way . . . so it all looks right . . . I mean, God, okay, I told you this was going to sound crazy."

"You heard what they said about this guy. He's

been in the studio, or wherever they do it, working on a film. Downstate, right? Doesn't he live in Bad Axe?"

"So they said."

"They interviewed him. They eliminated him as a suspect."

"Again, so they said. That's what the agents told us. But they're getting that information secondhand. Which means you and I are getting it thirdhand."

"So what are you suggesting?"

"When I was a cop," I said, "I always had this belief. Whether it was strictly true or not, I don't know, but I always felt that if I could confront somebody face-to-face, I would *know* if they were lying."

"You mean if you look them in the eye."

"Yes. You ask them the question, right to their face. 'Were you there? Did you do this?'"

"I've always felt the same way," Maven said. "I think any good cop does."

"It's a shame we didn't get the chance to do that here, Chief. That's all it would take. Go see this Clyde C. Wiley guy. Ask him point blank."

"We've already been down this road before," Maven said. "Interfering with an active investigation. We can't do that again."

"*You* can't do it," I said, standing up. "But guess what? I'm pretty sure *I* can."

And we're rolling . . .

. . . All right, you're gonna have to trust me on this one.

. . . After that last scene, we're gonna play this one soft.

. . . It'll be amazing, don't worry. You'll love the contrast. Just watch.

. . . That's right. Just like that. Nice and quiet.

. . . Like you're never going to wake up.

. . . Perfect. I love this.

. . . Good night, Dina. Sleep tight.

And cut.

CHAPTER FIFTEEN

I drove out of Paradise early the next morning. It looked like there was snow on the way again, but it didn't start falling until I was almost out of the Upper Peninsula. As I climbed the steady incline to the Mackinac Bridge, I looked down at the St. Ignace post, right there on the shoreline.

It was all open highway as I went down the middle of the Lower Peninsula's mitten. As I got near Indian River, I knew that there was some exact point in the road where Clyde C. Wiley had been arrested all those years ago. Some lonely, empty spot where he finally ran out of gas or gave up, or hell, maybe they even "pitted" him. PIT standing for pursuit immobilization technique, where you clip a vehicle from behind, just enough to make it lose control but not so much that you cause a major rollover. I'd never gotten the chance to do it myself, but then vehicle pursuits in the middle of a crowded city are a whole different animal.

Wherever the spot was where that arrest was made, I sped right by it and kept going, due south, through Gaylord and Grayling, three and a half hours of billboards and snow and just about nothing else until I finally got to Bay City. That's when I cut east and it was just another hour until I saw the sign welcoming me to Bad Axe, right in the middle of the Lower Peninsula's thumb. So that told me one thing straightaway. If my crazy gut feeling was right and Clyde C. Wiley was somehow involved in this case, it wouldn't take him more than four and a half hours or so to be right in the heart of the Upper Peninsula, where everything had happened.

I called Chief Maven on my cell phone as soon as I hit Bad Axe. He had promised me he'd find out everything he could about Wiley, without tipping our hand. God knows what the FBI agents would say if they found out I was down here on my own, snooping around.

"I listened in while Long and Fleury rehashed the interviews with the new guys on the team," Maven told me. "They talked about all three candidates, of course, but this is what I found out about Wiley. He's got a film company in Bad Axe called Grindstone Productions. They've been working on this movie, I guess it's like Wiley's life story or something, which is why he's supposedly been way too busy every day to even leave the studio. He's seventy-two years old, remember, so I don't know."

"Did you find out where this place is? What is it, Grindstone Productions?"

"Yeah, I looked it up on the Internet. There was a news story about this guy coming back to his hometown and buying the Bad Axe Theater, which is right there in the center of town, on

Huron Avenue. That's the mailing address for his film company, although I've got to believe they have other buildings if they're actually shooting movies."

"I got it, Chief. I'll check out the theater and ask around if I have to."

"Keep a low profile, eh? We don't need this getting back up here or we'll have our asses in a sling."

"Now that you've slept on it, do you still think this is worth doing?"

There was a long silence on the line. I started to wonder if I had lost him, but then he finally spoke.

"I still agree with what you said, McKnight. I got the same feeling you did looking at those photos. I wish I was down there to ask him in person. That's all we're going to do, right?"

"That's the idea, yes."

"Well, be careful, just in case it turns into more than that."

I told him I'd call him back later when I had any news. Then I ended the call and started looking for the Bad Axe Theater. It was a small city much like any other in Michigan, laid out flat with streets that ran perfectly north–south and east–west. There was snow on the ground but a hell of a lot less than in Paradise. Amazing how much different things can look in this state when you drive a little bit south. I knew that it would be cold when I finally got out of the truck, but it wouldn't be painful. It wouldn't be a physical trial with every breath.

As I got closer to the center of town, I saw my omen. It was right there next to the street, and whether it was a good omen or a bad omen, I couldn't say, but I felt like it meant something. The Bad Axe post of the Michigan State Police.

A few more blocks down, I saw the town hall on one side of the street, the Bad Axe Theater on the other. I parked the truck in the lot next door to the theater and got out. The lower floor was a classic old theater but the top three stories looked like a brick office building, with windows that had been covered over from the inside. It was the middle of a weekday, so the lot didn't have more than a half dozen cars in it. Nobody was lined up outside, but according to the schedule on the marquee the first matinee didn't start for another two hours.

I tried the door. It was open. I went inside and there was a kid vacuuming the carpet in the lobby. He had a pair of earphones on, so with whatever music he was listening to added to the sound of the vacuum cleaner there was no chance of him hearing me. I tapped him on the shoulder. The way he jumped, it was probably a good thing he was a teenager because otherwise he would have died of a heart attack.

"Sorry about that," I said. "I'm looking for Mr. Wiley."

He was pointing at the door before he could manage to speak. Finally, his breath caught up with him. "Try the studio. Across the street."

"Where's that? Which building are we talking about?"

He led me over to the door and pushed it open.

"Right there," he said. "Next to the town hall. You gotta buzz in at the front."

I thanked the kid and slapped him on the back. Then I walked across the street. There was a big brick building there and behind it I could see a great water tower rising above everything else in the town. Leon would have been proud of my detective skills, as I quickly figured out that this particular building had once been a Buick dealership. It had the wide front windows that you'd want if you were showing off cars, for one thing. My other clue was the big BAD AXE BUICK set in tile across the whole front of the building.

The only light I saw through the windows was a strange blue glow somewhere toward the back of the building. There was a small plate next to the door that read GRINDSTONE PRODUCTIONS. The *O* in Grindstone looked to be a gray, round grindstone, the kind they once made out of sandstone, I think, with a hole in the center. I had some dim memory that this was once grindstone country here in Michigan's thumb, but whatever.

There was a buzzer below the plate, so I pressed it.

I waited for a full minute. Finally, a man answered the door. He couldn't have been more than twenty years old and he was wearing a black T-shirt and jeans, weather be damned. He had one of those little rings sticking through his left eyebrow.

"I wonder if I can have a word with Mr. Wiley," I said.

He opened the door for me and I stepped inside. What had once been the Buick showroom was now a great open space filled with cameras and light poles and boxes to pack it all up in. One corner of the room had been walled off floor to ceiling, with a red light over the door that made me think it was probably a space for audio recording. In the other corner was a haphazard cubicle with chest-high walls, and that's where the blue glow I had seen was coming from. Through the gap in the walls I could just make out the corner of a video screen next to a desktop computer, plus a few other machines I couldn't have named if you put a gun to my head. There was a man sitting in front of the screen, and he seemed totally absorbed in what he was doing because he didn't so much as turn to glance in our direction.

"Somebody here to see you," the young man said.

"What? Who's that?" The other man kept watching whatever it was he was watching.

"I just need a minute of your time," I said.

Finally, the man turned around and looked at me. He got up from the blue glow and came to me through the middle band of darkness. As he came into the natural light filtering through the windows, I saw that he was not the man I was expecting to meet. This could not be Clyde C. Wiley.

He couldn't have been more than fifty years old, for one thing, although he was doing everything he could to look even younger. He was one of those guys who still have the long hair and the little soul patch goatee, a leather vest on over a blue denim shirt with the sleeves rolled up, trying to be half-hippie and half-biker at the same time, and not coming close to either. He was thirty pounds overweight at this point in his life, and he had faded Chinese characters or something equally nonsensical for a middle-aged white man tattooed on both forearms.

"I'm looking for Clyde C. Wiley," I said.

"And you are?"

"My name's Alex. I just want to have a word with him."

"Yeah, now's not a good time, okay? We're kinda busy here."

"It'll only take a minute. I came a long way today."

"Then I'm pretty sure you wasted your time. Have a good trip back to wherever you came from."

He started to turn away from me, but I sure as hell wasn't going to give up that easily.

"Look," I said, "I know the FBI was here. Day before yesterday, right?"

That stopped him.

"Who are you again?"

"I told you. My name's Alex."

"Yeah, Alex who? What exactly are you doing here?"

"I'm a private investigator. I just came to ask Mr. Wiley a few questions. That's all, I promise."

"We already answered all the questions we're gonna answer. Unless you've got a badge or something, I'm pretty sure we don't have to say shit to you. So why don't you hit the bricks?"

He put a hand on my shoulder to turn me toward the door. He had to rethink that idea when he saw I wasn't moving an inch until I was ready.

"You want to make me call the cops? I'm gonna do that in five seconds unless you get the hell out of here."

"Is Mr. Wiley even here?"

"None of your concern. Now get out."

I waited a few more seconds. More than five, no matter how slow he could count. It was pretty clear I wasn't going to get much further with this guy. I did a quick scan around the room to make sure Mr. Wiley wasn't lurking in a dark corner. Then I turned and went to the door.

"Don't come back," the man said. "You hear me?"

"You can throw me out," I said to him, "but you can't stop me from coming back. It would be easier on everyone if you just told me where he is so we can have our conversation."

He stepped up to me and I thought it might be time for something to happen, but he slid around me, opened the door, and held it for me. I could feel the cold air creeping in around my ankles. I went outside and he closed the door behind me.

"Well, that was interesting," I said.

As I crossed the street, I imagined him standing at the window, watching my back. I went to the parking lot next to the theater, but then it occurred to me that I'd be giving away an important piece of information if I got in my truck. So instead I kept walking down the street. I walked a full two blocks before I finally turned around. I couldn't see anybody in front of the Grindstone building.

So okay, I thought, now what the hell do I do?

Of course, I knew exactly what Leon would say about it if he were here. I doubled around the back of the block and came up parallel to the main street. As I got to the back of the theater parking lot, I watched the windows carefully for a full five minutes. I didn't see any movement.

So I slid into my truck, started it, and pulled out through the back exit, working my way around the block until I was facing in the right direction. About a block down, I tucked into a row of cars parked on the street, the theater up ahead on the right, the Grindstone building on the left. Now all I had to do was one of my very least favorite things in the world.

Sit there and wait.

Lunchtime had already come and gone when I started my little stakeout. Now as the clock closed in on two in the afternoon, I could feel my blood sugar dipping. If Leon were here, I thought, he'd have protein bars and water and a special container to piss in. Not to mention a fake beard and glasses.

There was a light stream of traffic on the street, but nobody had come out the door since I'd been escorted out of the Grindstone building. I spotted a little deli behind me, maybe half a block down the street. I figured I'd have to eat something soon or I'd pass out, so I slipped out of the truck. I ordered a sandwich, then used the bathroom while the girl behind the counter put it together.

As I was about to come back out, I heard the door to the deli open and then a familiar voice. It was the young kid who had come to the door first, before passing me off to Mr. Charming. I cursed my bad timing and then waited in the bathroom while he ordered two sandwiches and Cokes. Then there was some other conversation that made me think these two kids had a little something more going on besides buying lunch. Finally, they seemed to be done and when I was sure he had gone, I opened the bathroom door and came out.

I paid for the sandwich and a bottle of water, thanked the girl, and went outside just in time to see the young man going back into the Grindstone building.

He ordered two sandwiches, I thought. Not three.

I went back to the truck and kept waiting.

The afternoon slid by. The sun went down. Cars went up and down the street with their lights on while a soft light snow began to fall. Just another April evening in Bad Axe, Michigan. I sat in the truck and turned it on once in a while to run the heater for a minute, then I turned it back off. A Michigan State Trooper's car from the post down the street rolled by at one point and I thought he'd surely stop and ask me what the hell I was doing sitting there all day, but he kept going without even looking at me.

By six o'clock I started to get hungry again, but I didn't want to repeat my lunchtime performance so I stayed put. The streetlights came on and I had just enough light to see the front door of the Grindstone building. Right around seven o'clock I saw two figures come out the door. One of them locked the door and they crossed the street together and went into the theater's parking lot. I lost sight of them as they got into their separate vehicles. I saw a Jeep Cherokee pull out of the lot, followed by a Corvette. If I was going to follow either one of them, I wanted it to be the older man, and I figured he'd be the one driving the classic midlife crisis Corvette. So I pulled out and followed that car across town. The car stopped at a little apartment building, and now that we were in better light I could see it was an older model Corvette with peeling mint-green paint and a big dent in the rear fender. The young kid got out and went inside.

My first impulse was to just jump out and grab the kid, see if I could convince him to talk to me, but I figured that would be a bit of a gamble. It was a card I'd play if I didn't have any other choice. For now, I'd be content to just know where the kid lived.

I went back to the main street and pulled up in front of the Grindstone building. It looked dark and completely deserted, but I rang the bell just for the hell of it. Maybe the old man was still inside, I thought, working on his movie. But no, there was nobody home.

I had spotted a little motel on the way into town, so I went back there and checked in for one night. I went into my room and stripped off the bedspread. I may not know that much about anything, but I know never to lie on a motel bedspread. As I was setting the alarm clock, my cell phone rang. It was Chief Maven.

"I thought you were going to call me," he said.

"I was, if anything happened. So far I've just been sitting around and waiting."

"What are you talking about? Didn't you talk to Wiley?"

"I went to visit his film company, but he wasn't there. For somebody who's supposedly working day and night on his movie . . . I mean, I don't suppose that's the kind of work you can do at home, right?"

"Are you telling me this guy wasn't there at all today?"

"I'll go back tomorrow and see if he shows up. If not, I'll have to think of something else to try. I know one thing, the people who work for him aren't going to be much help. Not willingly."

"I don't know," Maven said. "I'm not down there, but I'm getting a funny feeling about this guy. More and more every time I think about it."

"What's going on up there, anyway?"

"More of the same. This new man, Special Agent Kozak, he wanted to talk to you today, just to go over what you did, going out to Misery Bay that first time, coming back and finding Raz. You know, your whole part in it."

"Agent Long or Agent Fleury could have filled him in on that."

"You know how these guys are. They want to hear it from the horse's mouth."

"So what did you tell him?"

"That I told you to take a long trip to get away from all of this. He wanted your cell phone number, but I told him you had a bad habit of not turning it on unless you were calling somebody. I also told him I had no idea where you are right now."

"That must have made him happy."

"Let him be mad at me, I don't care. If it gives you the chance to do your thing down there, then it's worth it."

"Well, I should have something by tomorrow," I said. "I sure as hell ain't gonna wait around all day and spend another night here."

"All right, well, let me know. Take care of yourself and I'll talk to you tomorrow."

"You too, Chief."

"It's strange being here alone, McKnight. I'm in this house where I've lived with my wife for thirty years. Where my daughter grew up. There's nothing left here now but the smell of murder."

"Sounds like you could use a motel yourself."

"I hate motels, McKnight, more than almost anything. I feel sorry for you that you have to be in one tonight."

On that bright note, I said good night. We were two men alone in two different places, three hundred miles apart. There wasn't much that made sense anymore, and we both knew we had a lot more work to do before things got any better.

And we're rolling . . .

. . . Hold on! This is all going too fast. Let me catch up here.

. . . I told you, you have to wait for your cue.

. . . It's all right, keep going. We'll get the aftermath here.

. . . That's a great effect, the red on the floor. Very striking.

. . . Close in on the face. I remember you!

. . . That's it. Just like that. Beautiful.

. . . How do you like us now, Trooper Razniewski?

. . . You're giving it your all, but next time wait for the cue, okay?

. . . Okay. We're good.

And cut.

CHAPTER SIXTEEN

I was back on the street when the sun came up. My two new friends didn't seem like early morning types, but maybe Mr. Wiley was. Maybe he'd be there putting in a half day's work before the other two even showed up.

I parked on the other side of the street this time, which meant I was facing away from the Grindstone building. I had my side-view mirror angled just right, so I could see the entrance. I had a bag of food and a bottle of water already in the truck, too. Plus a newspaper to duck behind if I needed to. Leon would have been proud of me.

I sat there while the whole town of Bad Axe woke up to another gray and blue April day. Cars began to roll by. I lay my head back and repositioned the mirror. Then I waited.

An hour passed. Two hours passed. I saw the young kid unlock the door and go inside. About a half hour later, I saw Mr. Charming come to the door. I'm sure he had a key, but he was apparently too lazy to dig it out so he just pressed the buzzer and then waited there for a few seconds, finishing his cigarette. When he finally went inside, I was left there to wait some more, and to start wondering if Clyde C. Wiley would ever show up.

Another hour passed. The sun tried to come out for a few seconds, but the clouds reassembled and then it was a normal Michigan sky again. Cars went by, one by one, kicking up slush. I stayed where I was, feeling like I was slipping into some sort of trance, but always with one eye on the side-view mirror.

Another hour passed. Certainly a mistake, this whole venture. Obviously and completely. No idea what I was thinking of. The man will never show up and I'll have no clue what to do next.

Then finally, lunchtime. The young kid came out and made his way down the street. The same routine as the day before, go to that same shop, get two sandwiches, go back. I thought it over for all of five seconds and then came to a decision.

Time to switch my tactics here. Do things the Alex way, for better or worse.

I got out of the truck and followed the kid into the shop. As I opened the door, he was standing in front of the counter, looking up at the menu board. A bit of a surprise as you'd figure he had the thing pretty much memorized today, but maybe he was branching out into new sandwiches. Then I saw that the girl from the day before wasn't behind the counter. Instead it was a man, thirty years older, wearing a big sloppy apron. Which explained why the kid was staring at the menu board today and not at the person making his sandwiches.

I went up and stood right next to him, and only then did he finally look at me. Another second passed before he recognized me and his polite smile disappeared.

"Can I ask you something?" I said.

"You're the guy from yesterday. What do you want?"

"I told you. I want to ask you something."

"I'm just getting sandwiches here, okay?"

"That won't keep you from answering one question."

"Just forget it," he said to the man behind the counter. "I'll come back later."

He pushed by me and made for the door. As he was about to open it, I asked him my one question.

"Did you know that lying to a federal agent is an automatic felony?"

A bit of an exaggeration, maybe, but I didn't have time for subtleties with this kid. He stopped dead in his tracks.

"No questions asked," I said. "Doesn't matter why, or where, or whether you're under oath or not. If a federal agent asks you a question and you knowingly tell him something that you know to be untrue, you are committing a felony and are subject to prosecution and prison time."

He didn't look back at me. He put his hand on the door.

"If you walk out that door," I said, "I can no longer help you."

He took his hand off the door. His whole body slumped like somebody had just put an eighty pound bag of cement on his shoulders.

"Oh, man," he said, so softly I could barely hear him.

"Give me five minutes, then I'll help you. I promise."

He turned around. I gestured to one of the three booths in the store. He came over and sat down. I slid in across from him. He was wearing a red sweatshirt today, getting closer to actual appropriate attire, at least. It looked like he had shaved since the day before. He almost looked like a nice, respectable kid now—even with the stupid ring through his eyebrow.

"What's your name?" I said.

"Sean."

"Sean, pleased to meet you. My name is Alex McKnight. I'm a private investigator, and for the past few days I've been working directly with the FBI."

Another exaggeration, but I had to keep him hooked.

"I understand that an agent came to visit you guys. When was that, a couple of days ago now?"

"Yeah, some guy named Davies."

"What did he ask you?"

The kid looked away and shook his head. "I can't believe this."

"It's okay. Just tell me what happened."

"He talked to CC first."

"Who's CC?"

"My grandfather. He doesn't like me calling him Grandpa or whatever. He says it makes him feel too old."

"Clyde C. Wiley. CC. I get it. Although I'm sorry, I didn't even realize you were his grandson."

"Don't you see the resemblance?" He sounded disappointed.

"I can't picture your grandfather in my mind, I'm sorry. But I'm sure the resemblance is there."

"You *should* know him," he said. "He's one of the best actors who ever lived."

"I'm sure you're right, but you were saying . . . he was actually here when the agent came?"

"Yeah, he was here that day. This agent guy took him into one of the back rooms and asked him some questions. I didn't know what was going on yet. When he came out, he asked me if he could ask me some questions, too. CC had a real funny look on his face, so I knew something was up. When this FBI guy got me alone, he asked me how much time CC had been spending in the studio. So right away, I figured, uh oh, this isn't good. The old man's about to go down again."

"Go down for what?"

"For the usual. Possession of a controlled substance. Or whatever. Gun charge, maybe. Either way, I had to make a snap call, so I told this guy that CC had been living on the set, then in front of the console, cutting the movie. I got kind of worried because I wasn't sure this guy was buying it, or hell, I don't know, if that was even the same story he was getting from CC and my father."

"Your father . . ."

"You met him yesterday. Conrad Wiley."

"CC's son. Okay, now I'm getting it. It's a real family business, eh?"

"The last couple of years, yeah. It wasn't always that way, believe me."

"Okay, but keep going. You were spinning this little tale for the FBI agent."

"I panicked, all right? I could see everything going down the tubes. The movie, the whole film company. Everything he came back here to build. After all those years, finally getting back together with his family . . ."

"You were looking out for your grandfather. Or at least you thought so. I understand."

"CC means the world to me. No matter what else happens, you've got to believe that. Whatever he's done over the years, he's the greatest man I ever met."

"Okay," I said, thinking maybe that doesn't say

much for your father. Or else you need to get out of town a little more. "So I take it this agent was getting the same message from everybody?"

"Well, yeah, he was. CC told him he was too busy working on the movie to be off doing anything else. My father told him that. I told him that. It's like we all agreed on the same story, without even having to talk about it beforehand."

"They didn't talk to anybody else?"

"Well, when we're actually shooting, there might be like thirty people around . . ."

"All in that one building?"

"Coming and going, yeah. Grips and sound guys and pretty much anybody who wants to be a part of making a movie. CC loves having a lot of young people around, giving them something to work on, you know, showing them how to make their own movies someday. He says he's trying to give people something he never had himself. Anyway, I think the agent said he'd try to track down a few of them, at least."

"I don't imagine any of them would be eager to drop a dime on your grandfather," I said. "But you said those people are only around when you're shooting?"

"Yeah, since we've been in post, it's pretty much just the three of us now."

"Okay, I get it. So the agent leaves and all three of you are congratulating yourselves on the snow job."

"It wasn't like that," he said. "It was more like we were all surprised as hell to find out what the agent was really here for. Apparently, some people in the UP ended up getting murdered or something. We were all like, damn, what the hell is that about?"

"CC was really surprised?"

"Well, yeah. Wouldn't you be?"

"Of course, you just said he was a great actor. But never mind. Let's get to the punch line. I didn't see your grandfather go into the office today. How much time has he really been spending there?"

"He's been there. Believe me, he's been there. I mean, this is his movie, right? When we were shooting, he was on the set pretty much constantly. I could tell it was really wearing him out."

"When exactly were you shooting?"

"We wrapped right before Christmas."

"Okay," I said, feeling an important piece of the puzzle fitting into place. "So as of New Year's Day or so, what did you say, you're in 'post' now?"

"Postproduction, yeah."

"But it's April. How long does that part take?"

"Post can run longer than the actual shooting. There's a million things to do with the editing and the sound, then the color correction and—"

"I get it," I said. "So how much time has he spent working on that?"

"Still a lot, but he's been taking some time off now and then. Like I said, the shooting really got to him."

"Taking some time off, meaning what? A few days at a time?"

"No, maybe like he'll work for five days straight and then go home for a couple of days. Show up the next Monday. That kind of thing."

"But meanwhile, you're here all the time."

"Me and my dad, yeah. We're the ones who're practically living here now. We actually have some mattresses in the back in case we run really late."

"Doesn't sound like much of a life."

"I wouldn't want to be doing anything else," he said. "My mom thinks I should've stayed with her and finished college, but come on. Where else am I gonna get a chance to work on a real movie like this?"

"Okay, I get it," I said. "But when CC goes away and then comes back a couple days later . . . will he say where he's been?"

"No. I mean, he's just home resting. So he'll come back and work some more, tell us what we should do next. Then he'll go home again."

I leaned back against the hard plastic booth. After so many hours sitting in the truck, my back was killing me. I had bigger things on my mind now than a sore back.

"You look like a decent kid," I said to him. "I

know you were only trying to do what you thought was best, but it wasn't the brightest move in the world."

"Am I gonna be in serious trouble for this?"

"I don't think so. If it comes to it, I'll vouch for you."

That didn't seem to make him feel any better. He sat there rubbing his hands together, looking out the window like he was still thinking about making a run for it.

"Tell me more about your grandfather," I said. "What's he really like?"

"That's what this whole movie is about," the kid said. "Him growing up here, and everything that happened. You ever see *Eight Mile*?"

"Was that another movie?"

"Yeah, that was Eminem. You heard of him, right?"

"He's the white rapper," I said. "From Detroit. That's about all I know. I confess I don't have any of his records."

"You sound like CC now. 'Records.' But anyway, Eminem made this movie about his own life, how he grew up in Detroit. I guess Eight Mile is an important street down there."

"It's the northern border." I didn't want to sidetrack him, but just hearing that name took me way back. Eight Mile Road, the line dividing Detroit from the suburbs. You cross that street and you go from one world to another.

"That movie was kind of a rags-to-riches story. But CC, his story was more like rags to insanity, to more rags to more insanity, to riches back to insanity again. It's just called *Bad Axe*. What do you think?"

"Sounds perfect. But what do you mean by insanity?"

"Well, he grew up right here in town, and apparently his mother and father . . . my great-grandparents, I mean . . . I never met them but I guess I didn't miss much. They were both absolutely batshit crazy. Like seriously delusional, psychotic, pretty much whatever you want to come up with. This was back in the old days, when they didn't take your kids away just because you were abusing them all the time. I guess he was hiding from them like every day, running away from home and getting dragged back there. The house is right over there on King Street. We even filmed there in the actual house, which must have been kinda weird for CC. If it was, he didn't show it. Anyway, he says it was the movie theater that saved him."

"The one right down the street?"

"That very one. He used to sneak into the movies all the time. Actually, the man who owned the place knew he was sneaking in and let him keep doing it. We filmed that scene, too. When CC came back from Hollywood, he bought the theater and fixed it up. Now he's trying to make this movie about growing up in the town and he's even talking about starting up a film festival here. Like they've got up in Traverse City. The Bad Axe Film Festival. Not bad, eh?"

"So when CC got arrested and went to prison," I said. "Did you film that scene, too?"

"Yeah, but that happened a lot later. When he was eighteen he finally escaped and ran off to California. Some guy saw him on his bike and liked the way he looked, and asked him if he wanted to be in the movies. I think CC told him to go jump in the ocean or something, but the guy was legit and that's how CC ended up doing *Road Hogs*. That was his very first movie, if you can believe it. Nowadays they'd never cast an unknown as the lead in a big film. I mean, you don't have a big name attached—"

"I don't mean to cut you off," I said, "but getting back to that arrest . . ."

"That was one of many arrests, actually. He got busted out there for marijuana. This was back before anybody could walk into one of those clinics and get it legally. Anyway, he ended up doing jail time and getting himself all messed up. You gotta remember, he came from a family of crazy people. Like he says all the time, it's in his blood. I've got bad blood, he says. I just can't help it sometimes. Which means maybe I've got some bad blood, too."

307

"So he's been arrested more than once, you say?"

"A few times, yeah. After he got bounced out of Hollywood, started making those low-budget horror films on his own. He was always his own worst enemy, but like he says, the movies were always there for him. They always kept him coming back from the edge of madness."

Now we're getting to it, I thought.

"So, this last arrest. It was about ten years ago."

"About that, yeah."

"It was up north here. He was coming down from the UP . . ."

"That was a tough couple of days, when we were filming that scene. He doesn't like to talk about it much, so you can imagine. I mean, it was really hard to relive it. I could tell it took a lot out of him."

"He played the part himself?"

"We had another actor playing the young CC, but the later years . . . yeah, a little makeup and he can still pass for sixty."

"Okay, so this scene with his daughter . . ."

"They let us use a holding cell over at the county jail. He had to take himself back to that day, when he found out. I swear he just about broke his hand on the wall all over again. And it wasn't even real this time."

"Maybe it's *always* real," I said. "No matter how many years have gone by."

"I was just a kid back then." He looked down at his hands. He was taking deep breaths now. Still scared, and now with this other family business . . . he was really starting to sweat.

"Don't bring it up with my grandfather," he said. "Okay? That's the one thing I have to ask you. He's relived it enough."

"Okay, I got it. Just tell me, where is he right now?"

"I don't know. He's probably at his house. Like I said before, just resting."

"Can you take me there?"

"My father would kill me if I did that."

"Can you just tell me where the house is?"

"My father would find out I told you. And he'd still kill me."

"Your father's a little crazy, too, I take it?"

"He's one-quarter crazy. That's the official amount, he says. Just ask him."

"So that means you're what, one-eighth crazy?"

"That sounds about right."

I couldn't help smiling at that. "Okay, well, I don't want to get you into any more trouble. Maybe I'll just go talk to your father. Conrad, you said his name is?"

"Yeah, but he goes by Connie. He hates it when anybody calls him Conrad."

"He's gonna hate a lot more than that today, I got a feeling."

"Just do me a favor," the kid said. "If you talk to my grandfather today—"

"Don't mention his daughter. I got it."

"No, besides that. Just take it easy on him, okay? He's really not in good shape these days."

"What's the matter with him?"

"Well, come on. He's seventy-two years old."

"There's young seventy-two and there's old seventy-two," I said. "I thought he was a real tough guy back in his day."

"He was, but after everything he's been through? Drugs and prison and whatever else? He's still getting his strength back, he says. But it might be too late."

"How's that?"

"Why do you think he's doing all this? Coming back here, making up with my father. You know, those two haven't exactly been close for a long time. My grandmother, she sorta took him away when things started getting too crazy. He was like seven years old then, so he didn't see much of his father for a long time. Once in a while, maybe, when CC was trying to get things together again. But now that CC's on his last lap, like he says, he's trying to make things right. Just these last couple of years, after he got out of prison. Getting back with whatever family he has left, buying the theater, making this movie. Telling his story, how he came through all the madness and the drugs and everything. It all makes sense, right?"

"It does. It's making more sense every minute."

"It's just like he told me," the kid said, summing it all up and sending an icy chill right down my back. "He doesn't have much time left, so he's finally doing all the things he should have done long ago."

That was all I needed to hear. It was time to go find Clyde C. Wiley.

And we're rolling . . .

. . . Let's get a nice buildup on this one, okay?

. . . Yes, that's it. Nice and slow.

. . . Where is he? He's in here somewhere! We'll get some really great music here.

. . . You can't hide, Sergeant Steele.

. . . There you are.

. . . Oh, and who's this?

. . . I don't believe your husband would approve of this, ma'am.

. . . Nice walk-on, by the way. We can use that. You're a natural.

And cut.

CHAPTER SEVENTEEN

The man behind the counter had the two sandwiches ready for Sean to take back to the studio. I told him to keep his money in his pocket, paid for both of the sandwiches myself, and gave him his.

"It sounds like you've been working pretty hard," I said. "You must really love this film business."

"Are you kidding? If you're a Wiley kid, CC gives you a camera as soon as you're old enough to hold one."

"I bet you really know how to use it. But as for right now, why don't you go on home. I think you just got the rest of the day off."

"That's not gonna go over very well. I should really talk to my father first."

"Trust me on this one, okay? You go home. I'll tell him I gave you no choice."

He still didn't look convinced, but eventually he agreed. I thanked him for sitting down and talking with me, then I sent him on his way. I took his father's sandwich with me and I headed down the street to the Grindstone building. When I got to the front door, I rang the buzzer. I heard the door unlock. I pushed the door open and went inside.

"What the hell took you so long?" the man

said. Just like the first time I'd been here, he was inside the little cubicle in the back of the big room, staring at the video screen, and he did not turn around to see me. He was wearing a different shirt today, but over it he still had the same leather vest.

"Sorry for the delay," I said. "Your son and I were having a little talk."

He spun around in his seat. "What the hell are you doing here?"

"It's time for you and me to talk now."

"Where's Sean? What did you do to him?"

"Nothing. I told him to take the rest of the day off."

"You can't just walk in here like that. I'm calling the police." He picked up the phone and started hitting the numbers.

"I'll tell you the same thing I told your son," I said. "It's a felony to lie to a federal agent. While you're calling your local police, I'll be calling the FBI."

He stopped dialing. "What are you talking about?"

"You know what I'm talking about," I said, taking out my cell phone. "Go ahead, make the call. How's your cell service here, anyway?"

I started hitting numbers on my phone at random. I could have looked up Agent Long's number if I really wanted to, but I was hoping I wouldn't have to.

"Not bad," I said. "Better than the UP. This call should go right through, no problem."

"Just hold on," he said. "Before we both go stirring up trouble."

"I want to see your father," I said, putting my phone away. "Right now."

"Why?"

"I just want to talk to him."

"About what?"

"About a matter that I'll discuss with him and not you."

He stood up from his console. He came over to me and he got way too close, and this was probably the sort of thing that had worked for him in the past. He was big enough, after all, and he looked scary enough. One-quarter crazy, like the kid said.

I didn't move. I didn't blink.

"I need to talk to your father, Conrad."

His eyes widened just a little bit at the sound of his given name.

"I understand you prefer to be called Connie?"

"I prefer that you'd get the hell out of here."

"It's not going to happen. One way or another, I'm going to talk to your father."

"As you can see, he's not here."

"Yeah, I got that part. Where is he?"

"He's at the house. He hasn't been well. I don't want you bothering him."

"This won't take long," I said. "I just need to

talk to him for a few minutes. That's all."

He stayed close to me. I was thinking he probably wanted me to make a move, give him a good excuse to sucker punch me.

I didn't. I kept my cool.

"I'm going to call him," he said. "I'll ask him if he wants to talk to you."

He took a step backward and pulled out his cell phone. He listened for a few seconds. He had the volume way up, so I could hear a man's voice on the other end, asking him to leave a message.

"He's probably asleep," he said. "He gets tired easy."

"How far away is the house?"

"Just across town, why?"

"Let's go, then," I said. "I'll even drive."

Better to keep an eye on him, I thought. Otherwise he'd call the cops on me, or call his father on another line to warn him off, or God knows what else he'd do.

"Why on earth would I agree to do that?"

"I'll give you one good reason," I said. "Because then I'll leave and you'll never have to see me again."

He sat in the passenger's seat with his arms folded. He looked at his watch and made a big deal of shaking his head and sighing.

"This won't take long," I said. "Just tell me where to go."

"Take a right here," he said as we came to the main intersection. "Then a left on Irwin Street."

I followed the road north, almost all the way to the edge of town, then I took the left and went down half a block. Connie nodded his head as we came to the house. It was one of the biggest houses in town, I was sure of that. An old Victorian, half-restored and begging to be finished, with most of the painting done but much of the trim still missing. I pulled into the driveway. There was a detached garage. The door was open.

"Where the hell is his car?" Connie said.

"He's not here?"

"If his car's not here, he's not here, genius."

I let that one go. We ended up sitting there another minute while he tried his cell phone again. I overheard the four rings and then the voice mail picking up.

"What the hell," he said, putting the phone down.

"Is there somewhere else he could be?"

"Yeah, I'm sure he's somewhere."

It was all I could do to not reach over and slap him in his smart mouth.

"He could be at the lake house," he said, "but what would he be doing up there? He knows we've got work to do today."

"Where's the lake house?"

"Up by Port Austin."

"How far away?"

"Twenty minutes, maybe."

I put the truck in reverse. "Let's go."

"Since when are you calling the shots?"

"Since I'm the one driving. I assume I keep going north here?"

"Yeah, that's where Port Austin is, last I checked."

I went back to the main road and went north. It was all empty farmland now, dusted white with the snow.

"Mind if I ask you a couple questions?"

"You can ask," he said. "I may not answer."

"When did you last see him?"

He didn't say anything. He kept looking out the window and I thought that was probably the only answer I was going to get.

"Couple of days ago," he finally said.

"That's the same day the agent came?"

"Yeah, I suppose it was."

"So the agent came and asked his questions. Then your father disappeared."

"He didn't *disappear*."

"I understand he's been doing that a lot. Ever since you finished filming."

He looked over at me. "My son tell you that?"

"Yes, he did."

"Then you've already got your answer."

"So ever since January, he's been gone off and on, for a couple days at a time. Is that fair to say?"

"He's been gone because he gets tired. He hates for other people to see him like that."

"I understand he's a pretty good actor. Is it possible he just *seemed* tired?"

He didn't even try to answer that one. Another minute of silence passed.

"Tell me about your sister," I said. "What was her name?"

"I swear to God," he said, "if you came down here to ask my father about Corina, you can just forget it right now. Do you understand me?"

"Relax," I said. "That's not why I'm here."

It wasn't a total lie. If Clyde C. Wiley was really the person hunting down former state troopers and their children . . . well, then the death of his daughter was obviously a big part of the reason why. But there was no specific reason why I'd have to bring her up now.

"Sounds like a sensitive topic," I said. "Doesn't he *ever* talk about it?"

Connie shook his head.

"He must have said something to you about it."

"What the hell is wrong with you?"

"Relax. I told you I won't bring it up with him. But he's not here now, right? You can talk about her."

"There's not much to say," he said. "I never really got to know her."

"Why's that?"

"Because he basically had two separate

families, okay? I grew up in California, after my mother walked out on him. Corina grew up in Michigan. She ended up getting married to the biggest loser in the world, which my father blamed himself for because the daughter always tries to marry a younger version of her father, and all that other crap. End of story."

"So you weren't around when she killed herself."

"No."

I was about to ask him why the hell he didn't try to help her, at least. Do something for his own sister or half-sister or whatever he wanted to call her. But I figured I wouldn't get very far with that.

I kept driving. It was another typical long, straight Michigan road. There was no snow on the pavement, so we were making good time. We saw the lake a few minutes later. The road ended in the small town of Port Austin, right at the very tip of the Lower Peninsula's thumb, extending out into Lake Huron. I saw a lot less ice than I'd seen on Lake Superior, but I still wasn't about to go swimming.

He had me make the right turn and head east, past driveway after driveway, each leading down to a small house near the water. Most of them were sealed up tight for the winter, I was sure. There wasn't much reason to be here in the middle of April.

"Why would he come up here?" I said.

"Various reasons. If he's not asleep, he'll probably be smoking. Just so you know."

"Smoking, as in . . ."

"What do you think?"

"I thought he was clean now."

"It's just pot," Connie said. "You want him coked up and getting in a fight with the police? Or hanging out watching old movies and smoking a joint?"

"I don't care what he does. I just want to talk to him. But you're telling me this is the designated smoking house?"

"It's the hangout house, yeah. Plus he keeps all his old stuff up here."

"What kind of old stuff?"

"He collects vintage film equipment. Spring-wound Bolex cameras, sixteen millimeter film. He even has an old Steenbeck up there."

"What's that?"

"It's an edit bay. From back when they had to splice actual strips of film together. It's like ancient history."

"So that's his other hobby, aside from the smoking?"

"It's his whole life," Connie said, an even harder edge to his voice now. "I know you wouldn't understand. Everything's digital now, but he still loves real film so much. He even develops the film himself sometimes. You know how hard that is to do?"

"No, I don't."

"Trust me. There aren't many people left who can do it."

We went down the road maybe a mile and a half, then he pointed to a driveway. It was unmarked and completely unremarkable. You'd definitely have to know where you were going to find this place. I could see a faint indentation where the last tracks had been made.

I stopped in front of the house. The weather had beat the hell out of the place. The siding was so split and worn, it was starting to fall right off the exterior walls. There was a big black vintage Cadillac parked haphazardly by the front door. A vintage car to go with his vintage film gear.

"He's here," Connie said. I could tell he was at least a little relieved. "Come on."

We got out of the truck and went to the door.

"I know it don't look like much from the outside," he said. "That's the way he likes it. Beat up all to hell, just like himself."

"Okay, whatever you say." Personally, I couldn't have slept one night in the place without going outside and working on that siding.

Connie tried the front door. It was locked.

"Since when do you lock the door?" he muttered to himself. He reached down under the little wooden front porch and grabbed a key off a hook. Not the most secure place in the world, obviously. As he unlocked the door and pushed it open, he called out to his father. There was no answer.

When I came in behind him, I could see he'd been right about the place. It looked like crap from the outside, but the inside was immaculate. There was a leather sofa in the front room facing a big hi-def television. Above the sofa was a framed poster for *Road Hogs*, with the young Clyde C. Wiley himself posed on the back of a Harley, looking ready to kick some serious butt.

I stood there for a moment, looking at the movie star with the tattoos and the arms rippling with muscles. He might be seventy-two years old now, I thought, but he's not ninety-two. I bet he could still put a hurt on you if he really wanted to.

As I turned around, I didn't see Connie anywhere. Might as well make myself at home, I thought. I took a quick look into the kitchen. It was small but well-appointed with high-end appliances. There was a small eating area with a glass table, and more framed movie posters. I was definitely picking up the faint, sweet odor of marijuana now. If anybody ever bought this place, they'd have to air it out for a month.

I went down the short hallway, past the bathroom, to the only bedroom in the place. There was a desk over by the big window, which looked out over the lake. There was a pile of manila folders on the desk, each of them stuffed with papers. I took a quick look down the hallway, but still didn't see Connie. So I started thumbing through the folders. I couldn't help myself. I had come this far and I had to see if my gut feeling about this guy could be validated.

The first two folders were a collection of court documents. They portrayed a lifetime of trouble with the law, and right there on top was the most recent record of all, an arrest record dated ten years ago. Clyde C. Wiley detained on a certain mile post of I-75, just north of Indian River. Arresting officers, Sergeant Dean Haggerty and Trooper Donald Steele, both of Michigan State Police Post 83, St. Ignace. I paged through the report, which listed the initial assault on a man named Darryl Bergman. Along with menacing and unlawful detention. There was an attempt to intercept Wiley at the Mackinac Bridge, then as I kept reading there were details of the pursuit itself, from the bridge down to Indian River, then a description of the extreme physical resistance offered by the arrestee once the vehicle had been stopped. There was some question about whether the resistance itself constituted lethal force, which would of course have upped the ante considerably. Then finally the list of items found in the car, the firearm, the cocaine residue, the three bottles of prescription painkillers. Stacked onto the probation violation from California, it was no wonder he got a stiff prison sentence for this little joyride. As a repeat offender, it was actually kind of amazing he didn't do a lot more time. He must have had a hell of a lawyer.

I didn't see any mention of Razniewski or Maven in the arrest report. We'd already been told that by the FBI agents, yet here it was in living color and I had to read through every word to make sure nothing was missed. There were no other officers assisting on the arrest. No other officers mentioned in any way.

I looked through the other folders, but they were all from earlier arrests and mishaps, and none of them had even taken place in the state of Michigan. It was all California and Oregon and Texas. This man certainly got around, I thought. And he seemed to make quite an impression wherever he went.

I put down the last folder and left the bedroom. "Hey, where did you go?" I said.

There was no answer.

I went back into the kitchen and stood there, trying to figure out where the hell Connie could be. That's when I noticed the leather portfolio sitting on the counter, right under the phone. I opened it and there on the right side was a pad of yellow legal paper. On the very top sheet there were three names written.

Steele.

Haggerty.

Razniewski.

That was it. Nothing else. No other information. Just three last names of three men who buried children and then who died themselves in the most violent ways imaginable.

Right there in the man's kitchen. Those three names.

I picked up the phone. I was about to start dialing. That's when I heard the sound. It was like a repetitive scraping. Over and over. It was coming from somewhere . . . below me? I looked over and saw the door to what had to be the basement. It was ajar. I hung up the phone.

The sound got louder as I opened the door. There were rough wooden stairs leading down to a concrete floor, and just enough light to see where I was going. I picked up the musty basement smell as I started to go down, along with something else—a faint chemical smell. When I finally reached the bottom of the stairs, there was almost too much to see at once. A single bulb burning in the center of the ceiling. Another light of some sort just around the corner ahead. A long table on my left, with cameras and tripods and a big glass cabinet with a million small parts. Cans of film, some the size of dinner plates. Others smaller. On the other wall a cork board almost completely covered with film strips. They were all tacked to the top of the board and many of them had slips of paper attached to them, with a jumble of letters and numbers.

I caught the chemical smell again and as I stepped down onto the concrete I saw that there was a small room built underneath the stairs. Through the open door I saw jerrycans and a high metal tub and even though I knew nothing about this I would have guessed this is where Clyde C. Wiley did his own developing, just as his son had boasted.

"Connie," I said, "are you down here?"

Still no answer, and now it was starting to get to me. The scraping sound was louder now. It got louder still with each step as I approached the other side of the L. As I turned the corner I saw the light coming from a single desk lamp. This was the old edit bay that Connie was talking about. There was a small monitor in the middle of the console. There was an empty film reel mounted horizontally on the left side. On the right side a full reel was still spinning, the end of the film licking at the metal guide post with each revolution. Scrape scrape scrape.

There was a chair. A man was sitting in it, facing away from me. Long hair hanging down the back. Connie was standing next to the man, looking down at him. Connie's mouth was open. No sound was coming out.

I stepped closer. The man in the chair . . . it had to be Clyde C. Wiley. After everything I had been through that day, I had finally come face-to-face with him. He was staring straight ahead at nothing. I pressed two fingers against his neck. His skin was cold. He had been dead for hours. But not days.

Connie didn't move. He was paralyzed.

"He's gone," I said to him. "Let's go upstairs and call somebody."

Connie let out a puff of air. He kept staring at his father's dead face. You never know how somebody's going to react in a situation like this. I'd seen every possible emotion back when I was on the night shift in Detroit. All those dead bodies on the hot pavement, and then whoever was left alive, usually a mother but sometimes a son or a daughter . . . they'd cry or they'd scream or they'd let out a high whooping noise that you might even mistake for laughter. Or else they'd shut down completely. Stand there like Connie was doing now, like they'd never be able to move again.

"Come on," I said. "Let's go."

"What was he doing down here?"

"Connie . . ."

"We were supposed to be working today. Why is he here?"

Before I could say another word, Connie found the switch inside himself and flipped it back on. He reached for the console, taking the full reel right off its post.

"You shouldn't touch that," I said, but he wasn't listening to me. He pulled out the end of the film and stretched it back to the empty reel. The film looked yellow and brittle.

"No," I said. "Leave that alone."

I tried to turn him toward the stairs, but he pushed me away. He pressed a button and the reels started turning fast. He was rewinding the film.

The hell with it, I thought. He's a zombie right now. I'm gonna go call the police.

Yet something made me hesitate. It didn't take long for the film to rewind, or for Connie to rethread it through the console. He hit another button and the monitor came to life.

I stood there and watched it with him.

There was a neighborhood, the camera panning down the street, one house after the next. Pausing on one house, then finally moving. An ordinary scene, but strange at the same time. There was no sound, for one thing. That would come later. Or at least that's what I assumed. Music and narration and whatever else, to complete the story. But for now as the film looped through the machine it was nothing more than a string of images, one after the other, rough and jittery and washed-out like something that had been filmed a hundred years ago.

I had to keep watching. I couldn't help it. I couldn't move.

From the neighborhood, to a woman standing in her garden. She looks up at the camera with mild annoyance. Then her face widens into alarm. Into genuine fright. She is looking past the camera now. The camera doesn't respond. We don't get to see what she's looking at.

The light shifting, the next scene indoors. The camera panning across a table. There's a man's belt. Then a large metal spoon. A broom handle. Then finally what looks like an old razor strop. The camera is shaking now. The focus is fading in and out. The scene goes black.

Then a flash of light. Sunlight. A bridge. The Mackinac Bridge? Yes, it is. There's no other bridge like it. It's a perfect summer day and we're looking at the bridge, like we've suddenly stumbled into somebody's normal home movie, taken by a normal person on a normal family vacation. It's so out of place here.

From the normal back to the strange. A long, almost loving shot of a knife. The camera slowly moves up the edge, barely staying in focus.

Then what's this? It's hard to even tell what's going on now. There's a thin shaft of light. It grows wider. We're looking through a door. A man is sitting in a chair. We can only see the back of his head. He tips his head back to drink something. A line of smoke curls above his head. He is jarred by something. He gets up. The camera doesn't go up to see the man's face. It stays at ground level. All we see are his pant legs and his feet. He comes closer and then everything goes black.

Then fire trucks. People running down the street. The camerawork seems a lot steadier now. It pans back and forth, zooming in on every detail. Flames coming out of a window. The firemen wrestling with the hoses. The camera follows the smoke, up and up, into the night sky.

I looked over at Connie. He was staring at the screen, his mouth half open. Between us the dead man. His father. Clyde C. Wiley. So close to me I could touch his neck again if I wanted to. His lifeless eyes still looking off at nothing.

This isn't happening, I said to myself. I'm not here in the basement of this man's house, watching these strips of film that have been pasted together into this bizarre sequence.

Then it got worse.

Misery Bay. Right there on the screen. Charlie Razniewski, the young man I never saw alive, is leaning against the back of his car. There's a light shining on him. Otherwise everything around him is dark. He seems drunk or half-asleep. The rope is around his neck. From somewhere off camera, the slack is taken up and the rope tightens. Charlie snaps awake and he's clutching at the rope. It gets tighter and tighter until finally Charlie's feet leave the ground. He's in the air now, kicking and struggling in vain against the rope. It's all silent still, and somehow it makes this all the more unreal. Charlie fights for a full minute until he finally starts to go limp. He hangs there for a long time. The camera finally moves. It comes closer. It circles him. It zooms in on his face.

I want to say something. I can't speak.

From the nighttime scene at Misery Bay, to daytime. Still winter, with a pale sunlight that makes everything seem to glow. The camera is in motion against the rough wall of a barn. It turns the corner and there's young Brandon Steele. His back is to us. He has a pistol extended in his right hand. From the recoil we can see he's shooting. There's a pair of acoustic earmuffs on his head. He's not aware of the camera approaching. Closer and closer. Slowly. Pan to the other weapon on the windowsill. A semiautomatic. A gloved hand reaches for it. The gun is pointed at the young man's head. The barrel is three inches away. Then the side of Brandon's head explodes. He goes down, pumping blood into the snow. The camera lingers on his body, recording every nuance. Then it cuts abruptly, as if the camera has just run out of film.

Immediately, we are indoors. It is dark. A sliver of light comes through a window and we can finally make out the features of a bedroom. There's a woman in the bed. She is sleeping peacefully. Haggerty's daughter. What's her first name again?

"No," I say, finally finding my voice. "Please."

As if I have the power to warn her. As if I can stop this from happening.

A helium tank. A hose. A plastic bag with a cord around the opening. The bag is carefully slipped over the woman's head. Dina is her name. It comes to me. Dina Haggerty. She stirs and turns a little but does not wake up. The cord is tightened. The valve on the helium tank is turned. The camera waits for a long time. The woman seems to be sleeping still. There's no discernable difference at all. Finally, the woman's arm is lifted by the cameraman. It falls back to the bed, lifeless. The helium tank is tucked into the bed beside her. The woman's arm is draped around the tank.

I'm standing there watching this. I feel like I could throw up at any moment.

Then Maven's kitchen. Charles Razniewski Sr. has already been attacked. His throat is already cut, the blood is already pooling on the floor. The camera can only play catch-up now. It zooms in on his dead face, and on the last gallon of blood as it leaves his body and spreads slowly across the floor.

Then a house. A door is pushed open. I've seen this house before. I've pushed open this very door myself. The camera goes inside. It seems to search, like it has no idea where it's going. It's disorienting to watch. Finally, a gun on the table. The gun is picked up. Another door is pushed open. An interior door this time. We see a man's back. We see the red flower blossom on his back. He goes down. Only now do we see the woman in front of him. She looks at the camera with confusion, growing into abject horror. She falls backward. The camera comes in close. The gun is aimed at her forehead. It fires. She lies there bleeding. The camera sees everything, then finally a hand reaches out. The same black glove. It takes the woman's arm and pulls it so that the woman's body is turned over. She is facing the floor now. The arm is hiding her face. The camera retreats. We see it all getting smaller and smaller, until we're back outside again. Cut to black.

The black resolves into the shapes of trees. There is deep snow. The camera moves forward slowly. In the distance, finally, we see the lights from a house. The camera approaches the back door. The door is pushed open. There is a man sitting in a chair. He seems to be asleep. The camera comes close. A white PVC pipe is placed against his forehead. The man wakes up. One second later, the pipe is jolted. The man has been shot in the head. The chair is thrown backward. The man is spread eagle on the floor. The hand behind the camera comes out, adjusts one arm so that his position is perfectly symmetrical. The camera watches the man for a few moments, then it goes back to the door, quickly now, and out into the night.

A sudden noise broke the spell. The film had looped all the way through and now it was spinning on the right-hand reel again, making that same sound I had first heard from upstairs. Scrape scrape scrape.

We both stood there for a long time. I didn't know what to say to him. I had absolutely no idea what combination of words would make any earthly sense at that moment.

Connie finally closed his mouth. He swallowed hard and then he looked down at his father.

"Did you really do this?" he said. "Did you?"

He closed his eyes. He started to sway like he was going to collapse. I took one step toward him and he put up his hand to stop me.

"Don't touch me," he said.

"I'm going to go call somebody."

He put his hand down. I turned and left him there. I left him there with his dead father, his murderous evil dead corpse of a father, and I went up the stairs to pick up the phone and to try to find the words to describe what I had just seen.

And we're rolling . . .

. . . Two miles through the snow. Uphill both ways, right? That's the old joke.

. . . Did I tell you the camera loves the snow? I believe I did. Even at night! All this hard work, it pays off. Keep going.

. . . Door left open, right on cue. Well done.

. . . Good to see you again, Sergeant Haggerty.

. . . Or should I say, Lieutenant Haggerty?

. . . Either way, time for your close-up.

. . . How do you like this thing? Pretty realistic, eh? I made it myself.

. . . Damn, that worked perfectly.

And cut.

CHAPTER EIGHTEEN

After I had answered all of their questions as well as I could, I sat in the waiting room of the Bad Axe post. Hours had gone by, a large part of the day, and as I finally sat there by myself, I went over it again in my head. I knew I'd be doing that for a long time to come.

Connie was still in the building somewhere, still talking to somebody. He had proven himself to be a complete jackass to me, in every possible way—right up until that exact moment when I had found him in that basement. Now I just felt sorry for him. For his son Sean, as well. I didn't know how they'd ever be able to deal with this.

A trooper came by and gave me a cup of coffee. He asked me if I wouldn't mind hanging around a little while longer. I told him I had no problem with that. I sat there with the coffee cup in both hands and watched the rest of the day go by.

I knew it was four hours from Sault Ste. Marie to Bad Axe. Another hour or two to get the full story. Maybe even see the filmstrip if you were properly prepared for the experience. Another few minutes to catch your breath. Maybe six hours total, and that's just about when Agent Long came through one of the inner doors and sat down beside me. I was glad to see her.

She didn't say anything for a while. Then she turned to me.

"Why didn't you tell us you were coming down here?" she said.

"I probably should have."

"Yeah, maybe."

"What would you have told me if I had? You'd already eliminated him as a suspect."

"I would have listened, Alex."

"I don't blame you guys for missing him. Not only was he seventy-two years old, he was a good enough actor to make people think he was on his last legs."

"So then it's kind of ironic," she said. "He may have fooled us into thinking he was too weak to do this, but then his heart gave out."

"Is that what happened? Cardiac arrest?"

"Yes. Before he had the chance to finish his masterpiece."

I shook my head. "Did you see it yet?"

"I just did, yes. You know, I'm not going to beat you up on this now, but what the hell were you thinking? You should have called somebody right away. What if you had accidentally erased the film or something?"

"It wasn't my idea," I said. "But once it started . . ."

"I get it. I'm sorry, I shouldn't have said anything. I probably would have done the same thing."

"No, you're right. It was a stupid thing to do, but that's not unusual for me. Just ask Chief Maven."

She smiled at that. We sat there for a few more minutes. Then we got up and she walked me to my truck. The state police had brought it back down from Wiley's lake house. It was parked on the street.

"So what's next?" I said. "Are you guys coming back up to the Soo?"

"I'm not sure. We may be all done up there now. We checked out of the hotel."

"Already?"

"That's one thing they teach you, an agent needs to be ready to move out at a moment's notice."

"That's too bad," I said. "I was going to buy you a drink at the Glasgow."

"I'll take a rain check. Next time I'm in the UP."

"You've got my number." I stood there for a moment, not quite sure what to do next. She put out her hand for me to shake. I took it in mine. Then I got in my truck.

I was about to drive off, but she motioned for me to roll down my window.

"How did you know?" she said.

"About Wiley? Just a gut feeling."

She shook her head. "That's a load of crap. There was something you saw that we didn't."

"Come up to Paradise and have that drink with me. I'll tell you all about it."

She smiled at me again. That slow, careful smile that was really starting to grow on me. I could only wonder if I'd ever see her again.

"Take care of yourself," I said. Then I rolled up my window. I watched her in the rearview mirror as I drove away.

A drink at the Glasgow, I thought. That's exactly what I need right now.

I pointed the truck due north and gunned it.

They closed the book on the murders of Charles Razniewski and his son Charlie, Donald Steele and his son Brandon, along with Donna Krimer, and Dean Haggerty and his daughter Dina. When they tried to write the very last page of that book, they cited the connection between Steele and Haggerty and the arrest of Clyde C. Wiley, ten years ago. They failed to find any concrete link to Razniewski, apart from the notebook I had found on Wiley's kitchen counter. They were beginning to suspect that no link would ever be found in the official records. However Wiley came to know Razniewski, it could have been nothing more than a chance encounter on a completely different day, either on the job during those few times when Razniewski was working on his own, or even off the job. A few harsh words spoken to a man who already had his own reasons to hate Michigan State Troopers, or who would soon come to have such a hatred . . . it might have been enough. They'd never know for sure because Wiley was probably the only man who could tell them.

The fact that Roy Maven's name did *not* appear in that notebook, along with the fact that Maven himself had no recollection of ever meeting Wiley—a meeting he would probably remember simply because of Wiley's celebrity—made it look less and less likely that Maven had ever been a target to begin with. Apparently, Wiley had done all the killing he was going to do. He just died before he could finish his film.

Maven's wife and daughter flew home from Amsterdam. As soon as they touched the ground, Maven's wife called him and told him that she would not sleep one single night in that house in Sault Ste. Marie. Not after what had happened on her kitchen floor. Maven put up a brief fight. He had ripped up the floor, cleaned everything in the house within an inch of its life, and so on. But I think even he knew it was a fight he'd never win. So he went outside with a sledgehammer and pounded a FOR SALE sign into the still-frozen ground.

His daughter was home safe and his wife was staying with her in Lansing, and Chief Maven went off his administrative leave and reclaimed his job as chief of police. He moved back into his windowless concrete office in the City-County Building, with no pictures or any other distractions of any kind on the walls. His spot on the lower end of the totem pole in Sault Ste. Marie was once again secure.

It was late April now. There was a false sense of spring while everything started to thaw for three days straight. Jackie was actually observed smiling. Then we got ten more inches of snow. I had drinks with Leon after his shift at the Cineplex one night and told him everything that had happened. When I finally dragged him home well after midnight, his wife was not happy. I don't know which one of us got in more trouble that night. I didn't regret it for a second, but Leon might have felt differently when he woke up the next morning.

I thought about calling Agent Long a few times, but whenever I picked up the phone I thought about how many miles there were between us. I wanted to see her again, but I knew it wouldn't be an easy arrangement for either of us.

The sun came back. The thermometer actually hit fifty for one brief day. Vinnie helped me do some of the remaining exterior trim work on the last cabin. Then it snowed another eight inches.

Things felt almost normal again, and I thought I might finally be ready to face that first cabin. Just go in, clean it out, reclaim it, banish all the bad memories of what had happened there. You do that and only the good memories will remain. At least that's what I was telling myself. I set a date and I promised myself that was the day I was going to do it.

It was time to get my life back.

Before that day could even begin, I got another one of those early-morning phone calls. The sky outside was still cold and dark and the sound of the phone ringing was like a jagged edge of a knife. I stumbled out of bed and answered it.

It was Agent Long. Sometime during the night, Olivia Maven had apparently ingested a lethal dose of the tranquilizer Pentobarbital. She was in the hospital, and Chief Maven was on his way down to see her. She had eventually thrown up much of the Pentobarbital, after it had been in her system for some unknown period of time. There was a chance this might have saved her life. But as of that moment, things did not look good.

I hung up the phone and closed my eyes.

Either Clyde C. Wiley was back from the dead, I thought, or else it was never him to begin with. Whoever the killer was, he was back at it. Or rather, he had never really stopped. He had just been waiting.

And we're rolling . . .

. . . Finally!

. . . I thought we'd never get this thing off the ground again.

. . . I still don't know where my film is. It better show up soon or there'll be hell to pay.

. . . On top of that, no edit bay for the time being. I even had to make my own developing tank!

. . . And Olivia was away for so long, I wasn't sure if she'd ever come back home.

. . . Just drink this and lie right back down. Act a little scared.

. . . Perfect. You took your time showing up, but at least you nailed the performance.

. . . It's good to be back in motion again, even with all the problems. Like they say, the show must go on.

And cut.

PART THREE

CHAPTER NINETEEN

I called Chief Maven's cell phone. It rang a few times, just long enough for me to question whether this was the right thing to do. He had enough on his mind, God knows. But before I could hang up, I heard his voice on the other end.

"What is it?"

"Chief, is that you?"

He didn't say anything. I could hear his engine racing. He was in his car, of course, on his way down to Lansing.

"Chief, are you driving? Please be careful."

"I can't talk now. I can't even—"

He broke off, swearing at another driver.

"Chief, it won't do you any good if you get killed on the way down there."

"What do you want, McKnight?"

"How is she? Do you have any other news yet?"

"No, I don't. I'll see when I get there."

"Do you want me to come down?"

More swearing on his end as he passed another vehicle. I don't know if he had a squad car with lights, or if he was driving his regular unmarked car.

"Chief, do you want me to come down there?"

"Ingham Hospital. In Lansing. I gotta go."

The line went dead. I hurried up and got dressed. Then I headed out to my truck and gunned it.

• • •

I couldn't go quite as fast as Chief Maven, and of course he already had a head start on me. I drove over the Mackinac Bridge again, into the Lower Peninsula. Straight south on I-75, just like my trip to Bad Axe, only this time I branched off at Grayling and headed straight for Lansing. I had left at about five in the morning, and I figured it would take me about four hours to get there. I stopped for gas and coffee and got right back on the road. When I got near Lansing I stopped again to ask for directions to the hospital. It was just after nine when I finally got there.

I went to the main reception desk and had a few minutes of tense wrangling with the woman about where Olivia Maven was and whether I could go anywhere near her. In the end, I called the chief on his cell phone again and he told me to come up to the Critical Care unit.

When I stepped out of the elevator, there was a nurse at the main station who didn't want me to go any farther, as only immediate family members were allowed in the unit. That's when Chief Maven came out of one of the rooms and flashed his badge at her. He didn't technically have any authority to do that, but it seemed to work, at least for the moment. He gave me a quick nod and I followed him over to a small waiting area.

"How's she doing?" I said.

"Better than a few hours ago."

His voice was tight. He wouldn't look at me. He wouldn't stand still.

"Why did I let her come back?" he said. "Will you tell me that, please?"

"The case was solved, Chief. It was over. How were you supposed to know this would happen?" I didn't know what else to tell him. I knew that whatever I said, it wouldn't help one little bit.

"For as long as I live," he said, "I will never forgive myself for being such an idiot. I don't care what anybody else says. It was up to me to look after her and I completely, totally failed."

He grabbed a magazine off the little table and threw it at the window. The nurse looked up from her station and was about to say something. Wisely, she decided against it.

"I understand what those other guys went through now," he said. "This is what it's like to see your child . . . just, I mean . . ."

He picked up another magazine. I grabbed him by the shoulders and sat him down. "Chief, tell me what happened."

He pushed me away from him, but he stayed in the seat.

"My wife was there, McKnight. She was in the guest room downstairs when he came in. He must have come in through the front door and walked right by her door. Gone upstairs, into Olivia's bedroom."

He started rocking back and forth as he went on.

"He went in there and . . . and I don't even know what happened next. Somehow he woke her up and got her to drink a glass of water with all these pills in it. Pentobarbital. You know what that is, right?"

"A tranquilizer."

"An old one. It's been around forever. It's what Marilyn Monroe took when she . . ." He stopped talking. He kept rocking back and forth in his chair.

"Chief, your wife didn't hear anything?"

"No. No, she takes her hearing aid out, and she just didn't . . ."

"So what's the prognosis right now, Chief? You said she's doing better?"

"Yeah, that's what they're saying. You want to know why? Because he made a mistake. It's the oldest trick in the book, right? You wait for them to make a mistake."

"What do you mean? What kind of mistake?"

"When you're going to kill yourself by taking a lot of tranquilizers or sleeping pills or whatever else, you know what you usually have to do first? If you really want to make sure it works? You take an antiemetic."

"*Anti*emetic, so you mean you don't—"

"So you don't throw it all back up, yes. That was his mistake, McKnight. He didn't realize that my poor Olivia's always had a nervous stomach. It probably didn't stay down for more than a few minutes. By that time, he must have been gone."

"What are they saying now?"

"They're still saying she could have some liver damage. It's too early to tell."

"Is she awake? Have you talked to her?"

"No, not yet. They said she'll be out for a while. Probably all day."

"But when you do . . . she should be able to tell us what happened, right?"

"Yes. You would think so. She should be able to tell us. I don't know."

He leaned all the way back in his chair, finally coming to rest for one second at least. He put two fingers from each hand on his temples and closed his eyes.

"But until she does that," I said, "we have no idea exactly what happened, right?"

"What are you getting at?" He opened his eyes. "Are you suggesting she might have really tried to kill herself?"

"No, Chief."

"Because if that's what you're saying—"

"All I'm saying is that we don't have any idea who to look for. That's all I meant."

"Whoever it is," he said, "he must be rattled now. After making a mistake like that . . ."

"What are you thinking? This has to be

somebody who was close to Wiley, right?"

"Probably. The film was in his basement. Which reminds me . . ."

"What?"

"Two agents were just here a minute ago," Maven said. "Not Long and Fleury, two other guys from Detroit. They went out to Bad Axe as soon as they found out about this. You know what they found?"

"What?"

"Somebody broke into that house on the lake. The feds had it all locked up tight, because they were still processing stuff. But sometime between yesterday evening and this morning, somebody got in, went down to the basement, and turned the whole place inside out."

"Looking for the film," I said. "Gotta be, right?"

"You would think. But whoever it was, he didn't find it."

"So what about Connie and Sean? Did the agents talk to them?"

"Naturally. Neither of them was alone last night. They both seem to have airtight alibis."

"They *seem* to?"

"Yeah, and neither of them has any idea who could have broken into the house. Of course, I'm getting all of this secondhand."

"We've been down this road before," I said.

"Last time around, secondhand wasn't good

enough for you, you mean. So you ran off to see for yourself."

"Pretty stupid thing to do. As usual."

He nodded slowly. "The kind of thing I'm always yelling at you for."

"You stay here with your daughter," I said. "I'll call you as soon as I can."

Bad Axe was about two hours away from Lansing. I took the expressway due east through Flint, but then I had to cut north on a smaller two-lane highway, all the way north into the thumb. So the last hour was hard driving.

When I finally hit Bad Axe, I knew exactly where to go. I parked in the lot next to the theater and went across the street. I pressed on the buzzer next to the Grindstone Productions plate, but nobody answered. I pressed again and took a peek through the window. It was dark inside. I rapped on the window a few times, then I turned and left. I went across to the theater and tried the door. It was locked. Not a big surprise. It wasn't even noon yet. I knocked on the door, but nobody answered.

Okay, think, I said to myself as I walked back to the truck. Where do I try next?

I played back my last trip down here and realized I knew exactly where Sean lived, at least. I had followed him home to his apartment that first night. It wasn't far from the theater, just a few blocks away from that motel I stayed in. I pulled out and retraced the route.

When I got to his building, I didn't see his green Corvette anywhere. Another swing and a miss, I thought. Not a good start. I got out and went to the front door, gave it a quick knock just for the hell of it. I was surprised when the door opened. A young woman stood there looking out at me. She looked vaguely familiar.

"Is Sean here?"

She shook her head. She was clearly upset about something.

"My name's Alex," I said. "Are you okay?"

She shook her head again.

"Can I come in and talk to you? It'll only take a minute, I promise."

She backed away from the door. She still hadn't said a word.

"Where have I seen you before?" I said. Then it came to me. "Wait a minute, you were the girl in the sandwich shop. Behind the counter, that first day I came in. I didn't realize you and Sean were . . ." I wasn't quite sure which word to pick, but it didn't seem to matter. She was looking down at the floor now and was obviously not listening to me at all.

"You weren't there in the shop the next day," I said, "when I sat down with Sean."

I leaned in closer to get her attention.

"We had a long talk," I said, "Sean and I. Did he say anything about it to you?"

"Yes," she said, finally finding her voice. "He told me a private investigator talked to him."

"Okay. Good. So tell me what's wrong."

"I . . . can't."

I took a step inside. She didn't stop me.

"Please talk to me," I said. "Maybe I can help."

She turned away from me and went to the center of the room. She had her arms folded around herself. As I followed her, I saw all the movie posters decorating their living room. *Casablanca*, *The Maltese Falcon*, *Chinatown*, and right there in the middle of it all, that same *Road Hogs* poster I had seen in Wiley's lake house.

Then I saw something else. On the bookshelf, occupying an obvious place of honor. An old movie camera.

I went up close to it and looked at it carefully without touching it. The body of the camera had a textured black surface, and the dials and buttons and lens were all gleaming silver. It was like a work of art.

"That's his Bolex," the young woman said.

"He got it from his grandfather, right? I remember what he told me when we were sitting in the sandwich shop. If you're a Wiley kid, the old man gives you a camera as soon as you're old enough to hold one."

"That's right."

"Let me ask you something. Does he ever let anybody else use it?"

"What, that camera? No way. He won't even let me touch it."

I turned to face her. "I'm sorry, I didn't get your name."

"Delaney."

"Delaney, that's a nice name. So tell me . . . I understand the FBI was here this morning?"

She looked at the floor again.

"You've got to talk to me," I said. "Where's Sean right now, anyway?"

She didn't answer.

"Come on, sit down."

As gently as I could, I guided her into one of the chairs. I got down on one knee, right in front of her. I didn't want to push her too hard, but at the same time I needed her to tell me what the hell was going on.

"You know I was trying to help Sean . . ."

She nodded.

"So let me help out again. Where's Sean?"

"He left." She wiped her nose with the back of her hand.

"Where did he go?"

"I don't know. He wouldn't tell me."

"When did he leave?"

"Right after he talked to the agents."

"Did you hear their conversation?"

"Only part of it. One of them took me aside and talked to me in the other room. They just wanted me to tell them where Sean was all last night and this morning."

"I understand. And he was with you the whole time?"

"Yes, he was. I swear."

"Okay, I got it," I said. "So what happened next?"

"I just heard the end of what they were saying, but it sounds like they were asking him if he knew anybody who might have broken into his grandfather's lake house. Sean was saying, 'No, sorry, I can't help you, I really don't know.' So they left."

"Then when did Sean leave? Right after that?"

"No, first he pulled out his cell phone, because I guess somebody had been calling him the whole time he was talking to the agents. He thought it was his father, but then when he looked at his phone, he was like, 'Who the hell is this?' He called the number back and that's when he ended up going outside."

"You didn't hear any of it?"

"Not really, but he was like, 'Hey, what's going on? What? What are you talking about?' And he got a real weird look on his face. He looked over at me and then that's when he went outside. I could see him pacing all over the place, walking up and down until he finally went and sat inside his car. He was really upset about something, I could see that from the window."

"You didn't get a name? Like did he say, 'Hey, so-and-so,' or anything like that?"

"No, I can't remember anything like that. But when he came back inside, he was still talking. It was like he was trying to end the call, but whoever was on the line wouldn't let him go, and Sean was just like, 'Okay, okay. Just go there and I'll meet you there. Yeah, you told me how to get there, I got it. Yeah, yeah, I'll bring it, I'll bring it. Don't worry. Just go there and don't do anything else.' "

"What was 'it'? What was he going to bring to this person?"

"He didn't tell me that. He just said he had to go see somebody right away. And that I should stay here and not talk to anybody about it. He promised me he'd call me as soon as he could."

"That's it? That's all he said?"

"That's all, I swear. He said he'd call me by the end of the day. He promised."

"Delaney, think hard. Do you have any idea where he might have gone? Who he needed to meet with?"

"No, I really don't."

I leaned back and let out a long breath.

"Did something happen to a woman in Lansing?" she said. "That's what the agents said. Did somebody try to kill her?"

"Yes, it looks that way."

"Is she okay?"

"It's too early to tell. But she's got a fighting chance."

"Oh, God," she said, looking away again. "I can't believe this is happening."

I got up off the floor, feeling a sharp pain in my knees.

"Do you think you can find him?" she said. "I'm really worried. Before he left, he was just so . . . I don't know. I've never seen him like this before."

I reached out and took her hand. "I'll do everything I can," I said. "Thank you for talking to me."

She wiped her nose with her free hand again and nodded.

"His father," I said. "Do you know where he is right now?"

"No. I have no idea."

"He wasn't at the studio. Do you have his home address?"

"He lives with CC, I think. I mean, he was when CC was still alive. In that big house on Irwin Street."

"I know where it is. I'm going to go there right now."

"When you find Sean," she said, "have him call me right away, okay?"

"I will. I promise."

"That's two promises I have now," she said. "One from him and one from you. So how come I get the feeling something horrible's going to happen today?"

"You can't think that way," I said. Yet even as I said it I knew I was sharing that exact same feeling. I thanked her again and I left her there. Then I headed out to find Conrad Wiley.

I drove up to the northern edge of town, to that big half-restored Victorian on Irwin Street. I parked in the driveway, got out, and knocked on the door. No answer. I was right back to my string of bad luck.

I got back in the truck and drove down to the center of town. I tried the Grindstone building again, but there was still nobody inside. I slammed my open hand on the door and said a few choice words. Then I went across the street for one more try at the theater. This time, finally, the door was unlocked. I pushed it open and saw a woman at the concession stand, going through a cash drawer.

"Movies don't start until four o'clock," she said.

"I'm looking for Connie Wiley."

"He's not here."

"Do you have any idea where he is?"

"He was across the street this morning, talking to some men in suits. It looked pretty heavy. If he's not there now, I think he was gonna go out scouting today."

"I'm sorry, I don't know what that means."

"Scouting locations for the new ending to his movie. I bet that's where he is now."

"You mean the movie he was making about his father? He's still working on it?"

"With the new ending, yeah. Kind of a different deal now, huh? I still can't believe it."

"So where exactly would he be?" I said.

"Well, he was going to film in the lake house eventually, but he can't get in there yet. Personally, I think that's a little morbid. You know what happened up there . . ."

"Yeah, I believe so."

"So if he's not there, I think he was gonna set up some of the outdoor scenes first. You know where Port Crescent State Park is? It's just about a mile down the road from the house. Take the left instead of the right and you can't miss it."

"Okay," I said, "I really appreciate it."

"Are you with the other film company? The one that's putting up all the new money?"

"No, I'm not. What, you're saying they're not only still making the movie, they're making it even bigger?"

"Biggest thing that ever happened to Bad Axe," she said. "Can you even imagine?"

I just shook my head at that one and got out of there.

• • •

It was strange to be driving up that same road again. I took the left instead of the right, like the woman had said, and headed west along the Lake Huron coast. It didn't take long to get to the park. It was mostly empty at this time of year, just a few cars in the parking lot and one unmarked van. Beyond that, just spring mud and dead grass, bare trees, and the cold water of Lake Huron in the distance. I parked and walked toward the water, passing empty picnic tables. I didn't see anybody at first. Then I finally spotted a small group of people to my left. They were all congregated down by a small clearing on the edge of the water.

As I made my way closer, I saw that Connie was among them. There were three other people, two men and a woman, all of them young. They were all looking up into the trees while Connie took a camera off its tripod. A modern camera, surely digital instead of film, nothing like the old Bolex camera I had just seen at his son's apartment. None of them heard me approaching on the wet ground.

I was ten feet away from them when I saw the rope hanging from the tree branch. That stopped me dead in my tracks. I stood there looking at the rope and the way the trees framed the view of the lake and it all hit me at once. The way this part of the land jutted out into the lake, we were even facing west. With the clearing and trees and everything else, it was as perfect a place as you could find to reenact the hanging, without actually driving all the way to Misery Bay.

Connie finally turned and saw me. "Oh great," he said. "I should have known. If the FBI comes around, that means you'll show up, too."

"Are you really doing what I think you're doing?"

"I'm finishing the movie, pal. I'm telling the story, no matter where it goes."

"No matter where it goes? Are you kidding me? Seven people were murdered."

"I know that. Don't you think I know that? I have to live with it every day."

"So why not turn lemons into lemonade, right?"

"What are you talking about?"

"I assume the agents told you what happened last night."

"Yes, they did. They talked to the woman I was with all night, too. So they know it couldn't have been me."

"I need a minute alone with you," I said. "Tell your crew they'll have to wait to film your sickening little scene here."

"We're not filming, genius. There'll be thirty people here when we do that. Have you ever seen a movie being made before?"

I stepped closer to him. "Tell them to leave us alone for a while."

He didn't even blink. "Take five, guys," he said.

The three kids all looked at each other, probably wondering where the hell they were supposed to go take their five. We were standing on the edge of a lake, after all.

"Go to the van," Connie said. "I'll let you know when we can get back to work here."

I waited for the kids to leave. "This is sickening," I said, nodding to the rope.

"I'm sorry if you disapprove. But it's not your family's story and it's not any of your business to begin with."

"Whatever, I don't care. I came to tell you something important about your son."

"He had nothing to do with this," he said. "And neither did I. We're both in the clear, and you know what? Think about it. Some other police officer's daughter takes a handful of pills? Are they gonna come back here every time somebody tries to kill themselves?"

"She didn't try to kill herself, you idiot."

He took one step closer to me. "How do you know? Did you talk to her personally? People do commit suicide, you know. I'm sorry if she did, but that's life. And that's all I have to say to you. You're not even a cop, remember?"

"You're right, I'm not. So guess what, I can go ahead and beat the hell out of you right here."

"How do you figure on doing that?"

"You're making this real easy," I said, taking my coat off. "I've been waiting a while for this, believe me."

He turned away from me, shaking his head. He put the camera down on the ground, carefully. Then he grabbed the tripod and collapsed it into a long rod.

"I've been waiting, too," he said, holding the tripod out in front of him like some kind of samurai sword.

"Put that down," I said. "You're gonna break it."

"I'm gonna break something all right."

He took a swing at me as I backed away. He took another swing. This one was hard enough to make a loud whoosh as it passed a few inches from my face.

"This isn't a fair fight," I said, taking another step backward. "Give me my own stick and we'll have something."

He was done talking for a while. He took another swing and I had to step back to avoid a tree. As long as he was taking big swings, I thought I'd probably be able to time my move, but now he was lining me up with one jab after another.

I tried to give him a head fake. He jabbed and just missed. Another fake and he caught me right in my bad shoulder. He smiled as he saw me wince in pain.

I tried to catch the next jab. I managed to knock the tip away but I couldn't grab it. I took a quick look behind me. I had about ten more feet until I'd hit a patch of mud and probably lose my footing.

Another jab, so close to my mouth I could practically taste the metal. Then another and I knew I'd have to try something soon while I still had the chance.

I've got to time this just right, I thought. Jab, miss, jab, miss. And go.

Just before he backed me up to the edge of the mud, on that very last jab I leaned one way, then spun back the other. He caught me in the bad shoulder again, making everything go dizzy for a second but it was too late now. I completed my little spin move and lashed out with my left hand, knocking the pole hard with my wrist. I kept moving forward as he tried to recover, but it was too late for him. It was too late and I was too pissed off and my shoulder hurt like hell and I had driven way too far to have this clown jabbing at me with a stick in the first place. I tackled him and drove him backward, across the rough ground until he lost his balance and went tumbling onto his back with me right on top of him. I twisted the stupid tripod out of his hands and brought it down against his neck. After all the waiting and watching and talking and driving myself crazy thinking about who'd be killed next, I admit it felt good to finally be doing something about it, to be pressing that cold metal against his skin.

"I should strangle you right here," I said. He had his hands on the tripod in a futile effort to push it away from his neck. I had all the leverage and I could have choked him right out with twenty seconds of even pressure.

"Get off me," he said, spraying my face with his spittle. "I swear, I'll kill you."

"How are you gonna do that?"

"I'll hunt you down like an animal. I swear."

"I don't think so. You're only one-quarter crazy, remember?"

I took the tripod away from his neck and tossed it aside. It landed next to the camera, knocking it over into the dirt.

"Watch it!" he said. "Do you know how much that thing cost?"

He started to get up, but I put one hand on his chest. "Do not move," I said.

"I'm getting all wet here."

He tried to get up again, so I really gave him a good shove this time. He was reaching for something else to swing at me. I grabbed him by the coat and put my face close to his.

"Your son is gone," I said.

"He was close to his grandfather. He's been taking it hard, so I told him to stay at home for a while."

"No, you don't get it. *Your son is gone.*"

"What are you talking about? The agents were at his apartment this morning. He was there."

"And then he left. His girlfriend has no idea where he was going."

That finally got to him. I let him sit up.

"Sean is gone?" he said. "I don't get it. Where would he go?"

"That's what we need to figure out. He left right after the agents talked to him. Apparently he got a phone call, and Sean promised this person, whoever it was, that he'd meet him somewhere and that he'd bring something for him."

"Bring what?"

"I understand somebody broke into the lake house this morning," I said. "They tore up the basement."

"That's what the agents said, yeah. I haven't seen it myself. They won't let me go near the place."

"Whoever it was, he was probably looking for the film. It was *his* film, not your father's . . ."

"Wait, hold on." He took out his cell phone and dialed. I knew he was calling his son. He held up his hand to me while it rang and rang. Eventually, he closed it.

"Tell me who else could have gotten into that basement," I said. "Not just today, but I'm assuming this goes back a while. Probably the last three months."

"That's what the agents wanted to know," he said. "We spent the whole morning making up a list."

"How big a list are we talking about?"

"Anybody who's ever worked for Grindstone knows how to get into that house. Hell, anybody who's even *been* there. It's like the resident party house for anybody in Bad Axe who knew my father."

I flashed back to Connie taking me into the house that day, and how he took the key off that hook under the front porch.

"So how many people did you come up with?" I said.

"It was like forty, fifty people? Those were just the ones I could think of. The agents said they were going to start working through them today."

"While you kept working on your little project here." I pulled the rope down from the tree and threw it aside.

"They told me to stay out of the way, so I am. Now where the hell is my son?"

"You're probably the only one who can figure this out," I said, "so keep thinking. Out of all those people on the list, who is he closest to?"

"I don't know. I can't think. My mind is just going around in circles here."

I ran back the scene in the apartment, trying to remember everything his girlfriend had said. I had a gut feeling that there was one more question I should have asked her. Meanwhile, Connie was running through every name he could think of.

"Brian, no. Craig, no way. Zack, no. Wait, Zack? No."

"Hold on," I said. "Whoever this is, he had to have access to a camera, right?"

"Yeah, I guess." He went back to the list in his head.

"Like that Bolex in your son's apartment. Delaney said he never let anybody touch it. Is that right? Nobody else could have used it?"

"I don't think so, no."

"So did this person take a camera from the basement?"

"Maybe," he said, waving his hand at me like I was a pesky fly. "I'm trying to think here, okay? No, to answer your question. I don't think so. My father would have noticed that. He would have freaked out, probably, if one of his beloved cameras was gone."

"Unless he gave one to somebody."

"That didn't happen very often, believe me. He'd give you a bag of weed or a thousand dollars cash if you needed it. But one of his old cameras?"

"He gave one to Sean, right? And he gave one to you . . ."

"No," he said. "Will you let me think, for God's sake? He never gave me a camera."

"Wait a minute, Sean told me a Wiley kid gets a camera as soon as he's old enough to hold one."

"My father wasn't even around when I was a kid, remember? I never got to do any of that stuff with him."

"So who else is Sean talking about?" I said. "If it was just him, he wouldn't say it that way."

I thought back on it. Sitting in that sandwich shop, the first time I had met him. Yes, that's what he said. A Wiley kid gets a camera as soon as he's old enough to hold one.

"What about your sister?" I said.

"Corina? No. No way. I think it's more of a recent thing. Just the grandsons. Now shut up for one minute, okay?"

He was still sitting on the ground. I was kneeling next to him. The water on the lake was gently lapping against the shore and I wanted to pick up the tripod and put it back on his neck. Just the grandsons, he says.

"What other grandsons are you talking about, Connie? Are you telling me Sean has a brother?"

"No, Corina's son. Bobby."

"Your nephew."

"My half-nephew."

I closed my eyes for a moment and rubbed my forehead. I counted to three.

"Your half-nephew," I said. "Bobby. What's his last name?"

"Bergman."

"That name is familiar. Where have I seen that name?"

"Hell if I know."

"Hold on," I said. "The court records in your father's room. The man he assaulted was named Bergman."

"Darryl Bergman, yeah. Bobby's father."

"The loser your sister married . . ."

"That's why my father beat the hell out of him, yeah. I think he felt bad that Bobby had to go through the same shit he did as a kid."

I waited for the quarter to drop. Connie just sat there looking up at me.

"Your nephew . . . ," I said.

"Half-nephew."

I had to close my eyes again.

"Wait a minute," he said, finally getting it. "Are you serious? Bobby Bergman? There's no way."

"Why not?"

"This kid's a marshmallow. He's afraid of his own shadow. He couldn't kill a mosquito, I swear to God. Now, will you just leave me alone for a minute?"

"Did you mention him to the agents, by any chance?"

"Of course not," he said. "Don't be ridiculous. I'm telling you, there's no way. That kid's like a beaten dog."

"Maybe there's more to him than you think,"

I said. "When's the last time you saw him?"

"I don't know. Like four years ago? Yeah, right after the fire."

It took me a moment to process those last words. It took him the same moment to realize what he had just said. We had both been in that same basement, watching that same film. We had both seen the same scene. The same fire.

"Oh my God," he said, his face turning white.

"What fire, Connie?"

"The fire that killed his father. Bobby was eighteen then. Sean was seventeen. He came down to stay with us for a couple of days. Hardly said a word the whole time."

"Came down from where?"

"From up north. He lived in Houghton then. I think he was getting ready to go to that college, the one in Houghton."

"Michigan Tech."

"Yeah," Connie said. "That's the one. Michigan Tech."

"Is he still up there?"

"I don't know. I guess. Probably."

"Does Sean still talk to him?"

"Maybe. Once in a while. He always felt bad for him, I know that."

"Unlike you, who couldn't give a damn about him. Your *half*-nephew."

"Screw you anyway," he said, "but wait, are we really both thinking—"

"Yeah," I said. "We're both thinking we just figured out who your son went to see."

"Hold on." He rolled over to get up. I could see his pants were soaked.

"We don't have any more time to waste," I said. "Do you have an address for this kid?"

"Why would he go see Bobby? That's insane! We have to find him!"

"Connie, do you have an address or not?"

"No! He wasn't even in college yet. I have no idea."

"A phone number? Anything?"

"No!"

"Okay, then I'll just start heading up there. I'll call the agents on the way."

"I'm coming with you."

"The hell you are," I said. "You've got a movie to finish, remember? Sorry to mess up your new ending, by the way. It looks like your father might not have been a murderer after all."

CHAPTER TWENTY

When I got back on the road, I picked up my cell phone and called Agent Long. All those times I'd been tempted to call her, this sure as hell wasn't the conversation I had in mind.

"Listen carefully," I said. "Did an agent talk to Sean Wiley this morning?"

"Alex, what's going on?"

374

"Just tell me. Did an agent talk to Sean Wiley?"

"That's the grandson. Yes."

"Did he say anything about his cousin?"

There was a moment of silence on the line.

"Alex, what cousin?" she said.

"God damn it."

"What are you talking about? What cousin?"

"Clyde C. Wiley has another grandson," I said. "From his daughter Corina. His name is Bobby Bergman, and apparently he's going to school at Michigan Tech."

"Where are you?"

"I'm on the road, just outside of Bad Axe. Did you hear what I said?"

"Yes. So let me get this information before I kill you. Bobby Bergman. Michigan Tech. How did you find this out?"

"Connie told me."

"Connie? What are you doing talking to him? I swear to God, Alex . . ."

"Just listen. Bobby's father's name was Darryl Bergman. When Wiley was arrested ten years ago? It all started with an attack on Darryl."

"I remember that part, yes. But I don't remember anything about a son . . ."

"You had no reason to look for that," I said, "but now you'll probably want to go dig up the full arrest record."

"I'll look into it. So you're on your way back home now, right?"

"That's one option."

"Alex—"

"I think Sean's headed up to Houghton," I said. "If you can find out where Bobby Bergman lives, you'd better send somebody out there right away. In fact, you know what, I talked to the Houghton County undersheriff when I was up there. You should give him a call and have him go find Bergman before something else happens."

"Okay, wait. If he's really at Michigan Tech—"

"That would be a hell of a coincidence, wouldn't you say?"

"Because one of our victims went to school there."

"Exactly. Plus there's a good chance Bergman has the right kind of camera to make that film."

Another silence.

"Tell me what you're really saying here, Alex. Are you saying this kid is the one we're looking for?"

"That's what we need to find out."

"If he did all of this . . . and filmed it . . . how did the film end up with Wiley?"

"He had the editing equipment, remember? So a little trip down to Grandpa's house. He knows how to find the place. I'm sure he knows where the key is."

"Then Wiley finds it and watches it . . ."

"And boom."

"Heart attack," she said. "He wasn't working on the film at all. He just watched it. One time."

"Yeah, I watched it one time and I'm surprised I didn't have a heart attack myself. Oh, and you know what else? You remember the fire?"

"In the film? One of the first few scenes? Yeah, we haven't been able to figure that one out yet, but—"

"Bobby Bergman's house burned down four years ago. It killed his father."

Another silence.

"We've been working through a long list of suspects," she said. "We would have come back to the family eventually. We would have found this connection."

"I know that. I'm not blaming you."

"And yet I feel like I'm defending myself whenever I talk to you," she said. "It's like you're always two steps ahead of me."

"Blind luck," I said. "Never mind. How's Maven's daughter?"

"No word yet."

"I'll have my cell phone here. Call me back as soon as you can."

"Alex, you're not going to Houghton, okay? Just go back home."

"I can't do that," I said. "Not now. Call me back. Please."

I hung up the phone and kept driving.

I stopped just north of Bay City to fill the tank and grab some food. It was about three o'clock in the afternoon now, on a cold but clear day. A great day for driving all over the state. I was three and a half hours from home. Or seven hours from Houghton.

It all goes back to that first death, I thought as I got back in the truck. It *has* to, right? Charlie Razniewski Jr. hanging from that tree in the middle of the night . . . it was the first death, and if you think about it, it was the one death that probably took a lot more planning than all of the others. With a clean getaway we still haven't figured out.

Yes, it was definitely the biggest and boldest death of them all. What better place to do that than a carefully chosen spot just down the road from where you live?

I checked my cell phone. I was still in the Lower Peninsula, so I still had good reception. Just call me, I thought. Tell me you sent somebody over there and picked up Bergman. He's behind bars as we speak. And Sean Wiley is safely on his way back home.

Call me and tell me that right now.

The phone stayed silent. I kept driving.

I was getting close to the Mackinac Bridge when my phone finally rang. It was just before six o'clock.

378

"What do you have?" I said.

"Where are you?"

"Just below the bridge. How's Maven's daughter now?"

"They're cautiously optimistic right now."

"Good," I said, letting out a breath. "That's good to hear."

"We're on our way up right now," she said. "We're about three hours behind you. So I think you should just stop and let us catch up to you."

"Did you find Bobby Bergman?"

"Not really, no."

"What do you mean, 'not really'?"

"Well, you were right about the Michigan Tech connection. He was definitely going to school there."

"He *was* going to school there?"

"He dropped out at the end of last year."

"Where is he now?"

"Unknown, Alex. I've got nothing on him at all since the end of the last school year."

"It's April now, so that's like a full year ago. Where the hell could he be?"

"He's not at Tech anymore. That's all I can tell you."

"Damn," I said. "So how do we find him?"

"Well, he did grow up in Houghton. He may still be in town, but we don't have an address for him. It's like he just disappeared off the face of the earth."

I let out another breath, feeling dead tired now. After so many miles today, and now I had no idea where I was going.

"Alex, are you still there?"

"I'm here."

"We confirmed what you said about the father. He died in that fire, four years ago."

"A house fire that was captured on film."

"Apparently so. It gets better. I went back and took a closer look at the daily logs. That day Wiley attacked his son-in-law, you know what else Steele and Haggerty did, besides making that arrest?"

"Tell me."

"They drove Bobby Bergman and his mother back home to Houghton, right after their shift ended."

"What? Why, were they in the car with Wiley?"

"No, that would have shown up in the arrest record. Apparently, the two of them ended up at the St. Ignace station somehow, and those two officers drove them home."

"That makes no sense."

"No, it doesn't. If you look at Darryl's sheet here, by the way, it's mostly minor stuff— possession, simple assault, general misdemeanors. But there were a few domestics, too. If Wiley came all the way out from California, he must have been trying to help them get away, right? Why would they end up going back home?"

"We'll just have to ask Bergman when we find him," I said. "But you really don't have an address? Is that what you're telling me?"

"No, we don't."

"Do you have any prior addresses?"

I heard muffled voices on the other end of the line.

"Janet, are you there? Is that Fleury?"

"We're on our way out there," she said. "Please just let us handle this, okay?"

"Just give me his last known address, then. I'm closer than you are."

"I can't do that, Alex."

I let a few seconds pass. I drove and I listened to the distant hum of static on the line.

"Hey," I said, "how come you didn't correct me this time?"

"What are you talking about?"

"I called you Janet and you let it slide."

"Alex, I'm serious. You need to stop right now."

"I'll see you in Houghton," I said. "Drive carefully." I ended the call.

My signal was starting to fade as I crossed the bridge. Before it disappeared completely, I went to my saved numbers and looked up Leon's cell phone. It rang twice and then he picked up.

"Leon," I said. "Are you at work?"

"No, I'm home. I actually have a night off for once."

"I'm sorry to bother you, but I just need you to look up an address for me if you can."

"Sure thing, just tell me what I'm looking for."

"The name is Bobby Bergman and the address is Houghton. The problem is, this address might be a little old. He hasn't lived there since last year."

I heard the clicking of keys, and then in the background I heard Eleanor's voice, asking Leon who was on the phone. I wasn't sure what the exact trouble threshold would be in that household, if just talking to me on the phone would get things going again.

"Eleanor says hello," Leon said, still working away at his keyboard. "She also says you need to stop by and have dinner some time."

"So she can kill me, right? Look, I don't want to get you in hot water again. I wouldn't be calling if this wasn't important."

"It's okay. It's just a phone call, and besides, we came to an agreement. She knows I can't help myself, so whenever you drag me into this stuff, it's all your fault, not mine. I'm just a helpless pawn in your wicked game."

"I really owe you, Leon. Yet again."

"Not a problem. As a matter of fact, I'm seeing three different addresses here."

"Three? What are you talking about?"

"I'm going back in time, Alex. On the Internet.

I can go back about ten years and see everywhere he lived."

"You can really do that?"

"You really need to get a computer. Can we set you up with one, please?"

"Then I'd have no excuse to call you," I said. "But seriously, can you tell me those addresses? And while you're at it, maybe help me find where they are?"

I pulled over for a minute and wrote everything down. When he was done, I thanked him, told him to kiss Eleanor for me, then thanked him again. I don't know how much of it he heard, because that's about when the signal cut out for good. I put the phone down and got back on the road, taking that first exit past the bridge, to that thin lonely U.S. Highway 2 that runs along the shores of Lake Michigan, straight west into the setting sun, toward Houghton.

It felt strange to be back in Copper Country, where everything had begun. Winter wasn't gone for good quite yet, but now it seemed to be fighting a losing battle. Where the snow had melted away there was dead ground and what deciduous trees there were looked like they'd never carry leaves again. I knew it would all come and it would come quickly, but tonight as my headlights swept across the empty road, the springtime felt like a fairy tale.

It was just after ten o'clock at night when I finally hit Houghton. There were lights now, and people driving around in their cars, but that empty feeling of foreboding I had brought with me didn't go away. Maybe I was just too tired now, but I'd spent so many hours on the road and I knew there was a good chance I'd find something horrible here, just as Sean's girlfriend had predicted.

As I went down the main street in Houghton, past the college buildings and the fraternities and everything else, I saw a lot more kids outside than I would have expected. They were walking up and down the sidewalks, some of them carrying beer bottles and most of them underdressed for the weather. I guess if you go to school in Houghton, an April night with the temperature just above freezing must feel like Bermuda.

I found the first address Leon had given me on the east side of town, not far from the college. This was the most recent address, I thought. This is where the trail will be warmest. I parked the truck on the street and sat there for a moment, still feeling the road and hearing the hum of the engine after so many hours of driving.

It was an old house, subdivided into several small apartments. I rang the doorbell. A young woman answered and told me that nobody named Bobby Bergman lived there anymore. It was all women now, as a matter of fact, and no, she had no idea where Bergman may have moved to. They pick up these rentals on a yearly basis, after all, and whoever lived there in previous years was nothing more than a foreign name to them. I thanked her and left.

The next address was right on campus. It was one of the main dormitories. I knew that would be even more of a dead end than the apartment.

The last address was over on the west side of town, away from the college. I wasn't sure what I'd be able to find out there, but what the hell. So I drove all the way through town, past the bridge, and made my way through the side streets until I found Waterworks Drive. I started tracking the house numbers. They were going up, so I was heading in the right direction. An even number, I thought, so definitely on this side of the street. Getting closer now. One more house.

Boom, here it is.

Nothing.

There was no house there at all, just an empty lot with a low mound of dirt where the house should have been. I rechecked the addresses on either side of the lot. This was it.

I parked the truck, got out, and then stood there looking at the empty lot.

This is the neighborhood, I thought, looking up and down the street. That first scene in the film, it was taken right here. Meaning that this empty lot was—

I sensed a movement to my right. I looked over at the house next door, saw a woman's face peering out at me from between the front window curtains.

Somebody's definitely awake next door, I thought, and she likes to know what's going on in her neighborhood. Maybe she likes to talk about it, too.

I went up her walkway and knocked on her front door. After a few seconds, I heard the deadbolt sliding and then the door opened up just a crack, with the little security chain rattling on its latch, making sure the door wouldn't open any farther. The same woman I had seen in the window was now looking at me. She was in her late sixties maybe, and she was wearing a pink robe and pink slippers. I could see a cat rubbing itself against the backs of her legs.

"I'm sorry to bother you, ma'am. Can I just ask you a couple of questions?"

"Who are you?"

"I'm a private investigator, ma'am." At that moment, I wished I had one of those stupid cards Leon had made for us, once upon a time. "Can I come inside for a moment?"

"I'd rather talk to you from here, if you don't mind."

"Fair enough." I wasn't about to point out to her that her little chain wouldn't have stopped any able-bodied person, if that person really wanted to come inside her house. "Can you tell me, did the house next door burn down?"

"It sure did."

"About four years ago, right?"

"Yep. Burned right to the ground. They had to come out with a bulldozer and clean it all out. Then they filled the foundation with dirt. It was two weeks of unholy racket, I'll tell you that much."

"The family who lived there," I said. "Those were the Bergmans, right?"

"The Bergmans, yes. The father's the one who died in the fire."

"Did you know them well?"

"I lived next door to that family for a long time, mister, but I think Darryl Bergman might have said three words to me the whole time. That man was as mean as a snake. I never meant to pry, but I couldn't help noticing what was going on over there. Police cars coming by, his wife with the bruises on her face, young Bobby always looking like he was afraid of his own shadow."

"There was a man named Clyde C. Wiley," I said. "An actor. He came out here one time, about ten years ago . . ."

"I sure remember that day, yes. He came over and beat up on Darryl, then the wife and kid went tearing down the street in Darryl's old truck. That was a hell of a day, I tell you. I've never heard such language."

"You saw it happen?"

"Sure did. I thought they were running away from the scary-looking biker guy, but then it turned out he was the father, just trying to help them get away. The wife and Bobby came right back, though, so I guess it didn't work. Things got even worse after that, let me tell you."

"So you were also here when Mrs. Bergman committed suicide?"

"Yes, sir. That was another heck of a day right there. The police came out and I thought they were just gonna talk to Darryl again, but then the ambulance showed up and they wheeled her out on a stretcher with a sheet over her head. I saw some of the blood seeping through the sheet, from where she cut her own wrists."

"That was about nine years ago, right? About a year after that other incident?"

"Has it been nine years already? I guess it has."

"You're being very helpful, ma'am. I appreciate you taking the time to talk to me."

"I know it's not a Christian thing to say, but I didn't mind it all that much when that house burned down with Darryl inside it. I truly didn't."

"I understand. I only have one more question for you. Do you have any idea where Bobby Bergman may be right now?"

"Haven't seen him since the fire," she said, shaking her head. "Poor kid. Some people shouldn't have to go through that much misery in their life, you know what I mean? I think that old camera of his was his only friend."

"An old movie camera?"

"An ancient thing, yes. He was always horsing around with it. He took a movie of me one day. I think I might have given him a funny look about it."

Of course, I thought. That was you. You were in that one scene, looking over the fence.

"Then I felt bad afterwards," she said. "I should have been a better neighbor to the boy."

"No, I'm sure you were just fine. Thanks again for talking to me. You have a good night."

She said something to her cat as she closed the door. As I left, I heard the deadbolt sliding back into place. After everything that had happened next door, I couldn't blame her for being a little scared, even if the house itself was nothing more than a memory now.

"Where are you now, Bobby Bergman?" I said, taking one last look at the empty lot. "And wherever you are, is your cousin with you?"

I got back in the truck. As long as I was here in town, there was one more place to go.

CHAPTER TWENTY-ONE

I drove back downtown, past the overflowing bars and up the hill toward Charlie Razniewski's old apartment building. Everything looked different without the waist-high snowbanks, but I found the building more or less where I remembered it. I parked the truck and took another breath of fresh air as I got out, hoping it would wake me up and help me get through the rest of this night.

I knocked on the door of the apartment. A few seconds later, the door was pulled open. It was Wayne, the kid I remembered as being Charlie's best friend, even if that friendship had been complicated by the business with Charlie's girlfriend. I blanked on her name for a moment, then it came to me. Rebecca.

"Mr. McKnight? What are you doing here?"

"Can I come in for a second?"

"Sure, of course."

He let me in and I had to step around a stack of boxes just to get in the place. The big television was gone now, along with all of the other equipment that had dominated the far wall of the living room. Nevertheless, I could hear the thump of some kind of rock music coming from one of the bedrooms.

"Don't mind the destruction here," he said.

"You sorta caught us in the middle of packing."

"What's going on? Is the school year over already?"

"Yeah, this is the last week of finals."

"Okay, now I get it. All the parties in town . . ."

"Yeah, it's kinda crazy, but I'm sorry, do you want to sit down or anything? I mean, what's going on? Is everything all right?"

"Sure, I'll sit down for one minute. I won't take up much of your time, I promise. I just have a couple more questions for you."

"Okay . . ." He looked confused, but he cleared off two chairs and half of the dining room table.

"How's Rebecca?"

"Oh, she's good. I'll be seeing her in a few minutes. At the Downtowner."

"That was the bar where I talked to everybody," I said. "All of Charlie's friends."

"Yeah, that's the one."

"Well, I'll get right to it, Wayne, so you don't miss your date. A lot of crazy things have been happening ever since I first came out here. I now have reason to believe that Charlie didn't really kill himself."

I watched that one sink in.

"I don't understand," he said. "What kind of crazy things are you talking about?"

"There were more deaths, in Sault Ste. Marie, in Marquette, a few other places."

"I didn't hear about anything like that.

Although, you know, I've got so much going on here at school . . ."

"Charlie's father was murdered," I said. "That's the first thing I should really tell you. It happened just after I came out here."

The color drained from his face. He tried to say something, but couldn't make the words come out.

"You didn't hear anything about that?" I said.

"Nobody told me. I swear to God."

"You know what, I should have called back out here myself. I apologize. I guess I just assumed you would have heard."

He shook his head. He was staring down at the table.

"So here's my question," I said. "I want to run a name by you . . ."

"Mr. McKnight, is that you?"

I looked up and saw one of the other roommates walking down the hallway toward us. It was the big kid, with the bad skin. He was carrying a framed poster of a woman in a bikini sitting on the hood of a red Ferrari.

"Bradley," I said, pulling the name out of nowhere. "You're Bradley, right?"

"That's right, you got a good memory. What brings you to town?"

"Just asking Wayne a couple questions here, and actually, if you've got a minute . . ."

"Yeah, hey, I'm sorry about the loud music.

Why didn't you guys tell me you were talking out here?"

He leaned the poster against some boxes and retreated down the hallway.

"Guys talking out there and they don't even tell me I should turn the music down . . ." His voice trailed off as he went back into his bedroom. That was the other thing I remembered about him. That kid was a real motormouth.

"He's actually a great guy," Wayne said. "You just have to put up with a few things. Like his fine taste in art."

I smiled at the comment and looked down at the artwork in question. Hot girl in bikini, hot sports car. How can you go wrong?

That's when I noticed what was behind it. It wasn't one framed poster he was carrying. It was two framed posters. He had fanned them out when he leaned them against the boxes. I got up and pulled the first poster so I could see the second in its entirety.

A young Clyde C. Wiley, sitting on his bike. It was the movie poster for *Road Hogs*.

"Okay, I'm all set," Bradley said as he came back down the hallway. "What kind of questions do you have for me? I hope it's not geography."

I put the poster down.

"Wayne," I said, "didn't you say you have to go meet Rebecca?"

"Well, yeah, but—"

"Go ahead. You don't want to keep her waiting."

"It's really okay, she's going to be—"

"Just get out of here," I said to him. "Tell her hello for me."

He stood there for one more awkward moment, then he grabbed his coat and left. Bradley had picked up on the sudden change of mood. He stood there looking at me and for once in his life he wasn't babbling away.

"Sit down," I said.

"What's going on?"

"Just sit down."

He did as he was told. I took my own chair back. I looked at him across the table and waited a few seconds.

"Mr. McKnight, tell me what's going on."

"You know, you complimented me on remembering your name, but you picked up my name right away."

"You came out here to ask all those questions about Charlie," he said. "Of course I remember you."

"But I had a lot more names to remember. That's what you're saying."

"You must have talked to a dozen people that night. So, yeah."

"I think Bradley's a fine name. Maybe that's why I remembered it."

"Um, okay. Thanks?" He was looking more rattled by the second.

"Good, strong name. Bradley. It's distinctive. Don't you agree?"

"Um, yes."

"Just tell me one thing," I leaned in for the kill. "Is Bradley your real name?"

"Yes." He said it without blinking, and he looked genuinely surprised at the question.

"Where'd you get that poster?" Time to switch gears.

"A poster shop. I know it's kinda dumb."

"Not the girl and the car. The other one."

"What, the movie poster?"

"Yes, the movie poster."

"RJ left it here."

"RJ?"

"Our other roommate. You met him. He left it here so I figured I could just take it. Is that a big problem? If you don't think I should have taken it, why don't you just—"

"Bradley," I said. "Shut up a second. Where's RJ?"

"I told you, he left."

"When?"

"Like a few weeks ago. Three weeks? Four weeks?"

"Okay, wait, stop." I had ten questions in my mind and I had to take a moment to put them in order. "Where did he go?"

"I don't know. He didn't say where he was going."

"He just left? Without saying a word?"

"Yeah, pretty much. It was kinda weird."

"Okay," I said. "Okay. RJ. Yeah, I remember him now. Tall guy, dark hair?"

"Yeah . . ."

"And those initials. RJ . . ."

I stopped dead. I didn't even have to ask him, but he told me anyway.

"Robert James," he said. "Everybody called him RJ."

"His last name?"

"Bergman."

"Son of a bitch." I slapped the table loud enough to make him jump.

"What's the matter?"

"I was right here. Right in this apartment. I talked to him. I asked him questions."

"You're starting to scare me here. What's going on?"

"This is very important," I said. "You have to help me figure out where RJ is right now."

"I told you, he left. He just didn't come back one day."

"Come back from where?"

"Well, he was always leaving for a few days at a time. He said he was going to the cottage for a while."

"The cottage?"

"Well, that's just it. He said he was watching a house for a professor of his who retired and moved down south, but he'd never say where the cottage was. I asked him about it once and he said he didn't want all of us going up there and trying to have a big party or something. He was kind of a strange guy sometimes—have I said that yet?"

"I believe you, but get back to that cottage. Do you think he could be up there right now?"

"Maybe. I don't know. It's just weird because I haven't seen him around at all since what, the beginning of the month? Like right after you came out here. But how do you just ditch all your classes like that?"

"I got news for you," I said. "RJ left school last year."

"That's impossible. He lived here. He was going to school. He went to class every day."

"Did you have him in any of your classes?"

"No. I'm electrical engineering. He was video production or something like that."

"So you never actually saw him attending an actual class."

"No—but wait, that's just weird, then. What kind of person would pretend to be in college and not go to any classes?"

"Let me ask you something else," I said. "How come RJ doesn't have this place listed as his official address?"

"Well, technically, we're only supposed to have three people in this apartment," he said, looking a little sheepish. "When RJ moved in, he offered to double up with me in my room, even though it only had the one desk."

"And you guys agreed to that?"

"He was paying the same amount of money, even though he didn't have a desk or much room for anything really. So it made everybody's rent lower. I know we probably shouldn't have done it."

"Don't worry about it," I said. "How did RJ and Charlie meet, anyway? Were you here then?"

"No, but it sounds like they went way back, to like freshman year. Funny, though, they never seemed to have that much in common. I'm not sure how they ever decided to live together."

Maybe one of them just had way too much motivation, I thought.

"One last thing," I said. "RJ's got a cousin named Sean Wiley. He lives down in Bad Axe. You ever see him up here?"

"No, but I think I've heard RJ talking to him on the phone."

"How often did that happen?"

"I don't know. Once every couple of months, maybe? I'd answer the phone sometimes when he called. He always seemed like a nice guy."

"Yeah, he is," I said. "There's a good chance he's with RJ right now. So is there any way we can figure out where that cottage is? You said he was looking after it for a retired professor. Do you know which one?"

"No, sorry."

"We'd have to go through his records and find out all the classes he took. Then we'd have to get hold of those professors . . ." I was working it through in my mind, talking it out, trying to find an angle.

"I think it's on a lake," he said. "Does that help?"

"Yes, it does. Which lake?"

"I don't know. He just said it that one time. The cottage is on a lake and 'I don't want anybody else coming up there having a big party and no, you can't come with me because I'm the only one who's allowed to go there.'"

"He said that? Those exact words."

"Pretty much."

"He said *a* lake. Not *the* lake."

"Yes. A lake."

"Because if he said *the* lake, it would be Lake Superior, right?"

"Right. There's only one *the* lake around here."

"Okay, so a smaller lake," I said. "And did he actually say, what did you just say, now, he didn't want you guys coming *up* there to have a party?"

"He said up, yes."

"You're sure?"

"Yes. He said up."

"What kind of car does he drive?"

"A junky old Subaru. Black."

"So a black Subaru," I said, "sitting next to a cottage on one of the inner lakes, north of Houghton. I wonder how many there are."

"You want to see a map?"

I smiled at him. My first real smile of the whole day. I was sure it would probably be my last, but for that one moment I felt almost human again.

"Bradley, you are a good man to have around," I said. "Don't let anybody ever tell you otherwise."

I was about to get up. Then I thought of one more thing.

"Do you remember that story you told me about how Charlie's father was giving him a hard time about switching to forestry?"

"Was that me?"

"Yeah, don't you remember? You said his father didn't understand why he'd give up law enforcement and go study forestry? It was a big thing between them? They had a big fight about it?"

Looking back on it, it sounded to me now like somebody was trying to make Charles Razniewski Sr. feel one hundred percent responsible for his son taking his own life. Like the ultimate twist of the knife.

"I have a bad habit of just saying stuff without thinking, Mr. McKnight. I really should have kept my mouth shut."

"But did Charlie really say those things?"

"What do you mean?"

"I mean, did Charlie really complain that much about his father?"

"Well, he didn't really say it to *me* so much."

"Didn't say it to *you?*"

"No, now that I think of it, it was RJ he talked to most of the time. I don't know, maybe RJ might have said something to me about it. Like I said, I should have kept my mouth shut."

But you didn't, I thought. RJ *knew* you wouldn't. In case it ever came up in the future . . . he didn't have to say a thing about it, just put a quarter in your slot and stand back. Like a director feeding lines to one of his actors.

A few minutes later, I was back in my truck. I had a good map of the Keweenaw Peninsula on the seat next to me. I called Agent Long on my cell phone.

"What the hell's going on?" she said. Her voice broke up slightly, making me believe she was still in her car. "Where are you?"

"Robert James Bergman is most likely somewhere north of Houghton right now. Sean could very well be with him. If they're up here, they're in a cottage on one of the interior lakes."

"Wait, what? What are you talking about?"

"Just listen to me. I assume you're pretty close by now, but you really need to get some other people up here right away. I'll keep my cell phone on, although I don't know how good the signal will be once I leave Houghton."

"Alex, damn it, I want you to stop right now."

"Just get up here. I'm the one with the head start, and we're gonna need all the manpower we can get. Bergman's car is a black Subaru. Sean's driving a vintage Corvette, mint-green."

"Alex—"

"A mint-green Corvette. Did you hear me? That should be easy to spot."

"I got it, I got it."

"Did you hear from Chief Maven?"

"It's looking better," she said, her voice softening. "They think his daughter will be okay."

"That's great to hear. Swing and a miss this time for the evil bastard, huh?"

"Alex, you sound like you're losing your mind. You've got to let us catch up to you. You shouldn't be up there alone."

"I shouldn't be up here at all, you mean. But thanks."

"For the last time—"

"Call me when you get here," I said. Then I ended the call.

It was almost midnight now. It was dark and I was exhausted and I had no real idea where I was going. No sensible person would have gone any farther. Not another foot.

I put the truck in gear and took off.

CHAPTER TWENTY-TWO

I crossed the bridge over the canal, which was really just the western arm of Portage Lake, thinking this was probably not the lake I'd be looking for. Even if you had a cottage on the other shore, you'd say it was "across the lake" or something like that. You wouldn't say it was "up on a lake."

I went up through Ripley and Dollar Bay, each town asleep now in the dead middle of the night. Not long after that, I started to see the dark water of Torch Lake to my right. It was the biggest lake on my list, and from the looks of the map it was completely surrounded by paved roads. It probably had more cottages on it than all the other Keweenaw lakes combined, but here again I started thinking that this wouldn't be the lake I was looking for. It was attached to Portage Lake, after all, and really still part of the greater Houghton-Hancock area. If you happened to have a cottage there, I still didn't think you'd say "up on a lake." It just didn't feel "up" enough. So I kept going, passing driveway after driveway, and eventually starting to regret my decision to skip all of them. It's a pretty damned long lake, I told myself. You've been driving a while and it's starting to feel kind of "up" now.

I stayed with my original call. If I had started

403

going down every driveway here, I would have never made it past this lake. So when I got to the top of it, I swung east and headed down the county road toward Rice Lake. The map showed it surrounded by maybe three or four miles of access road. When I got to it, I started nosing my way down each driveway until my headlights lit up the cottage and whatever vehicles might be nearby. It would have been a hell of a lot easier in the daytime, or even in the middle of winter when I'd be able to see which driveways had been plowed or driven down recently. In late April, with the snow mostly gone, it was a ridiculously slow process. Still, I kept imagining Bergman in one of these cottages, not even twenty-four hours gone by since the attack on Olivia Maven. And Sean Wiley on his way up here to find him, with a fair chance he knew exactly where to go.

Another driveway, another cottage. Most of them still closed up for the winter so I had that going for me, at least. A closed-up cottage meaning no vehicle most of the time. Although whenever I saw a garage, my heart sank, because that meant there was no way to know for sure unless I drove all the way down, got out of the truck, and peeked inside.

It was 1:30 in the morning now. I was starting to lose steam. I kept telling myself one more driveway, one more driveway. This next one could be it.

When I'd circled Rice Lake, I dropped down to Mud Lake. It was tiny and only a mile away, with a handful of cottages on the northern shore. I ran through those in a matter of minutes. Then I doubled back up through Calumet and left Houghton County. I was in Keweenaw County now, the end of the line, the only piece of land left, surrounded on three sides by Lake Superior. I started wondering where Agent Long was, whether she was close or still an hour away. But when I looked at my cell phone there was absolutely no signal at all.

It was two in the morning when I turned onto the long road to Lake Gratiot. I knew the lakeshores would be less and less populated now, which meant fewer cottages to check but more distance to drive between them. One thing I knew for sure—if you owned a cottage on one of these lakes, it was definitely *up on a lake*.

The cottages on Lake Gratiot were concentrated on the western shoreline, but I had to keep driving down separate access roads to get to them. I was halfway through the lake when I pulled down a driveway and saw an old black Subaru parked right next to a small cottage.

This is the one, I thought. As I got out and walked slowly down the rest of the driveway, it occurred to me that I had come this far with no good idea about what I'd actually do when I found the place. Another typical genius move on my part.

The car was unlocked, of course, because who locks a car at a cottage on a remote lake in the Upper Peninsula? It's not like somebody's going to drive up and break into it, even though that's exactly what I was thinking I'd need to do. It was either that or go look in the windows. I figured if it was me sleeping away in my cottage, I'd prefer the first choice over the second.

I opened up the passenger's side door and hit the button for the glove compartment. I found the registration and held it up to read the name in the interior light. Here's where the owner could come out shooting, I thought, if he happened to be going to the bathroom in the middle of the night and noticed the light coming from his car.

The car was registered to someone named Patricia Curry. I put the registration back in the glove compartment, closed the door, got back in my truck, and then got the hell out of there.

I kept working my way through the rest of the cottages on that lake, and when I was done it was going on three o'clock in the morning. The little voice in my head saying just one more, just one more had apparently gone to bed, so I stopped there on the side of that little road in the middle of absolute nothingness and I put my head down on the steering wheel. Just a few minutes to rest my eyes, I thought.

Then from out of nowhere a horrible insight came to me and I was jolted awake.

I flashed back to that day in the apartment, talking to Rebecca and Wayne and Bradley and RJ. All of us sitting there at the end of the night, drinking beer and thinking about Charlie. Rebecca asked me if she could talk to Charlie's father, and I told her that he was staying at his old friend's house in Sault Ste. Marie. She didn't end up calling him, but at that point I'd already given all of them the information. Charles Razniewski Sr. wasn't in Detroit, surrounded by fellow U.S. marshals, he was right across the UP, in a normal house in a normal neighborhood. If you could guess who his old friend was—which you obviously could if you already knew so much about his history—then you could find out exactly where that house was. You could go out to Sault Ste. Marie the very next day, when you knew that he'd probably be alone. If you went early enough, you could beat me there with hours to spare.

I sat there gripping the steering wheel and trying to find a hole in my logic, but I couldn't. I was the one who made it so easy for RJ to go to Sault Ste. Marie and to find Razniewski all alone in that house. I'm the one who made it happen.

Then the second insight, almost as bad as the first. RJ could have gone right to the door and said, "Hey, I'm Charlie's apartment-mate.

Maybe he mentioned me? So sorry about what happened. Can I come in and talk to you about Charlie?" He could have sat down with him at the kitchen table, put the man at ease. When the knife finally came out, Raz never would have seen it coming.

I pounded the steering wheel until my hand went numb. Then I put the truck back into gear and drove to the next lake.

There were two more interior lakes just to the east. The tiny Deer Lake and then the much larger Lac La Belle. On the map, the roads leading to them were nameless and so thin I could hardly trace their routes in the dim light of my truck's interior. I made my way on whatever road I could find leading through the trees, guessing my way here and there and just trying to stay pointed east. I eventually found Deer Lake, with one single access road that led down to a boat launch. I didn't see any cottages at all.

I cut back to Lac La Belle. It was after three in the morning now, and I worked my way around the lake—it was probably eight miles or so, but it might have been eighty or eight hundred. I nosed down every driveway, painting every cottage with a double beam of light. Back out and go to the next, do it all over again. Keep going, keep going.

It was after four in the morning when I finished

that lake. I had come up empty. As I drove back to the main road, I saw a police car flash by at high speed. I thought it might be a Michigan State Police car, but I was honestly too exhausted to see straight. If it was the state police, I thought, then they had come up here from the nearest post, in Calumet. Otherwise, it was a county car from Eagle River. They're out looking for me or they're looking for the cottage based on whatever information the FBI may have relayed to them. Probably both. It surprised me a little, just how much I didn't want to be found yet, and how much I wanted to find that cottage first. They had all the guns and manpower and everything else to do this right, but at that moment in the cold early hours I had an absolute physical hunger to finish what I had started.

Problem was, I was running out of lakes. I was going farther and farther north, to the absolute end of the earth, and on the map I could count only four more lakes—Lake Medora, Lake Bailey, Lake Fanny Hooe, and Schlatter Lake. If I tried those and failed, then I'd be forced to face the possibility that the cottage could be on one of the many tiny, unnamed lakes that might have only one or two driveways to serve them. Or that I had actually driven right by the cottage I was looking for without actually seeing it. Or that Bradley had been mistaken and it wasn't up here at all.

There was only one way to find out for sure. I took the right on the main road and kept going north, to Lake Medora. More trees, more nothingness, more total lack of any signs of civilization until I finally saw the water opening up on my left. There was a turnoff there, with a small parking lot and a boat launch. In the summer, in the actual daytime, I might have seen a person or two, but now the whole place was dark and empty. I stopped the truck for a moment and turned it off, then walked out onto the rickety dock next to the boat launch and looked out over the water. It was almost May and yet the lake was still half covered with ice. I could see cottages stretched out along the southern and eastern shorelines. I watched carefully, letting my eyes become accustomed to the dark, hoping that maybe I'd see a slight movement or a twinkle of light. After a few minutes, I got back in the truck and went up the eastern road.

I did my same routine, cottage by cottage, until I got to the end. Once again, no black Subaru, no mint-green Corvette. The road was a dead end so I had to turn around and retrace my steps. On to the southern road, I thought, and then I can check this lake off my list.

I happened to glance to my right for one single second. I kept driving another fifty yards or so. Then I stopped.

I put the truck in reverse and backed up, all the

way past the driveway. From there I could see a car next to the cottage. I hadn't seen it the first time because the driveway had brought me in at the wrong angle, but now through the trees I could see the shadow of a car. Nothing but a dark shape, but it was the shape that gave it away. Low to the ground, like a wedge in the front, the smooth rise of the roof in the middle, then the distinctive angled-in cut at the back. If you knew a little about American cars—and if you grew up in Michigan, you certainly knew more than a little—then you knew that shape.

It was a Corvette.

I didn't want to pull into the driveway again, so I kept going, all the way down that road, back to where I started. I parked in the lot by the boat launch again, got out of the truck, and grabbed the flashlight from my toolbox. I started walking back up toward the cottage. I figured it was probably a quarter mile.

I had a shot of adrenaline now. My heart was racing. For the first time in hours, I felt fully awake.

As I got closer, I slowed down and tried to stay as quiet as possible. I kept my flashlight off. It was going on five in the morning, late enough now that it was actually early. If there was somebody in that cottage, he could be out of bed in the predawn hours and getting ready for another day of God knows what.

I left the road and started going from tree to tree. There were still traces of snow that reflected the dull ambient light. When I had worked my way around the cottage, I went to the Corvette and ducked behind it. Now that I was close enough, I could see the color. Mint-green. But where was the black Subaru?

Okay, no matter, I told myself. You've found the house. Now it's time to call in the cavalry. I pulled out my cell phone and looked at it. It didn't even try to find a signal. If it could have laughed in my face, it would have. I put it back in my pocket.

A smart man would go right back out to the road, I thought. Drive south until you get a signal. But you don't see RJ's car here. So what if Sean's in the house by himself right now? Are you going to leave him here?

I stood up and made my way around to the back of the cottage. I just had to see for myself. The place looked dark and deserted, like nobody had been there in months. The furniture and the gas grill on the back patio were all covered with tarps. There was a boat on a trailer, but that was covered, too. Then I saw the second trailer. This one had a snowmobile on it.

That's one more question possibly answered, I thought. If he planned the apparent suicide at Misery Bay carefully enough, he might have brought down the snowmobile during the day and left it nearby. Then he could have gone out drinking with Charlie, somehow convinced him to come down to Misery Bay, left Charlie's car there in the lot, then taken the snowmobile back to wherever he had parked his car.

I inched my way to the back of the cottage and bent down beneath one of the windows. As I came up to peer in the window, I saw a blue glow and ducked back down again. I came back up and saw that I was looking into an empty kitchen. The blue glow was from the digital clock on the oven.

The only other option on the back of the cottage was the sliding glass door leading to the patio. I kept my back against the siding and slid over to the edge of the door. I paused there for a moment to catch my breath and looked down the backyard, toward the water. There was a boathouse. For all I knew, there could have been a black Subaru sitting in there, meaning maybe RJ was in the house after all, but now I didn't want to walk right past the glass door to go down and check. Instead I put one hand to the ground and leaned over to take a look through the door. I saw a desk with a small lamp on it, casting a narrow cone of light. Then I saw a bulletin board, just like the one I had seen in the basement of Wiley's lake house. This one had a single strip of film hanging from it.

I leaned a little farther to see more of the room.

I saw the floor-to-ceiling bookshelves along the back wall, an open doorway leading into darkness, and then a face staring right at me.

I threw myself back against the siding. I caught my breath for a few seconds, thinking about what to do next. Finally, I realized who I had just seen.

I bent down and took another peek through the glass door. That same face was there. It hadn't moved. I ducked back, switched on my flashlight, covered most of the beam with my hand and bent over one more time.

It was Sean Wiley. He was sitting on the floor, his back against an easy chair. He was staring straight ahead. He didn't move. He didn't blink. I could see the little ring in his left eyebrow. His chest was covered in blood.

I stood up and cast the full beam across the room. Everything else in the cottage was dark. I tested the handle. The door slid smoothly open and the smell of fresh blood came drifting out.

I stepped inside and looked at him more closely. He'd been dead for a couple of hours, at least. Maybe longer. It didn't matter. He was long gone and I could only think of his girlfriend sitting home in the apartment, waiting to hear from him.

"You stupid bastard," I said, my heart in my throat. "What the hell were you thinking?"

I took slow, careful steps through the rest of the cottage. There were no other lights on. There was

414

one bedroom, with a bed that had been slept in but was now empty. Another bedroom with a bed still made. The kitchen, then back to the sitting room or office or library or whatever you wanted to call it. Now it was just the room where Sean Wiley had gotten himself murdered for no good reason.

I went back to the kitchen and shined the flashlight along the wall until I saw the phone. I picked it up and heard a dial tone. Before I dialed 911, another odor came to me. I recognized it. A strong chemical smell . . . where was it coming from? The closet?

I opened the closet door and aimed my flashlight inside, expecting to see brooms and cleaning supplies all wedged into a tight space. Instead I was surprised to see a little room going back at least six feet. Somebody was standing there in what had just been utter darkness until I had opened the door. He was bent over a large metal drum and I realized at that moment exactly where I had smelled this odor before—in Wiley's basement, in the developing room under the stairs. As the man in the darkness stood up straight and looked at me, I realized I had seen him before, too.

It was RJ, Charlie's apartment-mate, otherwise known as Bobby Bergman.

He dropped the jerrycan he was holding and came at me, knocking me backward. The flashlight went off as it clattered across the kitchen floor.

He kicked me in the ribs, knocking the wind out of me. I swept my leg out, trying to trip him, felt the contact of ankle against ankle. He fell sideways. I rolled over and felt around for the flashlight, finally grabbing it and knocking it against my thigh until the lightbulb finally flickered on again.

I got to my feet just in time to see Bergman pointing the pipe at me. A white PVC pipe, the most unlikely thing in the world until I remembered what it was and where he had used it before. The homemade suppressor.

"What are you trying to do?" he said. "Ruin the film?"

Then he aimed the gun right at my chest and shot me.

CHAPTER TWENTY-THREE

I know this place. I've been here before. I am lying on my back and I'm looking up at the ceiling. Just like the last time . . . yes, I was in an apartment building then, in the middle of a city, people above and below me, down the hall and all around me in every direction. My partner was on the floor next to me, the light slowly going out in his eyes. There were sirens on the street below. It was hot.

Now I am alone on the floor, in a cottage next to a lake, in one of the most remote places I've ever seen. The man standing over me may be the only other person within miles. It is silent here and it is cold. Everything is different. Yet exactly the same.

There was a single shot. It made a strange alien sound as it came out of the white tube. I know in my mind, in that high place above everything else where I'm looking down and seeing it as it happens, that the slug was slowed by the wipe barrier, that the gases were trapped inside the tube, and that this is why the sound was so foreign to me. My ears are not ringing.

He has put the gun down on the counter. I am lying on the floor and I am looking up at him. He flips a switch and a light goes on. It hurts my eyes. Then he leaves the room and I reach toward the gun. I can see the black handle extending over the edge of the counter. It is four feet from my hand. I cannot reach it. I am bleeding.

He comes back into the room and now he has a black movie camera in his hands. There are knobs and dials and a lens that he points at me now. Around his chest he has slung another machine. A wire leads to a microphone and this he extends toward me. Both machines are smoothly humming, so softly I can barely hear the gears turning.

"Tell me who you are," he says to me.

I cannot speak. I am bleeding.

"Did you bring the film?"

I try to make a sound.

"You realize this entire project is *on hold* until I get that film back. It is *in limbo*. It is *dead in the water*."

He's staring at me, waiting for an answer?

"Please tell me you didn't come up here without bringing the film."

More staring. I am bleeding. I am—

"You know what? You look like a cop. You ever play a cop before? Have you ever played a state police officer, say? I bet you have."

The man closes his eyes for a moment. He shakes his head. But he keeps the machines still.

"You've got to be more careful when somebody's developing film, you know. You may have exposed it, which would not be good at all, believe me. I've had enough problems on this project without having to reshoot."

He turns off both machines, takes the strap off his shoulder, and puts everything down on the counter. He has to move the gun aside to make room. The gun is even closer to me now.

"I'll be right back," he says. "Don't go away."

He turns the light off. I am back in complete darkness. I hear him opening the door to the small room. The door closes behind him. I hear his voice from the room but I can't make out what he's saying.

I try to move my arms. My right arm, I can move. My left arm is numb. I wedge my right elbow underneath my side. I am bleeding. I try to push myself up. My head spins. I feel something shift in my rib cage and it makes everything go white for a second. Then black again. I try to push myself up again. A sound is coming out of my throat. I can taste blood in my mouth.

I try to lean my head forward. Push myself up even more. I can slide my right knee under me now. I can almost sit up. I try to reach with my left arm but I cannot move it. Lift the right arm. Keep my balance. Reach with my right hand. I cannot see anything. It's too dark.

The edge of the counter. Right there. Slide my hand this way. Nothing. Slide my hand back, feel the cold metal. I close my grip on it and the whole thing falls to the floor.

The door opens. He comes out, goes into the other room, comes back.

"It's okay, I can turn the light on now," he says. "The film is drying. We'll see how it turns out."

The light goes on and I see the gun with its long white homemade suppressor, right there in front of me. I reach for it but it's gone before I can touch it. He takes it away and he puts it back on the counter.

"You realize I have to develop the film here now. Everything's locked up down there in Bad Axe. No developing, no editing. So I can't put the new scenes in. I can't dub in the sound track. I'm totally stopped dead here."

He's down on one knee now, looking at me.

"Do you think Hitchcock ever had to develop his own film in a closet? Huh? You think?"

He's about to stand up, then he comes back down to my eye level.

"You've played a cop, right? Did I already ask you that? You sure look like one."

I'm dizzy. He's starting to waver back and forth in front of me.

"You played a Michigan State Trooper, right? So how many people did you put away in prison?"

I make a sound. There's more blood in my mouth.

"How many families did you tear apart, huh?"

I am starting to slide backward.

"Let me ask you this," he says. "Here's the big question. How many kids did you chase down, so you could drag them back to hell?"

I fall backward and feel the wood against my back. I'm half sitting, half lying. Half alive, half dead.

"How about it? How many kids did *you* personally stop from climbing out of hell, so you could drag them back and cast them *over the edge?*"

He sits back. He tilts his head.

"I'm not sure if we can use you," he says.

"What's the context here? How does it even fit?"

He laces his fingers together and rests his chin on them.

"Tell you what, let's see what you've got. If it's good enough, we'll find a way to use it."

He gets back up, goes to the counter, and slings one machine back over his shoulder. He picks up the other machine and now he has them both pointed at me again. I don't want him to be doing this. I am bleeding. I raise my right hand.

"Okay, action," he says. "Go ahead."

I'm trying to breathe. I'm leaning against the hard wood. I'm bleeding and I'm trying to breathe.

He doesn't move. He's silent. Time passes.

"Any day now," he whispers. "Come on, I'm going to run out of film."

Breathe. I'm trying to breathe.

"Here's my other problem," he says. "All I've got are old short ends. Real ancient stuff. It kept pretty well in the basement, but it's hard to shoot for more than a few minutes at a time. And I already used some this morning."

He gets down on his knees. He has the gun in his hand again.

"There's nothing like the look of film, though. Am I right? The most expensive digital video in the world, it can't *touch* the look of film. Just ask my grandfather. Or hell, ask my cousin. He's right in the other room."

He's pointing the gun at me. That white tube is aimed right at my forehead.

"Sean was supposed to bring the film up here with him. He specifically promised me that he would. Understand, it's not like he was supposed to bring twelve things and the film was just one of them. He was supposed to bring *one single thing and that was the film.*"

He moves the gun closer. It's inches away from me now. I try to reach for it.

"And now I have to reload. The camera, I mean. Ha ha, not the gun. If you'll excuse me."

He gets up off the floor. He takes both machines, and the gun, and he leaves the room. I can still hear him talking.

"One thing you were supposed to bring, Sean! Bring the film with you! One thing!"

I am going to die here. I will die here on this floor unless I get up.

I raise my right hand and I feel for the edge of the counter above my head. I grab on tight and I pull myself up. I weigh a thousand pounds. I slide against the wood and I can feel the blood slick against my back, until I have my chin up on the counter and then my elbow and my head is spinning again as I finally get both feet beneath me.

I stay there for a while and I see the thin line of blood running across the countertop. I know the gun is gone. I pull open the nearest drawer with the hand that still works. Batteries and old keys and junk. I pull open the next drawer and I see white plastic silverware and there, a knife with a long serrated edge. I take it out and now I'm ready to do something at least. Have some effect on the night instead of having it all taken away from me, gunned down like a stray dog in the gutter.

I take a step forward. I'm still leaning against the counter, using it as a rail now, moving forward along this straight line until I hit the edge of the refrigerator and almost go down again. I grab the handle of the refrigerator and drop the knife. I cannot bend down to pick it up. That would be impossible.

I can see through to the other room now. On the other side of the chair, Sean slumped on the floor. Dead and gone and three steps ahead of me. I grit my teeth and push myself toward him, find the back of his chair and now I'm leaning over him like I'm about to tell him a secret. I'm next, I'm next, wait for me.

I see the glass door and the night outside. The door still open an inch or two from when I came in. There's a new strip of film hanging on the board. Two of them now, with my own performance about to be added to them. It's a long way to the door but I'm up and moving now, almost floating it feels like, until I hit the glass and smear it with spit and blood and where the hell is he, anyway? He's loading the film but he must have heard me by now in this tiny house.

I wedge myself into the door's opening, thrust my arm through and then my shoulder, push it open with my head until my side touches the metal edge and everything flashes white again.

I fall through the doorway and now I'm spinning in the night air until I hit the gas grill and hold on to stop from falling to the ground. I see trees ahead of me and water in the impossible distance. If I can get to the trees. It is all I can think about now. I move across the rough ground and I slide through a patch of snow and feel myself touching its coldness with my right hand, pushing myself back up to rebalance and to keep moving forward.

I must breathe. I need air. I am bleeding.

I come to the first tree and I grab at the rough bark with my right hand and there is a low branch there to catch me. I slide around to the far side and lean my weight against it. I am in the dark now and I press against the pain in my left shoulder. Hand, shirt, coat, anything to stop the bleeding. I cannot stay here.

In my mind's eye, I see my truck. It is far away through an endless forest. Across a continent. But it is my only hope.

Breathe. Breathe.

I go to the next tree. I grab for another branch.

I lean against it and catch whatever breath I can find.

Then the next tree. And the next.

I see light. It is coming from behind me. I am casting a long shadow through the woods as I stumble from one tree to the next. The light is coming from behind me but I do not look backward.

I hear the voice now. The low whisper.

"Yes. This is good."

I will not let this happen. I cannot go down this way. I move to the next tree. The light follows me. The light and the voice.

"Perfect. Keep going."

I find a measure of strength from somewhere. It is impossible, but I suck in a breath of air and it seems to fill my lungs, finally. I push myself to the next tree, then the next. I am actually moving now. I am almost walking. I am finding branch after branch and then I trip and catch myself. I hang by one arm and I'm twisted around. I see the single bright light shining down on me. It is over his head. He is wearing it as he follows me through the woods. He has the camera. He has the audio recorder. He is a walking movie studio and he's following my every step.

I taste the blood in my mouth. I pull myself up and turn. I have so far to go.

No. It's not that far. I can see the truck. I am close.

Another tree, then another, and this time a broken branch scratches against my cheek. There is water at my feet and I feel it soaking into my shoes. It is cold and it comes up through my body like electricity. My left arm is still dead and useless and I'm swinging my right arm and hurling myself forward like something from a monster movie. Which is exactly what this has become. I know this. He is right behind me and there's no way I can get away from him. Unless . . .

I see the boat launch, the concrete slab angled down into the lake. I know if I take one step on it I'll go right in and never come out. I reach out and grab the rough wood of the dock. The platform over the water, where I first stopped to look at the edge of the lake and to wonder if he could possibly be here somewhere. My truck is just across the street here. A few yards away. It is waiting for me. If I can get in I'll find a way to put the key in. I'll turn it and I'll press the gas pedal and then steer down the long empty road until I reach something. That's my only way out of this.

I see my shadow in front of me again. The shadow grows shorter and I know he's close. I turn and try to swing at him but I feel myself going down onto the dock. I feel the wood against my face. I can't breathe again. I have to breathe.

"Bravo," he whispers to me. "I'm getting every second here. This is beautiful."

I roll away from him. I feel myself come to rest by the post at the end of the dock. I reach out for something to hold on to. Something I can grab and throw at him. Or plunge into his neck. There is nothing but the post and cold water, inches below me.

He comes closer. The light is getting brighter and brighter. He is wearing it on his head like a miner's helmet. As he bends over me, the audio machine pulls down from his chest, straining against the strap. The camera is on its own strap, looped around his neck now. He pushes the microphone closer to me.

I wave with my right hand. Come here.

"What a great scene," he says. "I'm so glad you showed up now."

I wave again. Come here.

He comes in for the close-up. Time to say good night.

I push myself up. I reach out and grab one of the straps. All I have is dead weight now, but it might be enough. I fall backward, bringing him with me. He collapses across my body and rolls right over me, head first into the water. I hear an instant of hiss as the hot light hits the cold water and then his body follows with a great splash. I am lying on the edge of the dock and I'm soaked and it is icy cold but it feels good. It wakes me up and lets me take one more breath. I'm still holding on to that strap. I roll all the way over so my arm is in the icy water and I'm reaching below the dock. I feel for a cross beam and I pull the strap through and around and then I pull back as tight as I can. He is thrashing now and for one second his head comes back above the water. He is spitting water and screaming and then he says his last words, "Cut! Stop rolling! Cut!"

I pull harder and he's back below the water. He's half under the dock and I hold on to that strap like it's the last good thing I'll ever get to do on this earth. I hold on to it for as long as I can until the thrashing grows quieter, until he is still and it's just me facedown on the dock, looking through the narrow slit between the planks and I see his dark form below me. I hear a drop of my blood falling into the water. Then another. Then another and I finally see another light moving across the water. It sweeps across my face and then it's dark again.

Then I sleep.

CHAPTER TWENTY-FOUR

Faces. Voices. Something covering my mouth, then the sensation of movement. More faces and voices. Lights shining in my eyes.

Then more sleep.

When I finally opened my eyes for good, I saw

Chief Roy Maven of the Sault Ste. Marie Police looking down at me. So I knew I wasn't in heaven.

"Where am I?" I said. I was leaning back at a forty-five-degree angle. My chest and left shoulder were wrapped in bandages, and there was a tube coming out of my side with blood draining through it. There was an IV drip in my left arm. I tried flexing the arm. It hurt like hell, but it moved.

"You're in the hospital," he said. "In Hancock."

"Your daughter . . ."

"She's fine. She'll be just fine. Don't worry."

"You should be down there with her."

"I'll go back down today," he said. "I just wanted to see what happened to you."

"What *did* happen to me?"

"A single .45-caliber slug through the upper lobe of the left lung. The doctors saw entry and exit wounds, but then they took an X-ray."

"Don't tell me."

"For a minute, they thought a fragment might have stopped near your heart," he said. "They didn't know this wasn't the first time for you. The agents gave me a call and I told them about your . . . previous history."

"I'll have to stop getting shot in the chest. It's going to catch up with me one of these days."

He smiled at that. Just a little bit, but it was the first smile I'd seen from him since this whole business started.

"I should be dead," I said. "He had me lined up straight in the chest, point-blank range."

"Good thing he's a bad shot."

"No, he still had his homemade suppressor on the barrel. That must have knuckleballed the shot."

"I guess he didn't take it off yet," Maven said, "because he was saving it to use on me."

I looked at him. "Yeah, that may have been the general plan."

Maven stepped closer. "It was the exact plan, Alex. The bullet that went through your chest was the bullet he was going to use to kill me."

I lay there and looked up at him.

"They found Sean Wiley in the cottage," he said. "He'd been shot in the chest, too."

I closed my eyes.

"They can increase your medicine if you want them to," he said. "Just say the word."

"I'm okay. Where are the agents, anyway?"

"They were here a while ago. They'll be back."

"How long have I been out?"

"Eight hours, give or take."

"Feels like longer," I said. "Hey, there's a young woman down in Bad Axe, Sean's girlfriend, she was waiting to hear from him."

"I believe some state officers went out there. Don't worry."

"I promised her I'd find him, Chief."

"You did, Alex. You found him."

"Come on . . ."

"You did everything you could have done."

"I don't know about that," I said. "But I'm glad your daughter's okay. That's the one thing that went right."

"No, the other thing that went right is that the agents had everybody out looking for you. One of them spotted your truck from the road."

"I'll thank them when I see them."

He nodded his head. He looked like he wanted to say something else, but couldn't find the words.

"What is it, Chief?"

"I still don't understand how I got put on this guy's list," he said. "It's driving me crazy. Did he happen to tell you why?"

"He didn't mention you specifically. Although he did say one thing."

"What was it?"

I tried to replay everything in my mind. I felt dizzy right about then and had to take a moment to breathe.

"Take it easy, McKnight. You don't have to do this right now."

"No, I have to remember. It was strange, because it was like he was just making a movie about everything. Like I was just an actor, and none of it was real."

"Okay . . . very strange, yes."

"At one point, he asked me if I had ever played

431

a state police officer. Then he asked me how many people I'd put in jail. How many families I had torn apart."

I kept going over it, moment by moment. The pain in my shoulder started to radiate across my chest.

"I'm getting the doctor," Maven said. "I'll be right back."

"No, wait." I reached out and grabbed him with my right hand. "He asked me if I had ever taken a kid who was trying to climb out of hell and thrown him back in."

"A kid? Like how old?"

"He didn't say that. But when Wiley was arrested, Bergman must have been around twelve years old."

"A twelve-year-old kid. Thrown back into hell. What could he have been talking about? I don't see how that could have had anything to do with me, I swear."

"I believe you."

"But this must be based on something."

"I don't know, Chief."

The doctor came in to examine me. I was ready to hear the whole story about the X-ray and the bullet and if the doctor had a sense of humor, how I should try to get shot in another body part next time. Maven got shooed out of the room, but I could see he was still working it over in his mind.

One minute later, he came charging back into the room.

"The governor's daughter!"

"You're gonna have to leave, sir," the doctor said.

"The governor's whole family was on Mackinac Island," Maven said, waving off the doctor. "There's a summer residence up there for the governor, and the governor's daughter had this horse show she was supposed to go to. The rest of the family would come down the next day, but on that day, they told me and Raz to run up there and pick her up and bring her back down to Lansing. That was the 'Admin' on our daily logs. But there were thunderstorms all over the area, so we knew the horse show would probably be cancelled, and we kept telling them that. This is a waste of time, you want us to drive all the way up there to bring the governor's daughter down here for nothing. Not to mention that's a total waste to begin with. A sergeant and a trooper driving four hundred miles round-trip so a teenager can ride a horse around some barrels."

I was mesmerized now, and I think the doctor was, too. I sat there on the bed and he stood there with the blood pressure cuff around my good arm, and we watched Maven go.

"I think we took one of the unmarkeds. That part I don't remember for sure, but I do remember both of us riding all the way up there while the black clouds are building up and the thunder's starting to roll in, and we're on the radio saying, hey, this is stupid, guys, but nobody wanted to actually go bother the governor to get the official word. So we get all the way up there and we go to Mackinaw City to catch the ferry. That's why St. Ignace wasn't registering, because if you come from the south you go out of Mackinaw City, right? Anyway, we get on the ferry and now we've gotta sit on that stupid boat like a couple of tourists and ride all the way out there, and then when we get there, there's one of the regulars from the governor's attachment, and he says, sorry guys, change of plans, no horse show after all. Except we can tell he's busting a gut trying so hard not to laugh. So we get right back on the boat and go back to the lot and get back in our cars and now we've got to drive all the way back to Lansing for nothing. No horse show, no daughter in the car, just a couple of idiots who obviously picked the wrong career. That part I remember now, because I think that might be the exact day I decided it was time for a change."

"But if you took the ferry from Mackinaw City, how did you ever get up to St. Ignace?"

"That's the part that comes later. That's the part I forgot, because I wasn't even thinking about picking up some kid. I was trying to remember actually *arresting somebody,* remember?"

"So what are you saying? You were the guys who picked up Bergman?"

He let out a sigh of exasperation. "Maybe. I mean, we picked up some kid on I-75, okay? We're driving back and we get a few miles and there's this kid hitchhiking right on the expressway. We pull over and we pick him up."

"Wait, he was alone?"

He squinted for a moment as he thought back on it.

"Yeah, it was really strange. He hopped in the back of the car like it was nothing, and he starts talking about nothing, I don't know, but then he realized we were cops. So I guess we must have been in the unmarked. But anyway, he gets real quiet then and he doesn't say one single word again. So we call in and they tell us to turn around and take him to St. Ignace."

"That's it? That's all they said?"

"The kid wouldn't give us his name or anything. We kept trying to talk to him, but he was just totally silent, so we had to call him in as a young John Doe and they said, oh yeah, we think we know who that is. Bring him up to St. Ignace. I don't think we ever found out why they wanted us to bring him all the way up over the bridge at that point. We probably didn't even care anymore. We just took him up and dropped him off and . . ."

"You used the bathroom."

"We used the bathroom. Naturally. It's a long trip. Got back in the car. We must not have stuck around to find out who the kid was, or how he ended up on the expressway. At that point, we had a long ride back and we were both pretty fed up with everything. We just got back in the car and went back to Lansing."

"But that would have been logged, right? Picking up the kid? It would be in your daily records."

"Well . . ." He closed his eyes and rubbed his forehead. "Maybe, maybe not. A day like that, that's the kind of day you might not even bother, you know? We didn't really do anything. We just went on this stupid errand and then we brought the car back and then we probably just went out and had a drink and bitched about the job. I think making sure all the paperwork was squared away was probably pretty low on our list of priorities. That wasn't the only time it ever happened, believe me."

"Wiley was trying to help them get away," I said. "He went up there and worked over his son-in-law, and the daughter and grandson were supposed to leave. They must have gotten separated from each other somehow."

"Wiley was helping them escape," Maven said. "My God. The kid made it all the way to the Lower Peninsula and we brought him right back. Just like he said, we dragged him back to hell."

"You had no way of knowing. You didn't do anything wrong."

"Tell that to the kid going back to hell."

"You don't have to feel guilty, Chief. You or especially any of those other men and their families."

"Okay," the doctor finally said. "Can we get back to treating your bullet wound now?"

Maven stood there for one more awkward moment, maybe trying to work it out, have it make sense, say something else about it, or God knows what. But the doctor went back to taking my blood pressure and Maven left the room.

The agents showed up later that day. Or at least they showed up for the first time since I was conscious.

"I'm getting the regular parade," I said. "It's like the end of *The Wizard of Oz*."

"Which one am I?" Agent Long said. "The scarecrow?"

"No, they were back to regular humans when Dorothy woke up, remember? Either way, I believe I owe you both a big thank-you."

"Going up there by yourself was probably not a great idea," Agent Fleury said.

"It seemed like the thing to do at the time."

"I'm serious," Fleury said, stepping a little closer to me. "It was reckless and stupid. But you sure as hell paid for it."

"He knows he's an idiot," Agent Long said. "Give him a break."

He kept standing over me, and I couldn't help but wonder if he was picturing a golden opportunity to take down Bergman himself going down the tubes. But then he surprised me.

"He filmed the whole thing," he said. "Every second."

"I know."

"We watched it. The film was a little wet, but we were able to get it developed."

"Already?"

"It doesn't take long."

"So how was my performance?"

He looked at me and shook his head. "I've never seen anything like it, Alex. I don't know many men who would have survived."

"No, I think Agent Long summed it up best. I'm just an idiot."

He put out his right hand. I shook it.

"Time to get some more rest," Agent Long said. Agent Fleury left first. She stuck around for another few seconds, just long enough to touch her hand to my face. She shook her head at me. Then she was gone.

Vinnie came out once to see me, bearing greetings from Jackie, along with a single bottle of Molson. Leon and Eleanor drove all the way out there, too. As soon as Eleanor saw me sitting there in that hospital bed, I could tell she felt terrible for me. I could also tell she felt vindicated in her belief that only men who are both single and mentally unstable should ever consider doing PI work. I knew Leon would be hearing about it all the way back home.

The doctor told me I was doing well. The wounds were healing and there were no signs of infection. He removed the tube from my side and let me actually get out of bed to use the bathroom.

On the fourth day, Agent Long came back into my room. This time she was alone.

"Where have you been? I was starting to worry about you."

"I'm here to take you home."

"Thanks, but I have my truck. They brought it down here for me."

"Yeah, and you can't drive it yet. So my partner dropped me off here. I'll take you to Paradise and then he can pick me up there. Then we'll go back to Detroit."

"You don't have to drive me. I'm serious. I'll be fine."

"Too late. He's already gone, so I'll need to ride with you, anyway. We can talk about the case on the way."

"Sounds like I don't have a choice."

"No," she said. "As a matter of fact, you don't."

The sun was shining in our eyes as she drove us to Paradise. It made my head hurt. More than anything, it felt strange to be sitting in the passenger's seat.

"Are you okay?"

"I'll be all right."

"It's okay to not be all right sometimes," she said. "You don't have to be such a man about it."

"Sounds like you've been around some men in your time."

"Only every working minute of every day."

"What about when you get off work?"

She thought about that one for a minute.

"I've given up a lot to stay in this job," she said. "Let's just leave it at that."

We rode on in silence for a while.

"I assume Maven talked to you," I finally said.

"About what he finally remembered, yes. You know who else I talked to?"

"Who?"

"A woman named Margaret Steele. I believe you met her."

"Sergeant Steele's wife? Yeah, we met her, all right. How's she doing now?"

"Good as can be expected. She appreciates all the help you tried to give her."

"All we did was ask painful questions about her son, and then find her dead husband in his girlfriend's house."

440

"Well, believe it or not," Agent Long said, "she actually remembers Bobby Bergman. I guess her husband talked about him quite a bit."

"Really?"

"That day Wiley was arrested, apparently he came all the way out from California and stuck a gun in Darryl Bergman's ear. He told his daughter and his grandson to take the truck and to get the hell out of there."

"So he really was trying to save them."

"In his own way, yes. But here's where it gets a little weird. After Wiley was done having his little man-to-man chat with his son-in-law, he left and tried to catch up with the truck. Bergman called the police, and that's how Wiley got flagged at the bridge. You know what happened next. But somewhere down the road, his daughter ended up parked at a rest stop. I guess she was waiting for her father, or I don't know, either she lost her nerve or else it sounds like she was high most of the time. Probably that day, too. It kinda ran in the family. Either way, they found her passed out in the truck a few hours later. Young Bobby was gone."

"What, you mean he tried to keep going on his own?"

"Who knows what he was thinking? Maybe he was planning on hitchhiking all the way to California. Living with his grandfather must have seemed like a much better deal for him."

"Damn," I said. "So that's when Maven and Razniewski picked him up."

"They called in and drove him back to St. Ignace. Steele and Haggerty drove him and his mother back home that night."

"Mrs. Steele remembers all this?"

"Her husband kept going back. Even after Haggerty transferred to Marquette, Steele would stop in every few weeks to see how the kid was doing. He tried to get Family Services involved, but I guess nothing ever came of it."

"This is the cop who tried to help him, you're saying. And years later, this is how he gets repaid."

"Obviously, young Mr. Bergman saw things a little differently."

"So I get how he'd remember Steele's name," I said, "especially if he kept coming by. But what about the other three? He gets picked up, driven back part of the way, then driven back home in another car. How does he remember all four names?"

"If he's a smart enough kid, and it means enough to him, he remembers. And if he remembers, he can go back and find them later if he really wants to."

"You're right about that," I said, thinking about how much information Leon was able to find on the Internet in a matter of seconds.

"But it was all about him," she said. "That's the

thing. This kid trying to escape and getting taken back. The whole business with his grandfather, that was secondary. That's why we never saw the connection with Razniewski and Maven. They had nothing to do with the arrest, but everything to do with what happened to Bobby Bergman."

"So what about that list I found at Wiley's house? Where did it come from?"

"It was just three names, right? Steele, Haggerty, and Razniewski. No Maven."

"Yeah?"

"Think about it."

I did. About a minute later, I let out a long breath and banged my good hand on the glass beside me.

"The agent who came out to question him," I said. "He *told* them those names. Wiley didn't know anything about it until then."

"I'm not sure if he told him the specific names or not, but it doesn't even matter. If he just said there's been some former state police officers killed up north, Wiley could have found out the names on his own. It's not like they were secret."

"You're right. Just search through the newspapers up here for the last few months. He's writing the names down. They start to look familiar—Steele and Haggerty, at least. So then he looks through his old court records and makes the connection."

"He knows his grandson is still up here . . ."

"So he starts thinking, what the hell's going on? Maybe he even calls him?"

"Maybe. Either way, he ends up down in his basement. That's when he sees exactly what his grandson's been working on."

"What about the fire?" I said. "Do you think Bergman set it to kill his father?"

"I don't know, although it's kinda funny how that fire happened right as he was going away to college," she said. "And if you think about it, that kid sure had a gift for making crimes look like something else."

"Yeah, I wouldn't bet against it."

Another mile of silence.

"So that's how he dealt with his life," I said. "He turned it into a movie."

"If it's a movie, it's not really happening."

"God damn . . ."

"The scene with Olivia Maven got ruined, by the way."

"Yeah?"

"The film was overexposed."

"I think that was my fault," I said. "Too bad."

She looked over at me. "Your scene, on the other hand, came out just fine."

"So you told me. Did you and Agent Fleury have popcorn while you were watching it?"

"I'm glad you can joke about it."

"What else am I going to do?"

Another minute of silence.

"I have it on my laptop," she said.

"What?"

"That old film is fragile, so we made a digital copy. I can show you it if you want me to."

"Are you serious?"

"It's up to you. You've earned the right to see it."

"I don't know," I said. "Let me think about it."

It felt like I'd been gone a long time, even though it was only a matter of days. Most of the snow was gone now. She drove up my road, past Vinnie's cabin, then past my first cabin.

"What's the matter?" she said.

"Nothing."

"Are you sure? You tensed up like you were in pain. Do you need your pills?"

"I'm fine. Really."

She shook her head, probably thinking I was just acting like a man again. I didn't want to get into the whole story with her.

She went up to the end of my road and stopped in front of the last cabin. I got out and felt a little dizzy as I walked across the muddy ground to the front door. She grabbed her laptop bag from behind the seat and followed me. I held the door open for her. When she was inside she stood around for a few moments, not looking entirely comfortable. Eventually, she took out her laptop and plugged it in.

"You're the one who told me not to look at those crime scene photos," I said.

"Yeah, but if you hadn't, he might still be out there killing people."

"Well, I'll tell you what," I said, coming closer to her. "I don't think I need to see the film of myself almost dying. I was there, and that's probably enough."

"Yeah, I guess that makes sense."

"So as long as you're here, what else can we do?"

I stood there looking at her. Eventually, I took another step toward her and felt a little dizzy.

"Alex, are you okay?"

When I opened my eyes, Agent Long was right there in front of me, holding both arms.

"Ouch," I said. "Watch the left side there."

"I think you need to lie down."

"No, I'm okay now. I promise. For real this time."

Her hand was still on my arm. My good arm. As I looked at her face, I felt a huge relief. I was glad she was there with me. I was glad she looked so good in that moment. I was glad I had at least half a working body left.

Then I laughed. It was hilarious to me that I was alive. That I managed to come through this and that now I was here in my cabin with this woman . . .

"What are we doing here?" she said.

I pulled her close to me. She smelled good. Better than good. This was the first woman I had touched since . . . well, since the thing that had happened in that first cabin. She wasn't resisting me. She was responding and I wanted to keep going, and then anything that happened after that we'd have to figure out when we got there.

Then I passed out.

CHAPTER TWENTY-FIVE

By the time I came to, Agent Long had called Agent Fleury. He said he'd be there in an hour.

"Call him back and tell him to meet us down at the Glasgow Inn," I said. "We need to have that drink, at least."

So she drove me down to the Glasgow and I introduced her to Jackie and Vinnie. I asked about Vinnie's mother and was glad to hear she was feeling a little better. Then we had some real Canadian beer and when Fleury got there, I made sure he had one, too. When they were ready to leave, I came out to the parking lot and I took Agent Long aside for a moment.

"Sorry about the clumsy pass," I said to her.

"That's all right," she said. "You're in a compromised state. Maybe next time it'll work out a little better for both of us."

"You'll come back up here sometime?"

"Maybe. Or maybe you can look me up if you ever get back to Detroit."

"I'll do that," I said, "but on one condition."

"What's that?"

"We can do dinner, but promise me one thing. No movie."

She laughed at that. "It's a deal."

"Okay then, take care of yourself, Agent Long."

"Call me Janet."

She kissed me on the cheek and got in the car. Agent Fleury was already behind the wheel. I waved to them as they took off.

Then I went back inside and collapsed by the fire.

"I suppose you'll be expecting me to bring your dinner to you," Jackie said.

"You are a perceptive man."

He walked away swearing at me. Things were already feeling normal again. The snow would finally melt for good. The summer would come. It would last for what would feel like five minutes, then the air would turn cold again. The lake would turn back into a monster. The snow would come to bury us and once again we'd ask ourselves why we lived up here. But we wouldn't leave.

None of us. Not Jackie, not Vinnie, not Leon, not Chief Roy Maven. Not me.

We would never leave this place.

• • •

The next morning, Vinnie came to the cabin early. He didn't knock. He just came in and made himself at home.

"What's going on?" I said, moaning as I turned over the wrong way.

"We've got lots of work to do today."

"That's what you think. I'm not doing anything."

"Okay, so *I've* got lots of work to do today."

"Vinnie, what are you talking about?"

"We're reclaiming your first cabin, Alex. You've avoided it long enough."

"No. Forget it."

"You can't stop me," he said. "That's the genius of my plan. You can complain all you want today, but in the shape you're in? What are you gonna do, kick me?"

"Vinnie, I swear to God . . ."

"I'm starting right after breakfast. With or without you watching."

I finally got myself out of the bed. "You're serious."

"Absolutely."

"Then give me a little more time," I said. "It'll take me at least an hour just to get dressed."

I insisted on being the one to actually open the door. This was the cabin I had helped build myself, all those years ago, my father and I

449

working side by side. Now there was a sad, stale odor in the air as I took my first step back into the place. I had moved out everything I could carry. The bed was unmade. The table was empty. The refrigerator and stove unplugged. The woodstove needed cleaning.

There on the floor. The stain.

"What first?" Vinnie said, stepping in right behind me.

I couldn't help thinking of Chief Maven, and everything he had done to reclaim his own house after what had happened.

"Only one place to start," I said. "The floor."

"How are we going to clean it?"

"We're not. We're gonna burn it."

A few hours later, we had about a hundred square feet of floor torn out. When I say we, I mean Vinnie. He pulled it out, slat by slat, and stacked it outside. When that entire section of the house was stripped down to the subflooring, we piled up the slats into a big teepee and filled the interior with wadded-up newspaper. Vinnie put some sage in with the paper. I didn't have to ask him why. I knew it was one of the four Ojibwa medicines.

Before I lit the match, I took one of the slats of wood and I rubbed the spot where the blood had seeped in forever. I said good-bye to Natalie Reynaud one more time. I kissed the wood once and then put it back on the pile. I lit the match and stood back to watch it all burn. I could smell the sage mixed in with the paper and the pine.

When it was all done, I stood there watching the embers for a long time. Vinnie came up to me finally and stood next to me.

"Feel better?" he said.

"It helps, yes. Thank you."

"You know what you really need?"

"What's that?"

"A sweat."

I looked at him.

"Tonight," he said. "As soon as the sun goes down."

"Can I bring somebody else? Somebody who needs it even more than I do?"

"Of course."

"I'll see you at sunset."

I probably wasn't supposed to be driving yet, but what the hell. I drove to Sault Ste. Marie, all the way to the river, to the City-County Building. I parked outside the front door and went in. The receptionist tried to say something to me, but I walked right by her. Down the hall, to the one office in the middle of the building with no windows. I opened the door without knocking.

"McKnight!" he said, the phone in his hand. "What the hell is wrong with you?"

That look on his face, it was just like old times.

"Hang up the phone," I said. "Get your coat."

"Have you lost your mind? Can't you see I'm working here?"

"I'm still recovering, Chief, so I can't pick you up and carry you. Get your ass out of that chair and let's get out of here."

"Not until you tell me where you think we're going."

"You'll see when you get there. For once in your life, will you just trust me?"

He sat there looking at me. He still had the phone in his hand.

"Please," I said. "Come with me."

He put the phone down, put on his coat, and followed me out the door.

"You want me to do what?"

"I want you to take your clothes off. Down to your underwear."

We were standing in Vinnie's cousin Buck's yard, with a half dozen of Vinnie's other relatives. Quiet men with long black hair hanging down their backs. All stripping down to their underwear. The sun had gone down. It was just below freezing.

"You really *have* lost your mind," Maven said. "I knew it was only a matter of time."

"Just shut up and disrobe, Chief."

Buck's was the only yard on the reservation that had a permanent sweat lodge. He had lashed some saplings together into a half circle about ten feet in diameter, then covered the saplings with canvas and every old rug he could find. Tonight he had a healthy fire going in the pit outside the lodge, and he was heating several rocks in the middle of it. When everything else was ready, he lifted the rocks one by one with a shovel and placed them inside the lodge.

"I feel ridiculous," Maven said, standing there shivering. "Not to mention how freakin' cold it is."

"But look at you. You're like some sort of glorious Greek sculpture."

"McKnight, so help me God, I'm going to smack you right in the face. I don't care how many bullets you took for me."

Buck lifted the flap and we all bent down to go inside. We took our places around the fire and Buck dipped a great iron ladle into a bucket of water and poured it onto the hot rocks. Then he tossed on a few sprigs of sage.

We all sat there in the dark as the steam surrounded us. I felt my muscles starting to unwind. Everything that had happened to me, I started to let go of it. Buck put more water onto the rocks. I was sweating now. The steam was filling my lungs.

The last time I had done this, I had opened my eyes and I had seen Natalie in the steam. I swear to God, I did. On this night, I didn't see anything, but then maybe this night wasn't about me at all.

I knew Maven was right next to me, but I couldn't make out if his eyes were open or closed. I didn't know what this experience was doing for him.

About thirty minutes later, we all came back out of the sweat lodge, into the sudden shock of cold air. It was like plunging into an icy lake, but it felt good. I knew I'd be okay now. I knew my injuries would heal and everything would go back to the way it was.

Well, maybe not everything.

"How did that feel, Chief?"

"It was good, Alex." He was putting his clothes on. "I admit it. That was exactly what I needed. I had no idea."

"What's it going to be like now?" I said. "I mean, who are you going to yell at?"

"I've got plenty of people to yell at, believe me."

"Yeah, but I was always your favorite."

"Just keep being yourself," he said. "We won't have to change a thing."

When he was finished dressing, we both got back in my truck and I took him back to the Soo. Neither of us said a thing on the way.

I pulled into the parking lot. We sat there for a moment, and then he opened his door. He didn't get out.

"Thank you for dragging me to that place," he said.

"My pleasure," I said. "I heard what you said there, by the way."

"What did I say?"

"You said, and I quote, 'I don't care how many bullets you took for me.'"

"Yeah, well. We both know I was next. We've already covered that."

Another moment of silence.

"Your daughter's okay?"

"She's okay. She'll be going back to work next week."

One more silence. The last one.

"We made a good team," I said. "Don't you think?"

"Put it this way," he said. "If we ever have to do it again, I wouldn't want to be the guy on the other side of the ball."

"Have a good night, Chief."

"You, too. I'll see you around."

He got out and closed the door. Then I drove back home to Paradise.

Center Point Publishing
600 Brooks Road ● PO Box 1
Thorndike ME 04986-0001 USA

(207) 568-3717

**US & Canada:
1 800 929-9108**
www.centerpointlargeprint.com